Perry Mason, Della Street, and Paul Drake were looking across the restaurant at the girl in the skin-fitting dress who was sitting with Harrington Faulkner. Abruptly, Faulkner arose and marched over to Mason's table.

"Mr. Mason," he said crisply, "that case I was trying to consult you about is not only about a goldfish. It also concerns a crooked partner, a secret formula, and a golddigger."

Mason looked intently at the girl Faulkner had left. "Who is she?"

"She's the golddigger. I'd give a thousand dollars to the man who would take her off my hands."

Much later in the case, when Sally Madison was in jail, charged with murder, Perry Mason knew that Faulkner had been a tightwad.

Two Complete Novels by
ERLE STANLEY GARDNER

PERRY MASON

2 in 1

The Case of
the Golddigger's Purse

The Case of
the Buried Clock

PUBLISHED BY POCKET BOOKS NEW YORK

PERRY MASON 2 IN 1

POCKET BOOK edition published October, 1976

The Case of the Golddigger's Purse

William Morrow edition published 1945
POCKET BOOK edition published July, 1951
16th printing......................August, 1976

The Case of the Buried Clock

William Morrow edition published 1943
POCKET BOOK edition published March, 1950
15th printing......................August, 1976

This POCKET BOOK edition includes every word contained in the original, higher-priced editions. It is printed from brand-new plates made from completely reset, clear, easy-to-read type.
POCKET BOOK editions are published by
POCKET BOOKS,
a division of Simon & Schuster, Inc.,
A GULF+WESTERN COMPANY
630 Fifth Avenue,
New York, N.Y. 10020.
Trademarks registered in the United States
and other countries.

ISBN: 0-671-80736-6.

The Case of
the Golddigger's Purse

Cast of Characters

1

Perry Mason, seated at the restaurant table, looked up at the tense, nervous face of the man who had deserted his spectacular companion to accost him.

"You said you wanted to consult me about a goldfish?" Mason repeated blankly. His smile was almost incredulous.

"Yes."

Mason shook his head. "I'm afraid you'd find my fees were a little too high . . ."

"I don't care how high your fees are. I can afford to pay any amount within reason, and I will."

Mason's tone contained quiet finality. "I'm sorry, but I've just finished with a rather exacting case. I have neither the time nor the inclination to bother with goldfish. I . . ."

A tall, dignified gentleman gravely approached the table, said to the man who was regarding Mason with an expression of puzzled futility, "Harrington Faulkner?"

"Yes," the man said with the close-clipped finality of one accustomed to authority. "I'm engaged now, however, as you can see. I . . ."

The newcomer's hand made a quick motion to his breast pocket. There was a brief flash of paper as he pushed a folded oblong into Faulkner's hand.

"Copy of summons, and complaint, case of Carson

versus Faulkner. Defamation of character, a hundred thousand dollars. Here's the original summons—directing your attention to the signature of the clerk and the seal of the court. No need to get sore about it. It's all in the line of work. If I didn't serve it somebody else would. See your lawyer. You have ten days to answer. If the other fellow isn't entitled to anything he can't get it. If he is, it's your hard luck. I'm just the man who serves the papers. No good getting mad. Thank you. Good night."

The words rattled along with such staccato rapidity that they sounded like a sudden, unexpected burst of hail on a metal roof.

The process server turned with quick, self-effacing grace, and merged himself into a group of diners who were just leaving the restaurant.

Faulkner, acting like a man who is in the middle of a bad dream and is being swept helplessly along by the events of his nightmare, pushed the papers down into a side pocket, turned without a word, walked back to his table and rejoined his companion.

Mason watched him thoughtfully.

The waiter hovered over the table. Mason smiled reassuringly at Della Street, his secretary, then turned to Paul Drake, the private detective who had entered a few minutes before.

"Joining us, Paul?"

"A big coffee and a slab of mince pie is all I want," Drake said.

Mason gave the waiter their orders. "What do you make of the girl?" he asked Della Street as the waiter withdrew.

"You mean the one with Faulkner?"

"Yes."

Della Street laughed. "If he keeps playing around with her he'll have another summons served on him."

Drake leaned forward so that he could look past the corner of the booth. "I'll take a look at that myself," he announced, and then after a moment said, "Oh, oh. *That's* a dish!"

Mason's eyes thoughtfully studied the pair. "Incongruous enough," he said.

"Notice the getup," Drake went on. "The skin-fitting dress, the long, long eyelashes, the burgundy fingernails. Looking in those eyes, he's already forgotten about the summons in his side pocket. Bet he doesn't read it until . . . Looks as though he's coming back, Perry."

Abruptly the man pushed back his chair, arose with no word to his companion, marched determinedly back to Mason's table. "Mr. Mason," he said, speaking with the crisp, deliberate articulation of a man determined to make his point, "it has just occurred to me that you may have received an entirely erroneous impression of the nature of the case about which I was trying to consult you. I think perhaps when I mentioned that it concerned a goldfish, you naturally considered the case one of minor importance. It isn't. The goldfish in question is a very fine specimen of the Veiltail Moor Telescope. The case also concerns a crooked partner, a secret formula for controlling gill disease, and a golddigger."

Mason regarded the anxious face of the man who was standing beside the table and tried not to grin. "A goldfish *and* a golddigger," he said. "After all, perhaps we'd better hear about it. Suppose you draw up a chair and tell me about it."

The man's face showed sudden satisfaction. "Then you'll take my case and . . ."

"I mean I'm willing to listen and that's all," Mason said. "This is Della Street, my secretary, and Paul Drake, head of the Drake Detective Agency, who quite frequently assists me in gathering facts. Won't you invite your companion to come over and join us, and we may as well . . ."

"Oh, she's all right. Let her sit there."

"She won't mind?" Mason asked.

3

Faulkner shook his head.

"Who is she?" Mason asked.

Without changing his tone in the least, Faulkner said, "She's the golddigger."

Drake said warningly, "You leave that baby alone at that table and you won't find her alone when you get back."

Faulkner said fervently, "I'd give a thousand dollars to the man who would take her off my hands."

Drake said laughingly, "Done for five hundred. It's cheap at half the price."

Faulkner regarded him with unhumorous appraisal, drew up a chair. The young woman he had left sitting at the table merely glanced over at him, then opened her purse, held up a mirror and started checking her make-up with the careful appraisal of a good merchant inspecting his stock-in-trade.

2

■

Mason said to Faulkner, "You haven't even read the papers that process server handed you."

Faulkner made a gesture of dismissal. "I don't have to. It's just part of a campaign to annoy me."

"What's he suing for?"

"A hundred thousand dollars, the man who served the papers said."

Mason said, "You're not interested enough to read them?"

"I'm not interested in anything Elmer Carson does to annoy me."

"Tell me about the goldfish," Mason said.

Faulkner said, "The Veiltail Moor Telescope is a prized goldfish. The uninitiated would hardly consider him a goldfish. He isn't gold. He's black."

"All over?" Mason asked.

"Even the eyes."

"What's a Telescope fish?" Drake asked.

"A species of goldfish that has been developed by breeding. They're called Telescopes because the eyes protrude from the sockets, sometimes as much as a quarter of an inch."

"Isn't that rather—unprepossessing?" Della Street asked.

"It might be to the uninitiated. Some people have called the Veiltail Moor Telescope the Fish of Death. Pure superstition. Just the way people react to the black color."

"I don't think I'd like them," Della Street said.

"Some people don't," Faulkner agreed, as though the subject held no particular interest. "Waiter, will you please bring my order over to this table?"

"Yes, sir. And the lady's order?"

"Serve it to her over there."

Mason said, "After all, Faulkner, I'm not certain I like that method of handling the situation. Regardless of what the girl is, you're dining with her, and . . ."

"That's all right. She won't mind. She isn't the least bit interested in what I'm going to talk about."

"What is she interested in?" Mason asked.

"Cash."

"What's her name?"

"Sally Madison."

"And she is putting the bite on you?" Mason asked.

"I'll say she is."

"Yet you take her out to dinner?"

"Oh, certainly."

"And walk away and leave her?" Della Street asked.

5

"I want to discuss business. She wouldn't be interested. She understands the situation thoroughly. There's no need of any concern about her."

Drake glanced at Perry Mason. The waiter brought him his mince pie and coffee, shrimp cocktails to Della Street and Mason and consommé to Harrington Faulkner.

Over at the table Faulkner had vacated, Sally Madison completed her make-up, sat with a carefully cultivated expression of demure rectitude frozen on her face. She seemed to have no further interest in Harrington Faulkner or the party he had joined.

"You don't seem to have any hard feelings," Mason said.

"Oh, I don't," Faulkner hastily disclaimed. "She's a very nice young woman—as golddiggers go."

Mason said, "If *you're* not going to read that complaint and summons, suppose you let me glance through it."

Faulkner passed it across the table.

Mason unfolded the papers, glanced through them, said, "It seems that this Elmer Carson says that you've repeatedly accused him of tampering with your goldfish; that the accusation is false and has been made with malice; that Carson wants ten thousand dollars as actual damages and ninety thousand dollars by way of punitive damages."

Faulkner seemed to have only a detached interest in the claims made against him by Elmer Carson. "You can't believe a word he says," he explained.

"Just who is he?"

"He was my partner."

"In the goldfish business?"

"Good heavens, no. The goldfish is just my own hobby. We have a real-estate business. It's incorporated. We each own one third of the stock and the balance is held by Genevieve Faulkner."

"Your wife?"

Faulkner cleared his throat, said with some embarrassment, "My former wife. I was divorced five years ago."

"And you and Carson aren't getting along?"

"No. For some reason there's been a sudden change in him. I've made Carson an ultimatum. He can submit a buy-or-sell offer. He's jockeying around to get the best price available. Those are minor matters, Mr. Mason. I can handle them. I want to see you about protecting my fish."

"Not about the slander suit?"

"No, no. That's all right. I have ten days on that. Lots can happen in ten days."

"Not about the golddigger?"

"No. She's all right. I'm not worried about her."

"Just about the goldfish?"

"That's right. Only, you understand, Mr. Mason, the partner and the golddigger enter into it."

"Why the concern about the goldfish?"

"Mr. Mason, I've raised this particular strain of Veiltail Moor Telescopes and I'm proud of them. You have no idea of the thought and labor that have gone into developing this particular fish, and now they're threatened with extinction by gill disease, and that disease has been deliberately introduced into my aquarium by Elmer Carson."

"He says in his complaint," Mason said, "that you accuse him of deliberately trying to kill your fish, and it's for that he's asking damages."

"Well, he did it all right."

"Can you," Mason asked, "prove it?"

"Probably not," Faulkner admitted glumly.

"In that event," Mason told him, "you might be stuck for a large sum by way of damages."

"I suppose so," Faulkner admitted readily enough, as though the matter held no immediate interest for him.

"You don't seem particularly worried about it," Mason said.

7

"There's no use crossing bridges like that before you come to them," Faulkner said. "I'm in enough trouble already. Perhaps, however, I haven't made my position entirely clear. The things Carson does to annoy *me* don't mean a thing to me. I am interested right now in saving my fish. Carson knows they are dying. In fact, it is because of him that they are dying. He knows that I want to remove them for treatment. So he has filed a suit, claiming the fish are the property of the corporation and not my individual property. That is, he claims the fish are affixed to the partnership real property and that I have threatened to and will, unless restrained, tear out the tank and remove the fish and tank from the premises. Because this constitutes a severance of the real property, he has flim-flammed a judge into giving him a temporary restraining order. . . . And hang it, Mason, he's right. The confounded tank *is* affixed to the property . . . I want you to beat that restraining order. I want to establish title to the fish and the tank as my own individual property. I want that restraining order smashed and smashed hard and quick, and I think you're the man to do it."

Mason glanced across to the girl at the table Faulkner had left. She seemed to be taking no interest in the conversation. A look of synthetic, motionless innocence was frozen on her face as painting is glazed on a china cup.

"You're married?" Mason asked Faulkner. "I mean you've remarried since your divorce?"

"Oh, yes."

"When did you start playing around with Sally Madison?"

Faulkner's face showed a brief flicker of surprise. "Playing around with Sally Madison?" he repeated almost incredulously. "Good heavens, *I'm* not playing around with her."

"I thought you said she was a golddigger."

"She is."

8

"And that she was putting the bite on you?"

"Indeed she is."

Mason said, "I'm afraid you're not clarifying the situation very much," and then, reaching a sudden decision, added, "if you people will excuse me, and there's no objection on the part of Mr. Faulkner, I think I'll go talk to the golddigger and get her ideas on the case."

Waiting only for Della Street's nod and not so much as glancing at Faulkner, Mason left the table and crossed over to where Sally Madison was seated.

"Good evening," he said. "My name is Mason. I'm a lawyer."

Long lashes swept upward, dark eyes regarded the lawyer with the unabashed frankness of a speculator looking over a piece of property. "Yes, I know. You're Perry Mason, the lawyer."

"May I sit down?"

"Please do."

Mason drew up a chair.

"I think," he said, "I'm going to like this case."

"I hope you do. Mr. Faulkner needs a good lawyer."

"But," Mason pointed out, "if I agreed to represent Mr. Faulkner, it might conflict with your interest."

"Yes, I suppose so."

"It might, therefore, cut down the amount of money you'd receive."

"Oh, I think not," she said with all the assurance of a person who occupies an impregnable position.

Mason glanced quizzically at her. "How much," he asked, "do you want out of Mr. Faulkner?"

"Today it's five thousand dollars."

Mason smiled. "Why the accent on today? What was it yesterday?"

"Four thousand."

"And the day before?"

"Three."

"And what will it be tomorrow?"

"I don't know. I think he'll give me the five thousand tonight."

Mason studied the expressionless countenance, heavy with make-up. His eyes showed he was taking a keen interest in the entire affair. "Faulkner says you're a golddigger."

"Yes, he *would* think so."

"Are you?"

"Perhaps. I really don't know. Probably I am. But if Mr. Faulkner wants to throw brickbats around, let him tell you about himself. He's a tight-fisted, miserly, over-bearing— Oh, what's the use! You wouldn't understand."

Mason laughed outright. "I'm trying," he said, "to make heads or tails out of this case. So far I don't seem to be having very much success. Now will you *please* tell me what it's all about?"

She said, "My connection with it is very simple. I want money out of Harrington Faulkner."

"And just why do you think Faulkner should give you money?"

"He wants his goldfish to get well, doesn't he?"

"Apparently, but I'm afraid I don't see the connection."

For the first time since Mason had seated himself, some expression struggled through the glazed make-up of her face. "Mr. Mason, did you ever see someone whom you loved sick with tuberculosis?"

Mason's eyes were puzzled. He shook his head. "Go on," he said.

"Harrington Faulkner has money. So much money that he'd never miss five thousand dollars. He's spent thousands of dollars on his hobby. Heaven knows how much he's spent on these black goldfish alone. Not only is he rich but he's *stinking* rich, and he hasn't the faintest idea of how to enjoy his money or how to spend it so it would do him or anyone else any good. He'll just keep on piling it up until some day he'll die and that granite-hearted

10

wife of his will fall heir to it. He's a miser except on his goldfish. And in the meantime Tom Gridley has T.B. The doctor says he needs absolute rest, freedom from worry, complete relaxation. How much chance does Tom stand of getting any of that while he's working at twenty-seven dollars a week, nine hours a day, in a pet store which is damp and smelly. . . . He hasn't had a chance to get out in the sunlight except a few brief snatches he can get on Sundays. That, of course, isn't enough even to help.

"Mr. Faulkner goes into spasms because a few black goldfish are dying of gill disease, but he'd watch Tom die of T.B. and simply ignore the whole thing as being none of his concern."

"Go on," Mason said.

"That's all there is to it."

"But what," Mason asked, "does Tom Gridley have to do with Harrington Faulkner?"

"Didn't he tell you?"

"No."

She sighed with exasperation. "That's what he went over there to tell you about."

Mason said, "Perhaps it's my fault. I got off on the wrong tangent. I thought *you* were trying to blackmail him."

"I am," she said with calm candor.

"But apparently not the way I thought," Mason explained.

She said, "Do you know anything about goldfish, Mr. Mason?"

"Not a darn thing," Mason admitted.

"Neither do I," she said, "but Tom knows all about them. The goldfish that are Mr. Faulkner's most prized possession have some sort of a gill disease and Tom has a treatment that will cure it. The only other treatment is a copper sulphate treatment that quite frequently proves fatal to the fish, and is of doubtful value as far as the

11

disease is concerned. Sometimes it works and sometimes it doesn't."

"Tell me about Tom's treatment."

"It's a secret, but I can tell you this much. In place of being a harsh treatment that shocks the fish, it's a gentle treatment that is thoroughly beneficial. Of course, one of the problems of treating fish by putting things in the water is that the remedy has to be thoroughly mixed with the water, and then, the minute you let it settle, it is apt to concentrate in the wrong places. If the remedy is heavier than water it will settle to the bottom, or if it's lighter it will rise to the top."

"And how does Tom get away from that?" Mason asked, interested.

"I can tell you that much. He paints the remedy he uses on a plastic panel which is inserted into the fish tank and then the panels are changed at certain intervals."

"And it works?" Mason asked.

"I'll say it works. It worked with Mr. Faulkner's fish."

"But I thought they were still sick."

"They are."

"Then it wouldn't seem that the remedy worked."

"Oh, but it does. You see, Tom wanted to go ahead and cure the fish entirely, but I wouldn't let him. I gave Mr. Faulkner just enough of the remedy to keep them from dying, and then I told him that if he wanted to finance Tom in the invention we'd let him have a half interest in it and he could put it on the market. Tom's one of these simple souls who trusts everyone. He's a chemist and is always experimenting with remedies. He worked out one remedy for distemper and simply *gave* it to David Rawlins, the man who was running the pet shop. Rawlins just said 'Thank you,' and didn't even give Tom a raise. Of course, you can't blame him very much because I can understand *his* problem. He doesn't have a large volume of business and there isn't a whole lot of money to be made out of pets unless you have a *huge* place, but he works Tom terribly hard and . . . Well, after all, the man's making some money out of this invention of Tom's for distemper."

"Those two the only things Tom's invented?" Mason asked.

"No, no, he's done other things but somebody always gyps him out of them . . . Well, this time I decided things would be different. I am going to take charge of the thing myself. Mr. Faulkner could give Tom five thousand outright and then pay him a royalty to boot. I'm willing to let the five thousand be considered as an advance payment against one half of the royalties, but *only* against one half."

"I don't suppose there are a great number of goldfish fanciers in the country," Mason said.

"Oh, but I think there are. I think that *lots* of people collect them as a hobby."

"But do you think there's enough gill disease to enable Mr. Faulkner to break even on an investment of that size?"

"I don't know, and I don't care. All I'm interested in is seeing that Tom gets a chance to go out into the country, some place where there's sunshine and fresh air. He's got to go where he can take life easy for a while. If he does, they tell me he can be cured absolutely. If he doesn't, things will go from bad to worse until finally it will be too late. I'm giving Mr. Faulkner an opportunity to cure those prize fish of his and to have a remedy that will enable him to build up his strain without danger of future infection, and that's worth a lot to him. When you consider what he's spent on them, I'm letting him off cheap."

Mason smiled. "But you're boosting the ante on him one thousand dollars a day?"

"Yes, I am."

"Why?"

"He's trying to blackmail me. He says Tom worked out his invention while he was working for Rawlins and

13

that, therefore, the invention belongs to Rawlins and unless Tom cures his fish, then Mr. Faulkner will buy an interest in Rawlins' store and sue Tom for his invention. Mr. Faulkner is a hard man, and I'm dealing with him in the only way he'll understand—the hard way."

"And just what is Tom Gridley to you?" Mason asked.

She met his eyes steadily. "My boy friend."

Mason chuckled. "Well," he said, "it's no wonder Faulkner thinks you're a golddigger. I thought from the way he talked that he'd been making passes at you and that you were holding him up."

Her eyes flickered somewhat scornfully over to where Harrington Faulkner was sitting, stiffly uncomfortable, at the table. "Mr. Faulkner," she announced with cold finality, "never made passes at anyone," and then, after a moment, qualified by adding, "except a goldfish."

Mason smiled. "The man's married?"

"That's what I mean. A goldfish."

"His wife?"

"Yes."

The waiter appeared with food on a tray. "Shall I serve you at this table?" he inquired of Mason.

Mason looked over to where Harrington Faulkner had turned to regard proceedings at the other table, apparently with anxiety. "If you don't mind," he said to Sally Madison, "I'll return to my table, and send Mr. Faulkner back to join you. I don't think I'll take his case."

"You don't need to send *him* back," Sally Madison said. "Tell him to send over his check for five thousand bucks, and tell him from me that I'm going to wait here until I get it, or until his damn black goldfish turn belly up."

"I'll tell him," Mason promised, and, excusing himself, returned to his own table.

Faulkner glanced at him questioningly.

Mason nodded. "I don't know just what you want," he

14

said, "but I'll at least look into the matter—after I've had something to eat."

"We could talk right here," Faulkner said.

Mason's nod indicated Sally Madison sitting alone at the other table. "After I've had something to eat," he repeated, "and I take it you didn't want me to try and work out any terms with Miss Madison, because, if you did, I'm not interested."

Faulkner said, "Sally Madison's proposition amounts to blackmail."

"I dare say it does," Mason agreed calmly. "There's a lot of blackmail in the world."

Faulkner said bitterly, "I suppose she's played upon your sympathies. After all, her face and her figure are her biggest asset, and how well she knows it!" And then he added even more bitterly, "Personally, I don't see what people can see in that type."

Mason merely grinned. "Personally," he announced, "I have never collected goldfish."

3
■

A thick pea-soup fog had settled down upon the streets of the city until it seemed that Mason's automobile was swimming slowly through a sea of watered milk. The windshield wipers were busily beating a monotonous rhythm of cold protest against the clammy surface of the windshield. Some fifty feet ahead, the red taillight of Harrington Faulkner's automobile served as a guiding beacon.

"He's a slow driver," Della Street said.

"An advantage in weather of this kind," Mason agreed.

Drake laughed. "Bet the guy never took a chance in his life. He's a cold-blooded, meticulous bird with an ice-water personality. I almost died when I saw him kick through over there at the table with that golddigger. How much did she nick him for, Perry?"

"I don't know."

"Judging from the expression on his face when he took out his checkbook," Della said, "it must have been just about what the girl asked for. *She* certainly didn't waste any time once she got her hands on the check. She didn't even wait to finish her dinner."

"No," Mason said, "she didn't make any bones about it. Her interest in Harrington Faulkner was purely financial."

"And when we get out to his house, just what are we supposed to do?" Drake wanted to know.

Mason grinned. "I'll bite, Paul, but he feels that he has to show us the location of the goldfish tank before we can understand his problem. It seems that's an important phase of the case as far as he's concerned, and when he gets an idea, he gets it all the way. As I gather it, Faulkner and his wife live in a large duplex house. One side is their living quarters and the other is where Faulkner and his partner, Elmer Carson, have their office. Apparently, Faulkner has various goldfish tanks scattered around the place and this particular pair of Veiltail Moors that is the cause of all the excitement is in part of the building that was used as an office. For some reason, Faulkner wants us to see the tank and the fish, and he has to have things done just so or not at all. It's just the way he's made."

Drake said, "Faulkner's a self-contained little cuss. You'd think it would take more than an ordinary jolt to send him running to a lawyer, all steamed up. What I mean is, he's the sort you'd expect to find making an appointment two days in advance and keeping that appointment to the exact second."

Mason said, "He evidently thinks more of that pair of Veiltail Moors than he does of his right eye. However, we'll get the details when we get out to his house. My own idea is there's something on his mind other than these fish and the affair with his partner, but I'm not going to stick my neck out until I see what's in the offing."

The taillight of the car ahead veered abruptly to the right. Mason piloted his car around the corner. They drove down a side street, pulled to a stop in front of a house which showed in misty outlines through the fog. Mason, Della Street and Paul Drake jumped out of the automobile, watched Harrington Faulkner carefully lock the ignition of his car, then lock the car door, following which he walked completely around the automobile, trying each of the doors to make sure it was locked. He even tried the trunk to make sure that it too was firmly bolted. Then he moved over to join them.

Having joined them, he took a leather key container from his pocket, carefully slid the zipper around the edges, took out a key and said in the precise tones of a lecturer explaining something to an audience in which he had only an impersonal interest, "Now, Mr. Mason, you will notice that there are two outer doors to this house, the one on the left bears the sign 'FAULKNER AND CARSON, INCORPORATED, REALTORS.' The door on the right is the door to my house."

"Where does Elmer Carson live?" Mason asked.

"A few blocks down the street."

"I notice," Mason pointed out, "that the house is dark."

"Yes," Faulkner said tonelessly, "my wife evidently isn't home."

"Now the particular fish about which you are mainly concerned," Mason went on, "are the black Veiltail

17

Moors which are in the tank or aquarium that is in the office?"

"That's right, and Elmer Carson claims the tank is an office fixture and that the fish are a part of the office furnishings. He's secured a restraining order keeping me from moving any fixture or even tampering with them."

"The fish were raised entirely by you?"

"Correct."

"Carson made no financial contribution?"

"None whatever. The fish were raised from a strain which I developed. However, the tank, Mr. Mason, *was* billed to the corporation as an article of office furniture, and it is so fastened to the building that it probably would be considered a fixture. It is, you understand, an oblong tank some three feet by two feet and four feet deep. There was a recess in the wall of the building, a place which was occupied by a china closet and which certainly added nothing to our office. I suggested that this closet could be removed and an aquarium inserted in the space. This was done with Carson's approval and co-operation. When the bills came in, without thinking, I okayed them as an office expense, and, unfortunately, they were so carried on our books and in our income tax report. The tank is undoubtedly affixed to the building, and the building is owned by the corporation."

"The entire building?" Mason asked.

"Yes. I have taken a lease on the other side of it where I live."

"Then how did it happen that you put such valuable fish in the tank that was a part of the office?"

"Well, you see, Mr. Mason, it's rather a long story. Originally, I put in a water garden in the bottom of the tank, a device to aerate the water and an assortment of some two dozen various types of interesting goldfish—the Fringetail, the Chinese Telescope, some Japanese Comets, some Nymphs and some Autumn Brocades. Then I developed these Veiltail Moor Telescopes, and suddenly found that other fish in another tank in which they were kept had developed something which looked suspiciously like gill fever, or rather a gill disease, since the fish really had passed the gill-fever stage. I wanted some place to move these Moors at once where I could have them under observation; and, without thinking of the possible legal complications, I cleaned out the other fish and inserted these Veiltail Moors in the office tank. Almost immediately my troubles commenced. The fish developed disease and Elmer Carson suddenly blew up and demanded that I pay him an exorbitant price for his interest in the business. He went to court and got a restraining order preventing me from moving that fish tank away from the premises, on the ground that it was a fixture. I simply can't understand what caused his sudden change of attitude, the bitter animosity with which he regards me. It happened almost overnight and followed an attempt on my life."

"An attempt on your life!" Mason exclaimed.

"Exactly."

"What happened?"

"Someone tried to shoot me. But after all, gentlemen, this is hardly the place to discuss these matters. Let's go on in and— Hello, what's this?"

"Seems to be a car stopping in front of the place," Mason said.

The automobile which had pulled in to the curb disgorged two passengers, a man and a woman. As the figures materialized through the fog, Faulkner said, "It's that Madison girl and her boy friend. This is a great time for *them* to be getting here! I gave her a key to the place. They should have been here thirty minutes ago. She started out fast enough. Didn't even wait to finish her dinner. I suppose it's that boy who held her up."

Mason lowered his voice and talked rapidly. "Look here, Faulkner, that *tank* may be a fixture and therefore a part of the building which can't be moved, but the fish

19

certainly aren't a fixture. They're swimming around in the tank. Get a bucket or a net and lift those fish out and leave the tank in place—then you can fight out the restraining order with Elmer Carson."

"By George, you've got something there!" Faulkner exclaimed. "Those fish are . . ." He broke off abruptly to turn to the couple who were hurrying up the walk. "Well, well," he said testily. "What was holding *you* up?"

The slender, somewhat bony-shouldered young man with Sally Madison said, "I'm sorry, Mr. Faulkner, but the boss had a case of gill disease to treat and I had to coat a tank so he'd have a place to . . ."

"Wait a minute, wait a minute," Faulkner interrupted. "Do you mean to say you're passing out the secret of this remedy right and left? Don't you realize I just paid for an interest in that invention? You can't tell a soul . . ."

"No, no," Sally Madison interposed hastily and soothingly, "he isn't *telling* anyone, Mr. Faulkner. The remedy is a secret, but you know Tom's been experimenting with it there at the pet shop and of course Rawlins knew what he was doing and— Well, you know how it is. But no one knows the secret formula, except Tom. It will be turned over to you and . . ."

"I don't like it," Faulkner snapped. "I don't like it at all. That's not the way to do business. How do we know that Rawlins isn't faking the whole business? He'll get hold of the material Tom is using to coat those panels and have it analyzed and then where will my investment be? I tell you I don't like it."

Faulkner angrily inserted a key in the lock of the door, snapped back the catch, flung the door open, reached inside, switched on a light and marched truculently into the room.

Sally Madison placed a hand on Mason's arm, said proudly, "This is Tom, Mr. Mason."

Mason grinned, said, "How are you, Tom?" and extended his hand, which was wrapped in the grip of long, bony fingers.

Gridley said, "I'm glad to know you, Mr. Mason. I've heard so much about you that . . ."

He was interrupted by an exclamation from Harrington Faulkner. "Who's been in here? What's happened? Call the police!"

Mason pushed through the doorway and followed the direction of Harrington Faulkner's angry eyes.

The tank which had been inserted in place of the china closet had been ripped from its fastenings and moved out to the extreme edge of a built-in sideboard. A chair had been placed in front of the sideboard, making a convenient step upon which some person had evidently stood. Water was splashed about on the waxed hardwood floor, and lying on the floor beside the chair was an ordinary long-handled silver soup ladle. To the handle of this ladle a four-foot section of broomstick had been attached so as to form a rude but effective extension.

The bottom of the goldfish tank contained an inch or two of small pebbles and sea shells with a few plants that stretched green shoots up toward the surface of the water. There was no sign of life in the tank.

"My fish!" Faulkner exclaimed, grasping the edges of the tank with his hands, pressing his face to within a few inches of the glass sides of the tank. "What's happened to the fish? Where are they?"

"They seem to have disappeared," Mason said dryly.

"I've been robbed!" Faulkner exclaimed. "It's a low-down dastardly attempt by Elmer Carson to . . ."

"Careful now," Mason warned.

"Careful!" Faulkner exploded. "Why should I be careful? You can see what's happened with your own eyes. It's as plain as the nose on your face. He's removed the fish from the tank and intends to use that as a club to make me come to his terms. . . . Hang it, it's just the same as kidnaping. I don't intend to stand for this. He's

21

gone too far now. I'm going to have him arrested! I'm going to get the police on the job and we'll settle this thing right here and right now."

Faulkner darted over to the telephone, snatched up the receiver, dialed Operator, and screeched into the mouthpiece, "Get me police headquarters quick! I want to report a burglary."

Mason moved over to the telephone. "Look here, Faulkner," he warned, "be careful what you say. You can call the police, tell them your story and let *them* reach any conclusions they want, but don't go making accusations and don't mention names. From a collector's standpoint those fish of yours are probably of considerable value, but so far as the police are concerned, they're just two more goldfish you . . ."

Faulkner motioned Mason to silence, said into the telephone in a voice that was tremulous with emotion, "I want police on the job right away. This is Harrington Faulkner. I've been robbed. My most priceless possession. . . . Get the best detectives on the force out here right away."

Mason moved back to join the others. "Let's get out," he said quietly. "If the police take this thing seriously they'll want to take fingerprints."

"Suppose they don't take it seriously?" Drake asked.

Mason shrugged his shoulders.

Over at the telephone, Harrington Faulkner repeated his name, gave the address and hung up. "The police say to get everyone out of the room." He fairly screeched in his excitement. "They told me . . ."

"I know, I know," Mason interpolated soothingly. "I've just told everyone to get out and leave the place as it is."

"You can come next door," Faulkner said. "That's where I live. We'll wait there for the police."

Faulkner ushered them out to the porch, across to the other door of the duplex house which he opened, and switched on lights. "My wife is out," he explained, "but if you'll just wait here. . . . Make yourselves right at home, please. Just be seated. The police say it will only be a few minutes before they have a radio car out here."

"How about the door to the other side of the house?" Mason asked. "You'd better see that it's locked and that no one gets in until the police arrive."

"There's a spring lock on it. It locks when you pull the door shut."

"You're certain that the door was locked when you arrived?" Mason asked.

"Yes, yes. You saw me insert the key and open the door," Faulkner said impatiently. "The door was locked and the lock hadn't been tampered with."

"How about the windows?" Drake asked. "Did you notice whether *they* were locked?"

"*I* noticed," Mason said as Faulkner scowled in an effort to concentrate. "All the windows in that room at least were locked. How many rooms are in the place, Faulkner?"

"Four. That room is our executive office where we have our desks. Then there's another room which we use as a filing room. We fitted up the kitchen so there's a little bar and an electric icebox. We can buy a customer a drink if the occasion seems appropriate. I'll go and look through those other rooms and see if I can find where anything's been disturbed. But I'm certain I'll find everything in order. The man who stole those fish opened the front door with a key and walked right in. He knew exactly where to go, what to get and just what he was doing."

"Better not go in there until the police come," Mason warned. "They might not like it."

The sound of a siren cut through the foggy darkness outside and throbbed ominously. Faulkner jumped up, ran to the front door and stood on the porch, waiting for the police car.

"Going in?" Drake asked Mason.

23

Mason shook his head, said, "We stick right here."

Tom Gridley moved uneasily. "I left a couple of plastic panels out in my car," he said. "They were painted and all ready to insert in the tank. I . . ."

"Your car locked?" Mason asked.

"No, that's the point, it isn't."

"Better go out and lock it then. Wait until after the police get in. I take it you're taking every precaution to keep your formula secret?"

Tom Gridley nodded. "I shouldn't have even told Rawlins I had a remedy."

Authoritative voices sounded from the outside. Harrington Faulkner by this time had regained control of his emotions and his voice was once more precise in its articulation. Steps moved across the porch. The door to the other house opened and closed.

Mason nodded to Gridley. "Better take advantage of this opportunity to run out and lock your car," he said.

Paul Drake grinned across at Mason. "The great goldfish case!"

Mason chuckled. "Serves me right for letting my curiosity run away with me."

"Wait until the police find out *you're* here," Drake said gleefully.

"And you," Mason retorted. "Particularly when they report the call to the press room."

The grin faded from Drake's face. "Hang it, I feel sort of sheepish."

"There's no reason why you should," Sally Madison said. "These goldfish mean as much to Mr. Faulkner as though they were members of his family. It's just the same as if he had had a son kidnaped. Is that someone coming?"

They listened, heard the sound of a car, then quick steps, and a moment later the front door opened.

The woman who stood on the threshold was a blonde somewhere in the middle thirties and making a valiant attempt to preserve a figure which had begun to fill out. The curves were still attractive, but were becoming ample, and there was a girdled smoothness about the fit of her skirt, a conscious elevation of the corners of the mouth, a determined effort at holding the chin high—all of which combined to give an effect of static immobility. The woman seemed somehow to have robbed herself of all her natural spontaneity in an attempt to stay the hand of time. Her every move seemed to have been rehearsed in front of a mirror.

Sally Madison said almost under her breath, "Mrs. Faulkner!"

Mason and Drake jumped to their feet. Mason moved forward. "Permit me to introduce myself, Mrs. Faulkner. I'm Perry Mason. I came out here at the request of your husband who seems to have encountered some trouble in the real estate office next door. This is Miss Street, my secretary, and Miss Madison. And may I present Mr. Paul Drake, head of the Drake Detective Agency."

Mrs. Faulkner swept on into the room. From the doorway a somewhat embarrassed Tom Gridley stood uncertainly as though debating whether to enter or to turn and seek refuge in the car.

"And," Mason observed, swinging around to include Gridley in his introduction, "Mr. Thomas Gridley."

Mrs. Faulkner's voice was well-modulated. It had a slow, almost drawling quality that was deep-throated and seductive. "Do make yourselves right at home," she said. "My husband has been very much upset lately and I'm glad that he has finally consulted a prominent attorney. I have been suggesting that he do so for some time. Do be seated, please, and I'll get you a drink."

"Perhaps," Della Street suggested, "I could be of some help."

Mrs. Faulkner turned wary, appraising blue eyes upon Mason's secretary, regarded her for a moment, then her face softened into a smile. "Why yes," she said graciously, "if you'd like to. It would be very nice."

Della Street followed Mrs. Faulkner out through the dining room into the kitchen.

Sally Madison turned to Mason. "See what I mean?" she asked cryptically, and then added parenthetically, "Goldfish."

Tom Gridley moved over to Sally Madison, said apologetically, "Of course, I *could* have kept Rawlins waiting on coating those other panels until after I'd put these panels in Faulkner's tank. I suppose I should have insisted."

"Don't be silly. It wouldn't have made a particle of difference. We'd have come dashing out here, and then *we'd* have been the ones to have found the tank empty. He'd have managed to blame us for that somehow, for . . . Say, you don't suppose the old buzzard's going to get technical about that check, now that his goldfish have been stolen?"

Gridley said, "I don't see any reason why he should. That formula is a safe and sure cure for gill disease. They've never had anything before that could come anywhere near touching it. Why, I can cure any case within forty-eight hours—well, make it seventy-two hours to be on the safe side, but . . ."

"Never mind, dear," Sally Madison said, as though cautioning him to silence. "These people aren't particularly interested in goldfish."

Paul Drake caught Mason's eye, closed his own eye in a slow wink.

Mrs. Faulkner and Della Street returned from the kitchen with glasses, ice cubes, scotch and soda. Mrs. Faulkner poured drinks, Della Street served them. Then Mrs. Faulkner seated herself across the room from Mason. She crossed well-curved legs and saw that the sweep of her skirt was just right across the knee. "I have," she said to Perry Mason with an artificial smile,

26

"heard a lot about you. I hoped that someday I'd meet you. I've read about all your cases—followed them with a great deal of interest."

"Thank you," Mason said, and had just started to say something else when the front door was pushed open and Harrington Faulkner, white with rage, said in a voice indignation had made harsh and rasping, "Do you know what they told me? They told me that there's no law against kidnaping fish! They said that if I could *prove* outside thieves got into the place it would be burglary, but since Elmer Carson owns a half interest in the place and has the right to come and go as he pleases, that if *he* wanted to enter the place and take my goldfish, the only thing I could do would be to start a civil suit for damages. And then one of the officers had the temerity to tell me that the damages wouldn't amount to much; that you could buy a whole flock of goldfish for half the amount I'd have to pay a lawyer to draw up the papers. The ignorance of the man is as annoying as it is unpardonable. A *flock* of fish! The ignoramus! You'd have thought he was talking about birds."

"Did you," Mason asked, "tell him that Elmer Carson was the one who had taken the fish?"

Faulkner's eyes shifted away from Mason's. "Well, of course I told him that I'd been having trouble with Carson and that Carson had a key. You see, whoever got in must have got in through the door."

"The windows all locked?" Mason asked.

"The windows were all locked. Someone had taken a screw driver or a chisel and pried open the kitchen door, but it was a clumsy job. As the officers pointed out, it had been done from the *inside,* and furthermore, the door on the screen porch was hooked shut. Whoever did it made a very clumsy attempt to make it seem that burglars had forced an entrance through the back door. No one would have been fooled by it. I don't know anything about

27

burglary, but just as soon as I looked at the marks on the door even *I* could tell what had happened."

Mason said, "I warned you not to make any charges against Carson. In the first place, you're putting yourself in a dangerous position making accusations which you can't substantiate, and in the second place, I felt certain that once the police got the idea that it was a feud between two business associates, they'd wash their hands of the entire affair."

"Well, it's been done now," Faulkner said coldly, "and personally I don't think the way you suggested that I handle it was the proper way to have handled it. When you come right down to it, Mr. Mason, my interest in the matter lies in recovering my fish before it is too late. Those fish are very valuable. They mean as much to me as my own family. The fish are in a very critical condition and I want them back so I can treat them and save their lives. You're as bad as the police, with your damned don't-do-this and don't-do-that."

Faulkner's voice rose to a rasp of nervous tension. The man's calm seemed so completely shattered that he might have been on the verge of hysteria. "Can't any of you understand the importance of this? Don't you realize that those fish represent the crowning achievement of something that has been my hobby for years? You all sit there doing nothing, making no constructive suggestions. Those fish are sick. They may be dying right now, and no one lifts a finger to do anything about it. Not a finger! You just sit here guzzling my whisky while they die!"

Faulkner's wife didn't shift her position or even turn her head to look at her husband. She said, over her shoulder, as though speaking to a child, "That will do, Harrington. There's nothing anyone could have done. You called the police, and apparently you botched things all up with them. Perhaps if you'd have invited *them* in to have a drink with us they'd have been inclined to look at the situation in an entirely different manner."

The telephone rang. Faulkner went to it, picked up the receiver, rasped, "Hello . . . yes, this is he speaking."

For several seconds he listened to what was being said at the other end of the line. Then a triumphant smile spread over his face. "Then it's all right. The deal's closed," he said. "We can sign the papers as soon as you can get them drawn up. . . . Yes, I'll expect you to pay for them . . . all the details of transferring title."

He listened a moment more, then hung up.

Mason watched the man curiously as he marched from the telephone to stand in front of Sally Madison. "I hate to be held up," he announced in a rasping voice.

Sally Madison moved only her long eyelashes. "Yes?" she asked in a drawling voice.

"*You* tried to hold me up tonight," Faulkner went on, "and I warned you I was a bad man to fool with."

She blew out cigarette smoke, said nothing.

"So," Faulkner stated triumphantly, "I'm stopping payment on that check I gave you. I have just completed a deal that has been pending with David Rawlins by which I have purchased his business outright, including the fixtures, the good will, all formulae, and all inventions he or any of his employees have worked out."

Faulkner turned swiftly to Tom Gridley. "You're working for me now, young man."

Sally Madison kept the dismay out of her eyes, but her voice held a quaver, "You can't do that, Mr. Faulkner."

"I've already done it."

"Tom's invention doesn't go with Mr. Rawlins' business. Tom perfected that on his own time."

"Bosh. That's what they all say. We'll see what a judge has to say about *that*. And now, young woman, I'll trouble you to return that check I gave you earlier this evening. I've bought the entire business for less than half of the amount you were holding me up for."

Sally Madison shook her head doggedly. "You closed the deal. You paid for the formula."

"A formula you had no right to sell. I should have you arrested for obtaining money under false pretenses. As it is, you'll either give me back that check or I'll stop payment on it."

Tom Gridley said, "After all, Sally, it doesn't amount to so much. It's only . . ."

Faulkner turned to him. "Not amount to so much, young man! Is that any way to talk about . . ."

Mrs. Faulkner's voice showed interest as her husband suddenly became silent. "Go on, dear," she said. "Let's hear how much. I'm wondering just how much you paid her."

Faulkner scowled at her and said savagely, "If it's any of your business, it was five thousand dollars."

"Five thousand dollars!" Tom Gridley exclaimed. "Why I told Sally to sell it for . . ." Abruptly he caught Sally Madison's eyes and stopped speaking in the middle of the sentence.

Drake hurriedly gulped down his drink as he saw Perry Mason put down his glass, arise from his chair, cross over to Faulkner. "I think," Drake said in a low voice to Della Street, who was watching Mason with amused eyes, "this is where we came in—and it's damned good whisky. I hate to waste it."

Mason said to Faulkner, "I don't think we need to trouble you further, Mr. Faulkner. Your case doesn't interest me in the least, and there's no charge for the preliminary investigation."

Mrs. Faulkner said hastily, "Please don't judge him too harshly, Mr. Mason. He's just a bundle of nerves."

Mason bowed. "And I'd also be a bundle of nerves—if I had him for a client. Good night."

4

■

Mason, attired in pajamas and lounging robe, stretched out in a reclining chair, a floor lamp shedding soft radiance on the book in his hand. The telephone at his elbow rang sharply.

Only Paul Drake and Della Street had the number of this telephone. So Mason promptly closed his book, scooped the receiver to his ear and said, "Hello."

Drake's voice came over the wire. "Remember the golddigger, Perry?"

"The one in the restaurant the other night?"

"That's right."

"What about her?"

"She's having a fit trying to get in touch with you. She's begging me to give her your number."

"Where is she?"

"Right now she's on the other telephone."

"What does she want?"

"Darned if I know, but *she* seems to think it's terribly urgent."

"It's after ten o'clock, Paul."

"I know it, but she's begging with tears in her voice to be permitted to talk with you."

Mason said, "Won't tomorrow morning be all right?"

"She says not. It's something terribly important. She's made a sale with me, Perry, otherwise I wouldn't have called you."

"Get a number where I can call her," Mason said.

"I've already done that. Got a pencil handy?"

"Okay. What's the number?"

"Columbia six-nine-eight-four-three."

"Okay. Tell her to hang up and wait for a call from me. Where are you, at the office?"

"Yes. I looked in on my way to the apartment to see if there was anything important, and this call came in while I was here. She'd called twice before within a period of ten minutes."

Mason said, "Okay. Better stick around there for a while, Paul, in case it turns out to be something really important. I'll call you in case I need you. Stick around for an hour anyhow."

"Okay," Drake said, and hung up.

Mason waited a full minute, then dialed the number Drake had given him. Almost immediately he heard Sally Madison's throaty voice saying, "Hello—hello—this is Miss Madison. Oh, it's Mr. Mason! Thank you *so* much for calling, Mr. Mason! Something has happened that makes it terribly important I see you at once. I'll come any place you say. But I must see you, I simply must."

"What's it about?"

"We've found the goldfish."

"What goldfish?"

"The Veiltail Moor Telescopes."

"You mean the ones that were stolen?"

"Well . . . yes."

"Where are they?"

"A man has them."

"Have you notified Faulkner?"

"No."

"Why not do it?"

"Because . . . because of the circumstances. I don't think . . . I think I'd better talk with *you*, Mr. Mason."

"And it won't keep until tomorrow?"

32

"No. No. Oh, please, Mr. Mason. Please let me see you."

"Gridley with you?"

"No. I'm alone."

"All right. Come up," Mason said, and gave her the address of his apartment. "How long will it take you to get here?"

"Ten minutes."

"All right. I'll be waiting."

Mason hung up the telephone, dressed leisurely, and had just finished knotting his necktie when a ring sounded at the outer door of his apartment. He let Sally Madison in, said, "What's all the excitement?"

Her eyes were bright with animation and excitement, but her face still retained its glazed veneer of expressionless beauty. "You remember that Mr. Rawlins wanted a tank built . . ."

"Who's Rawlins?" Mason asked.

"The man Tom Gridley is working for. He owns the pet store."

"Oh yes, I remember the name now."

"Well, that man who had Tom fix up a tank for him was James L. Staunton. He's in the insurance business and no one seems to know very much about him. I mean that he hasn't ever done anything with goldfish as far as anyone knows. He telephoned in to Mr. Rawlins Wednesday night and told him he had some very valuable fish that had gill disease and he understood the Rawlins Pet Shop had a treatment that would cure it, and he was willing to pay any amount if Rawlins would treat these fish. He finally offered a hundred dollars if Mr. Rawlins would promise to give him whatever was necessary for the fish. Well, that was too much money for Rawlins to pass up, so he got hold of Tom and insisted that Tom put a couple of panels in a small tank before we went out to Mr. Faulkner's that night. That's what detained us. You remember I didn't even finish my dinner, but went tearing out to get hold of Tom the minute I got the check, because I didn't want Faulkner's fish to die on us."

Mason nodded silently as she paused in her rapid-fire statement long enough to take a quick breath.

"Well," she went on, "Mr. Rawlins himself delivered the tank and Staunton told him his wife was ill and he didn't want to have any noise—and that he'd take care of the fish himself if Mr. Rawlins would just tell him how to do it. So Rawlins told him there wasn't anything to it, just to fill the tank with water, transfer the fish, and that sometime the next morning Rawlins would send out another panel to be inserted in the tank. You're getting this straight, Mr. Mason?"

"Go ahead, I think I'm getting it okay."

"Well, Tom painted up some panels and Mr. Rawlins took the second panel out the next morning. Once more Staunton met him at the door, told him in a whisper that his wife had had a very bad night, and that it would be better if Rawlins didn't come in. So Rawlins told him that there was nothing complicated about the treatment—to just slip the old panel out of the tank and gently put the new one in. He asked Mr. Staunton about how the fish were, and Staunton said they seemed to be better. He took the panel and paid Mr. Rawlins fifty dollars on account, and Rawlins told him a new panel would have to be put in the tank thirty-six to forty-six hours later."

Once more she stopped, partially out of breath, partially in preparation for the dramatic climax to her story.

Mason nodded for her to proceed.

"Well, tonight I was down at the store. Tom had been home sick, and I was helping Mr. Rawlins. You see, Mr. Faulkner really did buy out the store and Rawlins was taking inventory, and because Tom was sick today he needed someone to help him. Mr. Faulkner had been there from a little after five o'clock until around seven-thirty, making a lot of trouble. He'd even done something terrible that Mr. Rawlins wouldn't tell me about. It had upset Mr. Rawlins so that he'd quarreled—Rawlins said he'd tell me tomorrow—he'd taken something of Tom's. Well, all of this is just to explain why I promised to take out that treatment. You see, Mr. Rawlins was planning to go out to Staunton's house to put that last panel in the tank when Rawlins' wife called up and said there was a movie she wanted to see and wanted him to take her. When Mrs. Rawlins wants anything like that she doesn't want to be put off, and so Mr. Rawlins said he'd have to go and I told him I'd finish up, lock up the store and use my own car to take the panel out."

"And you did?" Mason asked.

"That's right. Mr. Rawlins was so nervous he was almost crazy. I finished the inventory and then just a short time ago took the panel out there. Mr. Staunton wasn't home, but his wife was there and I told her I was from the pet store and that I had a new panel to insert in the fish tank, that it would only take a minute or two to put it in. She was very gracious and told me to come right on in. She said her husband had the fish tank in his study. That he was out and wouldn't be back for awhile and that it would probably be better if I put the panel in, as she didn't want to take the responsibility."

"So you went on in with the panel?" Mason asked.

"That's right, and when I got in the study I found the tank contained a pair of *Veiltail Moor Telescopes!*"

"What did you do?"

"For a moment I was too flabbergasted to do anything."

"Where was Mrs. Staunton?"

"Standing right beside me. She'd shown me into the study and was waiting for me to change the panel."

"What did you do?"

"After a minute I just walked over to the tank, took the old panel out and slipped in the new one that was coated with Tom's remedy. Then I tried to start talking about the fish. You know, saying they were very beauti-

35

ful, asking whether Mr. Staunton had any other fish or not, and how long he'd had these."

"What did his wife say?"

"She thought the fish were ugly, and said so. She told me that her husband picked them up somewhere, that he'd never dabbled around with fish before and didn't know anything about them. She said that some friend had given him these two and that they hadn't been well when he got them. That the friend was giving him specific instructions, telling him just what to do. She said that personally she'd have liked it a lot better if her husband had started out with just a couple of plain goldfish. That these were supposed to be extra fancy—that they gave her the creeps with their long, sweeping black fins and tails, their swivel eyes and the funereal color. She said that somehow they seemed symbolic of death. Well, of course, *that* wasn't anything new because the fish have long been called 'The Fish of Death,' due to some ancient superstition and the peculiar appearance they have."

"Then what?" Mason asked.

"Well, I hung around and talked with her for a minute and lied to her a little. I told her I'd been sick and that there'd been a lot of sickness at the store. I talked along those lines for a minute and then she told me that she had been sick last year but that she hadn't even had so much as a headache since then—that she had taken some cold shots a year ago and started taking vitamins steadily, and that the combination seemed to have done wonders for her."

"And then?" Mason asked.

"Then I realized what I was up against, and suddenly became afraid Mr. Staunton would come back and I'd run right slap into him. So I got out just as fast as I could. I've been terribly afraid that if he came home his wife would tell him what we were talking about, and about the questions I'd asked, and then he'd get rid of the fish, or do something."

"What makes you think they were Faulkner's fish?"

"Oh, I'm certain they were. They're the same size and description and they were suffering from gill disease, although they're pretty well cured now and, of course, Veiltail Moors, particularly Telescopes, are very rare and it's inconceivable a man would start out with two fish like that, particularly if they were sick. And then, of course, there's all those lies he told about his wife being sick. All the things he did to keep Mr. Rawlins from getting a look at the fish."

"You've told Tom about this?" Mason asked.

"No, I've told no one. I got out of the house and went to your office and tried to get the night janitor to tell me where I could get in touch with you. He wouldn't do it—said he didn't know and then I was almost frantic. I remembered your secretary's name was Della Street, but I couldn't find her listed in the telephone book. Then I remembered you'd said Mr. Drake was the head of the Drake Detective Agency, so I looked *him* up in the book and found the number of his office. I called there and the night operator told me Mr. Drake was out but that he usually looked in at the office before he went home at night and that if he came in within the next hour they'd have him call me if I'd leave my number. I left my number but I also kept calling because I was afraid they might forget to give him the message."

"And you haven't told anyone about this?"

"No. I didn't even tell Mr. Drake. I decided I wouldn't tell him unless I had to in order to reach you."

"You didn't tell Tom Gridley?"

"No."

"Why?"

"Because Tom's been terribly upset. He's started running a high temperature every afternoon. You see, Mr. Faulkner has been exerting lots of pressure."

"Did he stop payment on his check?"

"Not that exactly. He put it up to me in another way.

37

He told me that the minute I cashed that check he'd have me arrested for obtaining money under false pretenses. He claims Tom developed the invention on Rawlins' time and that the whole secret of the thing is a part of the business that he's bought."

"He really bought the business?"

"Oh yes. He paid Rawlins two thousand for the business, the stock and the good will, and made Rawlins agree to stay on and run it for a small salary. Rawlins hates him. I think everyone hates him, Mr. Mason. And yet the man is *so* self-righteous according to his own code. He thinks the law is the law, and business is business. I presume he really thinks that Tom is holding out on him, and that I was trying to hold him up—and I guess I was."

"Has he made any offer by way of settlement?"

"Oh yes."

"What?"

"Tom is to turn over his formula. I'm to surrender the five-thousand-dollar check. Tom is to agree to keep on working in the pet store for a year at his present salary and to turn over all subsequent treatments or inventions he may work out. In return for all that, Mr. Faulkner will pay Tom seven hundred and fifty dollars and keep paying him the same salary."

"Generous, isn't he?" Mason said. "No provision for Tom to take a layoff for treatment?"

"No. That's what makes me so angry. Another year in that pet store and Tom would be past all cure."

"Doesn't Faulkner take that into consideration?"

"Apparently not. He says Tom can get out in the sunshine on week ends, and that if Tom is too sick to work now, he doesn't need to accept the position. He says Tom's at liberty to quit work any time he wants to, that Tom's health is Tom's own personal problem and that it's nothing to Faulkner. Faulkner says that if he went through life worrying about the health of his employees, he wouldn't have any time left to devote to his own business. Oh, Mr. Mason, it's men like that who make the world such a hard place for other men to live and work!"

"So you didn't tell Faulkner about finding his fish?"

"No."

"And you don't want to?"

She met Mason's eyes. "I'm afraid he'd accuse us of having stolen them or something. I want *you* to handle this, Mr. Mason. And I feel that somehow you might—well, might turn some of Mr. Faulkner's weapons against him—perhaps do something for Tom."

Mason grinned, reached for his hat. "It took you long enough to say so," he observed. "Come on. Let's go."

"You don't think it's too late—to do something tonight?"

"It's never too late to learn," the lawyer said. "And we're at least going to learn something."

5

■

The night was cold and clear. Mason drove rapidly through the late after-theater traffic. Sally Madison ventured a suggestion. "Wouldn't it perhaps be better to just start some detectives watching Staunton's house so as to make sure he didn't move the fish? And then wait until tomorrow?"

Mason shook his head. "Let's find out where we stand. The thing really has me interested now."

Thereafter they drove in silence until Mason slowed down as he came in sight of a rather pretentious stucco house with a red tile roof and wide windows. "This should be the number," he said.

"This is the place," Sally Madison declared. "They're still up. You can see there's a light in that side window."

Mason slid the car in to the curb, switching off the ignition, and walked up the cement walk to the three stairs which led to a tiled porch.

"What are you going to say?" Sally Madison asked, excitement raising her voice to a higher pitch than usual.

"I don't know," Mason told her. "It'll depend on what happens. I always like to plan my campaign after I've sized up my man." He pressed a bell button at the side of the door, and a moment later the door was opened by a tall, rather distinguished-looking gentleman in the middle fifties.

"Mr. James L. Staunton?" Mason asked.

"That's right."

Mason said, "This is Sally Madison from the Rawlins Pet Store, and I am Perry Mason, a lawyer."

"Yes. Oh yes. I was sorry I wasn't in tonight when you called, Miss Madison. I wanted to tell you that the treatment you had given the fish proved to be a great success and I suppose you want the rest of your money. I have it here all ready for you."

Staunton gravely counted out fifty dollars and, trying to make his voice sound very casual, added, "If you'll just give me a receipt, Miss Madison."

Mason said, "I think the matter has gone a little bit past that point, Mr. Staunton."

"What do you mean?"

"I mean there's some question about the ownership of the fish which you have. Would you mind telling us where you got them?"

Staunton drew himself up with a dignity so rigid that it might have been a mask to hide fright. "I certainly would, I don't consider it any of your business."

"Suppose I should tell you those fish had been stolen?"

"*Were* they stolen?"

"I don't know," Mason admitted frankly. "But there are some rather suspicious circumstances."

"Are you making an accusation?"

"Not at all."

"Well, it sounded to me as though you were. I've heard of you and I know you're a very able lawyer, Mr. Mason, but it occurs to me you had better watch what you say. If you'll pardon the suggestion, I'm quite capable of running my own business and it might be well if you'd devote *your* attention to *your* business."

Mason grinned, took his cigarette case from his pocket. "Have one?" he asked.

"No," Staunton said curtly, and stepped back as though to slam the door shut.

Mason extended the cigarette case to Sally Madison, said casually to Staunton, "Miss Madison asked my advice. I was about to tell her that unless you had some satisfactory explanation, I considered it was her duty to report the matter to the police. That, of course, might prove embarrassing. But if you want it that way, it's all right with me."

Mason snapped a match into flame, held it to the tip of Sally Madison's cigarette, then to his own.

"That sounds very much like a threat," Staunton charged, apparently falling back on a repetition of his previous charge.

By this time, Mason was sure of his man. He blew smoke into Staunton's face and said, "It does, doesn't it?"

Staunton drew back in startled surprise at the lawyer's insolent assurance. "I don't like your manner, Mr. Mason, and I don't care to stand here and be insulted."

"That's right," Mason agreed. "But you've already missed your chance to do anything about it."

"What do you mean?"

"I mean that if you hadn't anything to conceal about those fish, you'd have told me to go to the devil five

41

minutes ago and slammed the door. You didn't have
nerve enough to do it. You're curious as to what I know,
and afraid of what I'm going to do next. You're standing
there in a lather of indecision, wondering whether you
dare take the chance of slamming the door, rushing inside, and telephoning the man who told you to take care
of the fish for him."

Staunton said, "Mr. Mason, as a lawyer, you're doubtless aware that you're defaming my character."

"That's right. And as a lawyer, I know that the truth is
a defense to slander. So make up your mind, Staunton,
and make it up fast. Are you going to talk with me, or
are you going to talk to the police?"

Staunton clung to the doorknob for some two or three
seconds, then suddenly lost the dignified shell which had
been interposed as an ineffectual armor against the lawyer's attack.

"Come in," he said.

Mason stood to one side for Sally Madison to precede
him into the house.

From a living room on the right, a woman's voice
called, "What is it, dear?"

"A business matter," Staunton called, and then added,
"some insurance. I'll take them into the study."

Staunton opened a door and ushered his visitors into a
room which had been fitted up as an office, with an
old-fashioned roll-top desk, a safe, a table, a half dozen
steel filing cabinets, and a secretarial desk. On top of the
filing cabinets was an oblong glass container filled with
water. Two fish swam lazily about in this container.

Mason moved across to look at the fish, almost as soon
as Staunton had switched on the light.

"So these," Mason said, "are the Veiltail Moor Telescopes, sometimes referred to as 'The Fish of Death'."

Staunton said nothing.

Mason curiously regarded the dark fish, their long fins
sweeping down in black veils, regarded the protruding

eyes which were as black as the bodies of the fish. "Well," he announced, "as far as I'm concerned, anyone who wants my interest in them can have them. There certainly is something sinister about them."

"Won't you sit down?" Staunton ventured, somewhat dubiously.

Mason waited for Sally Madison to seat herself, then stretched himself comfortably in a chair. He grinned over at Staunton and said, "You can spare yourself a lot of trouble and nerve strain if you'll begin at the beginning and tell your story."

"Suppose you ask me what you want to know."

Mason jerked his thumb toward the telephone. "I've asked my question. If there's any more questioning to be done, it'll be done by the police."

"I don't fear the police. Suppose I should just call your bluff, Mr. Mason?"

"Go ahead."

"I have nothing to conceal, and I have committed no crime. I've received you at this unusually late hour because I know who you are and have a certain respect for your professional standing, but I'm not going to be insulted."

"Who gave you the fish?" Mason asked.

"That's a question I don't care to answer."

Mason took the cigarette from his mouth, casually moved his long legs, and walked over to the telephone, picked up the receiver, dialed Operator, and said, "Give me police headquarters, please."

Staunton said rapidly, "Wait a minute, Mr. Mason! You're going altogether too fast! If you make any accusations against me to the police you'll regret it."

Without looking around, still holding the receiver to his ear, Mason said over his shoulder, "Who gave you the fish, Staunton?"

"If you want to know," Staunton almost shouted in exasperation, "it was Harrington Faulkner!"

43

"I thought it might have been," Mason said, and dropped the receiver back into its cradle.

"So," Staunton went on defiantly, "the fish belong to Harrington Faulkner. He gave them to me to keep for him. I write a lot of insurance for the Faulkner-Carson Realty Company. I was glad to do Mr. Faulkner a favor. There's certainly no law against that, and I think you'll *now* appreciate the danger of your position in insinuating the fish were stolen and that I am acting in collusion with the thief."

Mason returned to his chair, crossed his long legs at the knees, grinned at the now indignant Staunton and said, "How were the fish brought to you—in the tank which is on the filing cases at the present time?"

"No. If Miss Madison is from the pet store, she'll know that's a treatment tank they furnished. It's an oblong tank made to accommodate the medicated panels which are slid down into the water."

"What sort of tank were they in when you got them?" Mason asked.

Staunton hesitated, then said, "After all, Mr. Mason, I don't see what that has to do with it."

"It might be considered significant."

"I don't think so."

Mason said, "I'll tell you this much. If Harrington Faulkner delivered those fish to you, he did so as part of a fraudulent scheme he was perpetrating, and as a part of that scheme he reported the theft of these fish to the police. Now the police aren't going to like that. So, if you have any connection with what happened, you had better get into the clear right now."

"I didn't have any connection with any fraudulent scheme. All I know is that Mr. Faulkner asked me to take charge of these fish."

"And brought them to you himself?"

"That's right."

"When?"

"Early Wednesday evening."

"About what time Wednesday?"

"I don't know exactly what time it was. It was rather early."

"Before dinner?"

"I think it was."

"And how were the fish brought to you? In what sort of a container?"

"That's the thing which I told you before was none of your business."

Mason once more got up, walked across to the telephone, picked up the receiver and started to dial Operator. There was a grim finality about his manner.

"In a bucket," Staunton said hastily.

Mason slowly, almost reluctantly, put the receiver back into its cradle. "What sort of a bucket?"

"An ordinary galvanized iron pail."

"And what did he tell you?"

"Told me to call the David Rawlins Pet Shop, tell them I had a couple of very valuable fish that were suffering from gill disease, for which I understood there was a new treatment furnished by the pet shop. I was to offer to pay them one hundred dollars for treatment of these fish. I did *just* that. That's all I know about it, Mr. Mason. *My* skirts are entirely clean."

"They aren't as clean as you claim," Mason said, still standing by the telephone, "and they don't cover you as much as you'd like. You forget about what you told the man from the pet shop?"

"What do you mean?"

"About your wife being sick and that she wasn't to be disturbed."

"I didn't want my wife to know anything about it."

"Why?"

"Because it was a matter of business, and I don't discuss business with her."

"But you lied to the man from the pet shop?"

45

"I don't like that word."

"Describe it by any word *you* like," Mason said, "but let's remember that you made a false statement to the man from the pet shop. You did that to keep him from coming in so that he wouldn't see the fish."

"I don't think that's a fair statement, Mr. Mason."

Mason grinned and said, "Think it over for awhile, Staunton. Think over how you're going to feel on the witness stand in front of a jury when I start giving you a cross-examination. You and your clean skirts!"

Mason stepped over to the window, jerked back the heavy drapes which covered the glass and stood with his back turned to the people in the room, his hands pushed down into his trouser pockets.

Staunton cleared his throat as though about to say something, then shifted his position uneasily in the swivel chair. The chair creaked slightly.

Mason didn't so much as turn around, but stood for some thirty seconds in utter silence, looking out at the section of sidewalk which was visible through the window, waiting while his very silence exerted a pressure.

Abruptly the lawyer turned. "I guess that's all," he said to the surprised Sally Madison. "I think we can go now."

A slightly bewildered Staunton followed them to the outer door. Twice he started to say something but each time choked off the sentence almost at the beginning.

Mason didn't look around or make any comment.

At the front door, Staunton stood for a few moments watching his departing visitors.

"Good night," he ventured somewhat quaveringly.

"We may see you again," Mason said ominously, and kept right on walking toward the parked car.

Staunton abruptly slammed the door shut.

Mason clasped his hand on Sally Madison's arm, pushed her over to the right across a strip of lawn and toward the stretch of sidewalk which had been visible from the window of Staunton's study.

"Let's watch him carefully," Mason said. "I purposely pulled the drapes to one side and left the telephone turned toward the window. We may be able to get some idea of the number that he dials by watching the motion of his hand. At least we can tell if it's a number similar to that of Harrington Faulkner."

They stood just outside of the oblong of light cast from the open window. From where they stood, they could clearly see the telephone and the fish in the tank on the top of the filing cases.

A shadow crossed the lighted oblong on the lawn, moved over toward the telephone, then stopped.

The watchers saw James Staunton's profile as he held his face close to the fish tank, watching the peculiar undulating motion of the black veils which hung down from the "Fish of Death."

For what might have been a matter of five minutes, Staunton regarded the fish as though held with a fascination that was almost hypnotic—then he slowly turned away, his shadow moved back across the oblong, and a moment later the lights were switched off and the room left in darkness.

"Do you suppose he knew we were watching?" Sally Madison asked.

Mason remained there watching and waiting for nearly five minutes, then he circled her with his arm, guided her toward the parked automobile.

"Did he?" she asked.

"What?" the lawyer asked, his voice showing his preoccupation.

"Know that we were watching."

"I don't think so."

"But you thought he was going to telephone?"

"Yes."

"Why didn't he?"

Mason said, "I'll be damned if I know."

"So what do we do now?" she asked.

"Now," Mason said, "we go to see Mr. Harrington Faulkner."

6
■

Mason escorted Sally Madison up the walk which led to Harrington Faulkner's duplex house. Both sides of the building were in the sedate midnight darkness of a respectable house in the residential district.

"They're asleep," Sally Madison whispered. "They've gone to bed."

"All right. We'll get them up."

"Oh, Mr. Mason. I wouldn't do that."

"Why not?"

"Faulkner will be furious."

"So what?"

"He can be very annoying and disagreeable when he's angry."

Mason said, "The man who handles his insurance has stated to both of us that Faulkner brought him those fish on Wednesday night. Some time after that, if this man's story is true, Faulkner made a great to do about finding the fish gone from the aquarium where they'd been placed. He called the police and made false statements to the police. Under the circumstances, he's hardly in a position to explode with righteous indignation."

Holding her arm, Mason could feel her shiver with apprehension. "You're—different," she said. "You don't let these people frighten you when they get angry. They absolutely *terrify* me."

"What are you afraid of?"

"I don't know. I just don't like anger and fights and scenes."

"You'll get accustomed to them before we go very much farther," Mason said, and jabbed his finger with insistence against the bell button.

They could hear the chimes sounding melodiously from the interior of the house. There followed an interval of some fifteen seconds while Mason and Sally Madison waited. Then Mason pressed his fingers several times against the button, causing the chimes to repeat their summons.

"That should wake them up," Sally Madison said, unconsciously keeping her voice lowered almost to a whisper.

"It should for a fact," Mason agreed, pushing the button twice more.

The last notes of the chimes were still sounding when the headlights of an automobile swung around the corner in a skidding turn. The car straightened, slowed abruptly as brakes were sharply applied, swerved into a right-angled turn, and headed up the driveway toward the garage. When the car was halfway up the driveway, the driver, apparently for the first time, saw Mason's car parked at the curb and the two figures on the porch.

Abruptly, the car slid to a halt. The door opened. A pair of well-curved legs flashed in a generous display, then Mrs. Faulkner slid out from the seat, across the running board to the ground, adjusting her skirts well after she had alighted.

"Yes?" she asked anxiously. "What is it, please? Oh, it's Mr. Mason and Miss Street. No, it isn't. It's *Miss Madison*. Isn't my husband home?"

"Apparently not," Mason said. "If he is, he's a sound sleeper."

"I guess he hasn't returned yet. He said he'd be out until quite late."

Mason said, "Perhaps we could wait for him."

"I warn you, Mr. Mason, he won't be in a good humor if he comes home and finds you waiting. Are you *quite* certain you want to see him tonight?"

"Quite certain—if it won't inconvenience you."

Mrs. Faulkner laughed melodiously, a laugh which seemed to have been practiced assiduously. She said, "Oh well, I'll let you in and if it's *that* important we'll have some drinks and wait for Harrington to come in. However, don't say I didn't warn you."

She inserted a key in the latch of the door, clicked back the lock, turned on lights in the hallway, and in the living room, and said, "Do come in and sit down. You're sure it isn't anything that you could tell me, and then let me tell Harrington in the morning?"

"No. We want to see him tonight. He should be coming in soon, shouldn't he?"

"Oh, I'm quite certain he'll be home within an hour. Do sit down, please. Pardon me a moment and I'll get myself organized."

She stepped from the room, taking off her coat as she went through the door.

They heard her moving around the bedroom. A door opened. There was a moment of motionless silence, and then her high-pitched, piercing scream knifed through the silence.

Sally Madison glanced inquiringly toward Mason, but the lawyer was already in motion. He crossed the room in four swift strides, jerked open the door of the bedroom and crossed the bedroom in time to see Mrs. Faulkner, her hands held over her face, stagger back from a bathroom which evidently communicated with another bedroom.

"He's . . . he's . . . in there!" she said, and wheeled blindly, then lurched into Mason's arms.

"Take it easy," Mason said, his fingers gently pulling her jeweled hands away from her eyes.

50

As his fingers touched her flesh, he realized that her hands were icy cold.

He supported her with one arm, moved toward the bathroom.

She pulled back. Mason released his hold, caught Sally Madison's eye and nodded. Sally Madison took Mrs. Faulkner's arm, gently piloted her toward the bed, said, "There, there! Take it easy."

Mrs. Faulkner moaned, slid down on the bed, her head on the pillow, legs trailing over the edge of the bed so that her feet were dangling halfway between the bed and the floor. Her hands were once more over her eyes. She kept saying, "Oh . . . oh . . . oh . . . !"

Mason moved to the bathroom door.

Harrington Faulkner lay motionless in death. His coat and shirt had been removed, leaving him attired in trousers and undershirt, and the front of the undershirt was a mass of blood. Back of the head was an overturned table, and on the floor fragments of curved glass caught the rays of the bathroom light and reflected them. A thin layer of water which had seeped over the floor had carried blood in a crimson stain to the far corners of the bathroom. On the floor near the figure were perhaps a dozen motionless goldfish, but as Mason looked, one of these goldfish gave a tired, dispirited flap of its tail.

The bathtub was half full of water and in this water a lone goldfish swam energetically back and forth, as though in search of companionship.

Mason stooped to pick up the lone fish which had shown signs of life. Gently he lowered it into the water of the bathtub. The fish kicked about for a moment, then turned half on its side, floated to the top of the water and remained motionless, save for a slight motion of the gills.

Mason felt the touch of Sally Madison's body, turned to find her standing just behind him.

"Get out," Mason said.

"Is he . . . is he . . . ?"

51

Mason said, "Of course he is. Get out. Don't touch anything. Leave a fingerprint here and it may make trouble. What's his wife doing?"

"Throwing a fit on the bed."

"Hysterics?"

"Not that bad, just a wild fit of grief."

"Does it mean that much to her?"

"It's the shock."

"Was she in love with him?"

"She was a fool if she was. You never can tell. I thought she didn't have any emotion at all. She had me fooled."

Mason said, "You don't ever show much emotion yourself."

Her eyes regarded him thoughtfully. "What's the use?"

"There isn't any," Mason said. "Go back to Mrs. Faulkner. Get her out of the bedroom. Call the Drake Detective Agency. Tell Paul Drake to get down here just as quick as he can, then, after you have done that, call police headquarters, get Homicide and ask for Lieutenant Tragg. Tell him you're speaking for Perry Mason and that I have a murder to report."

"Anything else?"

"That's all. Don't touch anything in the room. Get Mrs. Faulkner out of the bedroom and into the living room, then keep her there."

Mason waited until Sally Madison had left the room, then, moving backward away from the bathtub a few inches at a time, he carefully studied every part of the room, taking great care, however, not to touch any object with his hands.

On the floor, slightly to one side of the body, was a pocket magnifying glass consisting of two lenses, each approximately an inch and a half in diameter, hinged to a hard rubber case so that they would fold back out of the way when not in use. Back against the wall, almost directly under the washstand, were three popular magazines of approximately nine by twelve inches.

Mason bent over to notice the dates on the magazines. The top one was a current magazine, the one underneath that was three months old, and the bottom one four months old. On the top magazine was a smear of ink about half an inch in width by three or four inches in length and slightly curved in shape, trailing off almost to a point as it approached the end of the three-inch smear.

On a glass shelf over the washstand in the bathroom were two sixteen-ounce bottles of peroxide of hydrogen, one of them almost empty, a shaving brush, a safety razor, to the edge of which soapy lather was still adhering, and a tube of shaving cream.

The man had apparently been shot in the left side over the heart and had died almost instantly. When he fell he had apparently upset the table on which the goldfish bowl had been placed. One of the curved segments of broken bowl still held about half a cup of water.

On the floor, beneath the body of one of the goldfish was a pocket checkbook, and near by, a fountain pen. The cap of the pen lay some two feet away. The checkbook was closed, and bloody water had seeped against the edges of the checks. Mason noticed that about half of the checks in the book had been torn out, leaving the stubs of approximately half the checks in the front part of the book.

Faulkner had apparently been wearing his glasses when he was shot and the left lens had been broken, evidently when he had fallen, as the fragments of curved glass from that lens of the spectacles lay within an inch or two of the head. The right lens had not been injured and it reflected the bathroom light in the ceiling with a glitter which seemed oddly animate in the face of the death that tarnished the floor of the bathroom with its crimson stain.

Mason regarded the overturned table, stepping carefully backward and bending over to get a good look at it.

There were drops of water on this table, and a slight blob of ink, partially diluted with water.

Then Mason noticed something that had hitherto escaped him. A graniteware cooking pan of about two-quart capacity was in the bottom of the bathtub, lying on its side.

As Mason finished his careful inspection of the contents of the room, Sally Madison called to him from the bedroom. "Everything's been done, Mr. Mason. Mrs. Faulkner is waiting in the living room. Mr. Drake is on his way out here and I've notified the police."

"Lieutenant Tragg?" Mason asked.

"Lieutenant Tragg wasn't in, but Sergeant Dorset is on his way out."

Mason said, "That's a break," and then added, "for the murderer."

7

A siren, at first as muted as the sound of a persistent mosquito, grew in volume until as the police car approached the house it faded from a keen, high-pitched demand for the right-of-way to a low, throbbing protest, then lapsed into silence.

Heavy steps sounded on the porch and Mason opened the front door.

Sergeant Dorset said, "What the hell are *you* doing here?"

"Reception committee," Mason announced briefly. *"Do* come in."

Men pushed into the room, not bothering to remove their hats, gazing curiously at the two women: Sally Madison calm and collected, her face as expressionless as that of a doll, Mrs. Faulkner, her eyes red from crying, half sitting, half reclining on the davenport, emitting low, moaning sounds which were too regular to be sobs, too low in volume to be groans.

"Okay," Sergeant Dorset said to Mason, "what's the story *this* time?"

Mason smiled suavely. "No need to run a blood pressure, Sergeant. I didn't discover the body."

"Who did?"

Mason inclined his head toward the woman on the sofa.

"Who's she, the wife?"

"If you wish to be technically correct," Mason said, "and I'm certain you do, she's the widow."

Dorset faced Mrs. Faulkner, and by the simple process of tilting his hat toward the back of his head, gave her to understand that she was about to be interviewed. The other officers, having spilled through the house in a questing search for the body, congregated almost at once at the entrance to the bathroom.

Sergeant Dorset waited until Mrs. Faulkner glanced up. "Okay," he said.

Mrs. Faulkner said in a low voice, "I really did love him. We had our troubles, and at times he was terribly hard to get along with, but . . ."

"Let's get to that later," Dorset said. "How long ago did you find him?"

"Just a few minutes."

"How many? Five? Ten? Fifteen?"

"I don't think it's been ten minutes. Perhaps just a little more than five."

"We've been six minutes getting here."

"We called you as soon as I found him."

"How soon after you found him?"

"Right away."

"One minute? Two minutes? Three minutes?"

"Not as much as a minute."

"How'd you happen to find him?"

"I went into the bedroom and—and opened the door to the bathroom."

"Looking for him?"

"No. I had let Mr. Mason in and . . ."

"What was *he* doing here?"

"He was waiting at the door as I drove up. He wanted to see my husband."

Dorset seemed to glance sharply at Mason.

Mason nodded.

"We'll talk about that later," Sergeant Dorset said.

Mason smiled. "Miss Madison was with me, Sergeant, and had been with me for the last hour or two."

"Who's Miss Madison?"

Sally Madison smiled. "Me."

Sergeant Dorset looked her over. Almost unconsciously his hand strayed to his hat, removed it and placed it on a table. "Mason your lawyer?" he asked.

"No, not exactly."

"What do you mean by that?"

"Well, I hadn't fixed things up with him—you know, retained him, but I thought perhaps he could help me, thought he would, you know."

"Help you what?"

"Get Mr. Faulkner to finance Tom Gridley's invention."

"What invention?"

"It has to do with curing sick fish."

A voice from the bedroom called, "Hey, Sarge. Look in here. He's got a couple of goldfish swimming around in the bathtub."

"How many goldfish are swimming?" Mason asked.

"Two of 'em, Sarge."

Sergeant Dorset said angrily, "That wasn't me who asked you that last question. That was Mason."

"Oh," the voice said, and a broad-shouldered officer came to the door to stare belligerently at the lawyer. "I'm sorry."

Mrs. Faulkner said, "Please, I want to have someone come to stay with me. I can't bear to be here alone after all this. I—I think I'm going to be sick."

"Hold it, lady," the officer in the bedroom said. "You can't go in the bathroom."

"Why not?"

A certain delicacy caused the officer to keep silent.

"You mean you aren't going to . . . to move him?" Mrs. Faulkner asked.

"Not for a while. We've got to take pictures and get fingerprints and do lots of things."

"But I'm going to be sick. What . . . what shall I do?"

"Ain't there any other bathroom in the place?"

"No."

"Look," Dorset said, "why don't you go to a hotel for the night? Perhaps you can ring up some friend and . . ."

"Oh, I couldn't do that. I don't feel up to going to a hotel. I'm all upset. I'm . . . I'm nauseated . . . Besides, I don't think I could get a room in a hotel this hour of the night, just ringing up and telling them I wanted a room."

"Got some friend you could stay with?"

"No—not very well. She'd have to come over here. She and another girl share an apartment. There wouldn't be any room there for me."

"Who is she?"

"Adele Fairbanks."

"Okay. Ring her up."

"I . . . oh . . . !" Mrs. Faulkner clapped a hand over her mouth.

"Go out on the lawn," the officer in the doorway said.

Mrs. Faulkner dashed for the back porch. The men

57

heard the sound of retching, then the running of water in a set tub.

Sergeant Dorset said to the officer in the bedroom, "She's got a girl friend who'll be coming over. They'll be using the bathroom. Get busy on the fingerprints."

"They're taking 'em now, Sergeant, but the place is full of latents. You can't get 'em classified, photographed and all that by the time they're ready to move the stiff."

Sergeant Dorset reached a prompt decison. "Okay," he said, "lift 'em." Then he turned to Mason and said, "You can wait outside. We'll call you when we want you."

Mason said, "I'll tell you what you want to know now, and if you want any more information from me you can reach me at my office tomorrow."

Dorset hesitated, said, "Wait outside for ten or fifteen minutes anyway. Something may come up I want to ask you about."

Mason glanced at his watch. "Fifteen minutes. No longer."

"Okay."

Sally Madison got up from her chair as Mason started for the door.

"Hey, wait a minute," Sergeant Dorset said.

Sally Madison turned, smiling invitingly. "Yes, Sergeant."

Sergeant Dorset looked her over, glanced at the officer who was standing in the doorway. The officer closed his eye in a surreptitious wink.

"All right," Dorset said abruptly, "wait outside with Mr. Mason. But don't *you* go away." He strode to the door, jerked it open and said to a man in uniform who was on guard outside, "Mr. Mason's going to wait outside for fifteen minutes. If I want him within that time I'll call him. The girl is going to wait outside until I call her. She isn't to leave."

The officer nodded, said, "Fifteen minutes," and looked at his watch. Then he added, "A private dick's out here. I wouldn't let him in. He says the lawyer called him."

Sergeant Dorset glanced over to where Paul Drake was leaning against the side of the porch, smoking a cigarette.

"Hello, Sergeant," Drake said.

"What are *you* doing here?" Dorset asked.

"Keeping the porch from falling over," Drake drawled.

"How did you come—in a car?"

"Yes."

"All right. Go on out and sit in it."

"You're *so* good to me," Drake said humorously.

Sergeant Dorset held the door open until Sally Madison and Perry Mason had moved out to the porch, then slammed it shut.

Mason jerked his head toward Paul Drake and moved off toward the place where he had left his automobile. Sally Madison hesitated a moment, then followed. Drake joined them at the curb.

"How'd it happen?" Drake asked.

"He was in the bathroom. Somebody shot him. One shot. Dead center. Through the heart. Death must have been instantaneous, but the medical examiner hasn't said anything yet."

"Did *you* find him, Perry?"

"No, the wife did."

"That's a break. How did it happen? Wasn't she home when you got here?"

"No. She drove up just as I was ringing the bell. You know, Paul, she seemed to be in one hell of a hurry. There was a peculiar smell to the exhaust fumes. Suppose you can get over and take a look at her car before the officers start questioning her and perhaps get the same idea I have?"

"What idea?"

"Oh, I don't know. It isn't definite enough to be an idea, but she certainly slammed that car around the corner and up into the driveway. I don't know what gave

59

me the idea, Paul, other than the smell of the fumes from the exhaust—but I wondered if she'd driven the car a long ways, or whether she'd been parked around the corner somewhere. I remember there was something peculiar about the way the motor sounded, and I got the smell of all but raw gasoline when she slammed the car to a stop. How about taking a look at the choke?"

"Well," Drake said dubiously, "I can try."

"They can't hook you for trying," Mason said.

Drake moved away, starting toward the front porch. The officer grinned, shook his head and jerked his thumb. "Nothing doing, buddy," he said, and then added, "sorry."

Drake veered off to one side, made a few aimless motions, then strolled quite casually over toward the automobile Mrs. Faulkner had driven up to the house. Acting very much as though this were the automobile in which he had driven up, the detective settled down in the front seat and after a moment took a cigarette from his pocket and lit a match, delaying the application of the match to the end of the cigarette long enough to study the dashboard of the automobile.

"What do they mean by lifting fingerprints?" Sally Madison asked Mason.

"They dust objects with a special powder," Mason said, his eyes on Paul Drake. "That brings out what are known as latent fingerprints. Sometimes they use a black powder, sometimes a white powder, depending on the surface. Mostly when they lift fingerprints they use a black powder to bring out the latent, and then take a piece of adhesive, place it over the developed latent, rub it smoothly until every bit of powder has had a chance to adhere to the adhesive, and then pull off the adhesive. That definitely lifts the fingerprint from the object on which it was found."

"How long do fingerprints keep when they do that?"

"Indefinitely."

"How do they know where they took the prints from?"

Mason said, "You're asking a lot of questions."

"I'm curious."

"It all depends on the expert who's doing the job. Some of them make marks on the object from which the print was lifted, number the adhesive and put a corresponding number on the object. Some of them put the numbers in a notebook with a sketch or a description of the place from which the print was lifted."

"I thought they had fingerprint cameras and took photographs."

"Sometimes they do. Sometimes they don't. It all depends on who's doing it. Personally, I'd photograph all latents, even if the women *never* got the use of the bathroom."

Sally Madison looked at Mason curiously. "Why?"

"Because," Mason said, "if there were a lot of latents, the man's going to have a heck of a job keeping them all straight."

"I don't see the importance of that."

"You would if they found one of your fingerprints."

"What do you mean?"

"It might make a difference whether they found it on the doorknob or on the handle of the gun—a difference to you, anyway."

Paul Drake opened the door of the car Mrs. Faulkner had been driving, swung his feet around to the ground, stretched, yawned, slammed the door shut, and the red of his cigarette glowed in the darkness as he casually walked over to where Mason and Sally Madison were standing, talking.

"You played a hunch, Perry."

"What did you find?"

"Choke halfway out, motor temperature almost stone cold. Even making allowances for the fact that she's been here for twenty minutes or even half an hour, the motor wouldn't have cooled off that fast. It looks as though the

61

car hadn't been driven more than a quarter of a mile. Perhaps less than that."

Sally Madison said, "She was coming fast enough when she slewed around that corner."

Mason flashed Paul Drake a warning glance.

The door of the house opened, and Sergeant Dorset stood framed in the illumination of the doorway. He said something to the officer who was guarding the entrance to the house. The officer walked out to the edge of the porch and in the manner of a bailiff calling a witness to the stand, intoned, "Sally Madison."

Mason grinned. "That's you, Sally."

"What shall I tell them?" she asked in sudden panic.

"Anything you want to hold back?" Mason asked.

"No—I don't suppose there is."

"If you think of anything you want to hold back," Mason told her, "hold it back, but don't lie about anything."

"But if I held anything back I'd have to lie."

"No you wouldn't, just keep your mouth shut. Now then, the minute the police get done with you, I want you to call this number. That's Della Street's apartment. Tell her you're coming out there. The two of you go to a hotel, register under your own names. Don't let anyone know where you are. In the morning have Della telephone me, somewhere around eight-thirty. Have breakfast sent up to your room. Don't go out and don't talk with anyone until I get there."

Mason handed her a slip of paper with Della Street's number written on it.

"What's the idea?" Sally Madison asked.

Mason said, "I want you to keep away from the reporters. They may try to interview you. I'm going to try to get five thousand bucks for you and Tom Gridley out of Faulkner's estate."

"Oh, Mr. Mason!"

"Don't say a word," Mason warned. "Don't let the

police or anyone else know where you're going. Don't even tell Tom Gridley. Keep out of circulation until I have a chance to see how the land lies."

"You mean you think there's a chance . . ."

"There may be. It will depend."

"On what?"

"On a lot of things."

Sergeant Dorset spoke sharply to the officer on the porch and the officer once more intoned in his best courtroom manner, "Salleeeeeee Madisonnnn," and then, lapsing into a less formal manner, bellowed down at the trio, "cut out that gabbing and get up here. The sergeant wants to see you."

Sally Madison walked rapidly up toward the porch, her heels echoing her rapid, nervous step.

Drake said to Mason, "What gave you the hunch that she was parked around the corner, Perry?"

Mason said, "It may not have been around the corner, Paul. I had a hunch the car might have been running on a cold motor, judging from the way the exhaust smelled. And then, of course, the possibility naturally occurred to me that she might have been waiting somewhere around the corner for an auspicious moment to make her appearance."

"Well, it's a possibility, all right," Drake said, "and you know what it means if it's true."

"I'm not certain that I do," Mason said thoughtfully. "And I'm not even going to think about it until I find out whether it's true, but it's an interesting fact to file away for future reference."

"Think Sergeant Dorset will get wise to it?" Drake asked.

"I doubt it. He's too much engrossed in following the routine procedure to think of any new lines. Lieutenant Tragg would have thought of it if he'd been here. He has brains, Paul . . . Dorset is all right but he came up the hard way, and he relies too much on the old browbeating methods. Tragg is smooth as silk and you never know where he's heading from the direction in which he's pointed. He . . ."

Once more the door of the house opened. Sergeant Dorset didn't wait this time to relay his message through the guard at the door. He called out, "Hey, you two, come up here. I want to talk with you."

Mason said in a low voice to Paul Drake, "If they try to put skids under you, Paul, get in your car, and drive around the corner. Scout the side streets just for luck, then after the newspaper boys show up, grab one with whom you're friendly, buy him a couple of drinks and see what you can pick up."

"I can't do that until after he's phoned his story in to his paper," Drake said.

"No one wants you to," Mason told him. "Just . . ."

"Any old time, any old time," Sergeant Dorset said sarcastically. "Just take your time, gentlemen, no need to be in a hurry. After all, you know, it's only a murder."

"Not a suicide?" Mason asked, climbing up the porch steps.

"What do you think he did with the gun, swallow it?" Dorset inquired.

"I didn't even know how he was killed."

"Too bad about you. What's Drake doing here?"

"Looking around."

"How'd you get here?" Dorset asked Drake suspiciously.

"I told Sally Madison to call him at the same time she called you."

"What's that?" Dorset demanded sharply. *"Who* called me?"

"Sally Madison."

"I thought it was the wife."

"No, the wife was getting ready to have hysterics. Sally Madison put through the call."

"What did you want Drake for?"

64

"Just to look around."

"What for?"

"To see what he could find out."

"Why? You're not representing anyone, are you?"

Mason said, "If you want to get technical, I wasn't paying Faulkner a social call at this hour of the night."

"What's this about a man named Staunton having those stolen goldfish?"

"He claims Faulkner gave them to him to keep."

"Faulkner reported to the police that they'd been stolen."

"I know he did."

"They say you were here when the radio officers got here the night the fish were stolen."

"That's right. Drake was here too."

"Well, what's your idea? Were they stolen or weren't they?"

Mason said, "I've never handled any goldfish, Sergeant."

"What's that got to do with it?"

"Nothing perhaps. Again, perhaps a lot."

"I don't get you."

"Ever stand on a chair and dip a soup ladle down into a four-foot goldfish tank, try to pick up a fish and then, sliding your hands along a four-foot extension handle, raise that fish to the surface, lift him out of a tank and put him into a bucket?"

Sergeant Dorset asked suspiciously, "What's that got to do with it?"

Mason said, "Perhaps nothing. Perhaps a lot. My own idea is, Sergeant, that the ceiling of the room in that real-estate office is about nine and one half feet from the floor, and I would say that the bottom of the fish tank was about three feet six inches from the floor. The tank itself is four feet deep."

"What the devil are you talking about?" Dorset asked.

"Measurements," Mason said.

"I don't see what that has to do with it."

"You asked me if I thought the fish had been stolen."

"Well."

Mason said, "The evidence that indicates they were stolen consists of a silver soup ladle, to the handle of which was tied a four-foot extension pole."

"Well, what's wrong with that? If you were going to reach to the bottom of a four-foot fish tank you'd need a four-foot pole, wouldn't you? Or does your master mind have some new angle on that?"

"Only," Mason said, "that if you were lifting a goldfish out of water which was within a half inch of the top of a four-foot tank and that tank was already three and a half feet from the floor, the surface of your water would then be seven feet five inches above the floor."

"So what?" Dorset asked, his voice showing that he was interested, despite his elaborate attempt to maintain a mask of skeptical sarcasm.

"So," Mason said, "you would lower your four-foot ladle into the tank, all right, because you could slip it in on an angle, but when you started lifting it out you'd have to keep it straight up and down in order to keep from spilling your fish. Now let's suppose your ceiling is nine and a half feet from the floor and the surface of the water is seven and a half feet from the floor, then when you've raised the ladle, with its four-foot extension handle, some two feet from the bottom of the tank, the top of your extension handle knocks against the ceiling. Then what are you going to do? If you tilt your pole on an angle so you can get the ladle out of the tank, your fish slips out of the ladle."

Dorset got the idea. He stood frowning portentously, said at length, "Then you don't think the fish were stolen."

Mason said, "I don't think they were lifted out of that tank with any soup ladle and I don't think that soup ladle with its four-foot extension was used in fish stealing."

Dorset said somewhat dubiously, "I don't get it," and then added rather quickly, as though trying to cover his confession, "shucks, there's nothing to it. You'd have held the soup ladle with one hand straight up and down. The end of the pole would have been up against the ceiling, all right, but you'd have reached down into the water with your other hand and pulled out the fish."

"Two feet of water?" Mason asked.

"Why not?"

Mason said, "Even supposing you'd lift the fish from the bottom of the tank up to within two feet of the surface. Do you think you could have reached down with your other hand, caught the fish in your fingers and lifted him to the surface? I don't, and, furthermore, Sergeant, if you want to try rolling up your sleeve and picking something out of two feet of water, you'll find that you're rolling your sleeve pretty high. Somewhere past the shoulder, I'd say."

Dorset thought that over, said, "Well, it's a nice point you're making, Mason. I'll go in there and make some measurements. You may be right."

"I'm not trying to sell you anything. You simply asked me what I thought about the fish being stolen, and I told you."

"When did that idea occur to you?"

"Almost as soon as I saw the room with the fish tank pulled out to the edge of the sideboard and the soup ladle with its extension handle lying on the floor."

"You didn't say anything about that to the officers who came out to investigate."

"The officers who came out to investigate didn't ask me anything about that."

Dorset thought that over, then abruptly changed the subject. "What's this about this guy Staunton having the fish?"

"He's got them."

"The same fish that were taken out of the tank?"

"Sally Madison thinks they're the same."

"You've talked with Staunton?"

"Yes."

"And he said Faulkner gave the fish to him?"

"That's right."

"What would be the idea in that?"

"I wouldn't know."

"But you heard Staunton state that Faulkner gave him those fish?"

"That's right."

"Did he say when?"

"Sometime in the evening of the day Faulkner reported them as having been stolen—last Wednesday, I believe it was. He wasn't too definite about the time."

Dorset was thinking that over when a taxicab swung around the corner and came to a stop. A woman jumped out without waiting for the cab driver to open the door. She handed him a bill, then ran up the walk, a small overnight bag clamped under her arm.

The officer on guard blocked the porch stairway. "You can't go in here."

"I'm Adele Fairbanks, a friend of Jane Faulkner. She telephoned me and told me to come . . ."

Sergeant Dorset said, "It's all right, you can go in. But don't try to get into the bedroom yet and don't go near the bathroom until we tell you you can. See if you can get Mrs. Faulkner to calm down. If she starts getting hysterical, we're going to have to call in a doctor."

Adele Fairbanks was in the late thirties. Her figure had very definitely filled out. Her hair was dark but not dark enough to be distinctive. She wore thick-lensed glasses and had a nervous mannerism of speech which caused her words to spurt out in groups of four or five at a time. She said, "Oh, it's simply terrible. . . . I just can't believe it. Of course, he was a peculiar man. . . . But to think of someone deliberately killing him . . . If it was deliberate,

Officer . . . it wasn't suicide, was it? No, it couldn't have been. . . . He had no reason to . . ."

"Go on inside," Dorset interrupted hastily. "See what you can do for Mrs. Faulkner."

As Adele Fairbanks eagerly popped through the door and into the house, Sergeant Dorset said to Mason, "This Staunton angle looks to be worth investigating. I'm going to take Sally Madison out there. I'd like to have you as witnesses because I want to be damn certain he doesn't change his story about Faulkner giving him those fish. If he does change it, then you'll be there to confront him with the admission he made earlier in the evening."

Mason shook his head. "I've got other things to do, Sergeant. Sally will be all the witness you need. I'm going places."

"And that," Dorset said to Paul Drake, "just about leaves you with no excuse to be sticking around *here* any more."

Drake said, "Okay, Sergeant," with a docility that was surprising, and immediately walked over to his car, opened the door and started the motor.

The officer who was guarding the porch said suspiciously, "Hey, Sarge. That ain't *his* car. His car is the one parked there in the driveway."

"How do you know?" Mason asked.

"How do I know?" the officer demanded. "How do I know anything? Didn't the guy go sit in that car and smoke a cigarette? Want me to stop him, Sergeant?"

Drake turned his car out from the curb toward the center of the road.

"That's his car," Mason said quietly to Dorset.

"Then what's that other car out there?" the officer demanded.

"To the best of my knowledge," Mason said, "that car belongs to the Faulkners. At least it's the car in which Mrs. Faulkner drove up to the house."

"Then what was that guy doing in it?"

Mason shrugged his shoulders.

Dorset said angrily to the officer, "What the hell did you suppose I was leaving you out here for?"

"Gosh, Sergeant, I thought it was his car all the time. He walked across to it just as though he owned it. Come to think of it, I guess that car was there when we got here, but . . ."

Dorset said angrily, "Give me your flashlight."

He took the flashlight and strode over toward the parked automobile. Mason started to follow him. Dorset turned angrily and said, "You can stay right there. We've had enough interference in this case already."

The officer on the porch, trying to cover up his previous blunder by a sudden increase in efficiency, announced belligerently, "And when the Sergeant says you stay there, Buddy, it means you stay *right there!* Don't take even another step toward that automobile."

Mason grinned, waited while Sergeant Dorset's flashlight made a complete exploration of the interior of the car which Mrs. Faulkner had been driving.

After several minutes of futile search, Sergeant Dorset rejoined Mason, said, "I don't see a thing in the car except a burnt match on the floor."

"Drake probably lit a cigarette," Mason said casually.

"Yes, I remember that. He did for a fact," the officer on guard admitted readily enough. "He walked over to the car just as though he'd been going to drive off, lit a cigarette and sat there and smoked for awhile."

"Probably he just wanted a place to sit down," Mason observed, yawning, "and thought that was a good place to take a load off his feet."

"So you thought he was going to drive off," Sergeant Dorset said sarcastically to the officer.

"Well, I sort of thought . . . well, you know . . ."

"And I suppose if he'd driven that car off you'd have stood there with your hands in your pockets while this guy got away with what may be an important piece of evidence."

In the embarrassed silence which followed, Mason said placatingly, "Well, Sergeant, we *all* make mistakes."

Dorset grunted, turned to the officer and said, "Jim, as soon as they get done with those fingerprints in the bedroom and bathroom, tell the boys I said to go over that automobile for fingerprints. Pay particular attention to the steering wheel and the gearshift lever. If they find any fingerprints, lift them and put them with the others."

Mason said dryly, "Yes, indeed, Sergeant, we *all* make mistakes."

Once more Sergeant Dorset merely grunted.

8

Mason had started his car motor and was just pulling away from the curb when he saw headlights behind him. The headlights blinked significantly, once, twice, three times. Then the car slowed almost to a crawl.

Mason drove rapidly for a block and a half, watching the headlights in his rearview mirror, then he pulled in to the curb and the car behind him promptly swung in to a position just behind Mason's automobile and stopped. Paul Drake slid out from behind the steering wheel and walked across to Mason's car, where he stood with one foot on the running board.

"Think I've found something, Perry."

"What?"

"The place where Mrs. Faulkner was parked, waiting for you to show up."

"Let's take a look," Mason said.

"Of course," Drake added apologetically, "I haven't a lot to go on. When someone parks a car on a paved roadway you don't leave many distinctive traces, particularly when you take into consideration the fact that hundreds of automobiles are parked every day."

"What did you find?" Mason interrupted.

"Well," Drake said, "when I gave that car the once-over I did everything I could in the short time I had available. I noticed the choke was out, almost as soon as I got in; and then I lit the match to light my cigarette, turned on the ignition, and that gave me a chance to look at the gasoline gauge and the temperature gauge. The gasoline gauge didn't tell me anything. The tank was half full of gas and that of course just doesn't mean a darn thing. The temperature gauge showed the motor was barely warmed up and that was all I could find from the gauges, but I thought I'd better take a look in the ash tray, so I pulled it out and the darn thing was empty. At the time, it didn't register with me. I just saw the ash tray was empty and let it go at that."

"You mean there wasn't a single thing in it?" Mason asked.

"Not so much as a burnt match."

"I don't get it," Mason said.

"I didn't get it at first, myself. It wasn't until I had driven away from Faulkner's house that the thing began to register with me. Ever sit in a parked automobile waiting for something to happen and being a little nervous— not knowing what to do with yourself?"

"I don't believe I have," Mason said. "Why?"

"Well, I have," Drake told him, "lots of times. It usually happens on a shadowing job when the man you're tailing goes into a house somewhere and you just have to stick around and wait, with nothing in particular to do. You begin to get fidgety, and after a while, you begin to play around with the dashboard. You don't care to turn on the radio because a parked car with a radio blaring out noise is too noticeable, so you just sit there and fiddle around."

"And empty the ash tray?" Mason asked, his voice showing keen interest.

"That's right. You'll do it nine times out of ten, if you sit there long enough. You start thinking of all the little chores there are around a car and the ash tray is one of the first things you think of. You take it out and dump it out of the window on the left-hand side of the car, being sure you've got it all clean."

"Go ahead," Mason said.

"So," Drake told him, "after I drove away from Faulkner's place, I started looking for some place where you could park an automobile and still see the entrance to the Faulkner house."

"Some place straight down the street?" Mason asked.

"I looked there at first," Drake said, "but didn't find anything, so I swung around the corner and found there's a place on the side street where you can look across a vacant lot and see the front of the Faulkner house, and also the driveway to the garage. Just about as far up the driveway as the point where Mrs. Faulkner parked the car. You're looking across a vacant lot and between two houses but you can see the place all right. And that's where I found a pile of cigarette stubs and some burnt matches."

"What brand of cigarettes, Paul?"

"Three or four. Some with lipstick, some without. Different kinds of matches, some paper matches, some wooden ones."

"Any identifying marks on the paper matches?"

"To tell you the truth, Perry, I didn't stay there long enough to look. As soon as I found the place, I beat it back to tip you off. I thought perhaps you'd like to look at it. You were just pulling away from the curb, so I blinked my lights and tagged along behind. I was afraid to pull up alongside because I didn't want the cop in charge to think I'd discovered something important within four or five minutes after I'd driven away from the place. Not that I think the idea would have registered with him, but it *might* have, you never can tell. Want me to go back and make a more detailed examination?"

Mason tilted back the brim of his hat, moved the tips of his fingers through the wavy hair on his temple. "Hang it, Paul, if you can see the house from the place where the ash tray was emptied, then anyone standing in the front of the house or on the driveway can look back and see the place where we would be looking the stuff over. Your flashlight would be something they couldn't overlook."

"I thought of that," Drake said.

"Tell you what you do, Paul. Go back and mark the place some way so you can identify it. After that, get a dustpan and brush, sweep up the whole outfit and drop it in a paper bag."

"You don't suppose Dorset will think that's concealing evidence, do you?"

"It's preserving evidence," Mason pointed out. "It's what the police would do if they happened to think of it."

"But suppose they happen to think of it and the stuff is gone?"

Mason said, "Let's look at it from the other angle, Paul. Suppose they *don't* happen to think of it, and a street-washing outfit comes along and sluices the stuff down into the sewer."

"Well," Drake said dubiously. "Of course, we *could* tell Sergeant Dorset."

"Dorset has taken Sally Madison out to Staunton's place. Don't be so damn conscientious, Paul. Get busy and get that stuff in a paper bag."

Drake hesitated. "Why should Mrs. Faulkner have been waiting there for you to drive up, and then come

74

scorching around the corner as soon as she saw your car stop?"

Mason said, "It might mean she knew the body was in there on the floor and didn't want to be the one to discover it, all by herself. It must also mean that she knew Sally Madison and I were going to call at the house, and that in turn means that Staunton must have reached her on the telephone, almost immediately after we left his place."

"Where would he have telephoned her?"

"Probably at her house. She may have been there with the body on her hands and when she knew we were coming, she saw a chance to give herself a sort of alibi. You know, that she'd been absent all evening and arrived just about the same time we did. That brings us back to what must have happened out at Staunton's house. I pulled back the drapes on the window of Staunton's study so I could have a clear view of the telephone from outside the window. I thought he'd be certain to rush to the telephone and call the person who had given him the fish. All he did was switch out the lights in the study. That must mean there's another telephone in the house. Maybe an extension, maybe even a second line because he seems to do business from the house. I'm going to get a telephone book and look up the address of Faulkner's partner, Elmer Carson, and see if I can get there before the police do. You beat it up to your office, Paul, get a dustpan and a bag and sweep up that stuff from the ash tray. I'll drive up to the boulevard and cruise around until I find a restaurant or an all-night drugstore where I can get a telephone directory. Carson lives right around here somewhere. I remember Faulkner saying that while he leased one side of the duplex house from the corporation, Carson had a private residence a few blocks away."

"Okay," Drake said. "It'll take me fifteen or twenty minutes to get to the office, pick up the stuff and get back."

"That's okay. Dorset won't get back for half an hour, anyway; and the boys he's left in charge certainly won't think of scouting around the block and connecting up an empty ash tray in Jane Faulkner's car with a pile of cigarette stubs at the curb on a side street."

Drake said, "On my way," and walked back to his car.

Mason drove rapidly to the main boulevard, cruised along until he found an all-night lunch counter. He entered the place, had a cup of coffee, consulted the telephone directory and, to his chagrin, found that James L. Staunton had two telephones listed, one in his insurance office, one in his residence. Both at the same street address.

Mason then thumbed through the directory to find the residence of Elmer Carson and noted the address. It was exactly four blocks from Faulkner's residence.

Mason debated for a moment whether to call Carson on the telephone, then decided against it. He paid for his coffee, got in his automobile and drove to Carson's house. It was dark.

Mason parked his car, climbed to the porch and was ringing the bell for the third time when lights showed in the hallway. A man in pajamas, dressing gown and slippers was outlined for a moment against lights from an inner room. Then he closed the door, switched off lights in the hallway and, walking along the darkened passageway, reached a point where he could switch on the porch light.

Mason stood outlined in the brilliant illumination of the porch light, trying in vain to see through the curtained glass of the doorway into the darkened corridor.

From the inner darkness, a voice called out through the door, "What do you want?"

"I want to see Mr. Elmer Carson."

"This is a hell of a time to come punching doorbells."

"I'm sorry, but it's important."

"What's it about?"

Mason, conscious of the fact that his raised voice was audible for some distance, glanced somewhat apprehensively at the adjoining houses, and said, "Open the door and I'll tell you."

The man on the inside said, "Tell me and I'll open the door," and then added, "maybe."

"It's about Harrington Faulkner."

"What about him?"

"He's dead."

"Who are you?"

"My name's Mason—Perry Mason."

"The lawyer?"

"That's right."

The porch light clicked off. A light was switched on in the corridor. Mason heard the sound of a lock clicking back, then the door opened, and for the first time Mason had a good look at the man who was standing in the corridor. He was, Mason judged, around forty-two or three, a rather chunky individual inclined to baldness at the top and at the back. Such hair as he had had been left long so that it could be trained to cover the bald areas. Now that the man had been aroused from slumber, the long strands of hair hung incongruously down over the left ear almost even with the man's jawbone. It gave his face a peculiar one-sided appearance which was hardly conducive to the dignity which he tried to assume. His mouth was firm and straight. A close-clipped mustache was just beginning to turn gray. He was a man who wouldn't quit easily and wouldn't frighten at all.

Carson raised rather prominent blue eyes to Mason, said curtly, "Come in and sit down."

"You're Elmer Carson?" Mason asked.

"That's right."

Carson moved around to close the front door, then ushered Mason into a well-kept living room, scrupulously clean, save for a tray containing cigarette stubs, a champagne cork and two empty champagne glasses.

"Sit down," Carson invited, gathering the bathrobe around him. "When did Faulkner die?"

"Frankly, I don't know," Mason said. "Sometime tonight."

"How did he die?"

"That also I don't know. But rather a hurried inspection of the body leads me to believe that he was shot."

"Suicide?"

"I don't believe the police think so."

"You mean murder?"

"Apparently so."

"Well," Carson said, "there were certainly enough people who hated his guts."

"Including you?" Mason asked.

The blue eyes met Mason's without flinching. "Including me," Carson said calmly.

"Why did you hate him?"

"Lots of reasons. I don't see any necessity to go into them. What did you want with me?"

Mason said, "I thought perhaps you could help me ascertain the time of death."

"How?"

"How long," Mason asked, "would a goldfish live out of water?"

"Hell, I don't know. I'm sick and tired to death of hearing about goldfish or seeing goldfish."

Mason said, "Yet apparently you spent some money on a lawsuit trying to keep a couple of goldfish in your office."

Carson grinned. "When you start fighting a man, you hit his most vulnerable spot."

"And his goldfish hobby was Faulkner's most vulnerable spot?"

"It was the only one he had."

"Why were you hitting at him?"

"Various reasons. What's the length of time goldfish

78

could live out of water got to do with the time Harrington Faulkner was bumped off?"

Mason said, "When I looked at the body, there were some goldfish on the floor, one of them gave a feeble flick of its tail. I picked it up and put it in the bathtub. It started to turn belly up, but I understand a few minutes later it had come to life and was swimming around."

"When *you* looked at the body?" Carson asked.

"I wasn't the first to discover it," Mason told him.

"Who was the first?"

"His wife."

"How long ago?"

"Perhaps half an hour, perhaps a little longer."

"You were with his wife?"

"When we entered the house, yes."

The blue eyes blinked a couple of times rapidly. Carson started to say something, then apparently either changed his mind or hesitated while he searched his thoughts for some suitable phraseology. Abruptly he added, "Where had his wife been?"

"I don't know."

Carson said, "Someone tried to kill him last week. Did you know that?"

"I'd heard of it."

"Who told you?"

"Harrington Faulkner."

"His wife say anything about that to you?"

"No."

Carson said, "There's something strange about that whole affair. According to Faulkner's story, he was driving along in his automobile and someone took a shot at him. He claims he heard the report of the gun and that a bullet went whizzing past him and embedded itself in the upholstery of the automobile. That's the story he told the police, but at the time he never said a word to me or to Miss Stanley."

"Who's Miss Stanley?" Mason asked.

79

"The stenographer in our office."

"Suppose you tell me just what happened."

"Well, he came driving up to the office and parked his car out in front of the place. I noticed him take out his knife and start digging at the upholstery in the back of the front seat, but I didn't think anything of it at the time."

"Then what happened?"

"I saw him go into his house—you know, the other side of the duplex. He was in there for about five minutes. He must have telephoned the police from there. Then he came over to the office and, except for the fact that he was unusually nervous and irritable, you wouldn't have known anything had happened. There was some mail on his desk. He picked it up and read it, took the letters over to Miss Stanley's desk and stood beside her while he dictated some replies directly to the typewriter. She noticed that his hand was shaking, but aside from that, he seemed perfectly normal."

"Then what happened?" Mason asked.

Carson said, "As it turned out, Faulkner put the bullet down on Miss Stanley's desk when he signed one of the letters she'd written for him, and then she'd placed the carbon copy of the letter over the bullet. But she didn't notice it at the time and neither did Faulkner."

"You mean that Faulkner couldn't find the bullet when the police arrived?" Mason asked, his voice showing his keen interest.

"Exactly."

"What happened?"

"Well, there was quite a scene. The first thing that we knew about any shooting was a good twenty minutes after Faulkner came in. Then a car pulled up outside, and a couple of officers came pushing into the office and Faulkner spilled this story about having been driving along the road, hearing a shot, and then hearing something smack into the seat cushions within an inch or two of his body. He said he'd dug out the bullet, and the police asked where the bullet was. Then the fireworks started. Faulkner looked around for the bullet and couldn't find it. He said he'd left it on the top of his desk and finally as good as accused me of having stolen it."

"And what did you do?"

"As it happened," Carson said, "I hadn't moved from my desk, from the time Faulkner came in until the police arrived, and Miss Stanley could vouch for that. However, as soon as I saw what Faulkner was driving at, I insisted the police search me, and search my desk."

"Did they?"

"I'll say they did. They took me into the bathroom, took off all my clothes and made a thorough search. They didn't seem too enthusiastic about it, but I insisted they make a thorough job of it. I think by that time they had Faulkner pretty well sized up as an irascible old crank. And Miss Stanley was hopping mad. She wanted them to bring out a matron to search her. The police didn't take it that seriously. Miss Stanley was so angry she darn near took off her clothes right there in the office. She was white-faced with rage."

"But the bullet was on her desk?" Mason asked.

"That's right. She found it there late that afternoon when she was cleaning up her desk, getting ready to go home. She has a habit of piling carbon copies of stuff on the back of her desk during the day, and then doing all her filing at four-thirty. It was about quarter of five when she found the bullet. Faulkner called the police back again, and when they came, they told Faulkner quite a few things."

"Such as what?"

"They told him that the next time anybody shot at him, he should stop at the first telephone he came to and notify the police at once, not wait until he got to his home and not go digging out any bullets. They said that if the bullet had been left in the car the police could have dug it out and used it as evidence. Then they might have been able to identify the gun from which it had been fired. They told him that the minute *he* dug that bullet out, it ceased to be evidence."

"How did Faulkner take it?"

"He was pretty much chagrined over finding the bullet right where he'd left it, after making all that fuss and excitement."

Mason studied Carson for several thoughtful seconds. "All right, Carson," he said, "now I'll ask you the question you've been hoping I wouldn't ask."

"What's that?" Carson asked, avoiding his eyes.

Mason said, "Why did Faulkner drive to his house before he notified the police?"

Carson said, "I suppose he was frightened and afraid to stop."

Mason grinned.

"Oh well," Carson said impatiently, "your guess is as good as mine, but I suppose he wanted to see if his wife was home."

"Was she?"

"I understand she was. She'd been quite nervous the night before and hadn't been able to sleep. About three o'clock in the morning she'd taken a big dose of sleeping medicine, and she was still asleep when the officers went in."

"The officers went over there?"

"Yes."

"Why?"

"Faulkner didn't make too good an impression with the officers. I think they thought he might have fired the shot himself."

"Why?"

"Heaven knows. Faulkner was a deep one. Understand, Mason, I'm not making any accusations or any insinuations. All I know is that after a while the officers wanted to know if Faulkner had a gun, and when he said he did have one, the officers told him they'd go over and take a look at it."

"He showed it to them?"

"I presume so. I didn't go over with them. They were gone ten or fifteen minutes."

"When was this?"

"A week ago."

"What time?"

"Around ten o'clock in the morning."

"What caliber is Faulkner's gun?"

"A thirty-eight, I believe. I think that's what he told the police."

"And what caliber was the bullet that Faulkner dug out of the upholstery?"

"A forty-five."

"How did Faulkner and his wife get along?"

"I wouldn't know."

"Could you make a guess?"

"I couldn't even do that. I've heard him talk to her over the phone and use about the same tone he'd use to a disobedient dog, but Mrs. Faulkner kept her feelings to herself."

"There had been bad blood between you and Faulkner before this?"

"Not bad blood, exactly—a little difference of opinion here and there, and some friction, but we were getting along with some outward semblance of harmony."

"And after this?"

"After this I blew up. I told him either to buy or sell."

"You were going to sell out to him . . . to his estate, I mean?"

"I may. I don't know. I'd never have sold out to that old buzzard at the price *he* wanted to pay. If you want to know something about him in a business deal, ask Wilfred Dixon."

"Who's he?"

"He looks after the interests of the first Mrs. Faulkner—
Genevieve Faulkner."

"What interests?"

"Her share in the realty company."

"How much?"

"One third. That was her settlement when the divorce
went through. At that time Faulkner owned two thirds of
the stock and I owned a third. He got dragged into
divorce court and the judge nicked him for a half of the
stock he owned and gave it to the wife. Faulkner's been
scared to death of divorces ever since that experience."

Mason said, "If you hated him that much, why didn't
you and the first Mrs. Faulkner get together and pool
your stock and freeze him out? I'm asking just as a
matter of curiosity."

Carson said frankly, "Because I couldn't. The stock
was all pooled. That was a part of the divorce business.
The judge worked out a pooling agreement by which the
management was left equally in the hands of Faulkner
and myself. Mrs. Faulkner—that is Genevieve Faulkner,
the first wife—couldn't have any say in the management
of the company unless she first appealed to the court.
And neither Faulkner nor I could increase the expenses
of the company past a certain point, and we couldn't
raise salaries. The judge also pointed out that any time
the dividends on the stock fell below a certain point he'd
reopen the alimony end of it and take another bite if he
had to. He certainly had Faulkner scared white."

"The stock's been profitable?" Mason asked.

"I'll say it has. You see, we didn't handle things on a
commission basis alone. We had some deals by which we
took title in our own name and built houses and sold
them. We've done some pretty big things in our day."

"Faulkner's ideas or yours?"

"Both. When it came to making money, old Harrington
Faulkner had the nose of a buzzard. He could smell a
potential profit a mile away. He had the courage to back

up his judgment with cold hard cash and he had plenty of operating capital. He should have. Lord knows he never gave his wife anything, and he never spent anything himself, except on those damned goldfish of his. He'd really loosen up the purse strings on those, but when it came to parting with money for anything else he was like the bark on a log."

"And Dixon?" Mason asked. "Was he appointed by the court?"

"No. Genevieve Faulkner hired him."

"Faulkner was wealthy?" Mason asked.

"He had quite a bit of money, yes."

"You wouldn't know it from looking around his house," Mason said.

Carson nodded. "He'd spend money for his goldfish and that was all. As far as the duplex was concerned, I think Mrs. Faulkner liked it that way. After all, there were just the two of them and she could keep up this small duplex by having a maid come in a couple of days a week, but Faulkner certainly counted every penny he spent. In some ways he was a damned old miser. Honestly, Mr. Mason, the man would lie awake nights trying to work out some scheme by which he could trim you in a business deal. By that, I mean that in case you owned something Faulkner wanted to buy, he'd manage to get you in some kind of a jackpot where you'd lose your eyeteeth. He . . ."

The doorbell rang a strident summons, followed almost immediately by heavy pounding of knuckles and a rattling of the doorknob.

Mason said, "That sounds like the police."

"Excuse me," Carson said, and started for the door.

"It's okay," Mason told him. "I'm leaving. There's nothing more I can do here."

Mason was a step behind Carson when the latter opened the door. Lieutenant Tragg, backed by two plain-clothes officers, said to Mason, "I thought that was your car out front. You certainly do get around."

Mason stretched, yawned, and said, "Believe it or not, Lieutenant, my only interest in the case is over a couple of goldfish that really aren't goldfish at all."

Lieutenant Tragg was as tall as Mason. He had the forehead of a thinker, a well-shaped nose and a mouth which held plenty of determination but had a tendency to curve upward at the corners, as though the man could smile easily.

"Quite all right, Counselor. Quite all right," he said, and then added, "your interest in goldfish seems to be somewhat urgent."

"Frankly," Mason told him, "I would like to chisel some money out of Harrington Faulkner's estate. In case you don't know it, at the time of his death a young woman named Sally Madison was holding his check for five thousand dollars."

Tragg's eyes studied Mason with keen appraisal. "We know all about it. A check dated last Wednesday for five thousand dollars, payable to Thomas Gridley. And have you perhaps talked with Thomas Gridley lately?"

Mason shook his head.

There was a hint of a sardonic smile playing around the corners of Tragg's mouth. "Well, as you've remarked, Counselor, it's late, and I take it you're going home and go to bed. I don't suppose there's anything in connection with your interest in the case that will cause you to lose any sleep."

"Not a thing," Mason assured him cheerfully. "Good night, Lieutenant."

"And good-by," Tragg said, entering Carson's house, followed by the two officers, who promptly kicked the door shut.

9

■

Perry Mason struggled up through an engulfing sea of warm languor which seemed to make it impossible for him to move. Fatigue kept lulling him back to the blissful inertia of slumber; the strident ringing of the telephone bell insisted upon pulling him back to consciousness.

More than half asleep, he groped for the telephone.

"Hello," he said, his tongue thick.

Della Street's voice at the other end of the line knifed his brain to consciousness. "Chief, can you get over here right away?"

Mason sat bolt upright in the bed, every sense alert.

"Where?" he asked.

"The Kellinger Hotel on Sixth Street."

Mason's sleep-swollen eyes glanced at the luminous dial of his wrist watch, then he realized there was enough daylight filtering through the windows of his apartment to rob the hands of their luminosity. "As quick as I can make it, Della," he promised, and then added, "just how urgent is it?"

"I'm afraid it's terribly urgent."

"Is Sally Madison with you?"

"Yes. We're in six-thirteen. Don't stop at the desk. Come right up. Don't knock. The door will be unlocked. I'll . . ."

The receiver at the other end of the line was suddenly

slipped into place in the middle of the sentence, cutting off Della Street's words as neatly as though the wire had been severed with a knife.

Perry Mason rolled out of bed. Out of his pajamas, he was groping for clothes even before he switched on the lights in his apartment. Two minutes later he was struggling into a topcoat as he ran down the hall.

The Hotel Kellinger was a relatively unpretentious hotel which evidently catered largely to permanent guests. Mason parked his car and entered the lobby, where a somewhat sleepy night clerk looked up in a casual survey which changed to a frown of thoughtful inspection.

"I already have my key," Mason said hastily, and then added somewhat sheepishly, "darn near missed out on a night's sleep."

The elevator was an automatic. Mason noticed there were seven floors in the hotel. As a precaution, in case the doubtful scrutiny on the part of the clerk below should have ripened into skepticism, Mason punched the button which took the elevator to the fifth floor, and then, walking down the corridor, wasted precious seconds locating the stairway. During that time he heard the automatic mechanism of the elevator whirl into activity.

Mason ran up the uncarpeted stairs, located the room he wanted on the sixth floor and gently tried the knob of the door. The door was unlocked. He swung it open noiselessly.

Della Street, attired in a housecoat and slippers, held a warning finger to her lips and motioned toward the room behind her, then pointed to the twin bed near the window.

Sally Madison lay on her back, one arm flung out from under the covers, her fingers limp and relaxed. The girl's glossy dark hair streamed out over the pillow. The absence of shoulder straps and the curving contours which were visible indicated that she was sleeping nude. Her alligator-skin purse, which had evidently been placed under the pillow, had fallen to the floor and opened, partially spilling its contents.

Della Street's insistent finger pointed to the purse.

Mason bent over to get a look at the articles which were illuminated by a bedside lamp which had apparently been lowered from its normal position on a small table between the two beds to a point on the floor, where the light would not shine in Sally Madison's eyes.

He saw a roll of bills fastened together with an elastic band. The denomination of the outer bill was visible and showed that it was for fifty dollars. Back of the roll of bills there was the dull gleam of blued steel, where the barrel of a revolver caught and reflected the rays of the electric light.

Della Street glanced inquiringly at Mason. When she saw that the lawyer had fully appreciated the significance of the contents of the purse, she raised her eyebrows in silent inquiry.

Mason looked around the room, searching for some place where he could talk.

Della Street beckoned him around the foot of the bed and opened the door of the bathroom. She switched on the light, and, when Mason had entered, closed the door behind him.

The lawyer seated himself on the edge of the bathtub, and Della Street started talking in a whisper. "She clung to that purse like grim death. I wanted to get her some night things but she said she'd sleep in the raw. She got out of her clothes in nothing flat, was careful to put the purse under her pillow and then lay there watching me while I undressed. I switched out the lights and got into bed. Apparently she couldn't sleep at first. I heard her twisting and turning."

"Any sobs?" Mason asked.

Della shook her head.

"When did she get to sleep?"

"I don't know. I went to sleep first, although I had

intended to stay awake and make sure she was asleep and all right before I closed my eyes."

"When did you see the purse?".

"About five minutes before I telephoned you. Before she went to sleep she must have squirmed around so that the purse had worked over to a position near the edge of the bed—then when she turned in her sleep the purse fell out. I heard the jar and I was nervous enough so that I wakened suddenly and almost jumped out of my skin."

"Did you know what had wakened you?"

"Not right away, but I turned on the light. Sally was lying there sound asleep, just about as you see her now, but she was twitching restlessly and her lips were moving. The words she was uttering were all mumbled together so you couldn't distinguish anything. I could only hear some confused sounds.

"As soon as I turned on the light, I realized what had happened, and, without thinking, reached down to pick up the purse. First, I saw the rolls of bills and started to put them back in the purse. Then the tips of my fingers touched something cold and metallic. I immediately lowered the light to the floor so I could see what it was all about. At that time the purse was lying just as you see it now, and I left the light right there on the floor by the purse.

"Chief, I was just sick. I didn't know *what* to do. I didn't dare to leave her alone and go down to the lobby. Finally I took a chance on telephoning you because I knew that was all there was for me to do."

"Just what did you do?" Mason asked. "I mean how did you place the call?"

She said, "It was almost thirty seconds before I could get anyone to answer at the hotel switchboard, then I kept my voice just as low as possible and asked for an outside line. But the man downstairs told me all numbers had to go out through the hotel switchboard. And I saw then there was no dial on the telephone. I'd been so rattled I hadn't noticed that before. So I gave him your unlisted number. It was the only thing I could have done under the circumstances."

Mason nodded gravely.

"It seemed like an age before you answered," she went on. "And then I started talking to you, keeping my eye on Sally Madison all the while, so I could hang up in case she started to wake up."

"Is that why you were cut off in the middle of a sentence?"

"Yes. I saw her move restlessly and her eyelids fluttered. So I didn't dare to keep on talking. I slipped the receiver back into place and put my head back on the pillow so in case she opened her eyes I could pretend to be asleep—although, of course, the purse on the floor and the light by the purse would have been a giveaway. If she wakened, I was going to call for a showdown, but if I could postpone it until you got here I thought it would be better to play it that way. Well, she rolled her head around a bit and said something in that mumbled voice of a person talking in her sleep, and then she heaved a long sigh and seemed to relax."

Mason rose from his seat on the edge of the bathtub, pushed his hands deep into his coat pockets, said, "We're in a jam, Della."

Della Street nodded.

"She's supposed to be broke," Mason said. "If she has a roll of bills like that she must have got them from Mrs. Faulkner. I guess I played right into her hands. I wanted to be alone there in Faulkner's bathroom so I could take a good look at all the evidence. I didn't want her checking up on what I was doing, so I told her to take Mrs. Faulkner out into the living room and kid her out of her hysterics. I guess while she was out there, she must have put the bite on Mrs. Faulkner. That means she must have uncovered some evidence that escaped me. Or else, Mrs. Faulkner propositioned her to ditch the gun, and the golddigger ran true to form and wanted some heavy dough. In any event it leaves *us* in a mess.

"You can see what's going to happen now. I thought we were getting her out of circulation so the newspaper reporters wouldn't get hold of her, and so we could do something about building up a claim against the estate of Faulkner without having her spill any beans before we knew the lay of the land. That's what comes of being big-hearted and trying to help a guy who has T.B. and a golddigging girl friend.

"You've registered under your own name and under her name. If that gun happens to be the one with which the murder was committed, you can realize what a spot we're in. Both of us. What did she tell you when she telephoned?"

"She said you had told her to get in touch with me and had given her my number; that I was to take her to a hotel, stay with her and fix it so that no one would know anything about where she was until you got ready to let them find out."

Mason nodded. "That's exactly what I told her to do."

Della Street said, "I was asleep and the telephone kept ringing. It wakened me out of a sound slumber and I guess I was a little groggy. Sally Madison gave me your message, and one of the first thoughts that flashed through my mind was where I could find a hotel. I told her to call me back in about ten minutes, and then I got busy on the telephone and called half a dozen hotels. I finally found there was a room with twin beds here at the Kellinger."

Mason slitted his eyes in concentration. "Then she called you back in fifteen minutes?"

"I guess so. I didn't notice the exact time. I had started to dress as soon as I located the room. I was rushing around and I didn't notice the time."

"And you told her to meet you here?"

"That's right. I told her to come directly to the hotel,

92

and if she got here first to wait for me in the lobby; if I got here first, I'd wait for her in the lobby."

"Which was the first one here?"

"I was."

"How long did you wait?"

"I'd say about ten minutes."

"She came in a taxi?"

"Yes."

"What kind?"

"It was a yellow cab."

"Notice anything strange about the way she carried her purse?"

"Not a thing. She got out of the cab and . . . Wait a minute, Chief, I *do* remember that she had a bill all ready in her hand. She didn't have to take it out of the purse. She handed it to the cab driver and didn't get any change. I remember that."

"Probably a dollar bill," Mason said. "That would mean she had about an eighty-cent ride on the meter, and gave a twenty-cent tip."

Della Street, searching her memory, said, "I remember the cab driver looked at the bill—looked at it in a peculiar sort of way, then grinned, and said something, put it in his pocket and drove off. Then Sally Madison entered the lobby and we went directly to the room."

"You'd already registered?"

"Yes."

"Then Sally didn't have any occasion to open her purse from the time you first saw her until she got into bed and tucked it under her pillow?"

"That's right. I remember thinking at the time that she should take more care of her skin, but she just got out of her clothes and climbed into bed."

Mason said, "Of course she didn't want you to have any opportunity to see what was in the purse. All right, Della, there's only one thing to do. We've got to get that gun out of the purse."

"Why?"

Mason said, "Because it's got your fingerprints on it."

"Oh, oh!" Della Street exclaimed in dismay. "I hadn't thought of *that.*"

"After we get your fingerprints off of it," Mason said, "we're going to wake Sally Madison up and ask her some questions. What we do after that depends on the answers, but probably we're going to tell her to go back to her apartment, act just as though nothing had happened, and under no circumstances say anything to anyone about having spent the night here."

"Think she'll do it?"

"You can't tell. She may. The probabilities are they'll pick her up before noon. Then if they ask a lot of questions, she'll probably drag us into the mess. *But if your fingerprints aren't on that gun,* we don't have to tell anyone that we knew what was in her purse. We were simply keeping her out of the way of the newspaper reporters. She was going to be our client in a civil action we were about to bring against the Faulkner Estate in order to collect five thousand dollars for her boy friend."

Della Street nodded.

"But," Mason went on, "if your fingerprints are found on that gun, then we're in an awful mess."

"But when you take my fingerprints off the gun, won't you automatically remove all fingerprints that are on it?"

Mason nodded. "That's one of the things we've got to do, Della."

"Doesn't that constitute tampering with evidence or something of the sort?"

Mason said, "We don't even know that it's evidence, Della. It may or may not be the gun with which Harrington Faulkner was killed. Okay, here we go."

Mason opened the bathroom door, paused for a whispered word of caution to Della Street, and had taken one step toward the bed where Sally Madison was sleeping, when knuckles pounded loudly on the door of the room.

Mason stopped in dismay.

"Open up!" a voice called. "Open up in there," and knuckles once more banged on the panels of the door.

The noise aroused Sally Madison. With a half-articulate exclamation, she sat up in bed, threw one leg out from under the covers, then in the dim light of the room saw Perry Mason standing motionless by the doorway.

"Oh!" she exclaimed. "I didn't know *you* were here," and promptly grabbed the covers up to her chin and pulled her leg back into the bed.

"I just came," Mason said.

She smiled.

"I didn't hear you come."

"I wanted to make sure everything was all right."

"What's happening? Who's at the door?"

Mason said to Della Street, "Open it, Della."

Della Street opened the door.

The night clerk said, "You can't pull that stuff here."

"What stuff?" Della Street asked.

The man said, "Don't pull that line on me. Your boy friend went up to the fifth floor with the elevator, then sneaked up the stairs to the sixth floor. He thought he was being smart. I happened to remember that you'd put through a call from this room and thought I'd give it the once-over. I was listening outside the door. I heard the bathroom door open and heard you two whispering. This isn't the sort of a place you girls think it is. Get your things together and get out."

Mason said, "You're making a mistake, Buddy."

"Oh, no, I'm not. *You're* the one that's making the mistake."

Mason's hand slid enticingly down into his right-hand trouser pocket. "All right," he said, laughing, "perhaps I'm the one that's made the mistake, but it's getting daylight and it isn't going to hurt the hotel any if the girls check out after breakfast." Mason pulled out a roll of bills, peeled a ten-dollar bill from the roll, held it between his first and second fingers so the night clerk could get a good look at the denomination.

The man didn't even lower his eyes. "No you don't," he said. "That sort of stuff doesn't go here."

Mason glanced over to where Sally Madison was holding the sheet up under her chin. He noticed that she had taken advantage of the diversion to retrieve her purse from its position on the floor. It was now safely tucked out of sight.

Mason pushed the bills back into his pocket, took out his card case, produced one of his cards. "I'm Perry Mason, the lawyer," he said. "This is Della Street. She's my secretary."

The clerk said doggedly, "She'd have to be your wife to let you get by with this, and that's final. We're trying to run a decent place here. We've had trouble with the police before, and I'm not going to take any chances on having any more."

Mason said angrily, "All right. We'll get out."

"You can wait down in the lobby," the clerk told him.

Mason shook his head. "If we're going to be put out, I'll stay here and help the girls pack."

"Oh no you won't."

"Oh yes I will."

The clerk said, "Then *I'll* stay." He jerked his head at the girls. "Get your clothes on."

Sally Madison said, "You'll have to get out while I get something on. I'm sleeping in the raw."

The night clerk said to Mason, "Come on. Let's go down to the lobby."

Mason shook his head.

Della Street flashed an inquiring glance at Mason.

The lawyer's right eye slowly closed in a wink.

Almost imperceptibly, Della Street motioned her head toward the door.

Mason shook his head.

Della Street said suddenly, "Well, I'm not going to be put out of here at this hour of the morning. *I* haven't done anything wrong. It's bad enough to be disturbed in a night's sleep without getting put out of a second-rate hotel because your boss wants to give you some orders. *I'm* going back to bed. If you don't like it, call the police and see what they have to say about it."

Della Street pulled back the covers, kicked off her slippers and jumped into bed. Surreptitiously, she glanced at Mason.

Mason gave her an almost imperceptible nod of encouragement.

The clerk said gloomily, "I'm sorry but it won't work. I suppose if we hadn't had any trouble before this you could bluff us out, but the way it is right now, you either get out or I call the police. Make up your mind which you want."

"Call the police," Mason said.

The clerk said, "Okay, if you want it that way, that's the way you'll have it." He walked over to the telephone, picked it up, held the receiver to his ear, said, "Police headquarters," and then after a moment, "this is the night clerk at the Kellinger Hotel on Sixth Street. We've got some disorderly tenants in Room 613. I've tried to put them out and they won't go. Send a car around right away, will you? I'll be up here in the room. . . . That's right. The Kellinger Hotel, and the room number is six-thirteen."

The clerk slammed the receiver back into place, said, "I'm keeping my nose clean. Let me give you folks a friendly tip. You'll just about have time to take a powder before the police get here. Take my advice and beat it."

Perry Mason settled himself comfortably on the foot of Della Street's bed. He took a notebook from his pocket and scribbled a note to Della Street. "Remember that the telephones are only connected through the downstairs switchboard. My best guess is it's a bluff. Stick it out."

Mason tore the page from his notebook, handed it to Della.

She read it, smiled, and settled back against the pillow.

Sally Madison said, "Well, *I'm* going to get out. You two can do whatever you want to," and without more ado she jumped out of bed, snatched her clothes from the chair and ran into the little dressing room.

Mason casually leaned over and raised the pillow on her bed.

She had taken her purse with her.

Mason took a cigarette case from his pocket, handed Della Street a cigarette, took one himself. They lit up, and Mason once more settled back comfortably. From the little dressing room, came the sounds of Sally Madison hurriedly dressing.

Mason waited for nearly two minutes, then said to the clerk, "Okay, you win. Better get dressed, Della."

Della Street slid out of the bed, adjusting the housecoat around her. She picked up her overnight bag, entered the dressing room and said to Sally Madison, "Okay, Sally, I'm going with you."

"You're not going with me," Sally Madison said, the sound of her shod foot hitting the floor. "Personally, I don't like cops. As far as I'm concerned, you stuck around just a little bit too long. I'm on my way."

She had dressed herself with the facility of a lightning-change artist and now she stepped out from the dressing room ready for the street. Her hair was the only thing about her that bore witness to her hasty toilet.

"Wait a minute," Mason said. "We're all going."

Sally Madison, clutching the purse under her arm with the tenacity of a football player holding an intercepted pass, said, "I'm sorry, Mr. Mason, but I'm not waiting for anyone."

Mason played his trump card. "Don't let him bluff

you," he said. "There isn't any dial on that telephone. It would have to be connected through the downstairs switchboard before he could call anyone. He was just pretending to call the police."

The clerk, in a dispirited voice, said, "Don't think I haven't had to go through with this before. The minute I decided you were in six-thirteen, I plugged the line from this room through the switchboard to an outside line. I did that before I came up. Don't ever kid yourself that telephone wasn't connected."

Something in the man's manner carried conviction.

Mason said, "Okay, Della, do the best you can. I'm leaving you to take the rap. I'm going with Sally. Come on, Sally."

Sally eyed him with disfavor. "Wouldn't it be better if I went alone?"

"No," Mason said, and piloted her to the door.

The clerk hesitated a moment, deciding what to do.

Mason said to Della Street, "When the officers come, tell them that the clerk was trying to annoy you with his attentions."

The clerk promptly got up from his chair and followed Mason and Sally Madison out into the corridor. "I'll take you down in the elevator," he said.

"No need," Mason told him. "We'd rather use the stairs."

"Speak for yourself," Sally Madison told Mason in something of a panic. "I'm going down in the elevator. It's quicker."

They entered the elevator. The clerk removed the catch which had been holding the door open, and pressed the button for the lobby. "The bill's six dollars," he said.

Mason gravely took a five-dollar bill, a one-dollar bill, and a twenty-five-cent piece from his pocket, handed them to the clerk.

"What's the two-bits for?"

"A tip for checking out," Mason said.

The clerk calmly pocketed the twenty-five-cent piece, held the six dollars in his left hand. "No hard feelings," he said as he opened the door of the elevator on the lobby floor. "We have to keep the joint clean or we'll be closed up."

Mason took Sally Madison's arm. "You and I are due for a little talk," he said.

She didn't even look at him, but quickened her step until she was almost running across the lobby. They were halfway to the door when it was pushed open and a uniformed officer from a radio car said, "What's the trouble?"

Mason tried to edge past him. The man blocked the door, looked over Mason's shoulder to the clerk.

"Couple of girls in six-thirteen," the clerk said wearily. "They violated the rules of the hotel, receiving company in their room. I asked them to get out."

"This one of the girls?"

"That's right."

"Where's the other one?"

"Getting dressed."

"Who was the company?"

The clerk jerked his thumb toward Mason. The officer grinned at Mason, said, "We don't want you, but since I'm here, I think I'll ask a few questions of the girls."

Mason gravely produced a card. "The fault," he said, "lies with the hotel. My secretary was spending the night with Miss Madison, who is my client. I'm representing her in rather an important piece of litigation. I called to get some information."

The officer seemed duly impressed by Mason's card. "Then why didn't you tell that to the clerk and save us a trip?"

"I tried to," Mason said self-righteously.

"It's an old gag," the clerk said wearily. "You'd be surprised how many times I've heard that stuff. They're all secretaries."

"But this man is Perry Mason, the lawyer. Haven't you ever heard of him?"

"Nope."

The officer said, "I'll just check up on this thing, Mr. Mason. I guess it's all right, but seeing the call's been made, I've got to make a report on it, and I'd better make a check, and—let's take a look at the register."

Sally Madison started to push past him to the door.

"No you don't, Sister," the officer said, "not yet. Don't be in such a hurry. Wait five minutes and it'll all be cleared up and you can go get yourself some breakfast, or go back to your room, whichever you want. Let's just take a look at the register."

The clerk showed the officer where Della Street had signed.

"This Sally Madison your secretary?" the officer asked.

"No. Della Street is."

The elevator made noise in the shaft.

"She's up in the room?" the officer asked.

"That's right," Mason said.

The clerk said somewhat querulously, "I'm doing just what the Vice Squad told me to. They said that we could either get a house dick who would be acceptable to the Vice Squad, or we'd have to report every violation of rules in regard to visitors. I had a hunch not to let these two girls in in the first place. I'm going to be sore if I follow instructions and then you show up and pour a bucket of whitewash over 'em."

"What time did they check in?"

"About half past two this morning."

"Half past two!" the officer said, and gave Mason the benefit of a frowning scrutiny.

Mason said suavely, "That's why I wanted my secretary to keep Miss Madison with her tonight. It was late when we finished working on the case, and . . ."

The elevator rattled to a stop. Della Street, carrying

101

her overnight bag, stepped out, then stopped as she saw the trio at the desk.

"This is the other one," the clerk said.

The officer said to Della Street, "You're Mr. Mason's secretary?"

"That's right."

"I suppose you have something in your purse—social security card, or something of that sort."

Della Street said brightly, "*And* a driving license, a key to Mr. Mason's office, and a few other things."

"I'd better take a look," the officer said apologetically.

Della Street took out a small inner purse, showed him her driving license and her social security number.

The officer nodded to the night clerk. "Okay," he said. "You did all right under the circumstances. I'll report it. But you don't need to put these girls out. Let them go back to the room."

"I'm on my way," Sally Madison announced definitely. "I've had all the sleep I want, and right now I'm hungry."

Della Street looked to Mason for a signal.

Mason said, "I'm sorry your rest was disturbed, Sally. Drop into my office some time before noon."

"Thank you, I will," she said.

The officer, plainly impressed by her face and figure, said, "Sorry you were put to all this trouble, Miss. There isn't any restaurant near here. Perhaps we could give you a lift down to where there's a restaurant that's open."

"Oh no, thank you," Sally Madison told him, turning on her charm. "I *always* like to walk in the morning. It's the way I keep my figure."

"Well," the officer said approvingly, "you sure make a good job of it."

Mason and Della Street stood watching Sally Madison walk briskly across the lobby and out through the door. The officer, watching the lines of the golddigger's figure with evident approval, turned back to Mason only after the door was closed on Sally Madison. "Well, Mr. Mason, I'm sorry this happened, but it's just one of those things."

"Yes," Mason said, "it is. I don't suppose I could buy you a cup of coffee?"

"No thanks, we're on patrol. We'll be going. My partner's out in the car."

Mason moved his hand significantly toward his pocket. The officer grinned and shook his head, said, "Thanks all the same," and walked out.

The clerk said to Mason, "The room's all paid for. Go on back up if you want to."

Mason grinned. "Just the two of us?"

"Just the two of you," the clerk said dispiritedly. *"My* nose is clean. Stay as long as you want to—up until three o'clock this afternoon. That's checking-out time. Stay longer than that and you'll get charged for the room— *double."*

Mason relieved Della Street of her overnight bag. "We'll go now," he said. "My car is outside."

10
■

Mason and Della Street sat in a little all-night restaurant where the coffee was good. The ham was thin but had an excellent flavor and the eggs were cooked to golden perfection.

"Do you think we're in the clear?" Della Street asked.

"I think so," Mason said.

"You mean she'll get rid of the gun?"

Mason nodded.

"What makes you think she's going to do that?"

Mason said, "She was so anxious to get away. She certainly had something in mind. It doesn't take more than six guesses, you know."

"Didn't she have an opportunity to get rid of the gun last night?"

"Perhaps not," Mason said. "Remember that Sergeant Dorset took her out to see James Staunton. Did she tell you anything about the result of that interview?"

"Yes. Staunton insisted that Faulkner had brought him the fish. What's more, he brought out a written statement to prove it."

"The deuce he did!"

"That's what *she* said."

"A statement signed by Faulkner?"

"Yes."

"What was done with the statement?"

"Sergeant Dorset took it. He gave Staunton a receipt for it."

Mason said, "Staunton didn't tell *me* about having any written statement from Faulkner. What was in it?"

"Something to the effect that Faulkner had turned over these two particular fish to Staunton. That he wanted Staunton to care for them and secure treatment for them; that he absolved Staunton of all responsibility in case anything should happen to the fish, either death from natural causes or theft or sabotage."

"It was Faulkner's signature?"

"Staunton insisted that it was, and apparently there was nothing about it to arouse Sergeant Dorset's suspicions. He took the statement at its face value. Of course, I'm going by what Sally told me."

Mason said, "Now why do you suppose Staunton didn't produce that statement when *I* questioned him?"

"Probably because he felt your questioning wasn't official."

"I suppose so. But I thought I had him pretty well frightened."

"But if Faulkner himself took those fish out of the tank, what was the reason for the soup ladle and the four-foot extension on the handle?" Della Street asked.

Mason said, "I've already pointed that out to Sergeant Dorset. The ladle couldn't have been used to take the fish out of the tank."

"Why not?"

"In the first place," Mason said, "the surface of the water in the tank was about seven and a half feet from the floor, and I don't think the ceiling of the room was over nine and a half feet high. It's one of those low-ceilinged bungalow rooms. Now take a four-foot handle on a soup ladle, try to bring it out of the tank, and you've got two feet of handle that remain in the tank after the *top* of the handle is against the ceiling."

"But you can tilt the ladle, can't you? That is, you can take it out on an angle."

"Exactly," Mason said, "and when you do that, you lose your fish."

Della Street nodded, then frowned. She gave the problem thoughtful consideration.

"What's more," Mason went on, "I don't think you could lift a fish out of a tank with a soup ladle. I don't think the fish would stay in one position long enough to let you get him out. I think it would take something bigger than a soup ladle. Of course, I'm making allowances for the fact that these fish weren't as active as they might have been. But even so, I doubt if it could be done."

"Then what *was* the ladle used for? Was it just a blind?"

Mason said, "It could have been a blind. It could have been something else."

"Such as what?" Della asked.

105

"It could have been a device to get something out of the tank other than fish."

"What do you mean?"

Mason said, "Someone took a shot at Faulkner last week. At any rate he claims they did. The bullet missed him and embedded itself in the upholstery of the car. Of course, that bullet was valuable evidence. Police have worked out the science of ballistical detection now so that they can tell a great deal about the weapon which fired any particular bullet. And they can examine a bullet under a microscope and tell absolutely whether or not it was fired from any given gun."

"And what does all this have to do with the goldfish tank?" Della Street asked.

Mason grinned. "It goes back to something Elmer Carson told me. He was in the office when Faulkner came in carrying the bullet with him."

"The one he'd dug out of the car?"

"That's right. He'd recovered the bullet from where it had embedded itself in the upholstery, and he'd notified the police, although he didn't tell anyone in the real-estate office about it."

"And what happened?"

"The police came there and then Faulkner couldn't find the bullet."

"Oh, oh," Della said.

"Now Carson points out that he never left his seat at his office desk, and the stenographer there, a Miss Stanley, apparently corroborated his statement. However, police searched him, also his desk."

"So then what?"

"So then later on, along in the evening, when Miss Stanley was cleaning up her desk, she found *a* bullet under some paper on her desk."

"You mean it wasn't the same bullet?"

"I don't know," Mason said. "I don't think anyone else knows. It was simply a bullet. Everyone acted on the assumption that it was the same bullet Faulkner had brought in earlier in the day and had then misplaced. But as nearly as I can tell, there were no identifying marks on the bullet, so that it could not definitely be said to be the same one."

"I don't see just what you're getting at," Della Street said.

Mason said, "Faulkner thought that he had placed the bullet on the top of his desk when he came in. Then he'd gone over to dictate some correspondence, standing by Miss Stanley's desk."

"He must have been a pretty cool customer," Della Street said. "If someone shot at me, I don't think I'd dig out the bullet and then start dictating correspondence."

Mason said, "As I gather it, Miss Stanley noticed that his hand was shaking a little, but, aside from that, there were no other evidences of emotion."

Della Street looked at her employer as though trying to peer behind his eyes and penetrate his thoughts. "Personally I would have said that Faulkner was excitable. If someone had actually shot at him I'd think he would have been as nervous as a kitchen cockroach when a light is suddenly turned on."

"He was rather a complex character," Mason said. "Remember that night when the process server served the papers on him in Carson's suit for defamation of character?"

"Yes, I remember the occasion quite distinctly."

"Remember that he didn't get the least bit nervous. Didn't even read the papers, but pushed them down in his side pocket and kept his attention concentrated on the business of the moment—which was to get me to protect his precious goldfish by beating the temporary restraining order preventing him from moving the goldfish tank?"

Della Street nodded. "That's right. He took the service of those papers right in his stride. They seemed to constitute only a minor irritation."

"Despite the fact that the suit was for a hundred thousand dollars," Mason pointed out.

"You're getting at something, Chief. What is it?"

Mason said, "I'm simply sitting here sipping coffee and putting two-and-two together, trying to find out if perhaps someone may not have actually taken a shot at Faulkner while he was riding along in his automobile."

Della Street said, "But Faulkner hardly impressed me as a man who would have forgotten where he placed that bullet after he'd dug it out. That doesn't seem to be in keeping with his character."

"It wasn't," Mason conceded readily enough.

"Chief, what *are* you getting at?"

Mason said, "Let's consider another possibility, Della. A person seated at an adjoining desk, as Carson was, could have reached over to Faulkner's desk, picked up the bullet Faulkner had left on the desk and hidden it where it would never have been discovered."

"You mean without leaving his desk?"

"Yes."

"But I thought you said they searched Carson and searched his desk."

"They did."

"I don't see . . . oh! Now I get it! You mean he could have tossed it into the goldfish tank?"

"Exactly," Mason said. "The goldfish tank was right back of Carson's desk; was wide enough at the top so he could have tossed the bullet over his shoulder and been almost certain of having it light inside the tank, and then it would drop down to the bottom and be a relatively inconspicuous object among the pebbles and gravel at the bottom of the tank."

Della Street's eyes were sparkling with interest now. "Then when Faulkner thought attempts were being made to steal his goldfish . . . you mean it was actually someone trying to get the bullet back out of the tank?"

"Exactly," Mason said, "and the soup ladle would

108

have been an excellent instrument to have dredged down to the bottom of the tank, scooped up the bullet and eased it back out again. If someone had been reaching for the goldfish it wouldn't have been necessary to have tied a four-foot extension to the handle of the soup ladle. The goldfish would have been swimming around in the water, and by waiting for a favorable opportunity, they could have been fished out with a container that had a handle not over two feet in length."

"Then Carson must have been the one who shot at him and . . ."

"Not so fast," Mason said. "Carson had been in his office all that morning. Remember, Miss Stanley will give him an alibi. Or so Carson says, and he would hardly dare to falsify that, because he must know the circumstances incident to that first shooting are now to receive a lot of police attention."

"Then for some reason Carson was trying to confuse the issues."

"Trying to protect the person who had fired the shot, or the person *who he thought had fired the shot.*"

"You mean they may not have been the same?"

"It's a possibility."

"Would that account for the sudden animosity which developed between Carson and Faulkner?"

"The animosity had been there for some time. The thing that flared suddenly into existence was Carson's *open* hostility."

"And what did that have to do with it?"

Mason grinned and said, "Put yourself in Carson's position. He'd tossed a bullet into a fish tank. He'd evidently acted on the spur of the moment, looking for the best possible place of concealment. It was a simple matter to toss the bullet in, but it was a difficult matter to get the bullet out. Particularly when you remember that Faulkner was living in the other side of the duplex house and that he was suspicious of Carson and would have promptly rushed over to see what Carson was doing if Carson came to the office outside of office hours."

Della Street nodded.

"You can't reach down to the bottom of a four-foot fish tank," Mason said, "and pull out a lead bullet without making some rather elaborate preparations. And it was at this time that Carson suddenly realized Faulkner was concerned about the health of the goldfish and was planning to remove the entire tank to some place where the fish could be given treatment."

"But wouldn't Carson have been in a position to profit by that? Wouldn't he have stood more chance of getting the bullet if the tank had been moved?"

"Probably not. And you must also remember that he was running the risk of having the bullet discovered as soon as the tank was moved. Of course, once that bullet was discovered, it wouldn't take very much of a detective to piece together what must have happened, and Carson would find himself in quite a spot."

"I'd say he was in a spot anyway," Della Street said.

"He was," Mason told her. "And so it became necessary for him to take steps to prevent the goldfish tank from being removed from the office. *That* was the reason for his sudden flare-up of hostility and the filing of his initial action against Faulkner, the action which resulted in a temporary restraining order preventing Faulkner from removing the fish tank. Of course, Carson might have been left without a leg to stand on when he finally got into court, but that didn't bother him. He knew that by filing the action against Faulkner he could at least delay things until he had a chance to get that bullet out of the tank."

"That certainly sounds logical," Della Street admitted, "and would account for some of the things Carson did."

"And," Mason went on, "in order to make the filing of that injunction suit seem logical, Carson had to play the part all the way along the line. Otherwise, his sudden concern over the goldfish tank would have been so conspicuous that it might have aroused suspicion."

"So that accounts for his action for defamation of character?"

"Exactly."

"But what about the earlier attempts to steal the goldfish?"

"There weren't any. Carson had probably managed to get access to the fish tank for some rather limited period. At that time, he probably tried various methods of extracting the bullet and found that he was up against a tougher problem than he had anticipated. The size of the tank, the weight of the tank, and its position, made it something of a job to get that bullet out of the tank."

"And I suppose that the forty-five bullet which was subsequently found on Miss Stanley's desk was simply another bullet that had been deliberately planted."

"So it would seem," Mason said. "You will note that Miss Stanley vouched for the fact that Carson had not left the office *before* the police arrived, and that he had been seated at his desk during all of the time which had elapsed between Faulkner's entrance and the arrival of the police, but it's logical to assume that between the arrival of the police and the discovery of the bullet, Carson must have gone out—perhaps several times. He certainly must have gone out for lunch. He could easily have picked up another bullet then."

Della Street showed her excitement. "Chief, you've got it all figured out. It must have happened in exactly that way. And if it did, then Carson must have been the one who killed Faulkner and . . ."

"Take it easy, Della," Mason cautioned. "Remember that all I have at present is a beautiful theory, a logical theory, but nevertheless, *only* a theory. And remember that *we're in a jam.*"

"How do you mean?"

"Sally Madison had a gun in her purse. Let's hope

she's smart enough to either hide that gun where it won't be discovered, or to wipe all the fingerprints off of it, or to do both. In the event she doesn't, and if it should prove to be the murder gun, the police will find fingerprints on it and sooner or later they're pretty apt to discover they're *your* fingerprints. Then we're up against a serious charge. It will be a simple matter for the police to prove that we took Sally Madison out of circulation during a crucial period in the investigation. And if we try to plead innocence, or pretend that we didn't know she had the murder weapon in her purse, we will be confronted with your fingerprints on the gun. So, taken by and large, we're up against it *if* Sally Madison is caught before she gets rid of that gun."

"Chief, couldn't you have telephoned the police as soon as we'd found out that she had a gun in her purse?"

"We could have," Mason said, "and in the light of subsequent events, we undoubtedly should have. However, the police would have been skeptical, and at the time, it seemed like a better bet to wipe your fingerprints off the gun, wash our hands of Sally Madison, and step out of the case. The peculiar combination of circumstances which made that night clerk enter the room and decide to stay there couldn't very well have been foreseen."

"So what do we do now?" Della Street asked.

Mason said, "We keep our fingers crossed and . . ."

Abruptly, Mason lowered his coffee cup to the saucer. "Damn!" he said.

"What is it, Chief?"

"Don't look startled and don't act guilty," Mason warned. "Leave the talking to me. Lieutenant Tragg has just entered the restaurant and is headed this way, and if you think Tragg isn't the last person in the world I want to talk to just now, you've got another think coming."

Della Street's face changed color. "Chief, *you* keep out of it. Let *me* take the rap. After all, *I'm* the one whose

112

fingerprints are on the gun. They can't prove that *you* knew anything . . ."

Mason abruptly raised his head to look over Della Street's shoulder and said, with every semblance of surprise, "Well, well, well! Our old friend, Lieutenant Tragg! What brings you out here so early in the morning?"

Tragg placed his hat on a vacant chair, drew up another one and calmly seated himself. "What brings *you* here?"

"Hunger," Mason said, smiling.

"Is this your regular breakfast place?" Tragg asked.

"I think we'll adopt it," Mason told him. "The menu isn't large, but it's attractive. You'll find the coffee excellent, and the eggs are well cooked. I don't know about you, Lieutenant, but I particularly detest eggs that are fried in a pan so hot that a crust forms on the bottom of the eggs. Now, you take the fried eggs here, and they're thoroughly delicious."

"Exactly," Tragg said, and to the man behind the counter called out, "Ham and eggs, and a big cup of coffee now, and another cup of coffee when you serve the eggs."

Tragg shifted his position slightly, smiled at Mason and said, "And now, Counselor, since you've exhausted the subject of fried eggs, suppose we talk about murders."

"Oh, but I haven't exhausted the subject of eggs," Mason protested. "A great deal depends on cooking them at just the right temperature. Now, the yolk of a fried egg should be thoroughly warm all the way through, not cooked almost solid at the bottom but runny on top. Nor should . . ."

"I agree with you entirely," Tragg interrupted. "That also depends entirely on the temperature of the frying pan. But what do you think about Faulkner's murder?"

"I never think about murders, Lieutenant, unless I'm paid to do so. And in the event I'm paid for my thoughts,

I try to give only my client the benefit of them. Now you are in a different position . . ."

"Quite right," Tragg interposed calmly, reaching for the sugar as the waiter served his first cup of coffee. "I am paid by the taxpayers to think about murders at all times, and, thinking about murder, I somehow find my thoughts turning to a certain Miss Sally Madison. What can you tell me about her?"

"A rather attractive young woman," Mason said. "She seems to be devoted to her present boy friend who works in a pet store. Doubtless she has had other boy friends to whom she has been devoted, but I think that her present affair with Tom Gridley is, perhaps, more apt to result in matrimony."

"Something of a golddigger, I understand," Tragg observed.

Mason's face showed surprise. "Who told you that?"

"Oh, I get around. Is she a client of yours?"

"Now there again," Mason said smiling, "you are asking a difficult question. That is, the question is easy; it's the answer that's difficult."

"You might try answering it either yes or no," Tragg said.

"It isn't that easy. She hasn't as yet definitely retained me to represent her interests. But on the other hand, I think she desires to do so, and I am investigating the facts."

"Think you'll represent her?"

"I'm sure I can't say. The case she presents is far from being an easy one."

"So I would gather."

"You see," Mason went on, "as the agent of her boy friend, Tom Gridley, she may or may not have reached a contract with Harrington Faulkner. A contract involves a meeting of the minds, and a meeting of the minds in turn depends upon . . ."

Tragg held up his hand. "Please," he begged.

114

Mason raised his eyebrows in apparent surprise.

Tragg said, "You're unusually loquacious this morning, Counselor. And a man who can deliver such an extemporaneous dissertation upon the art of frying eggs could doubtless talk almost indefinitely on the law of contracts. And so, if you'll pardon me, I think I'll talk to your charming secretary."

Tragg turned to Della Street and asked, "Where did you spend the night last night, Miss Street?"

Della smiled sweetly. "That question, of course, Lieutenant, involved an assumption that the night is, or was, an indivisible unit. Now, as a matter of fact, a night is really divided into two periods. First, the period before midnight, which I believe was legally yesterday, and the period after midnight, which is today."

Tragg grinned, said to Perry Mason, "She's an apt pupil, Counselor. I doubt if you could have stalled for time any better if you had stepped in and answered the question for her."

"I doubt if I could have done as well," Mason admitted cheerfully.

"Now," Tragg said, suddenly losing his smile and becoming grimly official in his manner, "suppose we quit talking about fried eggs and contracts and the legal subdivisions of the period of darkness, and suppose, Miss Street, you tell me exactly where you were from ten o'clock last night until the present time, omitting nothing—and that's an official question."

"Is there any reason why she should have to answer that question?" Mason asked. "Even conceding that it *is* a legal question."

Tragg's face was as hard as granite. "Yes. In the event I get the run-around it will be an important factor in determining whether any connection Miss Street may have had with what transpired was accidental or deliberate."

Della Street said brightly, "Well, of course . . ."

"Take it easy, Della," Mason warned.

She glanced at him and at what she saw in his eyes the expression of animation fled from her features.

"I'm still waiting for an answer to my question," Lieutenant Tragg said harshly.

"Don't you think you should be fair with Miss Street?" Mason asked.

Tragg didn't take his eyes from Della's face. He said, "Your interruptions all go on the debit side of the ledger as far as I'm concerned, Mason. Miss Street, *where did you spend the night?*"

Mason interposed suavely, "Of course, Lieutenant, you're not a mind reader. The fact that you came to *this* restaurant means that you knew we were in the neighborhood. There are logically only two sources from which you could have acquired that information. One of them is that you received over the radio a report from a patrol car stating that it had been called to the Kellinger Hotel, where a complaint had been made that two young women were receiving a male guest as a visitor in violation of the rules of the hotel, and the police had been called to eject the tenants. You thereupon acted upon the assumption that you would, perhaps, find the parties who had been ejected in a near-by all-night restaurant, and by the simple process of cruising around, located us here."

Tragg started to say something, but Mason, slightly raising his voice, kept the conversational lead. "The other assumption is that you picked up Sally Madison on the street a few moments ago and questioned her. In which event you learned from her that we were in the vicinity. And if you questioned her, you doubtless made a rather complete job of it."

Mason's warning glance at Della Street conveyed the impression to her that in such event Lieutenant Tragg had doubtless examined the purse and by this time was fully familiar with its contents.

Tragg was still looking at Della Street. "Now that

116

you've been properly coached, Miss Street, *where did you spend the night?*"

"I spent part of it at my apartment. The rest of it at the Kellinger Hotel."

"How did you happen to go to the Kellinger Hotel?"

"Sally Madison called me on the telephone and told me Mr. Mason wished me to take her to some hotel."

"Did she say why?"

Della Street said quite innocently, "I can't remember quite definitely whether *she* told me why or whether I subsequently learned why from Mr. Mason. He wanted me to get her out of . . ."

"Out of circulation," Tragg prompted as Della Street's voice suddenly trailed away into silence.

"Out of the way of newspaper reporters," Della Street finished, smiling sweetly at Lieutenant Tragg.

"What time was this?" Tragg asked.

"That Sally Madison called me?"

"Yes."

Della Street said, "I really couldn't say. I don't think I looked at my watch, but doubtless the Kellinger Hotel can tell you approximately what time we arrived."

"What I am asking you now," Tragg said, "is what time you received this call from Sally Madison."

"I'm sure I can't say."

"Now then," Tragg said, "we're getting to the important part. Watch your answers carefully, because a great deal is going to depend on what you say. Did you notice anything unusual about Sally Madison?"

"Oh, yes," Della Street told him quickly.

Tragg's voice was grim and harsh. "What?" he asked, and the single word was as harshly explosive as the cracking of a whip.

Mason's eyes warned Della Street.

"Why," she said, "the girl slept in the nude." She smiled at Lieutenant Tragg and then went on rapidly, "That's rather unusual, you know, Lieutenant . . . I mean

117

she simply stripped her clothes off and jumped into bed. Ordinarily a young woman as beautiful as Sally Madison takes much more care of her personal appearance before retiring. She'll put creams and lotions on her face and usually . . ."

"That isn't what I meant," Tragg said.

"Of course," Mason interposed, "you've interrupted Della, Lieutenant. If you had let her keep on talking, she might have told you exactly what you had in mind."

"If I'd let her keep on talking," Tragg said, "she'd have been here until noon describing Sally Madison's bedtime habits. The question is, Miss Street, did you or did you not notice anything unusual about Sally Madison or did she make any confession or admission to you?"

"Remember, Lieutenant," Mason said, "that as a potential client, anything Sally Madison may have said was a privileged communication and as Della Street is my secretary, she can't be questioned concerning that."

"I think I understand that rule," Tragg conceded. "And it applies to anything that was necessarily said in connection with the matter on which Sally Madison was consulting you. Now I take it that matter related exclusively to a claim she had against the estate of Harrington Faulkner. I now want to know definitely, once and for all, whether Della Street noticed anything unusual or significant in connection with Sally Madison. Did you or did you not, Miss Street?"

Della Street said, "Of course, Lieutenant, I had only met the girl a day or two ago, and so I don't know what is usual about her. Therefore, when you ask me if I noticed anything unusual, it's hard to tell . . ."

"All this stalling around," Tragg said, "causes me to reach a very definite conclusion in my own mind. Miss Street, how did it happen Perry Mason came up to call on you at the hour of five o'clock in the morning?"

"Was it five o'clock?" Della Street asked, with some

show of surprise. "I'm certain that I didn't look at my watch, Lieutenant. I merely . . ."

Mason said, "There again, of course, the records of the Hotel Kellinger will be of some assistance to you, Lieutenant."

Tragg said, "Despite your repeated warnings to Della Street that she isn't to conceal any information which I can subsequently ascertain by interviewing the clerk at the Kellinger Hotel, I want to know whether you noticed anything unusual in connection with Sally Madison, anything in connection with her wearing apparel, what she had on, what she had with her, what she did, or what she said."

Mason said, "I'm quite certain, Lieutenant, that if Miss Street had noticed anything such as you have mentioned that was sufficiently unusual to be of any importance, she would have told me, so you can ask your question of me."

"I don't have to. I'm asking Miss Street. Miss Street, why did you call Perry Mason and ask him to come to the hotel?"

Della Street's eyes were suddenly hard and defiant. "That is none of your business."

"Do you mean that?"

"Yes."

"You know my business is rather inclusive," Tragg said, "particularly insofar as murders are concerned."

Della Street clamped her lips together in a tight line.

Abruptly, Tragg said, "All right, you two have sparred around here trying to find out how much I know. The very fact that you've been sparring for time convinces me that you do know the thing I wanted to find out. As Perry Mason so aptly pointed out, you could gamble with either one of two alternatives. One was that I'd received a report from the officers who answered the call to the Kellinger Hotel, and had cruised the neighborhood simply on the off chance of picking you up. The other was that I had first picked up Sally Madison and questioned her. You stalled for time, hoping that the first alternative was the correct one. You're wrong. I'd picked up the report from the officers when it came in as a routine radio report. I'd been up all night, waiting for a break in the case. That radio report looked like the break I'd been waiting for. I dashed out and picked up Sally Madison on the street. In her purse she had two thousand dollars in cash, the possession of which she couldn't explain. She also had a thirty-eight caliber, double-action revolver which had recently been fired, and which bears every evidence of having been the weapon with which Harrington Faulkner was murdered. Now then, Perry Mason and Della Street, if I can prove that either one of you knew of the contents of that purse, I'm going to stick you as being accessories after the fact. I gave you every opportunity to report to me and to communicate any significant information connected with the murder of Harrington Faulkner. You chose not to do so. And, so help me, Mason, if I can prove that you knew that gun was in Sally Madison's purse, I'm going to nail you to the cross."

Abruptly, Lieutenant Tragg pushed back his chair, said to the puzzled waiter, "Never mind the ham and eggs. I'll pay the check now."

And Tragg slammed money down on the counter and walked out.

Della Street's eyes, sick with dismay, caught those of Perry Mason. "Oh, Chief," she said, "I should have told him! I'm sick all over."

The lines of Mason's face could have been carved from stone. He said, "It's okay, kid. There were two possible alternatives. We took a chance and we lost. Now we'll carry on from there. It seems to be our unlucky day. We're in it together, and it's a sweet mess."

11

■

Perry Mason, Della Street and Paul Drake sat in Mason's office, grouped around Mason's big desk.

Mason finished his account of the events of the past few hours, and said, "So you see, Paul, we're in a jam."

Drake whistled softly. "I'll say you're in a jam. Why didn't you toss the jane overboard as soon as you saw that rod and call the cops?"

"Because I was afraid they wouldn't have believed us in the first place, and, in the second place I hated to throw her to the wolves without knowing what it was all about. I wanted to hear her side of the story first. And, if you want to know, I thought we could sneak out of it and get away with it."

Drake nodded, said, "Yes, it was a good gamble all right, only you seem to have lost with every throw of the dice."

"We did indeed," Mason said.

"Just where does that leave you now?"

Mason said, "If they can pin some part in the murder on Sally Madison, it leaves us right out on the end of the limb. If they can't, we'll probably squeeze out. What have you found out about the facts of the murder, Paul?"

Drake said, "They're putting an official hush-hush on the thing, but I can tell you this much—the medical examiner made a bad slip. The young deputy coroner who went out there was green, and Sergeant Dorset was helping to ball things up. The police have fixed the time of death within a very short time, but, as I understand it, the autopsy surgeon neglected to do the one thing that would have given the cops a perfect case."

Mason said, "That's good."

"I can tell you something else, Perry, that doesn't look so good."

"What?"

"This chap that works in the pet shop, Tom Gridley, seems to have been out there and got a check for one thousand dollars, and that check may have been about the last thing that Faulkner ever wrote."

"How do they figure that out, Paul?"

"There was a checkbook lying on the floor. The last stub in it had been partially filled out. It was a check for one thousand dollars, and Faulkner had been writing on that stub when all of a sudden his pen simply quit writing, but he had written 'Tom' and then the letters 'G-r-i.' Quite evidently he'd been intending to write 'Tom Gridley.' There was a fountain pen found on the floor."

Mason thought that over for a moment, said, "What did Tom Gridley say about it, Paul?"

"No one knows. The police swooped down on him as soon as they found that stub in the checkbook, and Gridley has been out of circulation ever since."

"When do the police think the murder was committed?"

"Right around eight-fifteen. Say between eight-fifteen and eight-thirty. Faulkner was to have attended a meeting of goldfish experts. He was to have been there at eight-thirty. About ten minutes past eight he telephoned and said that he'd been delayed by a business matter which had detained him longer than he'd expected; that he was just shaving and was going to jump in a hot bath, that as soon as he'd finished he'd be right over, but that he would be perhaps a few minutes late. He also said he'd have to leave probably at nine-thirty, as he had a

with photographing the position of the body, getting fingerprints and trying to reconstruct the physical evidence than in getting to work with body temperatures and all that sort of stuff. The detectives think it was a blunder on the part of the medical department and there's some feeling about it. Taking the body's temperature right at the time the police first arrived would have given them some fine corroborations. As it is, they have to rely on deductions."

Mason said, "Yes, I can see where that would make for considerable complications. It looks as though the police might be right. What's their theory about the overturned goldfish bowl?"

"Well," Drake said, "the goldfish *could* have been in a bowl on that overturned table, and Faulkner could have upset the whole works when the shot was fired and he fell down dead."

Mason nodded.

"Or," Drake went on, "someone could have been in the room some time after the murder was committed and upset the goldfish bowl either accidentally or on purpose."

"Any theories about that someone?"

"It could have been Mrs. Faulkner, who didn't like the looks of the thing, upset the goldfish bowl, either accidentally or on purpose, then got in her car and went around the corner to wait for you to show up."

"But how could she have known that I was coming?"

"As nearly as I can tell," Drake said, "it's the way you doped it out last night, Perry. Staunton must have given her a ring."

"In other words, she was in the house. She had already discovered the body. She had upset the goldfish bowl. Staunton rang up on the telephone. He wanted to talk with Faulkner. She told him Faulkner couldn't be reached at the present moment; was there any message she could take, and Staunton told her that Sally Madison and I were on our way out there."

Mason got up from behind his desk, started pacing the floor restlessly. "That, of course, presupposes the fact, Paul, that there was some inducement used to make Staunton keep his mouth shut. I mean about that telephone conversation. If Faulkner died at around eight-fifteen or eight-thirty, Staunton must have learned by this time from the police or the papers that Mrs. Faulkner was there in the house with her dead husband. . . . Hang it, Paul, what are we sticking around here talking for? Why don't we get in touch with Staunton and see what he has to say when we really start pouring it on him."

Drake didn't move from his chair. "Don't be silly, Perry."

"You mean the police have sewed him up?"

"Tighter than a drum. He won't get back into circulation until after he's made a complete written statement and sworn to it. By that time, he'll have sewed himself up in a sack. He won't dare to make any statement under any circumstances that would change the statement he gave the police."

Once more, Mason resumed his pacing of the floor, then he said, "Put men out to watch Staunton's house. As soon as the police let him get back into circulation, ask him one question."

"What question?" Drake wanted to know.

Mason said, "Last Wednesday Faulkner took these fish out to him and told him to telephone the pet store and ask for treatment. Find out what time the pet store sent out the treatment tank."

Drake showed surprise. "That's all?"

"That's all. There are other questions I'd like to ask him, but by the time the police get done with him, he won't answer. So just ask him that one question. Today's Saturday, and everything closes at noon. They'll probably keep Gridley and Staunton sewed up until it's too late to get any court orders. And the way things are now I don't dare to ask for a *habeas corpus* on Tom Gridley."

The telephone rang.

Della Street answered it, said, "It's for you, Paul," and handed the instrument over to Drake.

Drake said, "Hello . . . Okay, spill it . . . Right . . . You sure? . . . All right, give me everything you've got."

Drake listened for nearly two minutes while the receiver continued to give forth a continuous rattle of crackling, metallic sounds.

At the end of that time, Drake said, "Okay, I guess there's nothing much to do except keep a line on what's happening and let me know."

He hung up and turned to Perry Mason.

Mason took one look at the detective's face and asked, "Is it that bad, Paul?"

Drake nodded.

"What is it?" Della Street asked.

"You lose," Drake said.

"What?"

Drake said, "This is confidential, Perry. The police don't want it to leak out, but I've got it straight from one who knows. They took Sally Madison into custody. They found the gun and the roll of bills in her purse. They fingerprinted the gun and got some excellent latents. There were two fingerprints on top of the barrel, not complete fingerprints, but nevertheless enough to enable the police to make an identification. Tragg is nobody's fool. He closed up the room in the Kellinger Hotel, went to work on the bathroom mirrors and the doorknobs, got fingerprints of both Della Street and Sally Madison. Then he checked the prints on the gun. He found he had half a dozen fingerprints of Sally Madison, and two of Della Street. Then, after they'd photographed the gun, they turned it over to the ballistics department and fired a test bullet and compared that with the bullet they found in Faulkner's body. There's no question but what the gun they took from Sally Madison's purse was the weapon with which the murder was committed. And there's also no question but what that weapon belonged to Tom Gridley. It was a thirty-eight caliber revolver he'd purchased six years before when he was acting as messenger for a bank. The gun is registered with the police."

Della Street looked up at Perry Mason in dismay.

Mason said grimly, "All right, Paul. Put as many men on the job as are necessary to give it complete coverage. Find out where they've got Sally Madison held for inquiry if you can. Della, get out some blanks and fill out a writ of *habeas corpus* on behalf of Sally Madison."

Drake said, "It won't do you any good, Perry. They'll have wrung her dry by this time. There's no use trying to lock the stable after the horse has been stolen."

"To hell with the stable," Mason said. "There's no time for that now. *I'm* going after the horse!"

12

■

Paul Drake was back in Perry Mason's office within five minutes after he had left. He encountered the lawyer just leaving from the exit door of his private office.

"Where to?" Drake asked.

"Wilfred Dixon," Mason told him. "I'm going to check up on Dixon and on the affairs of the first Mrs. Faulkner. He is her lawyer. What's new? Anything important?"

Drake put his hand on Mason's arm, drew Mason back into the inner office and closed the door. "Sometime during the night," he said, "an attempt was made to get

127

that goldfish tank out of the office. It sure looks as though you called the turn on that business, Perry."

"Just when was the attempt made?"

"Police don't know. For some reason or other, they never looked into the other side of the duplex house, but confined their investigations to Faulkner's residence. Then, this morning, when Alberta Stanley, the secretary, opened up the real-estate office, she found the place something of a wreck. There was a long rubber hose which had evidently been used to siphon the water out of the empty goldfish tank. That is, it was empty of goldfish."

Mason nodded.

"After the water was siphoned out, the goldfish tank had been tipped over on its side and all of the mud and gravel in the bottom had been scooped out and left in a pile on the floor."

Mason's eyes narrowed. "Has it occurred to the police as yet, that someone was looking for that bullet Faulkner carried into the office?"

"You can't tell, Perry. It hasn't occurred to Sergeant Dorset, but you never know what Lieutenant Tragg is working on. Dorset shoots off his mouth to the newspaper boys and tries to get publicity. Tragg is smooth as velvet. He kids the boys along and prefers results to publicity."

"Anything else?" Mason asked.

Drake said, "I hate to do this, Perry."

"Do what?"

"Be hanging crepe all over things, but it's one of those cases where every bit of information you get is the kind you don't want."

"Shoot," Mason told him.

"You remember Faulkner had a reputation of being a man who would skin the other fellow in a business deal. He kept within his own standards of honesty but he was completely ruthless."

Mason nodded.

128

"Well, it seems that Faulkner was really anxious to get hold of that formula that Tom Gridley had developed for the treatment of gill disease. You remember he bought out Rawlins' pet shop? That was the first move in his campaign. Then, it turns out that Tom Gridley had mixed up a batch of his paste which was to be painted on plastic panels that were to be introduced into fish tanks. The trouble with Gridley is that he gets so interested in what he's doing and . . . well, he's just like a doctor. He wants to effect cures and doesn't care too much about the financial end of things."

"Go ahead," Mason said.

"Well, it seems that yesterday evening, Faulkner, who had, of course, got the combination of the safe from Rawlins, went down to the pet store, opened the safe, took out the can of paste that Gridley had mixed up and sent it to a chemist to be analyzed. Rawlins was there and tried to stop him but it was no soap."

"Faulkner certainly was a heel," Mason said.

"According to the police, it furnishes a swell motivation for a murder."

Mason thought the matter over and nodded his head. "Academically it's bad. Practically it isn't so bad."

"You mean the way a jury will look at it?"

"Yes. It's one of those things that you can play up strong to a jury. While technically it's a motivation for murder, it's such a flagrant example of oppression by a man who has money and power, who's picking on a chap in his employ . . . No, Paul, that isn't at all bad. I presume the theory of the police is that when Gridley found out about it he became terribly angry, took his gun and went up to kill Faulkner."

"That's about the size of it."

Mason smiled and said, "I don't think Tragg will hold to that theory very long."

"Why not?"

"Because the evidence is against it."

"What do you mean? It's Gridley's gun, there's no question of that."

"Sure, it's Gridley's gun," Mason said. "But mind you this: If the circumstantial evidence means what the police think it means, Tom Gridley effected a settlement with Faulkner. He may have gone up there *intending* to kill him, but Faulkner gave him a check for a thousand dollars. Faulkner wouldn't have done that unless he had reached some sort of a settlement with Gridley. Gridley certainly couldn't have killed him *before* the check was made out, and would have had no reason to have killed him afterward."

"That's right," Drake said.

"The minute Faulkner died, that check, and also the five-thousand-dollar check that Sally Madison has, weren't worth the paper they were written on. You can't cash a check after a man dies. I have an idea, Paul, that you'll find Lieutenant Tragg begins to think this motive isn't as simple as it appears to be on the surface. Hang it, if it weren't for the evidence against Sally Madison and the fact that Della Street's fingerprints are on that gun, we'd sit tight and tell the police to go jump in the lake. As it is, I've got to find out all the facts and be the first one to get the correct interpretation."

"Suppose Sally Madison bumped him off?"

"Then," Mason said, "the police have a perfect case against Della Street and me as being accessories after the fact."

"Think they'll press it?"

"You know damn well they'll press it," Mason said. "They'd like nothing better."

"Well, of course," Drake pointed out, "you can't blame them. You certainly do skate on thin ice, Perry. You've been a thorn in the flesh of the police for a long time."

Mason nodded. "I've had it coming to me once or twice," he admitted, "but what makes me sore is to think that they'd really hang it on me in a case where we were absolutely innocent and only trying to help a young fellow who had T.B. get enough money to take treatments that would cure him. Hang it, Paul, I'm really in a mess this time, and they've got Della roped into it. That's what comes of trusting a golddigger. Oh well, there's no use conducting post-mortems. By the time the police let me get in touch with Sally Madison she'll have been bled white. I'm getting out a writ of *habeas corpus* and that of course will force their hand. They'll have to put a charge against her. But by the time they do that, they'll have really put her through a clothes wringer. Keep working, Paul, and if you get anything new, let Della Street know. Work on this case as you've never worked on anything else in your life. We're working against time and we've got to find out not only the evidence, but we've got to interpret that evidence."

"Did the broken goldfish tank mean anything to you?"

"It means a lot," Mason said.

"How come?"

"Suppose Sally Madison isn't as dumb as she appears. Suppose back of that poker face of hers is a shrewd, calculating mind that isn't missing a bet."

"I'll go with you that far," Drake said.

"And suppose," Mason went on, "she reasoned out what had happened to the bullet that Faulkner had taken to the office. Suppose when Faulkner gave her the key there in the café at the time he made the deal with her and told her to get Tom Gridley and go out and treat his fish, Sally Madison went out instead and used the soup ladle to get the bullet out of the tank. Then suppose she very shrewdly sold that bullet to the highest bidder."

"Wait a minute," Drake said. "You've got something wrong there, Perry."

"What?"

"According to all the evidence, those goldfish must have been gone when Sally got there. Faulkner must have given her a complete double cross on that."

131

"All right, so what?"

"So when she went there to get the bullet, she would have known that the goldfish were gone."

"Not goldfish," Mason said, "a pair of Veiltail Moor Telescopes."

"Okay. They're goldfish to me."

"You won't think so after you've seen them," Mason said. "If Sally Madison went in there to get that bullet, the fact that the fish weren't there wouldn't have stopped her from getting what *she* was after."

"And then she went back and got Tom Gridley and came out the second time?"

"That's right."

"Well," Drake said, "it's a theory, Perry. You're giving that girl credit for an awful lot of sense."

Mason nodded.

"I think you're giving her too much credit," Drake said.

Mason said, "I didn't give her enough credit for awhile. Now I'm going to make my mistakes on the other side. That girl's batted around a bit, Paul. She knows some of the answers. She's in love with Tom Gridley. You take a woman of that type, when she falls for a man, it's usually a combination of a starved-mother instinct and a sex angle. My best guess is that that girl would stop at nothing. Anyway, I haven't time to stay here and talk it over now. I'm on my way to see Dixon."

"Be careful," Drake warned.

Mason said, "I'm going to be careful with everybody from now on, Paul, but it isn't going to slow me down any. I'm going to keep moving."

Mason drove to the address of Wilfred Dixon, found the house to be a rather imposing edifice of white stucco, red tile, landscaped grounds, a three-car garage and an atmosphere of quiet luxury.

Mason had no difficulty whatever in getting an immediate audience with Wilfred Dixon, who received him in a room on the southeast side of the house, a room which was something of a cross between a den and an office, with deep leather chairs, Venetian blinds, original oils, a huge flat-topped desk, a portable bar, and a leather davenport which seemed to invite an afternoon siesta. There were three telephones on the desk, but there were no filing cases in the room, no papers visible on the desk.

Wilfred Dixon was a short, chunky man with perfectly white hair, steel-gray eyes, and a face which was deeply tanned from the neck to the roots of the hair. His complexion indicated either considerable time spent on the golf links without a hat, or regular treatments under a quartz lamp.

"Won't you sit down, Mr. Mason," Dixon invited, after giving the lawyer a cordial grip with muscular fingers. "I've heard a great deal about you, and naturally it's a pleasure to meet you, although, of course, I can't understand why you should look *me* up. I presume it's connected in some rather remote way with the tragic death of Harrington Faulkner."

"It is," Mason said, giving Dixon a steady look.

Dixon met his eyes with calm assurance. "I have, of course, managed the affairs of Genevieve Faulkner for some years. She was the first wife, you know. But of course you *do* know."

And Dixon smiled, a disarming, magnetic smile.

"You knew Harrington Faulkner personally?" Mason asked.

"Oh yes," Dixon said, as though stating a fact which must have been well known and perfectly obvious.

"Talked with him occasionally?"

"Oh yes. You see, it was a little embarrassing for Genevieve to hold business conferences with her former husband. Yet the first Mrs. Faulkner—I'll call her Genevieve if you don't mind, Mr. Mason—was very much interested in the business transactions of the firm."

"That firm made money?" Mason asked.

133

"Ordinarily, Mr. Mason, I would consider that question involved Genevieve's private affairs. But inasmuch as an investigation in connection with the Faulkner Estate will make the whole matter public, I see no reason for placing you to the inconvenience of getting your information through more devious channels. The business was immensely profitable."

"Isn't it rather unusual for a real-estate business to make that much money under present conditions?"

"Not at all. It was more than a real-estate business. The business was diversified. It administered various other businesses which had been previously used as investment outlets. Harrington Faulkner was a very good businessman, a very good businessman, indeed. Of course, he was unpopular. Personally, I didn't approve of Mr. Faulkner's business methods. I wouldn't have employed them myself. I was representing Genevieve. I certainly was in no position to—well, shall we say, criticize the goose that was laying the golden eggs?"

"Faulkner was the money-maker?"

"Faulkner was the money-maker."

"What about Carson?"

"Carson was an associate," Dixon said suavely. "A man who had an equal interest in the business. One third of the stock was held by Faulkner, one third by Carson and one third by Genevieve."

"That still isn't telling me anything about Carson," Mason said.

With every simulation of candid surprise, Dixon raised his eyebrows. "Why, I thought that was telling you *everything* about Carson."

"You haven't said anything about his business ability."

"Frankly, Mr. Mason, my dealings were with Faulkner."

"If Faulkner was the mainspring of the business," Mason said, "it must have galled him to do the bulk of the work and furnish the bulk of the capital, and then receive only one third of the income."

"Well, of course, he and Carson had a salary—a salary that was fixed and approved by the court."

"And they couldn't raise those salaries?"

"Not without Genevieve's consent, no."

"And were the salaries ever raised?"

"No," Dixon said shortly.

"Was any request made to raise the salaries?"

Dixon's eyes twinkled. "Several times."

"Faulkner, I take it, didn't feel too friendly toward his first wife?"

"I'm sure I never asked him about that."

"I presume that originally Harrington Faulkner furnished most of the money which started the firm of Faulkner and Carson."

"I believe so."

"Carson was the younger man and Faulkner relied on him perhaps for an element of young blood in the business?"

"As to that, I couldn't say. I only represented Genevieve after the separation and during the divorce."

"You had known her before then?"

"No. I was acquainted with the attorney whom Genevieve employed. I'm a businessman, Mr. Mason, a business adviser, an investment counselor, if you wish. I try to be a good one. You really haven't stated the object of your visit."

Mason said, "Primarily, I'm interested in finding out what I can about Harrington Faulkner."

"So I gathered. But the reason for your interest is not apparent. Doubtless, many people would like to know something of the affairs of Mr. Faulkner. There's a difference between a casual curiosity, Mr. Mason, and a legitimate interest."

"You may rest assured I have a legitimate interest."

"Mr. Mason, I merely wanted to know what it was."

Mason smiled. "I will probably be the attorney for a claimant against the Faulkner Estate."

"Probably?" Dixon asked.

"I haven't as yet definitely accepted the case."

"That makes your interest rather—shall we say, nebulous?"

"I wouldn't say so," Mason said.

"Well, of course, I wouldn't have a difference of opinion with an attorney who has such an established reputation, Mr. Mason. So perhaps let us say you have your opinion and I will try to keep an entirely open mind. I'm perfectly willing to be convinced."

Mason said, "With two thirds of the stock and complete control of the corporation, Faulkner, I guess, controlled the corporation with an iron hand?"

"There's no law against guessing, Mr. Mason, none whatever. There are times when I find it a rather interesting occupation, although of course one hardly dares to reach a decision predicated solely upon a mere guess. One prefers to have facts to justify one's opinion."

"One does, indeed," Mason said. "Therefore, one asks questions."

"And receives answers," Dixon told him suavely.

Mason's eyes twinkled. "Not always the most definite answers that one would want."

"That's quite right, Mr. Mason. That's something I myself have found repeatedly in my business dealings. For instance, you'll remember I asked *you* about *your* interest in the unfortunate death of Harrington Faulkner. You stated, I believe, that you were considering representing a person who had a claim against the estate. May I ask the nature of that claim? I don't think you told me."

Mason said, "It involved a claim based upon a formula that was worked out for the cure of a fish disease."

"Oh, Tom Gridley's formula," Dixon said.

"You seem to know a good deal about the business, Mr. Dixon."

"As the person who represents a client whose financial eggs are virtually all in one basket, Mr. Mason, it behooves me to know a great deal about the details of the business."

"Now, to go back," Mason went on. "Faulkner was in the driver's seat until suddenly, and I presume out of a clear sky, Genevieve Faulkner sued him for divorce. Quite evidently she must have had the goods on him."

"The evidence in that case has all been introduced and a decision long since reached, Mr. Mason."

"That decision must have been gall and wormwood to Harrington Faulkner. In place of controlling the corporation he suddenly found that he was in the position of being a minority stockholder."

"Of course," Dixon pointed out somewhat smugly, "since under the laws of this state man and wife are presumed to be partners, if the marriage is dissolved it becomes necessary for some sort of a settlement to be made."

"And I presume," Mason went on, "that with the constant threat being held over Faulkner's head that you would go back into court and ask the judge to reopen the alimony settlement in the event of any failure on the part of Faulkner to accede to your wishes, you must have incurred Faulkner's enmity."

Once more the eyebrows went up. "I merely represent Genevieve's investments. Naturally, I represent her interests to the best of my ability."

"You talked with Faulkner occasionally?"

"Oh yes."

"He told you many of the details of the business?"

"Naturally."

"Did he come to you and tell you the details voluntarily, or did you ask him?"

"Well, of course, Mr. Mason, you'd hardly expect a man in Mr. Faulkner's position to run to me with every little detail about his business."

"But you were interested?"

137

"Quite naturally."

"Therefore, I take it you asked him?"

"About the things I wanted to know, yes."

"And that included virtually everything?"

"Really, Mr. Mason, I couldn't say as to that, because naturally I don't know how much I didn't know. I only know the things I did know."

And Dixon beamed at the lawyer with a manner that indicated he was trying his best to co-operate in giving Mason any information that was available.

"May I ask you when you last talked with Faulkner?" Mason asked.

Dixon's face became as a wooden mask.

"Of course," Mason said, "it's a question that the police will ask sooner or later."

Dixon carefully placed the tips of his fingers together, regarded his nails for a moment.

"I take it," Mason said, "that you talked with him sometime yesterday evening."

Dixon raised his eyes. "Really, Mr. Mason, what is the ground for that assumption?"

"Your hesitancy."

"I was deliberating."

Mason smiled. "The hesitancy may have been due to deliberation, but it was nevertheless a hesitation."

"A very good point, Mr. Mason. A good point, indeed. I'm frank to admit that I was deliberating and therefore hesitating. I don't know whether to answer your question or whether to reserve my answer until I am interrogated by the police."

"Any particular reason why you shouldn't tell me?"

"I was debating that with myself."

"Anything to conceal?"

"Certainly not."

"Then why conceal it?"

"I think that's unfair, Mr. Mason. I am not concealing

138

anything. I have answered your questions fully and frankly."

"When did you last talk with Faulkner?"

"Well, Mr. Mason, as you have so shrewdly deduced, it was yesterday."

"What time yesterday?"

"Now, do you mean when I talked with him personally, face to face?"

Mason said, "I want to know when you talked with him personally and I want to know when you talked with him over the telephone."

"What makes you think there was a telephone conversation?"

"The fact that you differentiate between a conversation with him face to face and another conversation."

Dixon said, "I'm afraid I'm no match for you, Mr. Mason. I'm afraid I'm in the hands of a very shrewd lawyer."

"I am," Mason said, "still waiting for an answer."

"You have, of course, no official right to ask that question."

"None whatever."

"Perhaps I wouldn't choose to answer it. What then?"

"Then," Mason said, "I would ring up my friend, Lieutenant Tragg, tell him that you had seen Harrington Faulkner on the day he was murdered, perhaps on the evening he was murdered; that you had apparently talked with him over the telephone. And then I would hang up, shake hands with you, tell you I appreciated your cooperation, and go away."

Once more, Dixon put his fingers together. Then he nodded his head, as though having reached some definite decision. But he still remained silent, a chubby figure with a masklike countenance, sitting behind a huge desk, slowly nodding his head in impressive acquiescence with himself.

Mason waited silently.

Dixon said at length, "You make a very powerful argument, Mr. Mason. You do indeed. You would make a good poker player. It would be hard to judge what was in your hand when you shoved your chips into the pot—very hard indeed."

Mason said nothing.

Dixon nodded his head a few more times, then went on to say, "I will, of course, be called on eventually by the police. In fact, I have debated with myself whether I should telephone the police and tell them exactly what I know. You will, of course, be able to get all this information sooner or later, else I wouldn't be talking to you. You still haven't told me your exact interest in finding out the facts."

Dixon looked up at Mason, his attitude that of a man who is courteously awaiting a reply to a routine question.

Mason sat absolutely silent.

Dixon drew his eyebrows together, looked down at his desk, then slowly shook his head in a gesture of negation, as though after giving the matter thoughtful consideration, Mason's refusal to be more frank had caused him to reverse his former decision.

Still Mason said nothing.

Suddenly the business counselor put both hands flat on the desk, palms down, the gesture of a man who has definitely reached a decision. "Mr. Faulkner conferred with me several times yesterday, Mr. Mason."

"In person?"

"Yes."

"What did he want?"

"That goes beyond the scope of your original question, Mr. Mason."

Mason said, "I am more concerned with the question than with the reason for asking it."

Dixon raised and lowered his hands, the palms making little patting noises on the desk. "Well, Mr. Mason, it's

140

asking for a good deal, but, after all—Mr. Faulkner wanted to buy out Genevieve's interest."

"And you wanted to sell?"

"At a price, yes."

"The price was in dispute?"

"Oh, very much."

"Was there a wide difference?"

"Quite a wide range. You see, Mr. Faulkner had certain ideas as to the value of the stock. To be perfectly frank, Mr. Mason, he offered to sell his stock to us at a certain figure. Then he thought that in case we didn't want to accept that offer, we should be willing to sell our stock at the same figure."

"And you weren't?"

"Oh, definitely not."

"May I ask why?"

"It's rather elemental, Mr. Mason. Mr. Faulkner was operating the company on a very profitable basis. He was receiving a salary that had not been raised during the past five years. Nor had Mr. Carson's. If Genevieve had purchased Mr. Faulkner's stock, Mr. Faulkner would then have been at liberty to step out into the commercial world and capitalize upon his own very remarkable business qualifications. He could even have built himself up another business which might well have been competitive to ours.

"On the other hand, when it came to fixing a price for which Genevieve Faulkner would be willing to sell *her* stock, I was forced to adopt the position that the value of the stock, so far as she was concerned, was predicated upon the income she was receiving from it, and if she were to sell out, she would want to get a sum of money which would draw an equal return. And, of course, investments are not nearly as profitable as they once were, nor do they have the element of safety. That made a wide difference, a very, very wide difference, Mr. Mason, between our selling price and our buying price."

141

"I take it that made for some bad feeling?"

"Not bad feeling, Mr. Mason. Surely not bad feeling. It was merely a difference of opinion about a business transaction."

"And you held the whip hand?"

"I'd hardly say that, Mr. Mason. We were perfectly willing to let matters go on in status quo."

"But Faulkner found it very galling to be working for an inadequate salary . . ."

"Tut, tut, tut, Mr. Mason. The salary wasn't inadequate, it was the same salary he had been drawing when he owned a two-thirds interest in the corporation."

Mason's eyes twinkled. "A salary which he had fixed so that Carson wouldn't be in a position to ask for any salary increases."

"I certainly don't know what Mr. Faulkner had in mind. I only know that the arrangement which was made by all parties concerned when the divorce decree was granted by the court was that salaries could not be raised without Genevieve's consent unless the court was called in to reopen the whole business."

"I can imagine," Mason said, "you had Harrington Faulkner in a position that was very, very disagreeable to him."

"As I have stated several times before, Mr. Mason, I am not a mind reader, and I see no reason for speculating upon Mr. Faulkner's ideas."

"You saw him several times yesterday?"

"Yes."

"In other words, the situation was approaching a crisis?"

"Well, Mr. Faulkner definitely wanted to do something."

"Of course," Mason said, "if Faulkner had bought Genevieve's stock, he would then once more have been a two-thirds owner in the company. Faulkner would have been in a position to have got rid of Carson, and firing

Carson would have been a perfect answer to Carson's lawsuit."

"As a lawyer," Dixon purred, "you doubtless see possibilities which, as a layman, I would not see. My own interest in the matter was simply to get the best possible price for my client in the event a sale was to be made."

"You weren't interested in buying Faulkner's interest?"

"Frankly, we were not."

"Not at any price?"

"Well, I wouldn't go so far as to say that."

"In other words, what with Faulkner's quarrel with Carson, the various and sundry suits Carson had been filing, and the situation in which your client found herself, you were in a position to force Faulkner to buy at your price?"

Dixon said nothing.

"It was something in the nature of a legalized holdup," Mason went on, as though thinking out loud.

Dixon straightened in the chair as though Mason had struck him. "My dear Mr. Mason! I was merely representing the interests of my client. There was no longer the slightest affection between her and Mr. Faulkner. I mention that merely to show that there was no reason for any sentiment to be mixed with the business matter."

"All right. You saw Faulkner several times during the day. When was the last time you talked with him?"

"Over the telephone."

"About what time?"

"At approximately . . . well, sometime between eight and eight-fifteen. I can't fix the time any closer than that."

"Between eight and eight-fifteen?" Mason said, his voice showing his interest.

"That's right."

"And what did you tell him?"

"Well, I told him that in the event any sale was going

143

to be consummated, we wanted to have the matter disposed of at once; that if the matter wasn't terminated before midnight, we would consider that there was no use taking up further time with discussions."

"And what did Faulkner say?"

"Faulkner told me that he would be over to see me between ten and eleven; that he wanted to look in very briefly on a banquet of goldfish fanciers, after which he had an appointment. He said that when he saw me he would be in a position to make us a final offer. That if we didn't accept the proposition he'd make us at that time, he would consider the matter closed."

"Did he say anything about anyone else being there with him at the time you phoned?"

"No, sir. He did not."

"That conversation might have been as late as eight-fifteen?"

"Yes."

"Or as early as eight o'clock?"

"Yes."

"Earlier than eight o'clock?"

"I'm quite sure it wasn't, because I remember looking at my watch at eight and speculating whether I'd hear any more from Mr. Faulkner that evening."

"And you don't think it was later than eight-fifteen?"

"At eight-fifteen, Mr. Mason, I tuned in a radio program in which I was interested, so I'm quite certain of the time there."

"There's no question but what it was Harrington Faulkner with whom you were talking?"

"No question whatever."

"I take it Faulkner didn't keep his appointment with you?"

"No, he didn't."

"That caused you some concern?"

"Well, Mr. Mason," Dixon said, running his chunky, capable fingers through his white hair, "I see no reason

144

why I shouldn't be frank with you. I was—disappointed."

"But you didn't call Mr. Faulkner back?"

"No indeed I did not. I was keeping myself in the position of—well, I didn't want to show any eagerness whatever. The deal which I had previously outlined to Mr. Faulkner would have been quite profitable if it had gone through."

"Can you remember exactly what Faulkner said over the telephone?"

"Yes, he said that he had planned on attending a rather important meeting that night and was just getting dressed to go out to it. That he would much prefer to attend that meeting, keep his appointment and conclude his deal with us some time today."

"What did you tell him?"

"I told him I didn't think that would be satisfactory to my client because today was Saturday. He then said he'd be here between ten and eleven."

"Would you mind telling me the amount of the price you had fixed?"

"I don't think that needs to enter into it, Mr. Mason."

"Or the price at which Faulkner was willing to sell?"

"Really, Mr. Mason, I'm quite certain it would have no bearing on the matter."

"How much of a difference was there between the two figures?"

"Oh, a very substantial amount."

"When was Faulkner here personally?"

"About three o'clock in the afternoon, I believe it was—the last time—for just a few minutes."

"You had already made Faulkner your proposition?"

"Yes."

"And he had made you his?"

"Yes."

"How long was the interview?"

"Not more than five minutes."

145

"Did Faulkner see his wife—I mean his former wife?"

"Not at that interview."

"Had he seen her at any other interview during the day?"

"I believe he did—the meeting was by chance. I think Mr. Faulkner called about eleven o'clock in the morning and, as I remember it, encountered his wife—that is, his former wife, on the porch."

"And they talked for awhile?"

"I believe so."

"Is it fair to ask what they talked about?"

"I'm quite certain, Mr. Mason, that's between Genevieve and her husband."

"And might I see Genevieve to ask her a few questions?"

"For a man whose interest in Faulkner's estate is as nebulous as yours, if you'll permit me to say so, Mr. Mason, you want to cover quite a bit of territory."

Mason said, "I want to see Genevieve Faulkner."

"Are you, by any chance, representing someone who is charged with the murder of Mr. Faulkner?"

"So far as I know, no one has been charged with the murder of Mr. Faulkner."

"You are, however, aware of the probability that someone *may* be charged with such murder?"

"Naturally."

"And that someone might become, or might even now be a client of yours?"

Mason smiled. "I might be tempted to represent some person who is charged with the murder of Mr. Faulkner."

Dixon said quite definitely, "I don't think I would like that."

Mason's silence was significant.

Dixon said, "Things which one would discuss without hesitation with a lawyer who was planning merely to represent a claim against the estate of Harrington Faulkner are hardly the same things which one would

146

discuss with a lawyer who was planning to represent a person who was going to be accused of the murder of Harrington Faulkner."

"Suppose that person were unjustly accused?" Mason suggested.

"That," Dixon said self-righteously, "is something that would be left to a jury."

"Let's leave it to the jury, then," Mason said, grinning. "I should like very much to see Genevieve Faulkner."

"I'm afraid that is impossible."

"I take it that she has no interest in the estate."

Dixon's eyes abruptly shifted to his desk. "Why do you ask that, Mr. Mason?"

"Does she?"

"I would say she had none—unless the will provided otherwise—which is very unlikely. Genevieve Faulkner has no interest whatever in the estate of Harrington Faulkner. In other words, she has no possible motive for murder."

Mason grinned. "That wasn't what I asked."

Dixon matched his smile. "That was, however, the answer I gave."

Knuckles tapped lightly and in a perfunctory manner upon the door, and a half second later, without waiting for any answer, that door was opened by a woman who entered the room with all the assurance of one who belonged there.

A frown of annoyance crossed Dixon's face. "I have no dictation today, Miss Smith," he said.

Mason turned to look at the woman who had entered. She was slender and very attractive, somewhere in that vaguely indefinite period which is between forty-five and fifty-five. And, for a brief instant, Mason caught the flicker of a puzzled expression on her face.

Mason was on his feet instantly. "Won't you sit down, Mrs. Faulkner?"

"No, thank you. I . . . I . . ."

Mason turned to Dixon. "You'll pardon me for reaching the obvious conclusion."

Dixon admitted somewhat dourly that the name "Smith" had perhaps been a bit unfortunate. "Genevieve, my dear, this is Perry Mason, an attorney, a very skillful, clever attorney who has called on me to secure information about Harrington Faulkner. He asked permission to see you and I told him that I saw no reason for granting an interview."

Mason said, "If she has anything to conceal, it's bound to come out sooner or later, Dixon, and . . ."

"She has nothing to conceal."

"Are you," Mason asked of Genevieve Faulkner, "interested in goldfish?"

Dixon said, "She is not interested in goldfish."

Mrs. Faulkner smiled serenely at Perry Mason and said, "It would seem that Mr. Mason is the one who is interested in fishing. And so, if you gentlemen will pardon me, I'll retire and return when Mr. Dixon isn't engaged."

"I'm leaving right now," Mason said, getting to his feet and bowing. "I wasn't aware that Mr. Faulkner had had such an attractive first wife."

"Neither was Mr. Faulkner," Dixon said dryly, and then stood rigidly erect and silent while Mason bowed himself out of the room.

13

∎

Mason called up his office from a drugstore that was within half a dozen blocks of Dixon's house. "Della," he said when he had Della Street on the line, "get hold of

Paul Drake at once. Tell him to look up all of the evidence in connection with Harrington Faulkner's divorce case. Somewhere around five years ago. I not only want all of the dope on the case, but I want a transcript of the evidence if we can get it, and I want to know what was actually behind it."

"Okay, Chief, anything else?"

"That's all. What's new?"

She said, "I'm glad you phoned. I filed the application for a writ of *habeas corpus* and Judge Downey issued a writ returnable next Tuesday. They've now booked Sally Madison on a charge of first-degree murder."

"I suppose they booked her as soon as they learned of the writ," Mason said.

"I guess so."

Mason said, "All right, I'm going up to the jail and demand an audience with her."

"As her attorney?"

"Sure."

"You're going on record as representing her without first knowing what she has to say?"

Mason said, "It doesn't make a damn bit of difference what she has to say. I'm going to represent her because I've got to. I have no other choice in the matter. What have they done with Tom Gridley?"

"No one knows. He's still buried somewhere. Do you want me to prepare an application for a writ of *habeas corpus* for him?"

"No," Mason said. "I don't *have* to represent him—at least not until after I see what Sally Madison has to say."

"Good luck to you, Chief," Della Street said. "Sorry I got you into this."

"You didn't. I got you into it."

"Well, don't pull any punches."

"I won't."

Mason hung up, jumped in his car and drove to the jail. The excessive politeness with which the officers

149

greeted him and the celerity with which they arranged for an interview between Sally Madison and the lawyer as soon as Mason announced that he was going to represent her as her attorney, indicated that the police were quite well satisfied with the entire situation.

Mason seated himself at the long table, down the middle of which ran a heavy-meshed steel screen. And a few moments later, a matron ushered Sally Madison into the other side of the room.

"Hello, Sally," Mason said.

She looked very calm and self-possessed as she walked across to seat herself at the opposite side of the table, the heavy screen furnishing a partition between the prisoner and the visitor.

"I'm sorry I walked out on you, Mr. Mason."

Mason said, "That's only about half of what you need to be sorry for."

"What do you mean?"

"Going out with Della Street when you had that gun and money in your purse."

"I shouldn't have done that, I know."

"Where were you when Lieutenant Tragg picked you up?"

"I hadn't walked more than four blocks from the time I left you. Tragg picked me up and talked with me a little while. Then he left me in the custody of a couple of officers while he went on a tour of the restaurants, looking for you and Miss Street."

"Have you made any statement to the police?"

"Oh yes."

"What did you do that for?"

"Because," she said, "I had to tell them the truth."

"You didn't have to tell them a damn thing," Mason said.

"Well, I thought I'd better."

"All right," Mason said, "what's the truth?"

She said, "I held out on you, Mr. Mason."

"Good Lord," Mason groaned, "tell me something new—at least give *me* the same break you gave the officers."

"You won't be angry?"

"Of course I'm angry."

"Then you won't—won't help me out?"

Mason said, "I have no choice in the matter. I'm helping you out because I've got to help Della Street. I've got to try to get her out of a jam, and in order to do that I've got to try to get you out too."

"Have I made trouble for her?"

"For her and for me and for everyone. Go ahead. What's the story?"

She lowered her eyes. "I went out to see Mr. Faulkner last night."

"What time?"

"It was right around eight o'clock."

"Did you see him?"

"Yes."

"What was he doing?"

"He was shaving. He had his face all lathered and he had his coat and shirt off. He was in his undershirt. There was water running in the bathtub."

"The bathroom door was open?"

"Yes."

"His wife was there?"

"No."

"Who answered the door?"

"No one. The door was standing ajar, open an inch or two."

"The front door?"

"Yes."

"What did you do?"

"I walked in. I could hear him in the bathroom. I called to him."

"What did he do?"

"He came out."

151

"You're sure the water in the bathtub was running?"

"Yes."

"Hot or cold water?"

"Why—hot water."

"Are you certain?"

"Yes. I remember there was steam on the mirror."

"Was Faulkner angry at you?"

"Angry at me? Why?"

"For coming to see him that way."

"I guess he was. But everything worked out all right."

"Go ahead," Mason said wearily, his invitation almost in the tone of a groan. "Let's hear the rest of it."

"Mr. Faulkner said he didn't want to have any trouble with me; that he'd like very much to get things cleaned up. He knew that Tom would do exactly as I suggested, and he said that we might as well come to terms."

"What did you say?"

"I told him that if he'd give me two thousand dollars we'd call everything square. That Tom would continue to work for him for six weeks and then would take a six-months layoff and then would come back to work for the pet store again; that if Tom worked out any inventions during the six months he was resting, Mr. Faulkner could have a half interest in them; that he and Tom would own them equally; that Faulkner would put Tom's remedies on the market and he and Tom would split the net profits. They'd be sort of partners."

"And what did Faulkner say?"

"He gave me the two thousand dollars and I surrendered the five-thousand-dollar check I had, and told him I'd go and see Tom and that I was certain it would be all right."

"Are you aware of the fact that Tom went to see him at quarter past eight?"

"I don't think Tom did."

"I think there's pretty good evidence he did."

"Well, I don't know anything about that, but I'm quite

certain Tom didn't go, because Tom had no reason to go. Tom had told me he'd leave everything in my hands."

"And the two thousand dollars you got, you received in cash from Mr. Faulkner?"

"That's right."

Mason thought for a moment, then said, "All right, how about the gun?"

She said, "I'm sorry about the gun, Mr. Mason."

"You should be."

"It's Tom's gun."

"I know."

She said, "I have no idea how it got there, but when I went in the bedroom with Mrs. Faulkner—trying to comfort her, you know—I saw this gun on the dresser. I recognized it as Tom's and—well, you know, I wanted to protect Tom. That was my first thought, my first instinctive reaction, and I just picked up the gun and shoved it into my purse. Knowing that a man had killed himself . . ."

"Been murdered," Mason supplemented.

"Knowing a man had been murdered," she went on, accepting his correction without protest, "I didn't want Tom's gun to be found on the place. I knew that Tom couldn't have had anything to do with the murder, but I didn't know how the gun had got there."

"And that's all?" Mason asked.

"I cross my heart and hope to die, Mr. Mason, that's all."

Mason said, "You told this story to the officers?"

"Yes."

"What did they do?"

"They listened."

"Did they question you?"

"Not much. A little bit."

"Was there a shorthand reporter there?"

"Yes."

"He took down everything you said in shorthand?"

153

"Yes."

"Then what?"

"Then they asked me if I had any objection to signing the statement and I told them certainly not, provided it was written up just the way I'd said it. They wrote out the statement and I signed it."

"Did they tell you you didn't have to say anything?"

"Oh yes. They recited some rigmarole in a sing-song voice saying I didn't have to say anything if I didn't want to."

"And that's the way your story stands on paper?"

"Yes."

Mason said, with a voice that was bitter with venom, "You little fool!"

"Why, what do you mean, Mr. Mason?"

Mason said, "Your story is so improbable on the face of it that it isn't even a good fairy tale. It's obviously something you thought up on the spur of the moment to protect Tom. But the officers were too smart to try to get you to change it right at the start. They reduced it to writing and got you to sign it. Now they'll begin to bring pressure to bear on you so you'll have to change it, and then you'll be in a sweet mess."

"But I don't have to change it."

"Think not?"

"No."

"Where did this figure of two thousand dollars come from—the one that you submitted to Faulkner?"

"Why, I thought that was just about a fair price."

"You hadn't mentioned it to him before?"

"No."

"And Faulkner was shaving when you got there?"

"Yes."

"Preparing to take a bath?"

"Yes."

"He was in the bathroom?"

"Yes."

"He came out of the bathroom when you went in there—into the bedroom?"

"Well, yes."

"Careful now," Mason said. "Did he come out of the bathroom or did he receive you in the bathroom?"

"Well, sort of in the door of the bathroom."

"And gave you two thousand dollars in cash?"

"Yes."

Mason said, "You asked him for two thousand dollars?"

"Yes."

"And he had two thousand dollars?"

"Yes."

"Exactly two thousand dollars?"

"Well . . . I don't know . . . he may have had more, but he gave me the two thousand dollars."

"In cash?"

"Certainly. That's where the money came from that was in my purse."

"And you found that gun of Tom Gridley's at Faulkner's house?"

"Yes. And if you want to know something, Mr. Faulkner was the one who took the gun there in the first place. Tom was keeping it at the pet store, and then yesterday evening about seven-thirty, Mr. Faulkner was down there prowling around, taking inventory, and—well, *he* took the gun. Mr. Rawlins can swear to that. He saw Mr. Faulkner take it."

"Did you tell that to the police?"

"Yes."

"That's in your written statement?"

"Yes."

Mason sighed. "Let's look at it another way. When I left you with Sergeant Dorset, he said he was going to take you out to call on James Staunton."

"That's right."

"Did he do so?"

"Yes."

"How long were you there?"

"I don't know. Some little time."

"And Staunton still stuck to his story that Faulkner had brought the fish to him?"

"Yes. He produced a written authorization from Mr. Faulkner to keep the fish."

"Then what happened?"

"Then Sergeant Dorset went back to Faulkner's house and took me with him."

"Then what?"

"Then after an hour or so, he told me I could leave."

"So what did you do?"

"Well, one of the men—I think he was a photographer—said that he was going downtown to police headquarters to get some films developed and I could ride along with him if I wanted. You know, said he'd give me a lift."

"So you went with him?"

"Yes."

"And then what?"

"Then I telephoned Della Street."

"Where did you find a telephone?"

"In an all-night restaurant."

"Near where this photographer let you out?"

"Yes, within a block."

"Then what?"

"Then Miss Street told me to call her back inside of fifteen minutes."

"So what did you do?"

"Had a cup of coffee and some scrambled eggs and toast."

"Can you remember where this restaurant was?"

"Yes, of course I can, and I think the night man in the restaurant will remember me. He was a man with very dark hair and I remember he had a limp when he walked. I think one leg had been broken and was quite a bit shorter than the other."

"All right," Mason said, "that has the ring of truth. You went back to Faulkner's house with Dorset. He kept you there for awhile and then decided he didn't need you any more and this photographer gave you a lift downtown. Did you talk any with him in the automobile?"

"Yes, of course."

"Tell him what you knew about the murder?"

"No. We weren't talking about the murder."

"What were you talking about?"

"Me."

"Was he making passes at you?"

"He wanted my telephone number. He didn't seem to be interested in the murder. If he hadn't been in such a hurry he said he'd have gone to the restaurant with me. He asked me if I wouldn't wait there for an hour or so until after he'd developed his films."

"That sounds natural," Mason said. "You're giving out stuff that has the ring of truth now. How long were you in the restaurant?"

"Just about fifteen minutes. I called Miss Street as soon as I went in and then she told me to call back in fifteen minutes, and in fifteen minutes I called back and she told me to go to the Kellinger Hotel."

"Then what?"

"Then I got a taxi and went to the Kellinger Hotel."

"You told the police this?"

"Yes, all of this."

"It's in your written statement?"

"Yes."

"Were there any other customers in that all-night restaurant when you were there?"

"No. It's just a little place—just a little lunch counter. Sort of a hole in the wall with a night man who does the cooking and then serves the food at the counter."

"And you got a good look at this man behind the counter?"

"Oh, yes."

"And he got a good look at you?"

"Yes."

"And you called Della Street twice from that restaurant?"

"Yes."

"Now then," Mason asked, "did you make any other calls?"

She hesitated.

"Did you?"

"No."

"That *doesn't* have the ring of truth," Mason said.

Sally Madison was quiet.

Mason said, "You got a taxicab there?"

"Yes, right near there."

"And went directly to the Kellinger Hotel?"

"Yes."

Mason shook his head. "From your description of where you were, the taxi ride to the Kellinger Hotel shouldn't have taken over two or three minutes at that hour of the night, and the meter should have been considerably less than a dollar."

"Well, what's wrong with that?"

"Della Street got there first," Mason said. "She had a lot farther to go than you did."

"Well, I . . . It took me a little while to find a taxicab."

"You didn't have one come to the restaurant?"

"No. I went out to look for a taxi stand. The restaurant man told me there'd be one right around there somewhere."

Mason said, "When Della Street got to the Kellinger Hotel, she sat in the lobby waiting for you. She saw you when you drove up in the taxicab. She saw you pay off the driver. You didn't open your purse. You had a bill all ready in your hand."

"That's right."

"Why did you do that?"

"Because, Mr. Mason, I had that gun in my purse and that big roll of bills, and I was afraid the taxi driver might see—well, you know, might see the gun or the roll of bills, or both, and think perhaps I was a stick-up artist and . . . well, you know how it was?"

"No, I don't know. How was it?"

"Well, I didn't want anyone to see what was in the purse, so I took this bill out of the purse when we were three or four blocks from the hotel, and I knew how much the meter was going to be."

"What was it," Mason asked, "a one-dollar bill?"

She started to say something, then instead of speaking, simply nodded.

Mason said, "Della Street said the man looked at the bill in rather a strange way, then said something to you and laughed and put it in his pocket. I don't think he'd have done that if it had been a one-dollar bill."

"What do *you* think it was?"

"A two-dollar bill," Mason said.

She said, "It was a one-dollar bill."

"Did you make any statement to the police about that?"

"No."

"Did they ask you?"

"No."

Mason said, "I think it was a two-dollar bill. I think the meter didn't show the fifty or sixty cents that it should have shown if you'd gone from the restaurant near police headquarters to the Kellinger Hotel. I think the meter showed around a dollar and eighty cents. I think that means you took a side excursion, and I'm making one guess as to where that excursion would have been."

She looked up at him defiantly.

"To Tom Gridley's boardinghouse or apartment—or wherever he lives," Mason said.

She lowered her eyes.

"Don't you see," Mason went on patiently, "the officers are going to trace every step you made. They're going to locate the taxicab that took you to the Kellinger Hotel; they're going to find out everything you did. They'll comb the city with a fine tooth comb. They'll find the man that took you to the Kellinger Hotel. He'll remember the trip—particularly if you gave him a two-dollar bill, and he made some comment to you about a two-dollar bill being unlucky."

She bit her lip.

"So," Mason said, "you'd better at least come clean with *me*."

"All right," she said defiantly, "I went up to Tom's place."

"And got the gun," Mason said.

"No, Mr. Mason. Honestly I didn't. I had the gun in my purse all the time. I found it just where I told you I did."

"And Sergeant Dorset was taking you around all that time with a gun in your purse?"

"Yes."

"And why did you go to Tom's place?"

"Because I knew it was his gun. You see, Mr. Mason, when I went to the pet store last night, I got there very shortly after Mr. Faulkner had left. I found Mr. Rawlins terribly upset. He told me he'd lost his temper and told Mr. Faulkner just what he thought of him. He told me Mr. Faulkner had taken some things that belonged to Tom, but he said he wouldn't tell me about what they were until today, because he said he didn't want me to do anything rash, and he didn't think Tom should know about it while he was having one of his bad spells.

"Well, at the time I didn't know what those things were. It was afterward that I learned from the police it had been this gun of Tom's and the can of remedy that Tom had mixed up and put in the safe. If I'd known Mr.

Faulkner had taken the gun I wouldn't have been so frightened when I saw it there on the dresser in Mr. Faulkner's house. But the minute I saw it, I recognized it as Tom's gun. You see, he'd etched his initials on the barrel with some acid. I used to shoot the gun a lot. I'm a pretty darn good shot with a revolver, even if I do say it myself. Well, when I saw that gun there on the dresser, and saw it was Tom's gun, I was panic-stricken. I just scooped it into my purse while you were there in the bathroom looking at the body on the floor.

"Then, just as soon as I could get away from the police, which was when I went into that restaurant, I called Tom up. I did that right after I'd called Miss Street. I told Tom that I had to see him right away, and to be sure that the door of his apartment was unlocked so I could get in."

"So what did you do?"

"I had the taxi take me down there. I went in to see Tom. I told him what had happened. He was absolutely flabbergasted. Then I showed him the gun and asked him if he'd had any trouble with Faulkner and he—he told me the truth."

"What was the truth?"

"He told me that he'd been keeping the gun at the pet store for the last six months; that Rawlins had told him there'd been some stickups in the neighborhood and that he wished he had a gun but he couldn't get one, and Tom said he had one, and Rawlins got Tom to bring it to the store. Then late yesterday afternoon, when Faulkner went down and took an inventory of stock that was in the store, and took that batch of fish remedy Tom had mixed up, Faulkner must have seen the gun there and decided that he wanted it and took it home with him. That, of course, was just what happened. Rawlins has said so, and the police were fair with me. They told me about it before I made my statement to them."

Mason studied her thoughtfully, said, "When Tom

found out that Faulkner had been down there and taken the jar of stuff containing his formula and sent it out to be analyzed, he became angry. He went up to Faulkner's house to try and effect a settlement. Faulkner gave him a check for a thousand dollars. . . ."

"No he didn't, Mr. Mason. Tom didn't go out to Faulkner's house at all, and he didn't know a thing about Faulkner taking the remedy. I didn't know it myself until the police told me. You can prove that by asking Rawlins."

"You're certain?"

"Absolutely."

Mason shook his head and said, "That doesn't check. Faulkner had made out a check for a thousand dollars to Tom Gridley. He was filling in the check stub when he was shot."

"I know that's what the officers say, but Tom didn't go out there."

Mason thought for a moment, then said, "If Faulkner found the gun in the pet shop and took it out to the house with him, how does it happen that Faulkner's fingerprints aren't on it?"

She said, "I can't tell you that. Mr. Faulkner picked it up at the pet shop. I don't think there's any question about that. Even the police say that."

Mason's eyes narrowed. "Look here," he charged, "when you found that gun there on the dresser, you became panic-stricken. You thought Tom had gone out there to have a showdown with Faulkner and had lost his temper and killed Faulkner, didn't you?"

"Not exactly that, Mr. Mason. I just didn't think it was a good place for Tom's gun to be. I was all upset, and when I saw the gun there—well, I didn't think."

"You did too," Mason said. "You picked that gun up and wiped all the fingerprints off it, didn't you?"

"Honestly I didn't, Mr. Mason. I just picked up the gun and dropped it into my purse. I didn't think about fingerprints. I just wanted to get that gun out of the way. That's all I was thinking of."

Mason said, "All right. Now let's get back to the two thousand dollars. Faulkner had that two thousand dollars in the pocket of his trousers, didn't he?"

She hesitated a moment, then said, "Yes."

"Just the two thousand dollars?"

"Yes."

"In the pocket of his trousers?"

"Yes."

"And what time did you get there?"

"Around—somewhere between eight and half past eight. I don't know exactly when."

"And you found the door open and walked in?"

"Yes."

Mason said, "You're trying to cover up for Tom, and it won't work."

"No, I'm telling you the truth, Mr. Mason."

Mason said, "Look here, Sally, your story just doesn't sound probable. Now you've got to face the facts. I'm talking to you not only for your own good, but for Tom's. If you don't do exactly as I tell you, you're going to get Tom into a mess. He'll be held in jail for months. He may be tried for murder. He might be convicted. But even if he's just held in jail, you know what that will do to Tom's health."

She nodded.

"Now then," Mason said in a low voice, "you've got to do one thing. You've got to tell *me* the truth."

She met his eyes steadily. "I've told you the truth, Mr. Mason."

Mason sat for some thirty seconds, his face a mask of concentration, his fingertips drumming on the table. Behind the heavy wire screen, the girl regarded him thoughtfully.

Abruptly, Mason pushed back his chair. "You sit right there," he said, and, catching the eye of the matron, he

163

explained, "I want to make a telephone call, then I'm coming back."

Mason crossed over to the telephone booth in a corner of the visitor's room and dialed Paul Drake's office. A few seconds later, he had the detective on the line.

"Perry Mason, Paul," the lawyer said. "Anything new on Staunton?"

"Where are you now, Perry?"

"I'm up at the visitor's room in the jail."

"Gosh, yes. I called Della a few minutes ago. She didn't know where to get in touch with you. The police have got a statement out of Staunton and have put him back into circulation. He won't talk about anything that's in the statement, but one of my operatives got hold of him and asked him the question you wanted to know, and he answered that."

"What was the answer?"

"On Wednesday night, after Faulkner had taken those fish out to Staunton's place, and Staunton had telephoned the pet shop, he said it was quite late before the pet shop came out with the treatment."

"Not early?"

"No. He said it was quite late. He doesn't remember the exact time, but it was quite late."

Mason heaved a sigh, said, "That's a break. Sit right where you are, Paul," and hung up the telephone.

The lawyer's eyes were glinting as he returned to face Sally Madison across the visitor's table. "All right, Sally," he said in a low voice, *"now* we'll talk turkey."

Her eyes regarded him with studied innocence. "But, Mr. Mason, I have been telling you the exact truth."

Mason said, "We'll think back to Wednesday night, Sally, when I first met you, when I came over and sat down at the table with you in the restaurant. Remember?"

She nodded.

Mason said, "Now, at that time, you reached an agreement with Harrington Faulkner. You'd been holding him up, but you'd been exerting sufficient pressure on him to make him pay the piper. His fish were dying and he knew it, and he would have paid a good deal to have saved their lives. He also knew that this treatment for gill disease Tom had worked out was valuable, and he was willing to pay something for that."

Again she nodded.

Mason said, "Faulkner gave you a check and a key to the office and told you to go out and treat the fish, didn't he?"

Again she nodded.

"Now then, where did you go?"

She said, "I went directly to the store to get Tom, but Tom was fixing up some treatment for some other fish that Mr. Rawlins had consented to treat. Rawlins was fixing up a treatment tank and he wanted Tom to finish getting some panels ready."

"That was the tank he took to Staunton's place?"

"Yes."

Mason said, "You've overlooked one thing, Sally. You didn't think anyone would ever bother to check up on that time element with Staunton. You're lying. Tom didn't fix up that tank for Rawlins to take to Staunton's until *after* he'd gone to Faulkner's place. You intended to rush right back to the pet store to fix up that other tank. But the fact that Faulkner's fish were gone and that he called the police delayed you materially. You didn't get back until quite late. And Rawlins, therefore, didn't deliver Staunton's tank until quite late. Staunton is positive about that."

"He's mistaken."

"Oh no he isn't," Mason said. "When Faulkner gave you the key to that office, it was the opportunity you'd been waiting for. You went out there with a homemade extension dipper consisting of a silver soup ladle to which had been tied a section of broomstick. You dredged something out of the bottom of that fish tank. Then you had to leave in a hurry because Tom tipped you off someone was coming. So you ran out, jumped in Tom's car, drove around the block, and then came driving up to the office again as though you'd just arrived from the pet store."

She shook her head in sullen, defiant negation.

Mason said, "All right, I'm telling you what's happened. You lied to me and you're sending Tom to his death. Do you still stick with your story?"

She nodded.

Mason pushed back his chair. "That settles it," he said. "When Tom dies, remember that you're responsible."

She let him take two steps before she called him back. Then she leaned forward so that her face was all but pressed against the heavy mesh. "It's true, Mr. Mason—everything you said."

Mason said, "That's better. Now suppose you tell me the truth. How did you know that bullet was in the tank?"

"How did you know it was a bullet?"

"Never mind," Mason said, "I'm asking you. How did you know it was in the tank?"

"Mrs. Faulkner told me."

"Oh, oh!" Mason said. "Now we're getting someplace. Go ahead."

"Mrs. Faulkner told me that she was satisfied I'd find a .38 caliber bullet somewhere in the bottom of that fish tank; that she knew Tom was going to be called on to treat those fish; that she wanted to have that bullet recovered, and she also wanted to be absolutely certain that she could prove where the bullet came from. She said that I must arrange it so that both Tom and I were present when the bullet was recovered. Well, that's about all there was to it, Mr. Mason. When Mr. Faulkner gave me the key, I got hold of Tom, and we intended to recover the bullet first and then come back *after* Mr. Faulkner had arrived, and treat the fish. But when we got there and let ourselves into the office, the fish weren't there. For a minute or two, I didn't know what to do. But then I went ahead just as we'd planned. I took the dipper and we got the bullet out and just then we heard a car coming."

"You didn't leave Tom out in the car to watch?"

"No. We both had to go in there. That was the agreement. But we felt certain we had plenty of time. The house next door was dark and I knew that Mr. Faulkner would be at the café for some little time—at least I thought he would. But we heard this car coming and it frightened us and we dashed out in such a hurry that we didn't dare to take the ladle with us."

"Then what did you do?"

"Then we drove around the corner and waited until we saw you and Mr. Faulkner drive up. And then we came around there and acted as innocent as possible, pretending that we'd just come from the pet store."

"And then what did you do with the bullet?"

"I gave it to Mrs. Faulkner."

"When?"

"Not until last night?"

"Why not until last night?"

"I telephoned her and told her I had it, and she said that it would be all right; that I could have the money all right but that I'd have to wait until the coast was all clear."

"And then last night?"

"Then last night I took the bullet out to her."

"Tom was with you?"

"No, I went alone."

"There was some identification mark on that bullet?"

"Yes. Tom had given me an etching tool and we'd both etched our initials on the base of the bullet. Mrs. Faulkner was very insistent that we do it just that way, and told us to be very careful not to mar the sides of the bullet because she wanted to be able to prove what gun had fired the bullet."

"How much were you to get?"

"She said that if a certain deal went through, we'd get five hundred, and if another deal went through we'd get two thousand."

"And then last night you took the bullet out to her?"

"That's right."

"When?"

"About half past nine, I guess it was."

"Half past nine!" Mason exclaimed incredulously.

"That's right."

"And where was she?"

"At her house."

"And she paid you the two thousand dollars?"

"Yes."

"And that's where the two thousand came from?"

"That's right."

"And this story about Faulkner paying you two thousand was all poppycock?"

"Yes. I had to account for two thousand some way, and I thought that was the best way to account for it, because Mrs. Faulkner warned me that if I ever said anything about that two thousand dollars that she wouldn't back me up at all, and the taking of that bullet would be burglary, a breaking and entering, and that both Tom and I would go to jail."

Mason said, "Wait a minute. By half past nine Faulkner must have been dead."

"Yes, I guess so."

"Lying there in the bathroom."

"Yes."

"Then, when you took the bullet out to Mrs. Faulkner, where was she sitting? In the living room? She must have known her husband was dead by that time, if she was there in the house . . ."

"Not *that* Mrs. Faulkner," Sally Madison explained. "Don't you understand, Mr. Mason? It was the first Mrs. Faulkner, Mrs. Genevieve Faulkner."

For more than ten seconds, Mason sat in utter silence, his eyes level-lidded, his brows knitted together. "Sally, you're not lying to me?"

"Not now, Mr. Mason. I'm telling you the absolute truth."

"Tom will back you up in your story?"

"About recovering the bullet and identifying it. But he doesn't know the person who was going to pay me the money. Those dealings were all through me."

Mason said, "Sally, if you're lying to me now, you're going to the death chamber just as sure as you're sitting there, and Tom Gridley will die in jail."

"I'm telling you the truth, Mr. Mason."

"You got the two thousand dollars at nine-thirty last night?"

"That's right."

"But you did call on Mr. Faulkner?"

"Yes. Between eight and eight-thirty. It's just like I told you. The door was open just an inch or two. I walked in. There was no one home except Mr. Faulkner. He was telephoning—I guess he'd just finished shaving because there was still just a bit of lather on his face— where the razor had left marks. There was hot water running in the tub and he only had on his undershirt above his trousers. I guess the running water prevented him from hearing the chimes when I pushed the bell button. I walked in because I felt I just had to see him, and his car was parked out in front so I knew he was there."

"What happened?" Mason asked.

"He told me to get out. He told me that whenever he wanted to see me, he'd send for me, and he was very abusive. I tried to tell him that Mr. Rawlins had told me

169

he'd taken something that belonged to Tom, and that that was just the same as stealing."

"And what did he do?"

"He told me to get out."

"Didn't he give you a check payable to Tom, and offer that as a settlement?"

"No."

"Just told you to get out?"

"That's right. He said if I didn't get out he'd throw me out."

"And what did you do?"

"I hesitated, and he actually pushed me out, Mr. Mason. I mean he came and put his hands right on my shoulders and pushed me out of the house."

"Then what did you do?"

"Then I telephoned his first wife and asked her when she wanted to see me, and she told me to telephone again in about half or three-quarters of an hour. I did so, and she told me to come right out; that I could have the money. I went out there and she gave me the two thousand dollars."

"Anyone else present?"

"No."

"Did you see a man by the name of Dixon?"

"No."

"Ever meet him?"

"No."

"Do you know a man named Dixon?"

"No."

"Mrs. Faulkner gave you the two thousand dollars. Then what did you do?"

"Then I went back to the pet store and got the panels to treat Staunton's fish the way I'd promised Mr. Rawlins I would, and—and well, you know the rest, Mr. Mason. I went out to Staunton's and then I telephoned you."

Mason said, "Sally, I'm going to take a chance on you

170

because I've got to take a chance on you. I want you to say three words for me."

"What are they?"

"See my lawyer."

She looked at him in puzzled perplexity.

"Say it," Mason said.

"See my lawyer," she repeated.

"You can remember that, all right?"

"Why yes, of course, Mr. Mason."

"Say it again," Mason said.

"See my lawyer," she said.

Mason said, "Sally, from now on those are the only three words you know. If you ever say anything to anybody else you're sunk. The police will be after you in an hour or so, brandishing that written statement of yours in front of you. They'll show you inconsistencies. They'll show you where it's wrong. They'll show you where you were lying. They'll prove this and they'll prove that and they'll prove the other. They'll ask you to explain why you lied about where you went in the taxicab, and they'll tell you that if you can explain so that the explanation satisfies them they'll turn you loose; that if you can't, the only thing that remains for them is to arrest Tom. Do you understand?"

She nodded.

"And what are you to say?" Mason asked her.

She met his eyes. "See my lawyer," she said.

"Now," Mason told her, "we're beginning to get some place. Those are the only three words in the English language that you know from now on. Can you remember that?"

She nodded.

"Can you remember that no matter what happens?"

Once more she nodded.

"And if they tell you Tom has confessed in order to save you and that you shouldn't let the man you love

171

take the rap and go to the death-house because he's simply trying to save you, what are you going to say?"

"See my lawyer," she told him.

Mason nodded to the matron. "That's all," he said. "My interview is finished."

14

■

Genevieve Faulkner lived in a small bungalow that was within half a dozen blocks of the place where Wilfred Dixon maintained his sumptuous bachelor residence.

Mason parked his car, ran up the steps and impatiently rang the bell.

The door was opened after a few moments by Genevieve Faulkner herself.

Mason said, "You'll pardon me for disturbing you, Mrs. Faulkner, but there are one or two questions I must ask you."

She smiled and shook her head.

Mason said, "I'm not fishing now, Mrs. Faulkner. I'm hunting."

"Hunting?" she asked.

"For bear," Mason said, "and I'm loaded for bear."

"Oh! I'm sorry I can't invite you in, Mr. Mason. Mr. Dixon says I'm not to talk to you."

Mason said, "You paid Sally Madison two thousand dollars for a bullet. Why did you do that?"

"Who says I did that?"

"I can't tell you that, but I'm stating it as a fact."

"When am I supposed to have paid her that sum of money?"

"Last night."

Mrs. Faulkner thought for a moment, then said to Mason, "Come in."

Mason followed her into a tastefully furnished living room. She invited the lawyer to sit down, promptly picked up a telephone, dialed a number and said, "Can you come over here right away? Mr. Mason is here." Then she dropped the receiver into place.

"Well?" Mason asked.

"Smoke?" she inquired.

"Thank you, I have my own."

"A drink?"

"I'd like an answer to my question."

"In a few minutes."

She settled down in the chair opposite Mason, and the lawyer noticed the supple grace of her movements as she crossed her knees, calmly selected a cigarette from a humidor and struck a match.

"How long have you known Sally Madison?" Mason asked.

"Nice weather we're having, isn't it?"

"A little cool for this time of year," Mason said.

"I thought so, but then on the whole it's nice.—You're sure you don't want a scotch and soda?"

"No, thank you, I just want an answer to that one question, and I warn you, Mrs. Faulkner, that you aren't playing around with blackmail any more. You're mixed up in a murder case up to your ears and if you don't tell me the truth here and now, I'm really going to turn on the heat."

"There's been quite a bit of rain. It's really nice to see the hills as green as they are now. I suppose we'll have rather a warm summer. The old timers seem to expect it."

Mason said, "I'm a lawyer. You're evidently relying for advice on Wilfred Dixon. Take a tip from me and don't do it. Either tell me the truth or get a lawyer, someone who knows the ins and outs of law and the danger you're running if you suppress facts in a murder case."

"It was really unusually cold around the first of the year," she said calmly. "Some of the people who have studied weather tell me *that* doesn't mean anything, but that if it's unusually cold around the *middle* of January it invariably means a cold summer. Personally I can't see any sense to that. I . . ."

Brakes sounded as a car slid to a stop out in front of the house. Mrs. Faulkner smiled benignly at Mason, said, "Excuse me, please," and crossed the room to open the door.

Wilfred Dixon came hurrying in.

"Really, Mr. Mason," Dixon said, "I had hardly thought that you would stoop to this."

"Stoop to what?" Mason asked.

"After I told you that I didn't care to have you interview my client . . ."

"To hell with you," Mason told him. "You're not a lawyer. You're a self-styled business counselor or investment broker or whatever you want to call yourself. But this woman is mixed up to her ears in a murder case. She isn't any client of yours as far as murder is concerned and you have no right to practice law. You go sticking your neck out and I'll push it back."

Dixon seemed completely nonplussed at Mason's belligerence.

"Now then," Mason went on, "Mrs. Faulkner bribed my client, Sally Madison, to get into the office of Faulkner and Carson and extract a bullet from a fish tank. Last night she gave Sally Madison two thousand dollars in cash for that bullet. I want to know why."

Dixon said, "Really, Mr. Mason, these statements of yours are *most* reckless."

"Play around with fire," Mason told him, "and you're going to get your fingers burned."

174

"But, Mr. Mason, surely you aren't making these accusations on the unsupported word of your client."

"I'm not making any accusations," Mason said. "I'm stating facts and I'm giving you just about ten seconds to come clean."

"But, Mr. Mason, your statement is absolutely unfounded. It's utterly ridiculous."

Mason said, "There's the telephone. Want me to call Lieutenant Tragg and let him ask the questions?"

Wilfred Dixon met his eyes calmly. "Please do, Mr. Mason," he said.

There was a moment of silence.

Mason said at length, "I've given this woman some advice. I'm going to give you the same advice. You're mixed up in a murder case. See a lawyer. See a good one, and see him immediately. Then, decide whether you're going to tell the truth or whether you want me to call Lieutenant Tragg."

Dixon indicated the telephone. "As you have so aptly remarked, Mr. Mason, there's the telephone. I can assure you that you're at liberty to use it. You talk about calling Lieutenant Tragg. I think we would be *very* glad to have you call him."

Mason said, "You can't monkey with the facts in a murder case. If you paid Sally Madison two thousand dollars for that bullet, that fact is going to come out. I'll drag it out if I have to spend a million dollars for detective fees."

"A million dollars is a lot of money," Dixon said calmly. "You were speaking of telephoning Mr. Tragg, Mr. Mason, or I believe *Lieutenant* Tragg is the title. If he's connected with the police I think it would be a good thing to call him. You see, *we* have nothing to conceal. I'm not, of course, certain about you."

Mason hesitated.

There was just a glint of triumph in Wilfred Dixon's eyes. "You see, Mr. Mason, I play a little poker myself."

Without a word, Mason got up, crossed to the telephone, dialed Operator, said, "Give me police headquarters," then he asked for Homicide and inquired, "is Lieutenant Tragg in? Perry Mason speaking."

After a few seconds, Tragg's voice sounded on the wire. "Hello, Mason. I'm glad you called. I wanted to talk with you about your client, Sally Madison. She seems to have adopted an unfortunate position. There are certain minor discrepancies in a written statement which she gave us, and when we asked her to explain those, she assumed a very truculent attitude and said, 'See my lawyer.'"

"I have nothing to add to that," Mason said.

There was genuine regret in Tragg's voice. "I'm really sorry, Mason."

"I can imagine you are, Tragg. I'm out at the residence of Genevieve Faulkner. She's Faulkner's first wife."

"Yes, yes. I had intended to interview her as soon as I could get around to it. I'm somewhat sorry you beat me to it, Mason. Finding out anything?"

Mason said, "I think you'd better question her at some length about whether or not she saw Sally Madison last night."

"Well, well," Tragg said, his voice showing surprise. "Does Sally Madison claim that she saw Mrs. Faulkner?"

"Any statements my client may have made to me are, of course, confidential," Mason said. "This is just a tip I'm giving you."

"Thank you very much, Counselor, I'll get in touch with her."

"At once, I would suggest," Mason said.

"At my earliest convenience," Tragg amended. "Goodby, Mason."

"Good-by," Mason said, and hung up. He turned to Wilfred Dixon and said, "That's the way I play poker."

Dixon beamed at him. "Very well done, Mason, very well done, indeed. But, of course, as you pointed out to

Lieutenant Tragg, you can hardly repeat to him any statements that your client made to you, and as I understand it, your client has already stated she received the two thousand dollars that was in her purse from Harrington Faulkner. It would be rather unfortunate if she should be forced to change her statement."

"How did you know she had made such a statement?" Mason asked.

Dixon's eyes twinkled. "Oh, I get around a bit, Mason. After all, you know, while I am not a lawyer, I have to represent the interests of my client—her business interests, you know."

Mason said, "Don't ever underestimate Tragg. Tragg will get a written statement out of you and you'll swear to it. And sooner or later, the true facts are going to come out."

"We'd be only too glad to have them come out," Dixon said. "You see, Mr. Mason, as it happens, Genevieve makes no moves without my advice, none whatever. I tell her what to do, but I don't bother her with details. She knows very little about the firm of Faulkner and Carson. She leaves that to me. She wouldn't have even seen this client of yours without me. I'm quite certain that this Lieutenant Tragg, whoever he is, will be only too glad to accept our statement, particularly in view of the fact that you are in no position even to suggest that the two thousand dollars held by your client was received from anyone other than Harrington Faulkner. And if you'll let me give you a little advice, Mr. Mason, it is that you should never put too much confidence in the word of a young woman of Miss Madison's type. I think if you'll investigate her past reputation you'll find that she's had considerable experience. A young woman who has from time to time been something of an opportunist. I won't say a blackmailer, Mr. Mason, but an opportunist."

"You seem to know a good deal about her," Mason said dryly.

"I do," Dixon told him. "I'm afraid, Mr. Mason, that to try and extricate herself and her friend from a very dangerous situation, she has given you some false information."

Mason got to his feet. "All right," he said, "I've told you."

"You certainly have, Mr. Mason. Unfortunately for you, as I have pointed out, you are in no position to make any direct accusation, and even if you were, Mrs. Faulkner's denial, supported by my corroborating statement, would effectually disprove the charges of this Sally Madison."

Mason said, "I don't give a damn what her past has been. I think she's on the square now, and I think she's genuinely in love with Tom Gridley."

"I'm satisfied she is."

"And," Mason said, "when she told me she got the two thousand dollars from Genevieve Faulkner, her statement had the ring of truth."

Dixon shook his head. "It's impossible, Mr. Mason. It couldn't have been done without my knowledge, and I assure you that it wasn't done."

Mason stood looking at the muscular figure of the chunky man, who met his eyes with such childlike candor. "Dixon," he said, "I'm a bad man to monkey with."

"I'm certain you are, Mr. Mason."

"If you and Genevieve Faulkner are lying about this, I'm likely to find it out sooner or later."

"But, Mr. Mason, why should we lie about it? What possible motive would we have? And why on earth should we want to pay two thousand dollars for—what did you say it was, a bullet?"

"A bullet," Mason said.

Dixon shook his head sadly. "I'm sorry for Miss Madison. I really am, Mason."

Mason asked abruptly, "And just how does it happen you know so much about her?"

"Mr. Faulkner bought an interest in a pet shop," Dixon said. "He used funds of the corporation. Naturally, I investigated the purchase, and, in investigating the purchase, I investigated the personnel."

"*After* he'd made the purchase?" Mason inquired.

"Well, during the time negotiations were pending. After all, Mr. Mason, my client is interested in the corporation and I like to know what's going on—and I have my own way of knowing every move that's made."

Mason thought that over. "Oh yes," he said, "Alberta Stanley, the stenographer—I begin to see a lot now."

Dixon hastily cleared his throat.

"Thanks for telling me," Mason said.

Dixon looked up, met the lawyer's eyes. "Not at all, Mason, not at all. It was a pleasure to be of assistance to you—but you can't pin that two thousand dollars on us. We didn't pay it and we won't be lied about. *Good*-day."

Mason started for the door. Mrs. Faulkner and Wilfred Dixon stood watching him in silence. With his hand on the doorknob, Mason turned. "Dixon," he said, "you're a damn good poker player."

"Thank you."

Mason said grimly, "You're smart enough to know that I can't make any definite accusation that the two thousand dollars came from Mrs. Faulkner. I'm a good enough sport to admit that I made a bluff and you called it."

A frosty smile twitched at the corners of Dixon's mouth.

Mason said, "And I think it's only fair that you should know where I'm going now."

Dixon raised his eyebrows. "Where?" he asked.

"Out after another stack of chips," Mason said, and pulled the door shut behind him.

15

∎

Mason's face was as grim as that of a football player backed up against his team's goal line, as he entered Paul Drake's office.

"Hello, Perry," Drake said. "Did that information on Staunton do you any good?"

"Some," Mason said.

"It's just about the only question Staunton will answer. The police have sewed him up on a written statement, and he isn't giving out any information whatever upon matters that are contained in that statement. As far as anything that transpired the night of the murder is concerned, Staunton is an absolute clam. And the same holds true of all the details concerning the delivery of the fish."

Mason nodded. "I rather expected that.—Look here, Paul, I want you to do something for me."

"Shoot."

"I want you to find out whether or not Sally Madison saw the first Mrs. Faulkner yesterday night. I want you to find out whether Mrs. Faulkner made any substantial withdrawal from her bank in the form of cash. I particularly want to find out whether she or Wilfred Dixon withdrew any cash from a bank in the form of fifty-dollar bills."

Drake nodded.

"That isn't going to be easy," Mason said, "and I don't expect it to be easy. I'll pay you any amount of money that you need to get that information, Paul. Damn it, I started playing verbal poker with Wilfred Dixon. I made a bluff and he called it so cold and so hard that I feel like a spanked kid. Damn him, I'm going to back that bird in a corner if I have to spend every cent I've got in order to do it."

"Dixon was there when you got there?" Drake asked.

"No. Why?"

Drake said, "I'm having him shadowed, not that it will do any good, but I'm working on every angle of the case. My man picked him up about eight o'clock this morning as he was coming from breakfast."

"Where did he eat, Paul?"

"At the corner drug store. He must be an early riser. He'd been there since seven o'clock."

"That's fine, Paul. Keep it up."

"He walked down there for his breakfast, then came right back, arriving home at eight-ten. I've got men watching the house. It's about all there is to do."

Mason glanced at the detective.

"What's the matter, Paul? You seem to be stalling around. What's the trouble?"

Paul Drake picked up a pencil, twisted it in his fingers. "Perry," he said quietly, "Sally Madison's past reputation isn't too good."

Mason flushed. "That's the second time today I've heard that. All right, so what?" Mason asked.

Drake said, "If Sally Madison told you she got that two thousand dollars from Genevieve Faulkner she's lying."

"I didn't say she told me that, Paul."

"You didn't *say* so, no."

"What makes you think she'd be lying if she had told me that?" Mason asked.

Drake said, "My men have just uncovered some new evidence.—That is, they didn't uncover it, they picked it up from a friendly newspaper reporter who, in turn, got it from the police."

"What is it?"

"Yesterday afternoon Harrington Faulkner went to his bank and drew out twenty-five thousand dollars in cold, hard cash. He went to the bank personally. He insisted on having the money in the form of cash and from the way he acted, the bank teller thought that perhaps he was being blackmailed. He wanted the money in thousand-dollar bills and hundred-dollar bills and in fifty-dollar bills. The teller made an excuse that it would take him a little while to get the cash together in just that form, and kept Faulkner waiting for a few minutes while he and an assistant stepped back into the vault and hurriedly took down the numbers of the bills, just in case something should turn up later. The two thousand dollars that Sally Madison had in her purse is money that was given her by Harrington Faulkner, and by no one else. And there's another twenty-three thousand dollars that she has cached away somewhere."

Mason said, "You're sure, Paul?"

"Not dead sure, Perry, but I have the information pretty straight and I'm passing it on to you just the way I got it. I think you'll find that it checks."

Mason's mouth was hard.

"Now then," Drake went on, "there's some news on the credit side of the ledger. That gun is Tom Gridley's gun, all right, but I guess there's no question Gridley took it to the pet shop and Faulkner picked it up there. The police have pretty well reconstructed Faulkner's day from the time he left the bank until the time he was murdered."

"I already know about the gun. What time did he leave the bank, Paul?"

"It was well after banking hours. Pretty close to five o'clock. He'd telephoned and they'd let him in the side door. He put the money in a satchel. He left the bank and picked up a taxicab at the hotel right across the street from the place where he banks. He drove to the pet store, got hold of Rawlins and started taking an inventory. While he was taking the inventory he found Gridley's gun and slipped it in his pocket. Rawlins told him that it belonged to Gridley but Faulkner didn't say anything. Of course, in the light of what we know now and knowing that Faulkner had twenty-five thousand dollars in cash in that satchel, it's only reasonable to suppose that he might have been interested in having a gun for his own protection."

Mason nodded.

"Anyway, he put the gun in his hip pocket. Then he went over and opened the safe. Remember, he had the combination from Rawlins."

"And what happened then?"

"There was a can of paste in there, and Faulkner wanted to know what that was."

"What was it, the fish remedy?"

"That's right. It was some of that compound that Rawlins had talked Tom Gridley into mixing up, because Rawlins had some fish of his own that had gill disease and he wanted to treat them. He'd had some difficulty getting Tom to do it, but had finally persuaded Tom by promising him that he wouldn't let anyone know about it."

"Where was Tom that afternoon?"

"Tom was in bed at home. He was having a bad spell, running a fever and coughing, and Rawlins had told him to go home."

"What did Rawlins do when Faulkner opened the safe?"

"Rawlins had a fit when he saw what Faulkner was up to. Faulkner took the can of paste, and right there in the store, telephoned to a consulting chemist whom he knew. It was after office hours—getting along toward seven-thirty by that time—and Faulkner telephoned this chemist at his home, told him he had something that he wanted analyzed; that he was coming right out with it."

Mason said under his breath, "The dirty so-and-so."

"I know it," Drake said, "but what I'm giving you now, Perry, is evidence. This is the thing you're going to have to fight in court. They'll account for every minute of Faulkner's time right from five o'clock in the afternoon to the time he was killed."

"Go ahead," Mason told him.

Drake said, "When Rawlins saw what was happening he had a fit. He almost took the can away from Faulkner by force. He told Faulkner that he had given Tom Gridley his own personal word that the can would only be used to treat some fish that were suffering from gill disease there in the pet shop."

"What did Faulkner do?"

"He told Rawlins that Rawlins was working for him, and that he didn't want to hear any criticism. So Rawlins then proceeded to quit his job and tell Faulkner just what he thought of him."

"What did Faulkner do?"

"He didn't even get mad. He picked up the telephone and asked to have a taxicab sent around to the pet shop. Rawlins raved and sputtered, called Faulkner just about everything he could lay his tongue to, but Faulkner just waited until the taxicab came, then picked up his satchel, tucked the can of medicated paste under his arm and walked out, with the revolver still in his hip pocket."

"I suppose police have located the cab driver?"

Drake nodded, said, "The cab driver took Faulkner to the residence of the consulting chemist. Faulkner told him to wait. He was in there about fifteen minutes, then Faulkner drove to his house. It was then just a little after eight o'clock. Apparently, Faulkner immediately started to undress, take a bath, shave and get ready to go to that meeting at eight-thirty."

"No dinner?" Mason asked.

"That meeting of the fish experts was a dinner," Drake said. "They were having a little banquet and some talks afterward by some experts on fish breeding. That ties together, Perry. It ties right up to the time that someone entered the house, apparently without knocking, and the chap to whom Faulkner was telephoning heard Faulkner tell that party to get out. At first the police thought it was Tom Gridley, but Tom's come pretty clean with them. He's satisfied the police. The police know now that it was Sally Madison. No one will ever know exactly what happened there. Sally Madison entered, Faulkner tried to put her out, that much is certain. Sally admits it. Remember that Faulkner had a satchel containing twenty-five thousand dollars, which was probably in the bedroom. He also had Tom Gridley's gun. It must have been lying on the bed or on the dresser. Faulkner's coat, tie and shirt were spread over a chair where he had peeled out of them in a hurry. The gun had been in his hip pocket. Naturally, he took it out and put it somewhere."

Mason nodded thoughtfully.

"Put yourself in Sally Madison's place," Drake went on. "Faulkner had robbed the man she loved. He had been guilty of despicable business practices. Sally was fighting mad and she was desperate. Faulkner was pushing her out when she saw the gun lying there. She grabbed it. Faulkner was frightened, he ran back to the bathroom and tried to close the door. Sally pulled the trigger—then probably, for the first time, she realized the enormity of what she had done. She looked around. She saw the satchel on the bed. She opened it. There was twenty-five thousand dollars in it. That meant a lot to her. It meant an opportunity to escape. It meant an opportunity to cure Tom Gridley of tuberculosis. She took two thousand dollars in fifties for get-by money. The big bills she hid somewhere because she was afraid to try to monkey with those big bills while the heat was on."

"It's a pretty theory," Mason said, "but that's all it is—a theory. Plausible, but just a theory."

Drake shook his head. "I'm not telling you the worst of it, Perry. Not yet."

"Well, get on," Mason demanded irritably.

"Police found the empty satchel under the bed. The satchel which the bank teller identifies as the one that held the twenty-five thousand dollars. Of course, when the police first found it last night, they didn't know that it had any particular significance, but they were grabbing fingerprints off of everything, and so they dusted the handle of that satchel. They found three latent prints on it. Two of them were prints of Harrington Faulkner's right hand. The third one was the right middle finger of Sally Madison's hand. That's the story, Perry. That's the story in a nutshell. I have a tip that the district attorney is going to give you a chance to let Sally Madison plead guilty to second-degree murder or perhaps manslaughter. He recognizes the fact that Faulkner had been a first-class heel and that there'd been a lot of provocation for the crime. Furthermore, now that he knows Faulkner was the one who took Tom Gridley's gun from the pet shop, he knows that Sally must have seen the gun lying on the bed and acted on the spur of the moment. So there you are, Perry. There's the thing in a nutshell. I'm no lawyer, but if you can cop a plea for manslaughter, you'd better jump at it."

Mason said, "If Sally's fingerprint was on that satchel, we're licked—that is if the satchel was *under* the bed."

"Are you going to try and get a plea?" Drake asked anxiously.

"I don't think so," Mason said.

"Why not, Perry? It's the best thing you can do for your client."

Mason said, "It puts me in something of a spot, Paul. The minute she pleads guilty to manslaughter, or to second-degree murder, Della Street and I are hooked. We then automatically become accessories after the fact, and it doesn't make a great deal of difference whether we're

186

accessories after the fact to manslaughter or to second-degree murder. *We* can't afford to take the rap."

"I hadn't thought of that!" Drake exclaimed.

"On the other hand," Mason told him, "I can't let my personal feelings influence my duty to my client. If I think a jury might stick her with a verdict of first-degree murder, I'll have to make a compromise if it looks as though I can serve her interests better by a compromise."

"She isn't worth it, Perry," Drake said earnestly. "She's two-timed you all the way along the line. I wouldn't consider her interests for a minute."

Mason said, "You can't blame a client for lying, any more than you can blame a cat for catching canaries. When a person of a certain temperament finds himself or herself in a jam, the natural tendency is to try and lie out of it. The trouble with Sally Madison was she thought she could get away with it. If she had, I probably wouldn't have condemned her too much."

"What are you going to do, Perry?"

Mason said, "We'll get all the facts we can, which probably won't be many, because the police have all the witnesses sewed up tight. We'll walk into court on the preliminary examination and turn everything wrongside out. We'll look around and see if we can't get a break."

"And if you can't?" Drake asked.

Mason said grimly, "If we can't, we'll do the best we can for our client."

"You mean you'll let her plead guilty to manslaughter?"

Mason nodded.

Drake said, "I hadn't realized before where that would leave you, Perry. *Please* don't do it. Think of Della, if you won't think of yourself . . ."

Mason said, "I'm thinking of Della. I'm thinking of her to beat hell, Paul, but Della and I are playing this thing together. We've played things together for a good many years. We've taken the sweet, and we'll take the bitter. She wouldn't want me to throw over a client, and by God I'm not going to."

16

■

There were only a few scattered spectators in the courtroom as Judge Summerville ascended the bench, seated himself, and the bailiff called the court to order.

Sally Madison, somewhat subdued, but with her face still giving no clue to her thoughts, sat directly behind Perry Mason, apparently completely detached from the tense, dramatic conflict of the trial itself. Unlike most clients, she didn't bother to whisper comments to her lawyer, and might as well have been a piece of beautiful furniture so far as taking any active part in her defense was concerned.

Judge Summerville said, "Time and place heretofore fixed for the preliminary hearing of The People versus Sally Madison. Are you ready, gentlemen?"

"Ready for the prosecution," Ray Medford said.

"Ready for the defense," Mason announced calmly.

The district attorney's office was quite apparently trying to sneak up on Mason's blind side.

So far, Tragg had said nothing about those incriminating fingerprints of Della Street's on the murder weapon. Ray Medford, one of the shrewdest men on the prosecutor's staff of trial deputies, was taking no chances with Perry Mason. He knew too much about the lawyer's ingenuity to overlook a single bet. But, on the other hand, he was very careful to treat the case merely as a routine procedure, one where the judge would bind the defendant over to answer, and the main contest would be made before a jury in the Superior Court.

"Mrs. Jane Faulkner will be my first witness," Medford said.

Mrs. Faulkner, clothed in black, took the witness stand, related in a low voice how she had returned from "visiting friends" and had found Perry Mason and Sally Madison, the defendant, waiting in front of the house. She had admitted them to the house, explained to them that her husband wasn't home, then gone to the bathroom and found her husband's body on the floor.

"Your husband was dead?" Medford asked.

"Yes."

"You are sure that the body was that of Harrington Faulkner, your husband?"

"Quite certain."

"I think that's all," Medford said, and then added with a disarming aside to Perry Mason, "Just to prove the *corpus delicti,* Counselor."

Mason bowed. "You had been with friends, Mrs. Faulkner?"

She met his eyes calmly, steadily. "Yes, I had been with my friend, Adele Fairbanks during the entire evening."

"At her apartment?"

"No. We had been to a movie."

"Adele Fairbanks was the friend to whom you telephoned after you had discovered your husband had been murdered?"

"Yes. I felt that I couldn't stay in the house alone. I wanted her to be with me."

"Thank you," Mason said. "That is all."

John Nelson was next called to the stand. He gave his occupation as a banker, stated that he had known Harrington Faulkner in his lifetime; that on the afternoon of the day on which Faulkner was murdered he had been at the bank when Mr. Faulkner had telephoned, stating that he desired rather a large sum of money in cash; that shortly after the telephone call had been received, Faulkner had shown up, had been admitted to the bank through the side door, and had asked for twenty-five thousand dollars in cash, which he had withdrawn from his checking account. It was, he explained, his individual account, not the account of Faulkner and Carson, Incorporated. The withdrawal had left Mr. Faulkner with less than five thousand dollars to his credit in his personal account.

Nelson had decided it would be a good plan to take the numbers of the bills, inasmuch as Faulkner had asked for twenty thousand dollars in one-thousand-dollar bills, for two thousand dollars in one-hundred-dollar bills, and for three thousand dollars in fifty-dollar bills. Nelson testified that he had called one of the assistant tellers, and, together, they had managed to list all of the numbers on the bills while they kept Mr. Faulkner waiting. Then the money had been turned over to Mr. Faulkner and he had placed it in a satchel.

Quite calmly and casually, Medford called for the list of numbers on the bills and that list was received in evidence. Then Medford produced a leather satchel and asked Nelson if he had ever seen it before.

"I have," Nelson said.

"When?"

"At the time and place I have referred to. That was the satchel which Mr. Faulkner carried with him to the bank."

"The satchel in which the twenty-five thousand dollars in cash was placed?"

"That's right."

"Are you certain that is the identical satchel?"

"Quite certain."

"You may cross-examine," Medford said to Mason.

"How do you know it's the same satchel?" Mason asked.

"I noticed it particularly when I put the money in it."

"You put the money in it?"

"Yes. Mr. Faulkner raised it to the little shelf in front of the cashier's window. I unlocked the wicket, swung it back on its hinges and personally placed the twenty-five thousand dollars in the satchel. And at that time, I noticed a peculiar tear in the leather pocket on the inside lining of the satchel. If you'll notice, Mr. Mason, you'll see for yourself that that tear is still there. It's a rather peculiar, jagged, irregular tear."

"And you identify the satchel from that?" Mason asked.

"I do."

"That's all," Mason said.

Sergeant Dorset was the next man on the witness stand. He testified to the conditions he had found at Faulkner's house when he arrived, the position of the body, the discovery of the satchel under the bed in the bedroom, the place where Faulkner's coat, shirt and tie had been found tossed carelessly on a chair, the safety razor on the shelf, still uncleaned, with the lather and hairs still adhering to the blade. The lather was partially dry, which, in his opinion, indicated that it had been "some three or four hours" since the razor had been used. The face of the corpse was smooth-shaven.

Medford desired to know whether Sergeant Dorset had seen the defendant there.

"I did, yes, sir."

"Did you talk with her?"

"I did."

"Did she accompany you upon any trip?"

"Yes, sir."

"Where did she go?"

"To the residence of one James L. Staunton."

"That was at your request?"

"It was."

"Did she make any objection?"

"No, sir."

"Was there a fingerprint expert present in the Faulkner house?"

"There was."

"What was his name?"

"Detective Louis C. Corning."

"Did he examine certain articles for fingerprints under your direction and supervision and in accordance with your instructions?"

"He did."

"You may take the witness," Medford said to Perry Mason.

"Just how did Mr. Corning examine the fingerprints?"

"Why, through a magnifying glass, I presume."

"No. That isn't what I meant. What method did he use in perpetuating the evidence? Were the fingerprints developed and then photographed?"

"No. We used the lifting method."

"Just what do you mean by that?"

"We dusted certain objects to develop latent fingerprints, and then placed adhesive over the fingerprints, lifting the entire fingerprints from the object, then covering the adhesive with a transparent substance so that the fingerprints could be perpetuated and examined in detail."

"Who has the custody of those fingerprints?"

"Mr. Corning."

"And he has had such custody ever since the night of the murder?"

"To the best of my belief, he has. However, I understand he's going to be a witness, and you can ask him about that."

"The method of perpetuating the fingerprints was suggested by you?"

"It was."

"Don't you consider that rather a poor method to use?"

"What other method would you have preferred, Mr. Mason?"

"*I* wouldn't have preferred any method," Mason said. "But I have always understood that it was more efficient and better practice to develop the latents and then photograph them in their position on the object, and, if the fingerprints seemed to be important, to bring the object into court."

"I'm sorry that we can't accommodate you," Sergeant Dorset said sarcastically, "but it happens that in this particular case the fingerprints were all over the bathroom of a dwelling house which was in use. We were hardly in a position to dispossess the tenants, and keep all fingerprints intact. We used the lifting method, which I believe is infinitely preferable to the other where the circumstances justify it."

"What circumstances justify it?" Mason asked.

"Circumstances such as these, where you are dealing with objects that can't readily be brought into court."

"Now what means did you use to identify the places from which the fingerprints had been taken?"

"I didn't use any, personally. That is entirely within the province of Mr. Corning, and you will have to ask him those questions. I believe, however, he prepared envelopes on which the exact location from which each print had been lifted were printed and kept the prints straight by that method."

"I see. Now, did you have occasion that night to look into the other side of the duplex house—the side which was, I believe, utilized as an office for the real-estate corporation of Faulkner and Carson?"

"Not that night, no."

"You did the next morning?"

"I did."

"What did you find?"

"An oblong glass tank, which had been apparently used as an aquarium or fish tank, had been drained of water, apparently by means of a section of long, flexible rubber tubing of an inside diameter of approximately one-half inch. The glass tank had then been turned over on its side and the mud and gravel in the bottom of the tank had been dumped out on the floor of the office."

"Did you make any attempt to get fingerprints from that tank?"

"No, sir. I didn't take any fingerprints from the glass tank."

"Did you try to take any?"

"I didn't personally, no sir."

"Did you suggest that anyone else do so?"

"No, sir."

"As far as you know, none of the police made any attempt to develop fingerprints from that tank?"

"No, sir."

"May I ask why?"

"For the simple reason that I didn't consider the overturned tank had any connection whatever with the murder of Harrington Faulkner."

"It may have?"

"I don't see how it could have."

"It is quite conceivable that the same person who murdered Harrington Faulkner might have drained that tank and overturned it?"

"I don't think so."

"In other words, because you, yourself, personally, didn't see how there could have been any connection between the two crimes, you let this evidence be destroyed?"

"I'll put it this way, Mr. Mason. In my capacity as an officer on the police force, it is necessary for me to make certain decisions. I take the responsibility for those decisions. Obviously, we can't go around fingerprinting everything. We have to stop somewhere."

194

"And this was your stopping place?"

"That's right."

"You usually take fingerprints in case of a burglary, don't you?"

"Yes, sir."

"Yet you didn't in connection with this one?"

"It wasn't a burglary."

Mason raised his eyebrows.

"Nothing was taken."

"How do you know?"

"Nothing was missing."

"How do you know?"

"I know," Dorset said angrily, "because no one made any complaint that anything was missing."

"The tank had been installed there by Harrington Faulkner?"

"So I understand."

"Therefore," Mason said, "the only person who could have made any complaint was dead."

"I don't consider anything was taken."

"You made an examination of the contents of the tank before it was upset?"

"No."

"Then, when you say you don't consider anything was taken, you're using a telepathic, intuitive . . ."

"I'm using my judgment," Dorset all but shouted.

Judge Summerville said placidly, "Is this overturned fish tank important, gentlemen? In other words, does the prosecution or the defense intend to connect it up?"

"The prosecution doesn't," Medford said promptly.

"The defense hopes to," Mason said.

"Well," Judge Summerville ruled, "I'll permit a very wide latitude so far as questions are concerned."

"We are not making any objection," Medford hastened to assure the judge. "We want to give the defendant every opportunity to establish any facts which may tend to clarify the case."

195

"When you entered the bathroom of Faulkner's house," Mason asked, "you found some goldfish in the bathtub, Sergeant?"

"I did, yes."

"Two goldfish?"

"Two goldfish."

"What was done with them?"

"We took them out of the tub."

"Then what was done with them?"

"There seemed to be no place where we could keep them, so we simply swept them out with the other goldfish."

"By the other goldfish, you mean the ones on the floor?"

"That's right."

"You didn't make any attempt to identify the two goldfish that were in the bathtub?"

"I didn't ask them their names," Sergeant Dorset said sarcastically.

"That will do," Judge Summerville rebuked the witness sharply. "The witness will answer counsel's questions."

"No, sir. I simply made note of the fact that two live goldfish were in the bathtub and let it go at that."

"There were goldfish on the floor?"

"Yes."

"How many?"

"I'm certain I couldn't say. I think the photograph will show the number."

"As many as a dozen?"

"I would say somewhere around that number."

"There was a shaving brush and a razor on the glass shelf above the wash stand?"

"Yes. I have already testified to that."

"What else was there?"

"There were, I believe, two sixteen-ounce bottles of peroxide of hydrogen. One of them was almost empty."

"Anything else?"

"No, sir."

"Now, what did you notice on the floor?"

"There were pieces of broken glass."

"Did you make an examination of those pieces of broken glass to determine if they had any pattern or if they had been originally a part of some glass object?"

"I didn't personally. I believe at a later date Lieutenant Tragg caused all of those pieces to be assembled and had them fitted together so that they formed a rather large curved goldfish bowl."

"You say that there was a checkbook on the floor?"

"There was."

"Near the body of the murdered man?"

"Quite near."

"Can you describe its appearance?"

Medford said, "Your Honor, I intended to introduce this checkbook in evidence by another witness, but if counsel wants to examine this witness about it, I'll introduce it right now."

Medford produced the checkbook, Sergeant Dorset identified it, and it was received in evidence.

"Calling your attention," Medford said to Judge Summerville, "to the fact that the last check stub in the book—that is the last one from which the corresponding check has been torn away along the perforated line, is a check stub bearing the same date as the day of the murder, with an amount of one thousand dollars written in the upper right-hand corner, and in the body of the stub a portion of a name has been written. The first name is completely written and the last name has been unfinished. Only the first three letters of that name appear. They are '-G-r-i.' "

Judge Summerville examined the check stub with keen interest.

"Very well, this will be received in evidence."

"Were any of the goldfish on the floor alive when you entered the room?" Mason asked Sergeant Dorset.

"No."

Mason said, "For your information, Sergeant, I will state that I noticed motion on the part of one of the goldfish when I entered the room—and I was, I believe, in the room some ten or fifteen minutes before the police arrived. I placed that goldfish in the bathtub and apparently it resumed life."

"That, of course, was something you had no right to do," Sergeant Dorset said.

"You made no test to ascertain whether there was some life on the part of any of the other goldfish?"

"I didn't apply a stethoscope to them," Dorset said sarcastically.

"Now then, you have stated that you asked the defendant to accompany you to the home of James L. Staunton?"

"I did, yes, sir."

"You had some conversation with Mr. Staunton there?"

"Yes."

"And Mr. Staunton gave you a statement purporting to bear the signature of Harrington Faulkner, the deceased?"

"He did."

Medford said, "Your Honor, I don't want to seem technical, but after all, this is a preliminary examination. The purpose of it is to determine whether there is reasonable ground to believe the defendant murdered Harrington Faulkner. If there is, the Court should bind her over to answer. If there isn't, the Court should dismiss her. I think that we have plenty of evidence to establish our case without carrying the inquiry far afield. These matters are entirely extraneous. They have nothing whatever to do with the murder."

"How do you know they have nothing to do with the murder?" Mason asked.

"Well, I will put it this way," Medford said. "They

have nothing to do with our case. We can establish our case by an irrefutable chain of evidence without dragging in all of this extraneous stuff."

Mason said, "Your Honor, I understand the law and I know the Court does, but I submit to the Court that under the circumstances of this case and in view of the very apparent mystery which surrounds the case, I should be permitted to show *all* of the surrounding circumstances which *I* contend played an important part in connection with the murder of Harrington Faulkner. I know that the Court doesn't want to hold this young woman over for trial if she is in fact innocent, regardless of the fact that it might be possible for the prosecution to establish a technical case. I also know that the Court is anxious to see that the real murderer is apprehended in the event this young woman should actually be innocent. Therefore, I submit to your Honor that it is better at this time, in view of the peculiar circumstances of this case, to let all of the facts come into the record."

"We don't have to put in all of the facts," Medford said angrily. "We only have to show enough of our hand to convince the Court that there is a reasonable cause to believe this defendant is guilty."

"That's just the trouble with the entire situation, your Honor," Mason retorted. "It is the attitude of the prosecution that it's playing some sort of a game; that it only needs to introduce a certain amount of evidence; that it can hold back the rest of its evidence as a miser hoards his gold, so that the defendant can be surprised when confronted with that evidence in the Superior Court. Now, that may be the way to secure a large number of convictions and to make a good showing for efficiency on the part of the district attorney's office, but I submit, your Honor, that it is hardly the way to clear up a rather puzzling and baffling mystery."

"It isn't a mystery to the police," Medford snapped.

"Certainly not. Because, as your Honor has just seen

from the attitude of Sergeant Dorset, he collected the evidence which he thought would result in a conviction of this defendant. Any evidence which tended to point to the guilt of some other person was disregarded. The police didn't think this other crime had any connection with the murder of Harrington Faulkner simply because it didn't involve this defendant."

Judge Summerville said, "I know it's somewhat irregular, but I'd like to hear from counsel just what the general surrounding facts of the case are."

"I protest that it's irregular," Medford said.

"I'm only asking counsel to make a general statement of his position," Judge Summerville ruled placidly. "I certainly have a right to know what is in counsel's mind before I rule on an objection the prosecution has made."

Mason said, "Your Honor, Harrington Faulkner had a pair of rather valuable fish, fish which were vastly more valuable to him personally than they would be on the market, but fish which were, nevertheless, of a rare strain. Harrington Faulkner rented one side of a duplex dwelling from the corporation which owned it. The other side was where the corporation had its office. Faulkner had installed a fish tank in the office and placed these two very valuable fish in that tank. He and Elmer Carson, the other active member of the corporation, quite apparently became mortal enemies. The fish in the tank were suffering from a fish disease that is nearly always fatal. Tom Gridley, whose name has been brought into the case, had a cure for that disease. The decedent tried, by various and sundry means, to get control of the formula by which young Gridley was able to cure the fish. Sometime prior to the murder, Elmer Carson had filed suit and secured a temporary restraining order preventing Harrington Faulkner from moving the fish tank from the real-estate office on the ground that it had been so affixed to the building that it had become a fixture. Before the hearing on the temporary restraining order and order to show cause, I understand Harrington Faulkner removed the fish without disturbing the tank, and took those fish to the residence of James Staunton. Now then, your Honor, in view of the peculiar circumstances, and in view of the fact that the defendant in this case was concededly what is known colloquially as the girl friend of Tom Gridley, and active in the store where Tom Gridley worked, a store which Harrington Faulkner subsequently bought in order to get control of Gridley's formula, I claim that *all* of these things are an integral part of the case."

Judge Summerville nodded his head. "So it would seem."

"Well, I submit that we are entitled to stay within our legal rights," Medford said angrily. "We didn't make the law, and I notice that learned counsel for the defense never hesitates to grab at any technicality which will advance *his* case. We have a law on the statute books. Let's conform to it."

"Quite right," Judge Summerville said. "I was about to make that statement when counsel interposed his comments."

"I beg the Court's pardon," Medford said stiffly.

"I was about to say," Judge Summerville ruled, "that under the law, the prosecution only needs to put on sufficient evidence to show that a crime has been committed and that there is reasonable ground to believe the defendant is the one who committed that crime. But, I want to go on record at this time as stating that under the circumstances of this case, and in view of the peculiar and rather mysterious incidents which seem to have surrounded it, after the prosecution has rested its case, the Court is going to permit the defendant to call witnesses and ask them any questions the defendant wants which may bring out the facts which counsel for the defense has just outlined to the Court."

Medford said, "The effect of that, if the Court please,

is to accomplish the same result. All of the extraneous facts will be dragged into this case."

"If they have a bearing on the question before the Court, I want to hear all of the things which you refer to as 'the extraneous facts.' "

"But the point I am making is that the effect is just the same as though they were brought in at this time."

"Why object to them then?" Judge Summerville asked urbanely.

Mason said, "I was only calling for a document which is in the possession of the police. I can, if I have to, subsequently put Sergeant Dorset on the stand as my witness and ask that the document be produced."

"But what earthly bearing does that document have on the murder of Harrington Faulkner?" Medford asked.

Mason smiled. "Perhaps a few more questions to Sergeant Dorset will clear up that part of the case."

"Ask him the questions," Medford said. "Ask him if the document has any bearing on the case. I defy you to ask him that question, Mr. Mason."

Mason said, "I prefer to ask my questions in my own way, Counselor." He turned to the witness and said, "Sergeant, after you discovered the body of Harrington Faulkner, you proceeded to investigate the murder, did you not?"

"I did."

"You investigated every angle of it?"

"Naturally."

"And during the course of the evening you questioned the defendant and also me about an interview we had had with James Staunton, and about whether the fish which Mr. Staunton had in his possession were actually the two fish which had been delivered to him by Mr. Faulkner, and which had been taken from the tank which was in the real-estate office, didn't you?"

"I asked questions, yes."

"And insisted upon answers?"

202

"I felt that I was entitled to answers."

"Because you thought that matter might throw some light upon who murdered Harrington Faulkner?"

"I thought so at the time."

"What has caused you to change your opinion?"

"I don't know that I have changed it."

"Then you *still* think that the circumstances you investigated in connection with James Staunton had some bearing on the murder of Harrington Faulkner?"

"No."

"Then you have changed your opinion."

"Well, I've changed my opinion because I know now who committed the murder."

"You know who you *think* committed the murder."

"I know who committed the murder, and if you'll quit throwing legal monkey wrenches in the machinery, we'll prove it."

"That will do," Judge Summerville ruled. "Counsel is questioning the witness for the purpose, I take it, of showing bias."

"That is right, your Honor."

"Proceed with your questioning."

"You demanded that the defendant accompany you out to the residence of James L. Staunton?"

"I did."

"At that time you had been advised by both Miss Madison and by me of all the facts which we had learned in connection with the possession of the fish by Staunton?"

"I suppose so. You said they were all the facts you had."

"Exactly. And, at the time those facts seemed sufficiently significant so you went out to verify them?"

"At the time, yes."

"What has caused you to change your mind?"

"I haven't changed my mind."

"You took from the possession of James L. Staunton a written statement signed by Harrington Faulkner?"

"I did."

Mason said, "I want that statement introduced in evidence."

"I object," Medford said. "It is not proper cross-examination. It's no part of the case. It's incompetent, irrelevant and immaterial."

"It's not proper cross-examination," Judge Summerville ruled calmly. "The objection will be sustained on that ground."

"That is all," Mason said.

Judge Summerville smiled. "And now, Mr. Mason, do you want Sergeant Dorset to remain in Court as a witness on the part of the defense?"

"I do."

Judge Summerville said, "The witness will remain in Court, and if the witness has in his possession any paper which he received from James L. Staunton relating to the fish which had belonged to Harrington Faulkner in his lifetime, the witness will have the statement ready to produce when he is called as a witness by the defense."

"This is going all the way around our elbow to get to our thumb," Medford said with some feeling.

"Apparently you object to reaching the thumb by any shorter route," Judge Summerville pointed out. "The Court doesn't want to be unduly harsh in its ruling so far as the prosecution is concerned, but it has always been the attitude of this Court that if any defendant in a preliminary hearing has any evidence to introduce which will tend to clarify the issues or throw any light upon a crime which has been committed, this Court wants to hear it. And that is going to continue to be the attitude of the Court. Call your next witness."

Somewhat sullenly, and with poor grace, Medford called the photographer who had taken the photographs showing the position of the body and the surroundings.

One by one, those photographs were introduced, and as they were introduced, they were carefully studied by Judge Summerville.

It was eleven-thirty when Medford said to Mason, "You may cross-examine."

"These photographs were all taken by you on the premises and all show the condition of the premises as they were at the time you arrived on the scene, is that right?"

"That's right?"

"Now you not only acted as photographer, but you also saw the things you photographed?"

"Naturally."

"And, therefore, are a witness to the things you saw?"

"Yes, sir, I so consider myself."

"These photographs, then, may be used to refresh your memory as to what you found at the scene of the crime."

"Yes, sir."

"I direct your attention to this photograph," Mason said, handing the witness one of the photographs, "and ask you if you noticed a granitewear container in the bathtub. I believe this photograph shows it."

"I did, yes, sir. It was a two-quart container and was lying submerged in the bathtub."

"There were two goldfish in the bathtub?"

"Yes, sir."

"On the floor were three magazines—I believe they are shown in this photograph?"

"Yes, sir."

"Did you notice the dates on those magazines?"

"I did not, no, sir."

Medford said, "As a matter of fact, your Honor, those magazines were carefully marked for identification and are in the possession of the prosecution, but I certainly hope that counsel is not seriously contending that those magazines have any bearing on the murder of Harrington Faulkner."

Mason said gravely, "I think, your Honor, those magazines will prove a very interesting and perhaps a vital link in the evidence."

"Well, we won't waste time arguing about them. We'll produce them," Medford said.

"Do you know which magazine was on top?" Mason asked.

"I'm sure *I* don't," Medford said. "And I don't know which goldfish was lying with his head facing south and which one was lying with his head facing south-southeast. As far as I am concerned, the police investigated the important angles of the case, and as a result of that investigation, reached a conclusion which is so logical it can't be questioned. That's all I know and that's all I want to know."

"So it would seem," Mason said dryly.

Medford flushed.

Judge Summerville said to Mason, "Do you contend that the position of the magazine is significant?"

"Very," Perry Mason said. "And I think if counsel will produce those magazines, we can examine the photographs with a magnifying glass and tell the relative position of those magazines. We can certainly tell which one was on top. This photograph which I hold in my hand shows that rather plainly."

"All right," Medford said, "we'll produce the magazines."

"Do you have them in court?"

"No, your Honor, but I can produce them after lunch, if the Court wishes to take its noon recess at this time."

"Very well," Judge Summerville ruled. "The Court will take a recess until two o'clock this afternoon."

Spectators, arising from the court benches, made the usual confused sounds of shuffling steps and low voiced comments. Sally Madison, without a word to Perry Mason, arose from her chair and stood waiting calmly for the officers to escort her from the courtroom.

17

■

Mason, Della Street and Paul Drake sat at lunch in a little restaurant near the courthouse where they ate frequently when trials were in progress. The proprietor knew them and kept reserved for them a small private dining room.

Paul Drake said, "You're doing okay, Perry. You've got Judge Summerville interested."

"It's a break for us that we drew Judge Summerville," Mason admitted. "Some judges like to get preliminary hearings over with as quickly as possible. They adopt the position that there's nothing very much to worry about because the defendant is going to have a trial before a jury anyway, so go ahead and bind 'em over and let it go at that. Judge Summerville has different ideas. He realizes that the function of the courts is to protect the rights of citizens at all stages of the proceedings, and believes that the function of the police is to investigate and perpetuate evidence while it's fresh. I happen to know from talking with him off the bench, and in casual conversation, that he is fully aware of the habit the police have of investigating a case until they pick on some person as the guilty one, and then disregard any evidence that doesn't coincide with their own opinions."

"Just what can you do?" Della Street asked. "Do you dare to put on all of this evidence, calling these witnesses as your own witnesses?"

207

"I don't dare to do anything else," Mason said.

"Well," Drake observed, "as I get the sketch, Sally Madison is lying. Her written statement contains falsehoods. She's lied to the police and she's lied to you and she's still lying to you."

Mason said, "Clients are all human—even the innocent ones."

"But that's no reason why they should be permitted to double-cross their own lawyers," Drake said with feeling. "Personally, I wouldn't have nearly such a broadminded attitude toward her."

Mason said, "I'm trying to keep an open mind, Paul. I'm trying to visualize what must have happened."

"Well, she's lying about one thing. She didn't get that money from Genevieve Faulkner."

"I didn't say that she said she did," Mason observed, his eyes twinkling.

"Well, you didn't need to say so, for me to draw my own conclusions," Drake observed dryly. "She got that money from that satchel, and there's another twenty-three thousand dollars salted away somewhere."

Mason said, "While we're looking at discrepancies, let's look at some of the other discrepancies. I can't imagine why Mrs. Jane Faulkner waited in her automobile for Sally Madison and me to show up unless she had been tipped off that we were coming. And no one could have tipped her off we were coming except Staunton. As a matter of fact, Paul, I'm well pleased with the way things are going. Medford played right into my hands. He's fixed it now so that I can put Staunton or any of these other hostile witnesses on the stand as my witnesses, and ask them leading questions, and Judge Summerville will permit it. That's going to give me a chance to examine Staunton about that phone call."

Drake said, "Well, even if you could prove that Jane Faulkner had been in the house before, discovered the body, and then had gone out and sat in her automobile and waited for you to come, so that she could go through all the motions of being surprised and hysterical, I still don't see that you're going to get anywhere."

Mason said, "If I get the opportunity to crucify her, I'm going to do it. You know as well as I do she's lying about having spent the evening with Adele Fairbanks. She pulled the wool over Sergeant Dorset's eyes there. She pretended to be ill and suffering *so* greatly from shock she simply had to have a girl friend come down to stay with her. She summoned the girl friend whom she knew she could depend upon to back her up in anything she said. And while Dorset was chasing around to Staunton's place with Sally Madison, Jane Faulkner and Adele Fairbanks were hatching up their cute little alibi about having been together and having gone to a movie. Lieutenant Tragg would certainly never have let Mrs. Faulkner slip one over on him like that."

"I'll say he wouldn't," Drake said. "That certainly was a raw deal."

Mason said, "Of course, Paul, *someone* must have been in that room with that corpse at least two or three hours after the murder was committed."

"On account of the one live goldfish?" Drake asked.

"On account of the one live goldfish," Mason said.

"It might have been one that happened to light in a low place in the bathroom floor where the water would collect in a little puddle and give him an opportunity to get just a little oxygen out of the water—just enough to keep him alive."

"It could have been," Mason said, and then added, "I consider the chances of that about one thousand to one."

"So do I."

"You take the fact that someone must have been in that room, coupled with the fact that we know Jane Faulkner was waiting around the corner where she could see us drive up to the house, and there's only one answer."

"I don't see what good it's going to do if you could prove that she was lying about having been in the room with the body," Drake said. "In any event, her husband must have been dead at that time."

Mason said, "They're pinning a murder on my client simply because she told a few fibs. I'd like to prove someone else was telling lies as well. It all gets back to Staunton and the fact that he must have telephoned Mrs. Faulkner we were coming."

Drake said, "I've got someone working on that, Perry. I won't burden you with details, but it occurred to me there was only one way to check Staunton's phone call."

"How was that?"

"Through his wife. And in doing that I found out a few incidental facts."

"Go ahead," Mason said. "What did you find and how did you do it?"

"There was only one way of going at it," Drake said. "That was to plant some good operative in the house who would take the part of a servant and who could pump Mrs. Staunton. I've got an operative right there in the house who's checking up on things. Mrs. Staunton is tickled to death. She thinks this girl is the best all-around maid she ever had." Drake grinned and went on, "What Mrs. Staunton doesn't realize is that she's getting maid service from a twelve-dollar-a-day detective and that the minute this girl gets the information she wants, she'll dust out of there, leaving Mrs. Staunton with a sink full of dirty dishes."

"Any reports on the phone call?" Mason asked.

"Nothing on that as yet," Drake said.

"Keep after it," Mason told him. "That's an important angle in the case."

Drake looked at his watch, said, "I think I'll give her a ring right now, Perry. I'm supposed to be her boy friend. Naturally, Mrs. Staunton is so tickled with the service she's getting, she makes no objection whatever when the maid's boy friend rings up. Of course, this girl may not be able to talk with me, but I have an idea she may be there all alone today. Staunton is hanging around, waiting to be a witness in this case, and there's a pretty good chance Mrs. Staunton is out. Let me give her a ring."

Drake pushed back his chair and went out into the main part of the restaurant where there was a phone booth.

Mason said to Della Street, "You know, Della, if it weren't for the time element in this case, we could bust it wide open."

"What do you mean?"

"The way the district attorney follows every move Faulkner made up to the time of his death. They pick him up at five o'clock when he went to the bank, and carry him right on through from there. From the bank to the pet shop, from the pet shop to the consulting chemist, from the consulting chemist to his home, and leave him just time enough to get his coat and shirt off when the call to the man at the banquet place is put through, and then Faulkner is heard ordering Sally Madison out. At that time, he's in a hurry to get dressed and shaved, and go to that banquet. He's evidently been in that house not over five or six minutes. He's partially undressed, turned hot water in the bathtub, has lathered his face, shaved and put the razor on the shelf. Hang it, Della, if it weren't for that fingerprint on the satchel. How I would like to prove that someone entered that house right after Sally Madison went out and pulled the trigger on that gun!"

Della Street asked abruptly, "Do you suppose Sally really got that bullet?"

"She must have. I had doped that out even before I talked with her in jail. I felt certain that she must have been the one who dredged that bullet out of the fish tank."

"You don't think she got it for Carson?"

"No."

"Why?"

"Because Carson didn't know that anyone had taken the bullet out of there"

"What makes you think that?"

"Because," Mason said, "Carson *must* have been the one who made that final desperate attempt to recover the bullet by siphoning the water out of the tank and turning the tank upside down. And he must have done that on the night Faulkner was murdered. Hang it, Della, let's go at this thing in an orderly way. Let's quit letting ourselves be confused simply because we're representing a client who is lying to us and who has got us into a jackpot. Let's quit being exasperated and use our brains as reasoning machines."

"No matter how you reason," Della Street said, "you always come back to the same focal point in the case that no matter how much others may have been mixed up in it, Sally Madison was the one who opened that satchel and took out the money, the one who threw the empty satchel under the bed, the one who was found in possession of a part of the money."

Mason started drumming with the tips of his fingers on the white tablecloth.

Paul Drake pushed open the door to enter the private dining room.

"Anything new, Paul?" Mason asked.

"This operative of mine is alone in the house, just as I thought. She's been there all by herself ever since nine o'clock. Naturally, she's been busy!"

"Prowling around?"

"That's right. She's stumbled across some interesting sidelights but nothing particularly startling."

"What are the sidelights?"

"Apparently Faulkner had been financing Staunton in some sort of a mining activity."

Mason nodded. "I had assumed all along that

Faulkner must have had some hold on Staunton; otherwise he wouldn't have taken the fish out there and told Staunton what to do—you know the fact that Staunton handled insurance business for the real-estate corporation isn't anything that would give Faulkner such a leverage. Of course, Staunton might have mentioned that when I was talking with him, but he probably thought it was none of my business and simply mentioned the insurance matter."

Drake said, "One thing my operative told me has me stumped."

"What?"

"Talking with Mrs. Staunton last night, she found out that on the night of the murder the telephone in the house had been out of order. Only the telephone in Staunton's study was working."

"Is she sure, Paul?"

"That's what Mrs. Staunton told her. Mrs. Staunton said she had to go to the study that night when she wanted to telephone. She mentioned it because she doesn't like the fish and didn't like to go in the room where the fish were. She said they gave her the creeps, staring at her with those queer, protruding eyes. But that her telephone had been out of order all afternoon and that the company didn't get it fixed until the next day; that the one in the study was a separate line and was working."

Mason said, "Hang it, Paul, do you suppose Staunton was smart enough to know what I was doing when I casually walked over and pulled the drapes back and stood looking out of the window?"

"I don't know," Drake said. "How long did you watch outside of the house after you went out, Perry?"

"It must have been four or five minutes. Staunton came back and stood looking at the fish. He seemed to be thinking of something—turning it over in his mind. Then he went back and switched out the light. We waited there

213

a few minutes after he'd turned out the light. Of course, he *could* have deliberately fooled us. I felt certain that if he had been going to telephone somebody, he'd have done the telephoning right then."

Drake said, "Well, we know that Mrs. Faulkner was out there watching. And you must be pretty certain that she upset that bowl of goldfish within, say, ten or fifteen minutes of the time you got there."

Mason said, "Of course, the other goldfish were dead, Paul. Only the one that I picked up had just a little life in him."

"All right, have it any way you want," Drake said. "The one goldfish was alive. Someone must have put that one goldfish on the floor."

Mason said thoughtfully, "There was a curved segment of the broken fish bowl that still had a little water left in it. I remember noticing that at the time, and I noticed it on one of the photographs this morning. Now, I'm wondering if that one fish couldn't have been in that segment that had a little water in it, and then flopped out."

"That, of course, would mean that the goldfish bowl *could* have been knocked over a long time before," Drake said. "Perhaps when Faulkner was murdered, right around eight-fifteen or eight-twenty."

"I wonder if a goldfish could live that long in such a small amount of water."

"Darned if I know," Drake said. "Want me to get a goldfish and try it?"

"I have an idea you'd better," Mason said.

"Okay. I'll phone my office and ask them to make the goldfish experiment."

Perry Mason looked at his wrist watch, said, "Well, I guess we've got to go back and take it on the chin some more. Lieutenant Tragg will probably be on the stand this afternoon, and Tragg is a smooth worker. How much of a mining deal was it that Staunton had with Faulkner, Paul?"

214

"I don't know, Perry," Paul Drake said, holding open the door of the dining room. "I may get a little more information later on in the afternoon."

"I don't imagine I'd have cared to have Faulkner as a partner in a mining deal," Della Street said.

"Or in anything else," Drake observed fervently.

They walked slowly back to the courthouse, and as Judge Summerville reconvened court at two o'clock, Ray Medford, with every indication of smug virtue, said, "I want the record to show that at this time we are turning over to counsel for the defense, for his inspection, three magazines which were found on the floor of the bathroom where the murder was committed. By carefully observing photographs which were taken and using a magnifying glass to bring out details, we are able to state that the magazines as now handed to counsel for the defense are in the order in which they were found on the floor."

Mason took the proffered magazines and said, "Calling the attention of the Court to the fact that the magazine which was on top, and which bears a peculiar semi-circular ink smear, is a current issue, while the bottom two are older numbers."

"Do you think there's some significance in that?" Medford asked curiously.

"I do," Mason said.

Medford started to ask some question, then caught himself in time and regarded Mason with thoughtful speculation as the attorney opened the magazine and riffled the pages.

"Our next witness will be Lieutenant Tragg," Medford said, "and . . ."

"Just a moment," Mason interrupted. "I call the attention of Court and counsel to a check which I have just discovered in the pages of this magazine which was on the top of the pile, a blank check which has not been filled in in any way, a check bearing the imprint of the Seaboard Mechanics National Bank."

215

Judge Summerville showed his interest. "That blank check was in the magazine, Mr. Mason?"

"Yes, your Honor."

Judge Summerville looked at Medford. "You have noticed the check, Counselor?"

Medford said, casually, "I think somebody did mention something about a book mark in one of the magazines."

"A book mark?" Mason asked.

"If it is a book mark," Judge Summerville said, "it might be interesting to note the place in the magazine where it was found."

"On page seventy-eight," Mason said, "which seems to be a continuation of a romantic story."

"I'm quite certain it has no significance," Medford said easily. "It was simply a blank check which had been used as a book mark."

"Just a moment," Mason said. "Has any attempt been made to get fingerprints from this check?"

"Certainly not."

"Your Honor, I want this check tested for latent fingerprints," Mason said.

"Go ahead and test it, then," Medford snapped.

Mason's eyes showed that he was excited, but with the ring generalship which had been learned from many courtroom battles, his voice showed no trace of emotion, only that clear resonance which enabled him to hold a courtroom completely spellbound without seeming to raise his voice.

"I call your Honor's attention," he went on, "to the fact that in the lower left-hand corner of this check there is a peculiar triangular point of paper adhering to the body of the check. In other words, the check was torn out of a checkbook along a line of perforations, but at the extreme bottom of the check the line of cleavage left the perforations, and a small triangular tongue of paper is adhering to the check."

Medford said sarcastically, "That happens about half

of the time when *I* tear checks out of a book. It merely means that the check was torn out in a hurry and . . ."

"I think counsel doesn't get the significance," Mason interrupted. "If the Court will notice the checkbook which has been introduced in evidence, and which has the stub showing an amount of one thousand dollars, and the name 'Tom' and then the three letters 'G-r-i', the Court will notice that in the lower *right*-hand corner of that stub, there is a little triangular piece of paper missing. It occurs to me that it might be well to compare this check with that stub and see *if this isn't the check which was torn from that stub.*"

Medford's face showed consternation.

"Let's see that check," Judge Summerville said abruptly.

Mason said, "May I suggest, your Honor, that the check be handled very carefully and only by one corner so that if there *are* any fingerprints remaining . . ."

"Quite right. Quite right," Judge Summerville said.

Mason, holding the check by one corner carried it up to Judge Summerville's desk. Judge Summerville took the checkbook which had been introduced in evidence from the clerk of the court, and while Medford and Mason leaned over his shoulders, the judge carefully placed the check against the perforations of the checkbook. There was no mistaking the keen interest on the judge's face.

"It fits," he said in a tone of finality. "That's the check."

"Of course," Medford started to protest, "that merely means . . ."

"It means that there is less than one chance in ten million that the jagged, irregular lines of that torn piece of paper would coincide with the place which was torn from the check stub unless that was the check that was torn from the book," Judge Summerville said sharply.

"Therefore," Mason interposed, "we are faced with a situation where the decedent evidently started to fill out the stub of a check showing a payment made to Tom Gridley of one thousand dollars, but tore the check which was attached to that stub out of the book and placed it within the leaves of this magazine. It is, therefore, quite apparent that the decedent never intended to fill out the check, but only to fill out a check stub, leaving it to appear that he had made a check to Tom Gridley."

"What would be the object in doing that?" Judge Summerville asked Mason.

Mason smiled. "At the moment, your Honor, the prosecution is putting on its case, and I will therefore leave the answering of that question to the prosecution. When the defendant puts on her case, she will endeavor to explain any evidence that she introduces. And in the meantime, I suggest that the prosecution explain the evidence it introduces."

"I haven't introduced it," Medford said testily.

"Well, you should have," Judge Summerville told him sharply, "and the evidence is going to be introduced if the Court has to do it on its own motion. But first we're going to turn that over to a fingerprint expert and see whether any latent fingerprints can be developed."

"I would suggest," Mason said, "that the Court appoint its own expert. Not that the police are at all incapable, but they may be somewhat biased."

"The Court *will* appoint its own expert," Judge Summerville announced. "The Court will take an adjournment for ten minutes, during which time the Court will get in communication with an expert criminologist and see what fingerprints can be developed on this check. In the meantime, the clerk will keep this check in his custody. I suggest that we run a pin through this corner and that the check be handled in such a way that any fingerprints *which may remain* on it will not be disturbed."

There was just enough accent on the words "which may remain" to make it apparent that Judge Summerville was expressing judicial irritation that the evidence had not been given proper consideration by the police at a time when there would have been a chance of developing latent fingerprints.

Judge Summerville retired with dignity to his chambers and left Medford free to engage in a whispered conference with Sergeant Dorset and Lieutenant Tragg. Dorset, quite plainly, was angry and irritated. But Tragg was puzzled and cautious.

Della Street and Paul Drake came up to stand beside Mason.

"Looks like a break, Perry," Drake said.

"It's about time," Mason told him. "It certainly has been a hoodooed case."

"But what does it mean, Perry?"

"Frankly," Mason said, "I'll be darned if I know. I guess there's no question but what that was Faulkner's handwriting on the check stub."

"I understand there's a handwriting expert who will swear to it," Drake said.

"A good one?"

"Yes."

"What I can't understand," Della Street said, "is why the man should write out the stub of a check and then tear the check out. Of course, Faulkner was equal to anything, and he may have intended to have it appear he had given Tom Gridley a thousand-dollar check."

"But it wouldn't make any difference if his books *had* shown he'd given Gridley twenty one-thousand-dollar checks. Not until Gridley cashed the check would there be any actual payment of money. There's something a lot deeper here than appears on the surface. And I've really overlooked a bet."

Paul Drake said, "I've just found out something, Perry. I don't know whether it will help or not, but somewhere around eight-thirty, the night of the murder, someone rang up Tom Gridley. He said he wanted to talk a little business, but wouldn't give his name. He said he wanted

219

to ask just one or two simple questions. He then went on to say that he understood Gridley was having a dispute over some money matters with Harrington Faulkner and that Faulkner had offered Gridley seven hundred and fifty dollars for a settlement."

Mason's eyes were alert with concentration. "Go on, Paul. What did Gridley say to that?"

"Said he didn't know why he should discuss his affairs with a stranger, and the man's voice said he wanted to do Tom a favor, that he'd like to know if Tom would settle for a thousand."

"Then what?"

"Then Tom, being sick and irritable, said that if Faulkner had a check for one thousand dollars in his hands before noon of the next day he'd settle, if it meant anything to anyone, and slammed up the phone and went back to bed."

"To whom has he told this?" Mason asked.

"Apparently to the police. He hasn't held anything back with the police and they're giving him what breaks they can. They tried for a while to fit that conversation in with the thousand-dollar check stub. Their best guess was that someone was acting as intermediary and had already got the thousand-dollar check from Faulkner and was trying to clean things up."

"But why?" Mason asked.

"Search me."

"And that conversation was around eight-thirty?"

"There we run into a snag. Tom Gridley had been in bed with fever. He was terribly nervous and all worked up over his dealings with Faulkner, and Faulkner buying the pet store and all that stuff. He had been just dozing off, and he didn't notice the time. A while later, after he'd thought things over a bit, he looked at his watch, and it was then around nine ten. He thinks the call was around a little more than half an hour before he looked at his watch. . . . That's a poor way to fix time. It might have been right around eight-twenty, or it may have been quite a bit later. The point is that Gridley swears it wasn't before eight-fifteen because he'd looked at his watch at eight o'clock and then had been awake for several minutes before he dozed into a light slumber.

"That's the story, Perry. The police didn't think much of it after they found they couldn't tie it in with the check for one thousand dollars, and particularly since Tom wasn't certain of the time."

"It wasn't Faulkner, Paul?"

"Apparently not. Tom said it was a strange voice, the voice of a stranger to him. The man seemed rather authoritative, as though he knew what he was doing, and Tom had thought it might have been some lawyer Faulkner had consulted."

"It could have been, at that," Mason said. "Faulkner had those lawsuits which demanded attention. But why wouldn't any lawyer have come forward? Hang it, Paul, the conversation must have taken place right about the time Faulkner was murdered."

Drake nodded, said, "On the other hand, it may have been someone who thought he had a chance to settle things, someone whom the wife had consulted, or perhaps someone Carson had asked to get things straightened out."

"I prefer the wife," Mason said thoughtfully. "It sounds like her. By George, Paul, it *must* have been someone the wife consulted! I'd certainly like to know where she *really* was the night of the murder."

Drake said, "I've had men nosing around, but we can't find a thing. Sergeant Dorset gave her the chance to frame that alibi, and the police are taking it at its face value."

"I'll bet Tragg smells a rat," Mason said.

"If he does, he's keeping his nostrils from quivering even the least bit," Drake replied. "He isn't going to stir up any stink in the department merely because Sergeant Dorset let a woman pull the line that she was going to have hysterics and so get a chance for a frame-up. You know, Perry, if Mrs. Faulkner had said she wanted to go out and *see* her girl friend before Dorset questioned her, they'd have given her the merry ha-ha, and then really given her a third degree. But she says she feels ill, goes out to the back porch, goes through the motions of being sick, and then starts having hysterics, and Dorset is so anxious to get her out of the way until he's finished his investigation that when she says she wanted to have one of her girl friends come over and stay with her, Dorset practically jumps down her throat telling her to go ahead."

Mason nodded, said, "I'm beginning to get an idea, Paul. I think that . . . Here's the judge coming back to the bench. Looks as though he had really taken things into his own hands . . . Bet *he's* going to give us the breaks from now on. He's certainly mad enough at the cops."

Judge Summerville returned to the bench, once more called court into session and said, "Gentlemen, the Court has arranged over the telephone with one of the best consulting criminologists in the city to take charge of that check and see what can be done toward developing latent fingerprints on it. Now do you gentlemen wish to go on with the case? I am frank to state that in view of the peculiar development, the Court will be inclined to give the defense an adjournment in case the defendant wishes it."

"I think not," Mason said, "not at the moment, anyway. Perhaps as the evidence progresses . . ."

"I don't think I'd like that," Medford interrupted. "In other words, the counsel for the defense is adopting the position that we've got to go on putting on our case and showing our hand and then, at any moment, when the defendant wants to, the defendant can call for an adjournment. I think if there's any question about it, we should

222

adjourn the case until after the fingerprints have been developed on that check."

Judge Summerville said crisply, "The Court's offer was made to the defense. I don't think that the prosecution is entitled to ask for an adjournment when a valuable piece of evidence, I may say a most valuable piece of evidence, has been permitted to all but slip through its fingers, and would have gone entirely unnoticed if it hadn't been for counsel for the defense. Proceed with your case, Mr. Medford."

Medford took the court's rebuke with the best grace he could muster. "Of course, your Honor," he said, "I am merely presenting the case as developed by the police. It is not the function of my office to . . ."

"I understand, I understand," Judge Summerville interrupted, "the fault undoubtedly lies with the police, but on the other hand, gentlemen, it is quite evident that it is not the function of the attorney for the defendant to come into court and point out evidence, the significance of which has been entirely overlooked, both by the police and the prosecution. However, that is neither here nor there. Mr. Mason says that he does not care for an adjournment at this time. The Court will state frankly that it will be inclined to give Mr. Mason a reasonable adjournment whenever it is made to appear that it would prejudice the defendant's case to go on with the examination before all of the evidence is in on that check. Call your next witness, Mr. Medford."

"Lieutenant Tragg," Medford said.

Tragg had never been in better form than when he got on the witness stand. In the manner of an impartial, skillful police officer who is only doing his duty and has no personal interest or animosity in the matter, he began to weave a net of circumstantial evidence around Sally Madison, and then, when he testified to the occasion of picking up Sally Madison on the street and finding the gun and the two thousand dollars in bills in her purse, he sprang the bombshell which Ray Medford had been so carefully preparing.

"Now then, Lieutenant Tragg," Medford said, "did you examine that weapon for the purpose of developing any latent fingerprints?"

"Certainly," Tragg said.

"And what did you find?"

"I found several latent fingerprints which retained sufficiently distinct characteristics so that they could be positively identified."

"And whose fingerprints were they?"

"Four fingerprints were those of the defendant."

"And the others?" Medford asked in a voice that held just a note of conscious triumph.

"The other two fingerprints," Lieutenant Tragg said, "were those of Miss Della Street, the secretary of Mr. Perry Mason, and the one who, at the request of Perry Mason, had taken Miss Sally Madison to the Kellinger Hotel in an attempt to keep her from being questioned."

Medford glanced quickly at Mason, not knowing that Paul Drake's detectives had already tipped Mason off to this point in the evidence, and thinking that he would encounter some expression of dismay.

Mason merely glanced casually at the clock, then looked inquiringly over at Medford.

"Have you finished with the witness?" he asked.

"Cross-examine," Medford snapped.

Judge Summerville held up his hand. "Just a moment," he said. "I want to ask your witness a question. Lieutenant Tragg, are you quite certain that the fingerprints you found on that weapon were actually those of Miss Della Street?"

"Yes, your Honor."

"Showing that she had touched that weapon?"

"That is quite right, your Honor."

"Very well," Judge Summerville said in a voice that

showed his appreciation of the gravity of the situation, "you may cross-examine, Mr. Mason."

Mason said, "You'll pardon me, Lieutenant Tragg, if I perhaps review some of your testimony, but as I understand it, you have made a very thorough check of the movements of Harrington Faulkner on the afternoon of the day he met his death?"

"From five o'clock on," Tragg said. "In fact, we can account for *every* move he made from five o'clock until the time of his death."

"And he went to the Rawlins pet store sometime after five o'clock?"

"Yes. He went to the bank, got the money and then went to the Rawlins pet store."

"And he was there some time taking inventory?"

"Around an hour and forty-five minutes."

"And while he was there he noticed this revolver?"

"That's right."

"And put it in his pocket?"

"Yes."

"And then, according to your theory of the case, when he went to his home he took the gun out of his pocket and put it down—perhaps on the bed?"

Tragg said, "The gun was in his hip pocket. He went home, took off his coat and shirt and started to shave. It's only natural to suppose that he took the gun out of his pocket."

"Then," Mason said suavely, "how does it happen that you didn't find any of Mr. Faulkner's fingerprints on the gun?"

Tragg hesitated a moment, said, "The murderer must have wiped all fingerprints off the gun."

"Why?"

"Obviously," Tragg said, smiling slightly, "to remove incriminating evidence."

"Therefore," Mason said, "if the defendant had been the one who committed the murder and had thought enough of the problem of fingerprints to have wiped all fingerprints off the gun she would hardly have gone ahead after that and left her own fingerprints on it, would she?"

Tragg was obviously jarred by the question. He said, "Of course, you're assuming something there, Mr. Mason."

"What am I assuming?"

"You're assuming that I know something of what was in the defendant's mind."

"You've already testified to what was in the mind of the murderer," Mason said. "You have testified that the murderer wiped the fingerprints off the weapon to remove incriminating evidence. Now then, I am asking you if that theory is consistent with the theory that Sally Madison committed the murder."

Lieutenant Tragg obviously realized the force of Mason's suggestion. He shifted his position uncomfortably.

"Isn't it far more likely that she is telling the truth, and that she picked up the gun in order to remove it from the scene of the crime, knowing that it was Tom Gridley's gun?"

"I'll leave that up to the court," Tragg said.

"Thank you," Mason announced, smiling. "And now, I want to ask you a couple of other questions, Lieutenant Tragg. It is the theory of the police, I believe, that Harrington Faulkner was writing this check stub and was about to write the name Tom Gridley in the check stub when he was shot?"

"That's right."

"The fact that he had written only the first three letters of the last name, and the fact that the checkbook was found where it had fallen on the floor, are the things on which you predicate your conclusion?"

"That, plus the fact that the fountain pen also fell on the floor."

"Don't you think that something else might have interrupted the deceased?"

"Such as what?" Tragg asked. "I'd be glad to have you mention something that would cause a man to stop writing in the middle of a name that way."

"Perhaps the ringing of a telephone?" Mason asked.

"Not a chance in the world," Tragg said. ". . . that is, if you want my opinion."

"I'm asking for it," Mason said.

"If the telephone had rung, the decedent would certainly have finished the name 'Gridley' before he answered the telephone. And he wouldn't have dropped the checkbook on the floor and wouldn't have dropped the fountain pen on the floor."

"Therefore," Mason said, "the thing that prevented the decedent from finishing writing the name 'Gridley' was the fatal shot?"

"I think there's no other conclusion."

"You have talked with a gentleman named Charles Menlo?"

"Yes."

"And, without anticipating Mr. Menlo's testimony, I believe you know that Mr. Menlo will state that he was talking with the decedent on the telephone at the time when someone, apparently the defendant, entered the house and was ordered out by Mr. Faulkner?"

"This, of course, is very irregular," Medford interposed.

"I think counsel is simply trying to save time," Judge Summerville said. "Do you want to object to the question?"

"No, I think not. There's no question about Mr. Menlo's testimony."

"That's right," Lieutenant Tragg said.

"Therefore," Mason went on, "if it had been the defendant who entered the house at that time . . ."

"She admits that she did," Tragg said. "Her own written statement covers that point."

"Exactly," Mason went on. "And if she found the door open and entered, encountered Harrington Faulkner in the bedroom, talking on the telephone, and if Faulkner then tried to eject her and she snatched up the gun and shot him, she could hardly have shot him while he was writing a check stub in the bathroom, could she?"

"Wait a minute. How's that again?" Tragg asked.

Mason said, "It's quite obvious, Lieutenant. The police theory is that Faulkner was telephoning when Sally Madison came into the room. Faulkner still had some lather on his face. He was running water in the bathtub. He ordered the defendant out. There was a struggle. She saw the gun lying on the bed and picked it up and shot him. Now then, if she had shot him while he was struggling with her in the bedroom, she couldn't have shot him while he was writing that check stub in the bathroom, could she?"

Tragg said, "No," and then after a moment added, "I'm glad you brought up that point, Mr. Mason, because it makes the murder a deliberate, cold-blooded murder instead of one committed in the heat of rage."

"Just how do you reason that out?" Mason asked.

"Because Faulkner must have gone back to the bathroom and picked up the checkbook and started writing the check stub when she shot him."

"That's your theory now?" Mason asked.

Tragg said, smiling, "It's *your* theory, Mr. Mason, and I'm now beginning to think it's a good one."

"And when Faulkner fell as the result of that shot, did he upset the table containing the bowl in which the goldfish were swimming?"

"He did."

"But," Mason said, "there was a graniteware container and one goldfish in the bathtub. How do you account for those?"

"I think one of the fish must have fallen into the bathtub."

Mason smiled, "Remembering, Lieutenant, that at that time Faulkner was drawing *hot* water for a bath. How long do you think the fish would have lived in *hot* bath water and how do you think the graniteware container got in the bathtub?"

Tragg frowned, thought for a few seconds, then said, "I'm not a mind reader."

Mason smiled courteously. "Thank you, Lieutenant, for that concession. I was afraid that you *had* been trying to qualify as such. Particularly in regard to your comments as to the fingerprints of Della Street on the gun. For all you know, those prints might have been put on the gun before the murder."

"Not the way *you've* explained it," Tragg said. "The murderer must have wiped all fingerprints off the gun."

"Then, the murderer could hardly have been Sally Madison."

Tragg frowned. "I want to think that over a bit," he said.

Mason bowed to Judge Summerville. "And that, your Honor, is the point at which I will terminate my cross-examination. I would *like* to let Lieutenant Tragg think it over a little bit—think it over a whole lot."

Judge Summerville said to Medford, "Call your next witness."

"Louis C. Corning," Medford announced. "Please come forward, Mr. Corning."

Corning, the fingerprint expert who had lifted the fingerprints from the various objects in Faulkner's house, testified in detail as to the fingerprints he had found, and paid particular attention to a fingerprint of Sally Madison which had been found on the handle of the satchel under the bed—a fingerprint which was introduced in evidence and marked, "F. P. No. 10."

"Cross-examine," Medford said to Perry Mason, as

soon as the witness had positively identified that particular fingerprint.

"Why," Mason asked on cross-examination, "did you use the so-called lifting method?"

"Because," the witness answered defiantly, "that was the only method to use."

"You mean that you couldn't have used any other?"

"I mean that it wouldn't have been practical."

"What do you mean by that?"

The witness said, "Attorneys for the defense always try to hold a field day with an expert who has lifted fingerprints. But when you're called on to investigate a crime of that sort, you have to lift the fingerprints, and that's all there is to it. Lifting enables you to make a complete examination and a careful examination, and to avoid the mistakes which are sometimes made by the use of too much haste—such as when a person is trying to examine and classify a lot of latent fingerprints in a short time."

"It took you some time after you had lifted these prints to examine them?"

"I worked on them for a good many hours, yes."

"You found a fingerprint of the defendant—the one that has been introduced as the People's Exhibit F. P. No. 10—on the handle of the satchel, which has also been introduced in evidence?"

"I did."

"How do you know you found that fingerprint there?"

"How do I know anything?"

Mason smiled.

Judge Summerville said, "Answer the question."

"Well, I knew it because I took an envelope, wrote on the outside of it, 'Fingerprints taken from satchel,' and I then proceeded to dust the satchel and wherever I found a latent I pulled it off and dropped it into this envelope."

"And what did you then do with the envelopes?"

"I put them in my briefcase."

"And what did you do with your briefcase?"

230

"I took it home that night."

"And what did you do with it then?"

"I worked on some of the fingerprints."

"Did you find F. P. No. 10 that night?"

"No, I didn't find that until late the next morning."

"Where were you when you found it?"

"At my office."

"Did you go directly from your house to your office?"

"I did not."

"Where did you go?"

"At the request of Lieutenant Tragg, I went out to the residence of James L. Staunton."

"What did you do there?"

"I took some fingerprints from a fish tank."

"By the lifting method?"

"By the lifting method."

Mason said, "And what did you do with *those* fingerprints?"

"I put them in an envelope marked 'Prints lifted from fish tank at residence of James L. Staunton.'"

"And that envelope was also put in your briefcase?"

"Yes."

"Is it possible that you made a mistake and that one of the fingerprints of the defendant which was actually lifted from this tank was placed inadvertently in this envelope labeled 'Fingerprints taken from satchel'?"

"Don't be silly," the witness said scornfully.

"I'm not being silly," Mason said. "I'm asking you a question."

"The answer is an unequivocal, absolute, final and emphatic *no*."

"Who was present when you were taking these fingerprints?"

"No one except the gentleman who had admitted me."

"Mr. Staunton?"

"That's right."

"How long did it take?"

"I would say not over twenty to thirty minutes."

"Then you went back to your office?"

"That's right."

"And how soon after that did you finish checking the fingerprints and find this exhibit F. P. 10?"

"I would say about three hours afterwards."

Mason said, "That's all."

As the witness left the stand, Mason said, "Now, your Honor, I think I would like to request that recess which the Court has previously suggested might be in order. I would prefer to know the result of the examination of that blank check for fingerprints before I go on with the cross-examination of witnesses."

"The Court will adjourn until tomorrow morning at ten o'clock," Judge Summerville said promptly. "And, for the benefit of counsel, it will be noted that the Court has advised the criminologist who is examining the blank check for fingerprints to notify both counsel immediately upon the completion of his examination. Until tomorrow morning at ten o'clock."

Sally Madison, without the slightest change of her facial expression, said in a low voice to Perry Mason, "Thank you." Her voice was as calmly impersonal as though she had been expressing her gratitude for the lighting of a cigarette or some similar service. Nor did she wait for the lawyer to make any reply, but instead arose and stood waiting to be escorted from the courtroom.

18

■

Late afternoon sunlight was throwing somewhat vague shadows from the palm trees on the lawn against the stuccoed side of the residence of Wilfred Dixon when Mason parked his car, walked up the steps to the porch and calmly rang the bell.

Wilfred Dixon opened the door, said rather formally, "Good afternoon, Mr. Mason."

Mason said, "I'm back."

"I'm engaged at the moment."

"I have," Mason announced, "more chips. I want to sit in the game again."

"I'll be glad to accommodate you some time this evening. Perhaps around eight o'clock, Mr. Mason?"

"That," Mason announced, "won't be satisfactory. I want to see you now."

Dixon shook his head. "I'm sorry, Mr. Mason."

Mason said, "The last time I saw you I made a bluff and you called it. This time I've got more chips and I think I have better cards."

"Indeed."

Mason said, "Thinking back on your conversation, I am impressed by the very skillful way in which you led me to believe that you never for a moment considered *buying* Faulkner's interest in the company, but only selling Genevieve's interest to him."

"Well?" Dixon asked, acting as though he were on the point of closing the door.

Mason said, "It was a rather clever piece of work, but the only reason you would have had for being interested in the bullet which Carson had concealed in the fish tank would have been because you wanted to have some definite hold on Carson, and the only reason that I can think of for wanting to have such a hold would be either because you or Genevieve had fired the shot, or because you intended to buy out Faulkner, and when you bought him out wanted to have a strangle-hold on Carson so you could freeze him out without his being able to fight back."

"I'm afraid, Mr. Mason, that your reasoning is entirely fallacious. However, I'll be glad to discuss it with you this evening."

"And," Mason said, "so that the deal would look better for income tax purposes, you arranged to give Faulkner a check for twenty-five thousand *more* than the price that was actually agreed upon and have Faulkner bring you twenty-five thousand dollars in cash."

Wilfred Dixon's eyes closed and opened three times, as though they might have been regulated by clockwork. "Come in," he invited. "Mrs. Genevieve Faulkner is with me at the moment. I saw no reason to disturb her, but perhaps we'd better get this over with once and for all."

"Perhaps we had," Mason said.

Mason followed Dixon into the room, shook hands with Genevieve Faulkner, calmly seated himself, lit a cigarette and said, "So, of course, having received the twenty-five thousand dollars from Faulkner in a deal which was completely fraudulent because it had for its primary purpose an attempt to defraud the Collector of Internal Revenue, you inadvertently paid Sally Madison two thousand dollars in cash from the twenty-five thousand which Faulkner had previously delivered to you. Now, that means that you must have seen Faulkner either at his house or at some other place, subsequent to the time Sally Madison left Faulkner's residence, and *before* you paid the money over to Sally Madison out here."

Dixon smiled and shook his head at Genevieve Faulkner. "I don't know just what he's driving at, Genevieve," he said calmly. "Apparently it's some last-minute theory he's using to try and get his client acquitted. I thought perhaps you'd better hear it."

"The man seems to be crazy," Genevieve Faulkner said.

"Let's go back and look at the evidence," Mason said. "Faulkner was very anxious to attend a banquet where some goldfish experts were to talk and where he was to mingle with some other goldfish collectors. He was in such a hurry that he wouldn't even discuss matters with Sally Madison. He rushed her out of the house. He had drawn the water for his bath. He had shaved but part of his face, still had lather on it. It's reasonable to suppose that after he put Sally Madison out, he washed his face. Then, before he had had a chance to clean his razor, before he had had a chance to take off his clothes and hastily jump into his hot bath, the telephone rang.

"Whatever was said over the telephone was something that was of the greatest importance to Harrington Faulkner. It was something that caused him to forego his bath, to put on his shirt, tie and coat and go dashing out to meet the person who had telephoned. That person must have been either you, Genevieve, or both. He paid over the twenty-five thousand dollars, and then returned to his house. By that time it was too late to attend the banquet. The water, which had been hot in the bathtub when he had drawn it some time before, had now become cold.

"Harrington Faulkner had another appointment he didn't care to miss. But he had an hour or so before that appointment. He decided that he'd treat a fish that had tail rot, and then segregate that fish from the others. The treatment for tail rot is to immerse the fish in equal parts of hydrogen peroxide and water. So Faulkner once more took off his coat and shirt, went to the kitchen, got a graniteware pot, put equal parts of hydrogen peroxide and water in it, immersed the fish in that water, and then, when the treatment was finished, put that fish in the bathtub.

"At that point, Faulkner remembered that he had given a thousand-dollar check payable to Tom Gridley, which he hadn't entered on the stub of his checkbook and therefore hadn't deducted from his bank account. In view of the twenty-five-thousand-dollar withdrawal, the balance in his checking account had been diminished materially, and he wanted to be certain that he kept right up to date on it. So he got his checkbook, took his fountain pen from the pocket of his coat, and picked up a magazine to use as a backer so he could write. He found that one magazine wasn't enough, so at random, he picked up two old magazines. There was some reason why he remained in the bathroom to write that check stub. It probably had to do with the exact timing of his fish treatment. He was writing on the stub of that check when he was killed."

Dixon yawned and politely stifled the yawn with his forefinger. "I'm afraid, Mr. Mason, you're not getting anywhere with that theory."

Mason said, "Perhaps not, but my own idea is that once the police start questioning Mrs. Genevieve Faulkner along the lines of that theory of mine, they'll either force her to disgorge that other twenty-three thousand dollars and make a statement which will clarify the situation, or they'll start searching the place and find the twenty-three thousand dollars."

With elaborate courtesy, Dixon moved over toward the phone. "Would you like to have me call the police and suggest that to them?"

Mason looked him squarely in the eyes. "Yes," he said, "and when you make the call, ask for Lieutenant Tragg."

Dixon shook his head sadly. "I'm afraid, Mason, that you want us to play into your hands. On second thought, I've decided that I'm simply not going to have anything to do with this."

Mason grinned. "You made a bluff, just as I did yesterday, and this time *I'm* calling it. When you called me, I actually telephoned Tragg. Now go ahead and be as good a sport as I was."

"You're too anxious," Dixon said, and walked back to his chair.

Mason said, "All right, if you won't do it, I'll do it."

"Go right ahead."

Mason moved over to the telephone, turned back over his shoulder and said, "That one-thousand dollar check to Tom Gridley is the payoff. You didn't want to buy the business and have any possible claims outstanding that might involve litigation. So you telephoned Tom Gridley and asked him if he'd accept a thousand dollars by way of a complete settlement. Gridley said he would. So you had Faulkner sign a check for that amount right here, which you mailed to Gridley. But when you learned Faulkner had been murdered, you had to get that check back. At the time you didn't realize you were gambling with Sally Madison's life. You only knew that if you could keep it from becoming known that Faulkner had rushed out here, you would be in a position to keep twenty-three thousand dollars in cold, hard cash, and still have plenty of opportunity to buy the business at your own price from Faulkner's estate."

Dixon said, "Come, come, Mr. Mason. This is being said in the presence of a witness. Tomorrow I shall sue you for defamation of character. You must have *something* on which to pin such a fantastic story."

Mason said, "I have the word of my client."

Dixon smiled. "For a veteran lawyer, you're *most* susceptible to feminine charm."

Mason said, "And I also have some shrewd deduction. You got up this morning and went to the corner drug store for breakfast. You were there an hour. That's a long time to eat a light breakfast at a corner drug store. When I drove up, I looked the drug store over. There's a mail box in front of it. The hour of the first mail collection in the morning is seven forty-five. I think the mailman who collects the mail will be able to testify that when he opened the box you were there with a plausible story and a bribe. You had inadvertently mailed a letter to Thomas Gridley. It had a check in it, but there was a mistake on the check. You wanted to rectify it. You convinced the man of your identity, of the fact that you had mailed the letter. . . . That is a hunch, but when I play poker, I play hunches. And now I'm going to call Lieutenant Tragg."

Mason picked up the telephone receiver, dialed Operator, and said, "Get me the police. This is an emergency."

For a moment the room was completely silent, then suddenly a chair overturned. Mason looked back over his shoulder to see the squat, athletic form of Wilfred Dixon coming at him with a rush.

The lawyer dropped the receiver, swung in a body pivot, and at the same time jerked his head to one side.

Dixon's punch missed Mason's chin, went harmlessly over Mason's shoulder. Mason's right hand sank into the pit of Dixon's stomach. Then, as the business counselor folded up, Mason jerked back his arm, raised his shoulder, and caught the man a terrific uppercut.

Dixon dropped to the floor with a thud that was as inanimate as the sound of a flour sack falling to the floor.

Mrs. Genevieve Faulkner sat very calmly, her knees crossed, eyes slightly narrowed, an expression of concentration on her face. She said, "You're a rough player, Mr. Mason—but I always did like men who could take care of themselves. Perhaps you and I could talk a little business."

Mason didn't even bother to answer. He picked up the dangling receiver, said, "Police headquarters? Get me Lieutenant Tragg of Homicide, and get him in a hurry."

19

It was after seven o'clock when Lieutenant Tragg entered Mason's office.

"Some people are born lucky," Tragg said, grinning. "Others achieve luck, and others have luck thrust upon them."

Mason nodded. "I did have to put it on a silver platter and dump it in your lap, didn't I?"

Tragg's grin faded. "I was referring to you. I'd really have hated to have done it to you, Mason, but you've slipped it over on us so often, that when you left yourself wide open, I wouldn't have had any other choice. I was going to put the skids under you."

"I know," Mason said, "I don't blame you. Sit down."

Tragg nodded to Della Street. "No hard feelings, Della. It was all in the line of duty." He sat down and said, "How about one of your cigarettes, Mason?"

The lawyer gave Tragg a cigarette.

"Well," Tragg said, "we've got most of it in the bag. We're going to turn your golddigger loose. I wondered if you wanted to be on hand for the ceremony."

"Of course I do."

"I don't blame you. It'll be impressive. The deuce of it is I haven't got a really good case as yet."

"Suppose you tell me just what you've found out."

Tragg said, "I'd like it a lot better if you'd tell me how you knew what had happened."

"We held out a little evidence on you, Lieutenant."

"Such as what?"

Mason said, "I deduced that Carson must have picked up that bullet from Faulkner's desk and tossed it over his shoulder into the fish tank. Now, the only reason he would have done that would have been because he wanted to protect the person who fired the shot."

"Meaning that he fired it?"

Mason said, "No. Meaning that someone else had, and he wanted to protect that person."

"Who?"

Mason said, "When we went to Faulkner's house the night of the murder, Mrs. Faulkner came tearing up in an automobile. She seemed in the devil of a hurry, but the way the exhaust smelled, I thought the choke must be nearly all the way out. That meant she'd been running with a cold motor, and that in turn meant she hadn't come very far. So Paul Drake examined the car and found that the ash tray was empty. As he pointed out, a nervous person will almost invariably empty the ash tray of a car if there's a long wait under tension."

Tragg nodded and said, "I've done it myself."

"Drake found the place where the ash tray had been emptied. It was a place from where you could see the front of the Faulkner house."

"You mean Mrs. Faulkner was waiting for you to drive up?"

"That's what I thought at the time," Mason said, "and I damn near got a client convicted because the true solution didn't occur to me."

"What was it?"

"I was right in deducing that she had only come a short distance," Mason said. "Her car had been parked earlier that evening at the spot where the ash tray had been emptied. I made the mistake of picking on the obvious

240

© Lorillard 1975

C'mon

Come for the filter.
You'll stay for the taste.

KING SIZE

KENT
WITH
THE FAMOUS MICRONITE FILTER

KING SIZE

KENT
WITH
THE FAMOUS MICRONITE FILTER

Newport

Alive with pleasure!

Newport

20 CLASS A CIGARETTES

MENTHOL KINGS

17 mg. "tar", 1.2 mg. nicotine, av. per cigarette, FTC Report Apr. '75.

Warning: The Surgeon General Has Determined That Cigarette Smoking Is Dangerous to Your Health.

and jumping at the wrong conclusion. It had been much earlier in the evening. It had been between five and seven instead of around the hour Sally Madison and I arrived."

"And why should she have parked there at that time?"

"Because her husband had gone out, and Elmer Carson had taken advantage of his absence to go into the real estate office and start looking for that bullet. And Jane Faulkner, who had fired the shot at her husband in an attempt to get him out of the way, had been sitting there in her car, where she could see the entrance to the house, and blow her horn and warn Carson in the event Faulkner returned unexpectedly. In that event, Carson would have slipped out of the back door, gone through the alley, joined Mrs. Faulkner in her automobile, and been whisked away."

Tragg's eyes narrowed. "You think Mrs. Faulkner took that shot at her husband?"

"I'm satisfied she did. She pulled that sleep medicine stuff as a species of alibi. She'd managed to plant herself where she knew her husband was going to be driving his automobile. She planned to fire the shot, jump into her own car, take a dose of quick acting sedative, drive back to the house, undress, and go to bed. She fired the shot at her husband, all right, but she hadn't realized the difficulty of shooting at a man in a moving automobile. She missed him by inches. The evidence shows that the only possible explanation of what happened is that Carson was protecting the person who tried to commit the murder. Obviously, Carson didn't do it. Therefore, who was the person who had made the attempt, and whom Carson was trying to protect? I should have known when Mrs. Faulkner came driving up in her automobile in a terrific hurry and with the motor almost cold. She was trying to get home before her husband returned from that banquet, and her car was cold, not because she had been parked around there watching the house, but because she had been spending the evening in the arms of Elmer Carson, who lived, you will remember, within four blocks of Faulkner's house."

Tragg stared steadily at the pattern of the carpet as he correlated these points in his mind.

"That doesn't make sense, Mason."

"What doesn't?"

"That elaborate attempt at getting the bullet earlier in the evening when they knew that Faulkner was going to be out after eight-thirty. They'd have waited until then."

"No they wouldn't," Mason said. "They knew that he was going to be at the pet store while there were still some minutes of daylight. They wanted to drain that fish tank and try and find the bullet, which seemed to have eluded them, while they still had daylight. If Faulkner had driven up and found the lights on in the office, it would have been a give away. And you'll remember that since the duplex side of the building was to be used as an office, there were no curtains on the windows, merely Venetian blinds on the south and west windows."

"Well," Tragg admitted, "you called the turn on Dixon. They telephoned Faulkner, told him they'd make the deal promptly at eight-thirty, but that he had to be there with the twenty-five thousand dollars; that if he wasn't there at that exact moment, they wouldn't make the deal.

"What I can't figure out, though, is why Faulkner paid out twenty-five thousand in cash and trusted to Dixon's good faith to go through with the deal."

"He had no alternative," Mason said. "Besides, he knew Dixon *wanted* to buy his interest in the company."

"Well, anyway, Faulkner dropped everything to rush out there. When he got out there, they raised the point about Tom Gridley. They weren't buying any lawsuits. So Dixon called up Tom Gridley, and reached a deal with him over the phone by which Faulkner was to mail him a check for a thousand dollars. But how did Dixon and

Genevieve Faulkner know all about that bullet business? I neglected to get that cleared up."

Mason said, "How did they know everything else that went on in the company? There's only one answer. Alberta Stanley, the secretary for the company, was in Dixon's employ. When she told him about the bullet, he deduced what must have happened—just as I did when I heard of it."

Tragg nodded. "Of course. The Stanley girl is the answer to lots of things."

"What became of the check?" Mason asked.

Tragg grinned. "Just as you deduced, that was the one weak spot in Dixon's armor. The postman was talked and bribed into giving the letter back to Dixon when the mail was collected. But I'm still a long way from pinning the murder on Wilfred Dixon."

"Pinning the murder on *him!*" Mason exclaimed.

"Why, yes."

"You can't pin it on *him*," Mason told the officer. "Use your head. The person who killed Faulkner went to Faulkner's house. He found Faulkner treating a goldfish for tail rot. He got Faulkner to stop his treatment of the goldfish and go get his fountain pen so that he could write some document, or sign some document. And then, after that document had been signed, and while Faulkner still had his fountain pen in his hand, Faulkner remembered about that check to Gridley and decided he'd make a stub that would cover the amount of the check. So he tore the check out of the book, started making out the stub, and was shot in cold blood by a man who had started to leave the house, but who saw Gridley's gun lying on the bed, and couldn't resist the temptation to use it.

"Faulkner fell down dead. When he fell, he upset the bowl of goldfish that was on the table in the bathroom. The bowl broke. One segment of the bowl contained a little water. One of the fish lived in there until he had exhausted the oxygen in the water, and then in his strug-

243

gles, flopped out onto the floor. Taking the evidence of that goldfish, I'd say that the crime must have been committed somewhere around nine-thirty, and you'll remember Faulkner said that he had an appointment at around that time.

"Wilfred Dixon and Genevieve Faulkner weren't above rigging their books so that they had a twenty-five thousand dollar profit that wouldn't show on their income tax. They weren't above throwing the hooks into Faulkner and forcing him to sell out. They weren't above getting the bullet Carson had tossed into the fish tank, proving that Carson must have put it there, and black-mailing Carson into letting go of his own holdings for a fraction of their value; but they weren't the type that deliberately kill a man without any motive. Once they'd got Faulkner's twenty-five thousand dollars, they certainly had no interest in bumping him off. They didn't realize that keeping silent would doom Sally Madison—not at first. By the time they did, they were in so deep they had to carry on. Dixon couldn't tell the truth without implicating himself and Genevieve Faulkner in a fraudulent transaction. So they decided to keep quiet. But *they* certainly weren't the ones who followed Faulkner home and murdered him."

"Then who the devil did?" Tragg asked.

"Use your head," Mason told him. "Remember there's a blot on the magazine, an ink smear. What makes an ink smear? A fountain pen that's almost empty. And James L. Staunton had a written release from Faulkner which he showed you when you started crowding him, but which he didn't show to me when I questioned him. Why didn't he produce it sooner? Why didn't he show it to me? Because the ink was hardly dry on it, and probably because a portion of the blot that had fallen from the almost empty fountain pen when Faulkner took it out of his pocket had stained one edge of the document."

Tragg abruptly got up and reached for his hat. "Thanks, Mason."

"Did that written statement have a blot on it?" Mason asked.

"Yes, on one edge. And like a damn fool I didn't have the ink analyzed. I could have done it when I first saw the statement, and it would have shown that it had been written the night before, instead of at the time Faulkner brought the goldfish. I'm afraid, Mason, I've been so hypnotized by the fact that I was dealing with a girl who happened to have the murder gun in her purse, that I closed my eyes to everything else."

"That's the big trouble with being an officer," Mason agreed. "You have the responsibility of getting the evidence which will support a conviction. Once you make an arrest, you have to put in all of your energies getting evidence which will insure the conviction of the arrested person. Otherwise you're in bad with the D. A."

Tragg nodded, then half way to the door turned and said, "How about that fingerprint—that F. P. No. 10?"

Mason said, "That fingerprint shows the danger of the lifting method. Every bit of evidence shows that Staunton was a shrewd man and a cunning man. Sergeant Dorset must have let it drop while he was out there with Sally Madison that they were lifting fingerprints at the scene of the murder. After they had left, Staunton, whom you will probably find knows something about fingerprinting, himself, knew that Sally Madison's fingerprints would be on the glass tank where she had handled it while treating his goldfish. He simply lifted one of her fingerprints off of that tank and had it all ready, looking for a chance to slip it into the collection of lifted fingerprints. When Louis Corning came out to Staunton's house to fingerprint the tank, it gave Staunton the opportunity he'd been anticipating. While Corning was taking fingerprints from the fish tank and completely absorbed in what he was doing, Staunton saw the collection of envelopes which Corning had so obligingly taken from his briefcase, and slipped Sally's fingerprint in where he thought it would do the most good."

"I don't believe he could have done that," Tragg said.

"Ask him," Mason said, grinning. "And when you ask him, tell him that you've found his fingerprint on the lift that carries Exhibit F. P. 10."

"Why did Staunton kill him?" Tragg asked after he had thought over Mason's suggestion for a second or two.

Mason said wearily, "Go find out. Good Lord, do you want me to do *everything* for you? Faulkner and Staunton had been secret partners in a mining deal. I'll bet you ten to one that Faulkner had Staunton over the barrel. Faulkner had just been forced by Dixon to sell out his business for less than it was worth, and you'll probably find that Faulkner was passing the bite on to Staunton. Hell, I don't know, and I'm not paid to think about it. My job was to get Sally Madison out of jail and I'm getting her out of jail. Della Street and I are going out on the town. We're going to eat. Maybe we're even going to drink!"

"More power to you," Tragg said. "Where will you be?"

Mason wrote the names of three night clubs on a slip of paper, handed it to Lieutenant Tragg. "We'll be at one of those three places, but don't try to reach us to report anything except a confession from Staunton and the time at which you're going to release Sally Madison from jail. We don't want to be disturbed over minor matters."

20

■

The orchestra was playing one of the old-time waltzes. Lights had been turned down and blue spotlights shining on the dome above the dance floor gave the place the appearance of summer moonlight, showing the forms of couples waltzing slowly.

Mason's lips brushed Della Street's cheek. "Happy?" he asked.

"Yes, darling," she said softly. "And it's lovely not to be going to jail!"

A waiter came hurrying toward them, caught Mason's eye, made frantic signals.

Mason guided Della Street over toward him, then, on the edge of the dance floor they ceased moving their feet but kept swaying to the rhythm of the music. "What is it?" Mason asked.

"A Lieutenant Tragg has called up. Says he's from Homicide and to convey the message to you that you win all the way along the line, and that Sally Madison is to be released at midnight. He wants to know if you care to talk to him?"

Mason grinned. "He's on the line?"

"Yes."

Mason said, "Kindly give him my thanks—tell him that I'll be there in time for the ceremonies, and that I'm too agreeably engaged at the moment to talk with anyone except my partner."

The waiter turned away. Mason guided Della Street back toward the center of the dance floor.

"Poor Sally Madison," Mason said, "she was willing to take a chance on the death chamber in order to save the man she loved."

Della Street looked up at him. "You can't blame her for that. It's . . . it's feminine nature."

Mason said, "It surprises some people, Della, to think you find as much loyalty in the Sally Madisons of the world as you do in women who have followed all the rules."

Della Street lowered her eyes. "It's the way a woman's made, Chief. She'll do anything for the man she loves—anything." Then she added hastily, "What time is it, Chief? We don't want to be late getting to the jail."

"We won't," Mason assured her, circling her waist with his arm, as the music ended. "I even think," he added as the lights blazed into brilliance and they started back toward their table, "that Lieutenant Tragg might be grateful enough to delay things a few minutes for us. And the next time you go places with a golddigger, Della, take a look in the purse first."

Della Street laughed. "I probably won't," she said. "You and I learn everything from our adventures except prudence."

"That's the way I like to have it," Mason said, grinning at her.

The Case of
the Buried Clock

CAST OF CHARACTERS

1

The coupe purred up the winding highway. Adele Blane's dark eyes, usually so expressive, were now held in a hard focus of intense concentration as she guided the car around the curves. She was twenty-five, but, as her sister Milicent had once said, "Adele *never* looks her age. She either looks five years younger, or twenty years older."

At her side, Harley Raymand held the door handle, so that swaying around the curves wouldn't swing his weight over against his left elbow. The Army surgeons had managed to fix up the joint. "It'll be stiff for a while," they had told him, "and it'll hurt. Try and work that stiffness out. Keep from jarring it as much as you can."

A few hundred feet below the car, jumping from foam-flecked rocks to dark, cool pools, a mountain stream churned over boulders, laughed back the sunlight in sparkling reflections, filled the canyon with the sound of tumbling water.

The road crossed the mountain torrent on a suspension bridge, started a slanting climb up the other side of the canyon, mounted at length to a pine-clad plateau.

Off to the left, the Southern California sunlight turned the towering granite mountains into a dazzling brilliance which made the shadows below seem as blotches of ink. The road wound along a plateau region where pine trees oozed scent into the warm dry air. Far off to the right, the heat-haze which enveloped the lowlands looked like molten brass whipped up to a creamy consistency and poured into the valley.

"Tired?" Harley Raymand asked Adele.

"No—a little worried, that's all."

She negotiated a sharp turn, concentrating on the road. Then, on a brief straightaway, flashed him a glance. "I'll bet *you're* tired," she said suddenly. "Almost your first day home, and I drag you up here to Dad's cabin. . . . And you had your talk at the luncheon club, too."

Harley said quietly, "No, I'm not tired. . . . I'd just forgotten there were places like this, and now I'm getting reacquainted with them."

"Didn't your talk at the luncheon club tire you?"

"Not me," he laughed, "only the audience."

"Harley, you know I didn't mean it that way."

"I know."

"What did you tell them?"

"I guess they expected the usual flag-waving. I didn't give it to them. I told them this time war was a business —and they'd have to work at it just as they worked at their businesses, without fanfare and bands and hullabaloo. And I told them we'd get licked if we *didn't* work at it."

Adele Blane said suddenly, "Harley, are you going to work for Father?"

"He telephoned me to drop in and see him when I had a little time and knew what I wanted to do."

"He needs someone like you, someone he can trust . . . not like— Oh well."

"Jack Hardisty, eh? Didn't that turn out all right, Adele?"

"Let's not talk about it," she said shortly. Then, apologizing for her shortness, "No, it definitely didn't turn out all right, but I'd rather not discuss it."

"Okay."

She flashed him a quick glance. The indifference in his

2

voice was new to her. In many ways this man was a stranger. A year ago she had known his every mood. Now he could surprise her. It was as though the Kenvale world were being viewed in his mind through the wrong end of a telescope, as though things which loomed important in her mind seemed merely trivial in his.

The road entered another steep canyon, climbing sharply. At the summit of this grade Adele turned sharply to the left, ran up a grade to a plateau where the cabin, nestling at the apex of a triangular slope, looked as though it had grown there as naturally as the pine trees.

It was one story, with a wide porch running across the front and one side. The rail of the porch and the pillars were of small logs from which the bark had been removed. The outside was of shakes, and the weather had aged them until the cabin blended into the green of the background and the brown pine needles of the foreground.

"Look natural?" she asked him.

He nodded.

For a moment she thought he was bored, then she caught sight of his eyes.

"I've thought about this place a lot," he said. "It represents something that's hard to find these days—tranquillity. . . . How long will we be up here?"

"Not long."

"Can I help?"

"No, it's just a checking up, looking over the canned goods, seeing what needs to be done. You stay out in the sunshine and rest."

She watched him get out of the car, saving his left elbow. "You know your way around," she said. "There'll be some cold water in the spring."

She hurried on into the cabin, opening windows, airing the place out. Harley walked around the trail to the deep shadows where crystal-clear, cold water trickled out of the spring. He used the graniteware cup to take a deep drink, then strolled out to a patch of sunlight beside a flat rock. His view took in the long slope across the deep canyon, now beginning to fill with purple shadows. There wasn't enough wind to start the faintest murmur in the tops of the pines. The sky was cloudless blue. The mountains rolled in undulating pastels except where jagged crags ripped their way into glittering pinnacles.

Harley propped his head back against a pine-needle cushion, half closed his eyes, experiencing that sudden fatigue which comes to men whose reserve strength has been sapped by wounds. He felt as though the effort of moving even an arm would require a superhuman expenditure of energy.

"Tick-tick-tick-tick-tick-tick-tick-tick."

Harley opened his eyes. A fleeting expression of annoyance crossed his face. He wanted so much to have utter silence, for just a few moments . . .

"Tick-tick-tick-tick-tick-tick-tick-tick."

Surely his watch couldn't be making that much noise. The thing seemed to be coming from the ground right by his ear.

He shifted his position and folded his coat into a pillow. The sound of the ticking was no longer audible. He was lying flat now, looking up at the lacework of pine branches traced against the blue sky. He was completely, utterly weary, wanting only to lie there, as though he were a pine needle which had drifted down to the ground to soak up oblivion.

He wakened with a start, opened his eyes, caught the lines of a shapely ankle and leg, the hem of a sport skirt.

Adele Blane, sitting on the rock beside him, smiled down at him with that tenderness which women have for men who are recuperating from wounds received in combat. "Feel better?"

"Heavens, yes. What time is it?"

"Around four."

"Gosh, I must have been asleep for a couple of hours."

"Not much over an hour, I guess. Did you go to sleep right after I left you?"

"Yes. I—I felt as though someone had pulled a plug in my feet and let all my vitality run out."

They both laughed. "And you're feeling better now?"

"Like a million dollars! That nap brought back my strength. . . . Ready to start back?"

"Uh huh, if you are."

He raised himself to a sitting position, shook out the coat, asked, "What's the clockwork mechanism for, Adele?"

"What clockwork mechanism?"

"I don't know. It probably regulates something. You can hear it over at the corner of the rock. That's why I moved."

He caught the significance of her glance and laughed outright. "Do you really think I have spells of delirium?"

She joined his laughter at once, but her laughter lacked spontaneity.

Slightly irritated, Harley said, "You can hear it for yourself, over at that corner of the rock."

She bent down, more as a courtesy than out of curiosity, quite evidently expecting to hear nothing.

He was watching her face when her detachment gave way to a sudden flare of puzzled bewilderment.

"That's what I meant," Harley said with dignity.

"It sounds—Harley, it sounds like a clock! It *is* a clock! It's right here!"

He scooped away the pine needles, clearing a small section of earth, and disclosed the lid of a lacquered tin box which had been buried with great care in the soil. He raised the lid.

Within the box, held securely upright by wooden blocks, a small-sized alarm clock was ticking steadily. It was, Harley saw, a clock made by one of the best-known manufacturers. Aside from the peculiar bracing, there seemed to be nothing unusual in its appearance. There were two small holes in the lacquered box.

Harley consulted his watch. "It's exactly twenty-five minutes slow. You wouldn't think it would be *that* far off. It's a good grade of clock. Notice this lid. It's almost flush with the ground. Just a few pine needles and a little moss have been placed over it."

"What a strange way to bury a clock!" Adele exclaimed.

Raymand laughed. "I don't know just what *is* the standard of normal in clock-burying. Personally, it's the first time I've ever heard of a buried clock. Are we—"

The sound of an automobile engine reached their ears, the motor of a car that was climbing rapidly.

Harley listened, said, "Sounds to me as though they're taking the road up here. Let's just drop the clock back into the box, put the pine needles over it, and stroll up toward the cabin. Perhaps whoever is coming in that car will—"

"Go ahead," she said. "You'll have to hurry."

Harley dropped the lid back on the box, deftly replaced the pine needles and little fragments of moss. "All ready," he said, taking Adele's arm.

Momentarily a clump of brush masked them as a car swung around the curve in the roadway to emerge on the little plateau. For a moment it was merely an indistinct object moving through the afternoon shadows cast by the trees. Then, as it debouched into a sun-flecked opening, it resolved itself into a two-tone blue coupe.

"It's Jack Hardisty's car!" Adele exclaimed.

Abruptly the car came to a stop. The door opened.

6

Jack Hardisty scrambled out to the needle-carpeted clearing.

Adele Blane's hand rested on Harley's arm as he started to move out from behind the brush. *"Don't!* Wait here, *please!"*

They stood motionless, watching Hardisty reach into the interior of the car, pull out a long-bladed garden spade, and start toward the outcropping of rock. Then he stopped abruptly as he saw the indistinct figures behind the brush.

For a moment the pair were gripped in that rigid immobility that comes with discovery. Then they broke into the stiff action pattern of those who are trying consciously to act naturally—and making a dismal failure of it.

"Walk out from behind the brush as though we hadn't seen him," Adele coached in a low voice.

Harley Raymand felt the pressure of her hand on his arm. They moved awkwardly from behind the brush into the patch of afternoon sunlight. From the corner of his eye, Harley saw Jack Hardisty hastily push the spade back into the car. Adele, now in plain sight, registered a surprise which, to Harley's self-conscious embarrassment, seemed as obvious as the overdone pantomime acting of the silent screen.

"Why, there's a car—it's Jack!"

She had raised her voice so it would carry, and her attempt at surprise left Harley with no alternative save to follow suit.

Hardisty came walking toward them.

He was narrow across the shoulders, pinched in the face, but his double-breasted gray suit had the unwrinkled neatness which is found only in the clothes worn by thin men whose pores exude a minimum of body moisture. His nose was prominent, high-bridged, and supported bowless glasses.

"Well, *well!*" he exclaimed. "It's our hero returned from the wars! How *are* you, Harley? Hello, Adele."

The hearty, man-to-man enthusiasm of Jack Hardisty was overdone. He hadn't the capacity of lusty emotions, and his attempt to put punch into his greeting was so synthetic it carried its own stigma of insincerity.

Harley Raymand couldn't bring himself to respond to Hardisty's vociferous cordiality. Adele Blane held herself aloof, and the first rush of sentences stagnated into a slow-flowing trickle of conversation.

"Well," Hardisty said, "I want to get on up to the cabin. Lost my favorite knife when I was up here a week ago. . . . Thought I might have left it out around the grounds, or perhaps it dropped down behind the cushions in that big chair."

"A week ago," Adele said musingly. "Why, I didn't think anyone had been up here for ages. The cabin didn't look as though it had even been opened."

"Oh, I didn't straighten it up any, just ran up for a few hours' rest. . . . Like to get away from the noises and the blare of radios. It's peaceful up here, helps you reach a decision when—"

He became abruptly silent.

Adele said with dignity, "We were just leaving. I was looking the place over. Dad is coming up tomorrow night. Are you ready, Harley?"

He nodded.

"Hope you find your knife," Harley said politely, as they started toward the place where Adele had left her car.

Hardisty became instantly effusive. "Thanks, old man! Thanks a lot! Hope that arm doesn't give you any trouble. Take care of yourself. Don't try to do everything all at once. Take it easy, boy. Take it easy."

It was not until after they had reached the foot of the grade and were on the straight stretch leading to Kenvale, that Adele suddenly gave vent to her feelings. "I *hate* him," she said.

"He'd do a lot better if he acted naturally," Harley agreed. "Someone's sold him on the idea of impressing people with his personality. He just hasn't that kind of a personality. It's as though a dummy tried to do a strip tease."

"It isn't that," she said. "I can stand that stuff, because I think he has an inferiority complex; but it's what he's done to Father."

Harley started to ask a question then thought better of it.

Adele said, "He's short over ten thousand dollars at his bank. You know as well as I do, it was Dad's money and Dad's influence that got him in over there."

"I'm afraid I'm a little out of touch with things," Harley apologized.

"Dad started a bank in Roxbury, made a six-thousand-dollar-a-year job for Jack—just because he was Milicent's husband."

Harley remained silent.

"Jack Hardisty," Adele went on, "has been reading books on salesmanship and on influencing people. He hides his half-starved, whimpering soul behind the mask of a big, bluff, backslapping paragon of pep. . . . It's all I can do to keep my hands off of him."

"The shortage known?" Harley asked.

"Only the bank directors and the bonding company. Dad had guaranteed the bonding company against loss on Jack's policy. They didn't want to write it—something in Jack's past. I suppose Dad's got to make it good and hush it up and—I shouldn't have shot off steam about this, Harley. Forget it, will you?"

Harley smiled at her. "It's forgotten."

She realized that a year ago this would have absorbed his thoughts and dominated their conversation. Now he

9

apparently dismissed it from his mind as a minor matter. She said, "That's why Dad needs someone he can *trust*."

He might not have heard her, or hearing, might not have realized the implications to himself. He merely asked, "Why did Jack bury that clock up at the cabin?"

"Do you think he did?"

"He certainly was starting over toward that granite outcropping, and he'd taken a shovel from the car."

She said, "I've been trying to think that out. I can't understand it. I—why, here comes Milicent's car! She—"

Adele broke off talking, to wave frantically at an approaching light convertible. The car slowed to a stop. Milicent Blane's eyes regarded them from behind neat-fitting, rimless spectacles. Impatient with the life of idleness which was open to her as the daughter of Vincent Blane, she had studied to become a registered nurse. Her marriage had interrupted her career, filling her at first with a radiant happiness which had withered almost as it bloomed. Her face, never very expressive, had become a mask of grave immobility.

"Hello! Been up to the cabin? Why, hello, *Harley!* I didn't recognize you for a minute! Well, *how* are you?"

Harley Raymand opened the door of Adele's car, walked around to shake hands with Milicent.

"It certainly *is* good to see you. They told us you were pretty well shot up. . . . Are you feeling all right now?"

"Tough as taxes. I'm glad to see you again."

She turned to Adele. "Been up to the cabin?"

Adele nodded.

"Did you—I mean—was . . . ?"

"Yes," Adele interrupted, reading her thoughts. "He came up just as we were leaving."

Milicent's attempt to be courteous, to show a polite interest in Harley's return yet get started for the cabin

10

without so much as a minute's delay, made her rather confused.

"Well, it's nice to have seen you," she said, slipping the car into gear and holding out the clutch. "I hope we'll be seeing you. Hope you see us—I mean I hope you'll—oh, we'll get together."

Her foot slid back. The car lurched ahead.

Adele watched her dubiously for a few moments, then started on toward Kenvale. "The rat," she muttered savagely under her breath, "isn't good enough to be her doormat."

"She knows about what's happened?"

"I don't think so. I certainly hope not."

"Then why was she in such a dither to locate her husband?" Harley asked.

"Because there are—domestic troubles, too. Let's not talk about Jack. . . . Where are you staying, Harley?"

"At the hotel."

Adele's foot pushed down on the throttle. After the tire-conserving pace at which she had been operating the car, the new speed seemed terrific, although the speedometer showed it as only fifty-five miles an hour.

She laughed apologetically. "I just thought of an appointment I had. I'm going to be late. . . . That's the trouble with you, Harley: you make me forget things. And here it is almost sunset."

2

■

Harley Raymand showered, stretched out on the bed, and almost instantly sank into exhausted lethargy. The speech at the luncheon club, his trip to the cabin, had used up energy, and he was being forced to a realization that his available store of energy was limited. Those bullets had sapped more of his strength than he had thought possible.

The telephone rang sharply, and the convulsive start with which he regained wakefulness made him realize just how nervous he was. He switched on the lights, answered the phone.

The voice of the switchboard operator advised him that a Mr. Vincent P. Blane was waiting in the lobby.

"Blane!" Harley repeated, in surprise. "Tell him— Tell him I'm dressing. It'll be ten minutes before I can join him in the lobby. If he's in a hurry, he can come on up here."

Harley dropped the receiver into place, put on his shirt and trousers, and was just putting on his shoes when he heard Blane's knock at the door.

It had been but little more than a year since Harley had last seen Adele's father, yet he was shocked at the change in the man. Definitely, he was older, more worried. There was still the same charm of manner—that courteous interest in others which was neither effusive on the one hand, nor patronizing on the other, but had the graciousness of dignity about it.

Harley knew that Blane's errand was important, could

see that he was under a great strain, yet the man wouldn't think of mentioning his problem until after he had done those things which were demanded by courtesy: an apology for his intrusion, a solicitous inquiry after Harley's health.

"I'm sorry," Blane began, "if I wakened—"

"It's all right," Harley interposed, trying to make things easier. "I'm just a little lazy these days. Was there something I could do for you, Mr. Blane?"

Under the bushy eyebrows, Blane's keen gray eyes showed gratitude. "Mighty nice of you to make such a suggestion, Harley. . . . As a matter of fact I'm a little worried about Adele."

"What about her?"

"You were with her this afternoon?"

"Yes. We went up to the cabin."

"What time did you come back?"

Harley looked at his watch. "Why, I've been here in the hotel for about an hour and a half, I guess, perhaps two hours."

"She hasn't been home. I was rather expecting her."

"She said she had an appointment she'd forgotten about," Harley explained reassuringly. "She was speeding up a bit to get me here. . . . Won't you sit down, Mr. Blane?"

"I feel that I've put you to a lot of trouble," Blane apologized. "I shouldn't have disturbed you. I—"

Harley laughed. "I was just digesting some of the health I absorbed up at your cabin this afternoon. I think it's the first time I've really relaxed."

Blane nodded in mechanical acquiescence, his mind apparently occupied with something else. Then suddenly he shot a quick glance at Harley. "How'd you like to stay up there for a few days?"

"At the cabin?"

"Yes."

13

"Why—wouldn't that inconvenience you?"

"Not at all."

"I understood you had a meeting—"

"I'd prefer to hold it at my house. I'd like to have you up there, Harley. Of course, you'd have to do your own cooking, but—"

Harley smiled as Blane hesitated. "If you're really serious, there's nothing I'd like better."

"See anyone up at the cabin this afternoon?" Blane asked, trying to make his voice sound casual.

"Why, yes. Jack Hardisty came up there."

Blane gnawed at his close-clipped, gray moustache. "Notice anything strange about him?" he asked abruptly.

Harley said, "His manner seemed to be much the same as usual."

"Yes, yes, I know," Blane said. "Reminds you of a firecracker trying to pretend it's a cannon. I want you to do something for me. You'll be well paid, and a little later on, we can talk about something permanent. I want you to go up to that cabin now, tonight. Keep an eye on anything that goes on up there."

Harley hesitated.

Blane, noticing that hesitancy, said, "You can rest assured that whatever compensation—"

"It isn't that," Harley interpolated. "I'm wondering exactly what I'm supposed to do."

Blane said, "I'll tell you a secret. Adele doesn't know it. Milicent doesn't know. . . . Jack Hardisty is short ten thousand dollars over at the Roxbury bank. Adele probably told you that. Here's what she *doesn't* know. Jack expected, of course, I'd make his shortage good in case he was discovered, and hush the whole thing up. I fooled him. I told him I was damned if I was going to. . . . Damned little pipsqueak! I don't consider him one of the family. I know how it would hurt Milicent to have a scandal like that, but it's better to have it happen

14

now and get it over with. He's just a cunning little adventurer who insinuated himself into the family by sweeping Milicent off her feet. Milicent hadn't had much attention paid to her by the local boys. She'd never had any experience with what we call fortune hunters. . . . I didn't have the heart to tell her. No one did. . . . You *couldn't* tell her. There was just a chance Jack really was all wrapped up in her. He said he was. She thought he was. She wanted him—oh, well, you're not interested in all this."

Harley started to say something, but Blane held up his hand. "Here's the low-down. I told Hardisty I wasn't going to make good. He could face the music. . . . Know what he did?"

Harley shook his head.

"That's what comes of not having him thrown in jail like a common criminal. He cleaned out everything in the bank—about ninety thousand dollars in cash. Then he telephoned me and told me what he'd done; said that if I wanted to make good the ten thousand, I'd get the rest of the assets back; that if he was going to jail he'd as soon be hung for a sheep as a lamb, and he was going to make it worth his while. He'd have a stake when he came out. . . . That's the kind of a cur he is.

"If he went up to the cabin, he quite probably went up there to find a hiding place for the stuff. If he's buried it there, we'll have to find it. How about going up and—"

Harley Raymand opened the closet door, pulled out his coat.

"I'm ready to start any time, Mr. Blane."

Blane said, "You haven't had dinner. You go to the dining room and get yourself some dinner. Don't hurry. It will be at least an hour or an hour and a half before I'm ready to leave. I'll drive you up there myself. Just take your time. . . . I'd appreciate it if you'd be waiting in the lobby so you can hop right in when I come back. . . . And I'm deeply grateful, my boy. Having you up there will take a load off my mind."

3
■

The cabin was more isolated than ever at night. The absolute silence out on the porch made one conscous of his ears, set up a vague ringing rhythm within the eardrums. The blazing stars seemed to hang just above the tops of the pine trees. Harley had the feeling that he could stand on the porch with a .22 rifle and shoot them down, as though they were lighted Christmas tree ornaments hanging from the dome of the sky.

The evening had turned chill, with that peculiar penetrating cold which comes at night in the high places, which gets into the blood and settles around the marrow of the bones.

Mr. Blane had left at once, and Harley laid a fire in the wood stove and lit it. The dry pine crackled into cheery flame. When the warmth touched him, Harley realized how cold he had really been, and began to shiver. He took blankets from the windowseat in the front room, and made up a bed on the spring cot on the front porch.

He had returned to the warmth of the fire, when a board on the porch creaked. Listening, he felt certain he heard the sound of cautious steps.

Harley slipped through the doorway into the kitchen, closing the connecting door to shut out the light, and stood with his face pressed against the window.

16

There was someone on the porch, someone who moved with catlike stealth, trying to peer through the side windows without being seen.

Harley tried in vain to recognize the figure. He closed his eyes for a few seconds to adjust them to the darkness. When he opened them again, the figure was still there peering in at the side window. Apparently the man had found a crack of visibility between the drapes, because Harley could see a very faint line of light across his face, a thread-like strip which looked as though it had been ruled with a luminous pencil.

When Harley was on the point of going out to challenge the intruder, he saw the figure move cautiously around to the front of the house.

"Halloooooo! Anybody home?"

The voice was almost instantly swallowed up in the unechoing silence.

Harley went at once to stand by the front door, but didn't open it.

"Who is it?" he called.

"There's been an accident."

"Where?"

"Down the road a piece."

"Were you hurt?"

"No, but I need your help."

Harley flung open the door.

The man who stood facing him was twenty-seven or twenty-eight years old. He had a somewhat whimsical smile, but his eyes stared with disconcerting steadiness. The mouth was well formed, the hair black and tangled, pushed back and partially held in place by a broad-brimmed, battered felt hat. He was short—not over five feet three or four inches—and slender, but he carried himself with an air, and his motions indicated a hard, muscled body.

17

"I didn't know anyone was living here," he explained apologetically.

"I haven't been here very long," Harley admitted, and then added quickly, "You seem familiar with the property."

The other laughed. "I'm a next-door neighbor—in a way of speaking. My cabin's on down the road half a mile."

Harley extended his hand, introduced himself. The other said, "I'm Burton Strague. I'm a writer of sorts. My sister and I have rented the Brigham cabin. We're heating it with rejection slips."

"I think I know the place," Harley said. "Won't you come in?"

"Thanks, but I'm looking for help. A car went off the road down here. I was going up to see if Rod Beaton would come along and give us a hand. Then I saw your light and wondered who was in here. The cabin hasn't been tenanted for months. . . . Belongs to a Vincent Blane, doesn't it?"

"Yes. . . . Who's this other man you mentioned?"

"Rodney Beaton, the artist, naturalist and wild-life photographer. It was through him we came up here. I became acquainted with him by correspondence. He bought one of the cabins up here not very long ago. . . . How about coming along and giving a hand with that car?"

"How far is it," Harley asked, and then added quickly by way of explanation, "I'm convalescing."

The other looked at him quickly, sudden respect in his eyes.

"Army?"

"Yes."

"Gosh, how I wanted to go, but I'm T.B. All right, I guess, as long as I stay quiet, but—a man hates to stay quiet while there's shooting going on. . . . That accident's

18

about a quarter of a mile down the road. You hadn't better tackle it if you're not feeling fit. It's getting a little crimpy outside."

"A quarter of a mile," Harley said. "That would put it right down—"

"Just beyond where this road joins the main highway. Fellow must have been going pretty fast and missed the curve. A two-tone blue job. I don't think anyone's under it, but we ought to make sure. We'll have to get help to lift the car. That's why I'm—"

"I'll go," Harley said, trying to keep expression from his face as he realized the description of the car was that of the one Jack Hardisty had been driving. "You don't think the driver's pinned under the car?"

"I doubt it," Strague said. "Sis is staying down there so in case there are any sounds of life under the car she can tell the injured driver help is on the way. If you want to go down, I'll run up to Beaton's place and we'll join you within a half hour."

"All right," Harley said, "I'll start just as soon as I get on my coat and take a look at the fire."

Harley went back to the kitchen and closed the dampers on the stove. He returned to the front room, turned off the gasoline lantern, belted his heavy overcoat about him and took the precaution of locking up. He slipped a flashlight in his pocket and started down the roadway.

As he descended into the little draw, it became measurably colder. Occasionally he used the beam of his flashlight to guide him through some shadowed twist in the road. Then, almost before he knew it, he was at the intersection with the main road. . . . If a car had gone off, it must have been right at the turn, about ten yards below. . . . A two-tone blue job. That certainly sounded like Jack Hardisty's automobile.

Raymand switched on his flashlight, holding the beam down in the road, looking for tracks. He found, without

19

difficulty, where the car had gone off. The tracks were plain, once you started looking for them, although he certainly hadn't noticed them when Mr. Blane had driven him up to the cabin. . . . In a way, he shouldn't have left that cabin. And yet, if this should turn out to be Jack Hardisty's car, and—

"*Yoohoo,*" a feminine voice called from the darkness down below the bank.

"Hello," Harley called. "Are you Miss Strague?"

"Yes."

He saw her, then, standing about halfway down a steep declivity, her shoulder resting against a tall pine. "You hadn't better try coming straight down," she warned. "You can go down the road about twenty or thirty yards and work your way down a little ridge. Even then you'll have to be careful."

Harley said, "Your brother and the man he went to get should show up soon. I'm from the Blane cabin up here. . . . How far is the wreck from where you're standing?"

"It's directly below me, thirty or forty feet. I don't think anyone's in it."

Harley walked down the road and found the sharp ridge the girl had mentioned. Even with the aid of his flashlight, it took him several minutes to get down to join Burton Strague's sister.

She was tall and slender. He could tell that much about her, although he couldn't see her features distinctly, much as he wanted to. Courtesy demanded he keep the beam of his flashlight from her eyes. Her voice sounded cultured, the voice of a young woman who is well poised and very certain of herself.

Harley Raymand introduced himself. He tried to avoid mentioning his military service, but he felt the searching gaze of her eyes. Then she said suddenly, "Oh yes,

20

you're from the Army. I should have known. You're the man we read about in the Kenvale paper."

Harley tried to detour the subject by moving over to where he could inspect the car. It was Jack Hardisty's car beyond question. It was lying on its top, the wheels in the air, the body jammed down between huge boulders.

"I haven't heard the faintest sound," Lola Strague said. "If anyone's in it, he must be dead. . . . So you're *the* Harley Raymand I've been reading about!"

There followed ten or fifteen minutes during which Harley found himself answering polite, adroit, but pointed, questions. Then they heard the sound of an automobile on the road above, the slamming of a car door. Someone stumbled, and a little rock rolled and clattered down the steep slope to plunge with a rattling escort of loose gravel to a final resting place in the canyon.

"Cease firing," Lola Strague called with a laugh. "Did you bring an ax?"

Burt Strague's voice sounded from above. "I brought an ax, a flashlight, and a rope from the house. I couldn't get Rod. There's a note on his door saying he's gone to town for the evening. I waited five or ten minutes, hanging around the place, hoping he'd show up. . . . Did Mr. Raymand find you?"

"I'm here," Harley Raymand called.

"Well, I think the three of us can do the job. I'll double the rope around a tree and slide down it. Look out, here I come. I—wait a minute, I think I hear a car coming."

They listened, and could hear the sound of an automobile coming rapidly up the grade. Then, after a moment, they saw the reflections of headlights shining against the tops of trees, shifting from the bank on the left of the grade to the dark abyss of blackness which marked the canyon. A few moments later the headlights steadied, to send a stream of brilliant illumination flow-

21

ing directly along the road above. The motor abruptly changed its tempo. There was the sound of brakes and then Burt Strague's voice calling, "I wonder if you can give us a hand. There's a car down here and—"

Masculine laughter boomed from above. There was the sound of a car door slamming, then a deep bass voice said, "Well, don't be so damned formal about it."

Lola Strague said, parenthetically, to Harley Raymand, "That's Rod Beaton now. He must be coming back from town."

A woman's voice said, "Why, hello, Burt."

"Hello, Myrna."

Lola Strague added, "Myrna Payson," and with sudden bitterness, "our local glamour girl."

From the road above there drifted down low-voiced conversation, the boom of Rodney Beaton's heavy laughter. Harley Raymand caught also the tinkle of Myrna Payson's light laugh. Standing in the darkness, apparently forgotten by those above, Harley had an opportunity to appreciate the significance of what Lola Strague had said. Myrna Payson's presence seemed to distract the attention of both men from the car at the bottom of the canyon and the people who waited there.

Lola Strague made no further comment, but in the rigid formality of her seething silence, Harley Raymand could feel her anger.

For what seemed almost two minutes, the little group up on the roadway chatted and laughed. Then Harley Raymand saw a broad-shouldered giant silhouetted against the illumination of the headlights. Rodney Beaton, standing on the edge of the embankment, looking down into the darkness called good-naturedly, "What have you got down there?"

"A wrecked car," Lola Strague said crisply, and added nothing whatever to those three essential words.

At the tone of her voice, Rodney Beaton seemed suddenly anxious to make amends for his apparent neglect. He became instantly the energetic executive, assuming complete control.

"All right, Burt, you say you have a rope. Let's double it around this tree. I'll slide down it and you can follow. Then we'll pull the rope down after us. . . . You'd better stay here and watch the road, Myrna."

Beaton's voice was quietly authoritative. He somehow had the knack of getting things done. The scene almost instantly became efficiently active.

Rodney Beaton came down the rope first, sliding and slipping directly down the steep declivity, sending a shower of loose gravel rattling on ahead of him. Burt Strague followed, and Myrna Payson came to the edge of the roadway to stand outlined against the illumination reflected back from the car's headlights.

Harley Raymand had a confused overlapping of impressions: the young woman standing up on the side of the roadway; the headlights faintly silhouetting her figure through her clothes, an attractive young woman who might not have been entirely unaware that the illumination was turning her skirt into a shadow gown—Burt Strague, slender, seeming somehow inefficient as he floundered and scrambled down the rope, his feet shooting out from under him on two or three occasions—Rodney Beaton, a good-natured giant, making every move count. . . . Then Lola Strague was performing introductions and Harley's hand was gripped by Rodney Beaton's powerful fingers.

Harley saw that Beaton was some ten years older than Burt Strague. He was tall, powerful, loose-jointed, not fat, but thick. He had a smiling mouth, a firm jaw and was wearing a western hat of the type generally referred to as a "five gallon."

In the light reflected from the beam of the five-cell flashlight Rod Beaton was holding, Harley had a chance to get a better look at Lola Strague. She was blonde, not

23

more than twenty-two or twenty-three, attired in a heavy checkered woolen shirt, open low at the throat, a plaid woolen jacket, trousers and laced boots. She gave the impression of being quite competently a part of the out-doors, of wearing clothes that were warm, strong, and made for service.

The beam of the flashlight darted down into the black canyon, licked over boulders and fallen trees, then came to rest on the overturned car.

Rod Beaton seemed thoroughly at home, thoroughly capable of handling a situation such as that. He said, "We won't try any salvage work, just make sure there's no one in the car and then quit. . . . I think we can cut down the tree, Burt. If you'll hold the flashlight, I'll swing the ax. We'll use it as a lever and raise the car so we can see the interior."

Strague held the flashlight. Beaton swung the light ax with a smooth rhythm of powerful shoulders, the gleam-ing blade biting deep into the wood with every swing. It seemed to Harley that it took no more than four or five swinging blows to sever the tree neatly through. Then Beaton trimmed off the little limbs and the top, and had a pole some fifteen feet long and ten inches in diameter at the butt.

Calmly, competently, he assumed command, issuing quiet instructions, treating Harley Raymand with the same assurance he displayed toward Burt and Lola Strague.

"Now, Raymand, if you'll get out on the far end of that pole. Just sit on it. Don't try to use that bad el-bow. . . . Burt, you and Lola get on each side as near the end as you can. Let me guide this end of it. . . . All right, now put a little pressure on it."

They came down on the end of the pole. The car groaned and scraped, then raised up. Beaton blocked it with rocks, said, "All right. Take the pressure off the

24

pole. Let me give you a new purchase. . . . Okay, here we go again."

Once more the car moved.

Beaton said, "We can see in it now," and the beam of his spotlight showed windows that were cobwebbed with glass fractures and illuminated an empty interior.

"No one in here," Beaton said. "Let's take a look and see if he was thrown clear."

The flashlight swung around in ever widening circles.

"No sign of him," Beaton said.

Abruptly Harley asked, "Can you get a good look at the interior of that car, Beaton, and see if there's a spade in there?"

At the sudden, complete silence which greeted his request, Harley realized how peculiar it sounded.

"You see," he added, by way of explanation, "I think I know that car. If it's the one I think it is, there should be a spade in back of the front seat."

"Okay, I'll take a look," Beaton said. "You don't know the license number?"

"No," Raymand added somewhat lamely. "It was a car that was up at the cabin this afternoon."

"I see. . . . No, there doesn't seem to be any spade in it."

Lola Strague said, "Well, we've discharged our duties as Good Samartians. I guess there's nothing to do now except get back to the road."

Rodney Beaton climbed up the steep slope as far as he could, then, coiling the rope, said to Myrna Payson, "Catch an end of this and loop it around that tree, will you, Myrna?"

With a heave of his powerful shoulders, Beaton sent the rope snaking up against the glow of the headlights, and as Myrna Payson caught the end and doubled it around the tree, she moved with a certain lithe grace, a deft co-ordination of arms and legs that accomplished her

25

task and sent the loose end of the rope back down to Rodney Beaton in a surprisingly short time.

With the aid of the rope, they went up the steep incline to the road with relative ease.

Harley Raymand was left until last. He called up, "I'm afraid to trust this arm. I think I'd better—"

"Not at all," Beaton interrupted heartily. "Just loop the rope around your waist and knot it with a bowline. . . . Can you tie a bowline?"

"I think so," Harley said.

"Wait a minute. I'll tie one and toss it down to you."

Beaton's hands made two or three swift passes over the rope, then a loop came down to Raymand. He stepped inside it, raised it to his waist, took hold with his right hand, and leaning against the rope and using his legs, was pulled up the steep pitch.

At the top he was presented to Myrna Payson, who was, as Rodney Beaton gravely explained, a neighboring cattle rancher. One look at Myrna Payson's wide-spaced, laughing eyes, her full, vivid-red lips, and Harley knew why Rodney Beaton and Burt Strague had been so preoccupied up there on the road. Her skin showed the result of care. Her clothes followed the lines of her figure with a well-fitting grace that to a woman would mean she "could wear anything." Men would see only the effect. As Harley studied her, Myrna Payson's eyes in turn took him in from head to toe and made a careful and frankly personal appraisal of him.

In the quick burst of general conversation which followed the introduction, Harley gathered that the car, an old model coupe, belonged to Rodney Beaton; that, in the interest of "conserving rubber and gas," he had "picked up his neighbor" in the early evening for a trip to town. Harley also gathered that Lola Strague definitely resented this. . . . Then of a sudden, Harley felt

26

too utterly wearied to remain interested in the affairs of this little group.

"I'm going to say good night, if you don't mind," he said. "I've had rather a trying day."

"Oh, but let me drive you up to your cabin," Burt Strague said quickly.

Harley didn't look forward to the walk with any degree of pleasure, yet he said, "Oh that's all right. I'd just as soon walk."

"Nonsense," Lola said firmly. "Burt will drive you up. Come on. Get in."

Lola Strague jumped into the car in the middle of the front seat. Harley climbed in beside her, and Burt twisted himself in behind the steering wheel. Rodney Beaton seemed, for a moment, ill at ease. It was as though he had hoped to get Lola Strague off to one side for a word in private before leaving. But Myrna Payson called out, "Come on, Rod. We've got to get our car out of the way so they can turn around."

Beaton still hesitated.

Burt Strague said, "The nearest telephone is at the ranger station three miles up that road, Rod. I'll drive Raymand up to his cabin. You might go on up to the ranger station and notify the sheriff."

After that it seemed a good five seconds before Beaton said, "I guess that's the thing to do. Good night, everyone."

No one tried to make conversation as Burt Strague piloted the car up to the cabin. And Harley was glad of it. He felt too tired even to talk.

They deposited him in front of the cabin. Burt said good night, and added something about hoping to see more of him and trusting the experience hadn't been too much for him. Lola Strague gave him her hand, said, "Hope you'll be all right, and we'll be seeing you again."

There was someting of finality in her comments, but

Burt waited for two or three seconds, then said, "Well, good night," and turned the car.

Harley felt positive that Burt had been hoping for an invitation to come in.

Harley, climbing the three steps to the porch, realized that once more he was completely exhausted. He had intended to look for the buried clock, but felt able to do no more than crawl into the bed he had made out on the porch. He fell asleep almost instantly.

It was an hour before sunrise when he opened his eyes to find the air crisp with cold. He snuggled down into the warm blankets and amused himself by fastening his eyes upon one particular star, trying to keep it from receding to nothing in the growing light. But the star eluded him, vanished, and Harley couldn't find it again. Smiling drowsily over his failure, he drifted off to sleep once more. The sun was warm on the porch when he finally awakened.

Harley knew as soon as he threw back the covers that he was feeling much stronger. The fresh mountain air had drained poisons from his system, and for the first time in weeks he actually wanted food—and lots of it.

He lit the oil stove, cooked coffee, eggs, bacon, toast and cereal—and then thought of the buried clock.

While the dishwater was heating, Harley went out to the porch, and then walked down the sloping, needle-carpeted grounds. He found the spot he wanted without difficulty and swept away the covering of pine needles.

The clock was ticking merrily away.

Harley compared it with his watch.

The clock was still exactly twenty-five minutes slow.

Harley replaced the box, carefully put the pine needles and moss back into place and returned to the cabin. The water was not yet hot enough for the dishes. There were no dishtowels in sight, but Harley remembered that linen was stored in a big cedar chest in the back bedroom. He opened the door of the bedroom, conscious of the fact that the chill of the night still clung to this room on the north side of the house. He was half-way to the cedar chest before he noticed that the bed was occupied.

For what must have been several seconds, Harley stood motionless with surprise, not knowing whether to withdraw quietly or to speak. Suppose Milicent or Adele had gone to the cabin, exhausted, had climbed into bed, knowing nothing of his subsequent arrival. Harley could sense complications.

The sleeper was facing the window, away from the door. The covers were pulled up in such a way that the head was completely concealed. Harley decided to get it over with.

"Good morning!"

The figure didn't move.

Harley raised his voice, "I don't want to intrude, but I'd like to know who you are." The figure gave no sign of having heard.

Harley walked over to the bed, let his hand fall on the covers over the shoulder—and instantly knew something was radically wrong. . . . He jerked with his right arm, pulling the motionless form toward him.

It was Jack Hardisty.

He had been dead for hours.

4

Perry Mason hummed a little tune as he strolled down the corridor to his office, moving with the leisurely, long-legged rhythm characteristic of him. Walking to meet the adventures of the day, he didn't intend to be too hurried to enjoy them.

He latchkeyed the door of his private office, and caught Della Street's smile as she looked up from the mail.

"What ho!" Mason said. "Another day. . . . How about the dollar, Chancellor of the Exchequer."

Della Street bowed with mock humility. "The dollar awaits, my lord."

Mason lost his bantering tone. "Don't tell me you've scared up a new case."

"We have a potential client."

"In the outer office?"

"No. He's not the type who waits in outer offices." Della Street consulted a memorandum on her desk. "He's a Mr. Vincent P. Blane, a banker and department store owner at Kenvale. He called on long distance, three times within thirty minutes. The first two times he wouldn't talk with anyone except Perry Mason. The third time he consented to talk with Mr. Mason's secretary."

Mason hung his hat in the closet, crossed over to the big desk, selected a cigarette from the office humidor, and said, "I don't like him."

"Why not?"

"He sounds pot-bellied and self-important. What does he want?"

"His son-in-law was murdered in a mountain cabin sometime last night."

Mason scraped a match on the under side of the desk, devoted his attention to lighting the cigarette before asking, "Who's elected as the official suspect?"

"No one."

"Who's nominated?"

"They haven't even made a nomination."

"Then what the devil does Blane want *me* for? I'm not a detective, I'm a lawyer."

She smiled. "It seems there are several family skeletons Mr. Blane wants kept safely in the closet. Naturally, he didn't dare say much on the phone. Both of Mr. Blane's daughters were up at the cabin yesterday afternoon. Mr. Blane himself was also up there. . . . And well, after all, the man has money."

Mason said, "Oh, I suppose I've got to handle it, but it sounds like a legal chore, one of these uninspiring, routine family murders."

Della Street once more consulted her memorandum. "There is, however, one redeeming feature," she added, her eyes twinkling.

"Della, you've been holding out on me!" Mason charged.

"No. I only saved the dessert until last."

"All right, let's have the dessert."

"A buried clock," she said, "which is running about twenty-five minutes slow. It's buried somewhere near the cabin where the murder was committed, a small-edition alarm clock in a lacquered box. It—"

Mason started for the cloak closet.

He called to Della Street as he grabbed his hat. "The clock does it. . . . Come on. Let's go!"

5

■

Mason was advised in Kenvale that the deputy sheriff, a representative of the coroner, Vincent Blane and Harley Raymand had left for the scene of the crime only a few minutes earlier; that Mason could probably catch up with them if he "stepped on it."

Mason duly stepped on it, arriving at the cabin just as the little group was getting ready to leave the chill north bedroom where the body lay just as Raymand had left it.

Mason was acquainted with Jameson, the deputy sheriff, and so was permitted to join the group without question, a tribute to Mason's reputation as well as Blane's local influence.

The lawyer had a glimpse of a cold bedroom, rustic furniture, knotty pine walls, clothes thrown over a chair, shoes placed at the side of the bed, and the stiff, still form of the little man, who, in his lifetime, had tried so desperately to be a magnetic, dominant personality. Now, in death, he seemed shriveled to his true stature, a cold corpse in a cold bedroom.

Mason made a swift survey of the room. "Don't touch anything," the deputy warned.

"I won't," Mason assured him, studying the room carefully.

"He must have undressed, gone to sleep and been killed while he was sleeping," the coroner's representative said.

The deputy sheriff said, "Well he's dead, all right, and

it's murder. I'm going to close this room up and leave things just as they are until someone from the Los Angeles office can get here. . . . Now, let's take a look at this buried clock—although I don't see where it enters into the picture."

The deputy ushered them out of the room, closed and locked the door, and followed Harley out to the warmth of the sloping, sun-bathed clearing.

Harley walked over to the granite rocks. "Now, the clock is buried right about here. You can hear it ticking if you listen."

"Let's take a look," the deputy sheriff said.

Harley got down on his knees, scraped away moss and pine needles. He placed his ear to the ground, then straightened and looked puzzled. "I'm certain this is the place," he said.

The deputy's tone was frankly skeptical. "Doesn't look as though anything had ever been buried there."

"Perhaps it's a little deeper," Blane suggested.

Harley, scraping a wider clearing in the ground, said, "No, the lid of the box was quite close to the surface."

The deputy sheriff kicked the ground with the toe of his boot. "Doesn't look to me as if this place had been disturbed since last winter."

Harley bent over once more to place his ear against the ground.

The deputy sheriff flashed a glance at the coroner's representative.

"I don't hear it ticking now," Harley said.

"You're certain about that clock?"

Harley flushed. "I had it in my hands, took it out of the box. Adele Blane can vouch for that."

Jameson seemed reluctant to extend belief. "And it was there this morning?" he asked.

"Yes."

"*After* you'd found the body?"

"No, just before I found the body."

"But after Hardisty had been killed?"

"Oh yes."

"Well," the deputy said, in the tone of one who wishes to be rid of a matter which may prove embarrassing, "then Jack Hardisty couldn't have taken it, and that's pretty apt to mean it isn't connected with the murder. Now, how about Hardisty's car. You haven't any idea how it got down in that canyon?"

"No."

"Now, I'm just asking this as a question," Jameson said. "There's no call to get up on your ear about it, but it's a question I want you to answer, and answer truthfully. You won't have a second chance at this, Raymand. Your answer's got to stand for all time. . . . You didn't get on the running board of Jack Hardisty's automobile, get it going at a good clip, then step off the running board and let the car go over the grade, did you?"

"Absolutely not."

"Why did Blane ask you to stay up here at the cabin?"

"He wanted the place watched."

"Why was that, Mr. Blane?" the deputy asked.

Before Blane could answer, Harley Raymand said, with a smile, "I think it was an attempt on Mr. Blane's part to be magnanimous. He thought a period of rest and recuperation up here at the cabin would do me good, and he tried to make a job out of it so I wouldn't feel under obligations to him."

Blane started to say something, then apparently changing his mind, smiled enigmatically. After a moment he said, "Now if you'll excuse me, while you're getting additional details from Harley, I'll have a chat with Mr. Mason."

Blane motioned to Mason, and the lawyer, Della Street and Blane walked around the big granite outcropping to a sequestered clearing where they were out of earshot.

"Mr. Mason," Blane said, "I can't begin to tell you how relieved I am now that you're here. Thank you for coming."

"The buried clock did it," Mason told him. "What do *you* know about that clock?"

"Harley Raymand mentioned it to me for the first time this morning. Adele confirmed his story. The clock was there, all right."

"There where he had scraped away the pine needles?" Mason asked.

"Raymand *may* have mistaken the place," Blane admitted.

"All right, that can wait. Tell me just what you want me to do and why you want me to do it. Hit the high spots. That deputy will be back here in a minute with more questions."

Blane spoke with nervous rapidity, all but running his words together, in his anxiety to give Mason the picture.

"Jack Hardisty was my son-in-law—married Millicent. She was a girl who wanted a career—studied nursing. She's clever—the sort people always praise for their intellect. . . . Then along came Jack Hardisty, handed her a new line—the passionate, fervid, romantic line—swept her off her feet, married her. Put him in a bank over at Roxbury—a damned four-flusher, a half-pint of nothing. Been breaking Milicent's heart, chasing around with a milliner over there—ten thousand short in his accounts —found it out and told him to face the music. . . . Before I could do anything about it, he took a couple of suitcases and cleaned out everything in the bank, nearly ninety thousand altogether. Rang me up, told me if I made good the ten thousand I'd get the rest of it back. If I didn't, there wouldn't be a dime in the bank when it opened this morning."

"What did you do?" Mason asked.

"What *could* I do?" Blaine asked. "I was stuck for it."

"How about the bonding company?"

"That's just it. The bonding company held off on his bond. There'd been a little something in Jack's past. At the time I thought the bonding company was being too damn technical—told them to go ahead and write the bond, and I'd guarantee they never lost a penny on it—signed a paper to that effect. . . . Damn fool—serves me right."

"All right. Go ahead."

"My other daughter, Adele, came up here with Harley Raymand yesterday afternoon. Before they left, Jack Hardisty showed up. He didn't see them. Raymand says Hardisty had a spade in the car. . . . They started back for Kenvale and met Milicent on the road. She asked if Jack was up here.

"Adele didn't think much of that until after Milicent had started on for the cabin. Then she got frightened. She told Harley she had another appointment, rushed him to his hotel, turned around and dashed up here to the cabin."

"After Milicent?" Mason asked.

Blane nodded.

"Find her?"

"Yes."

"Here at the cabin?"

"No, down by the main highway."

"What was she doing there?"

"Having a spell of nerves."

"Where was her husband?"

"No one knows. Milicent hadn't gone to the cabin. She'd parked her car at a wide place in the road, and started to walk up to the cabin."

"Why not drive all the way up?"

"She told Adele she didn't want her husband to hear her coming."

"Did she say why?"

"No."

"All right, she didn't get to the cabin?"

"No, her nerves went back on her. She must have had hysterics. She had a gun in her purse. She dropped it over the embankment at the edge of the road."

"Why?"

"She told Adele she was afraid to trust herself with it."

"Afraid she'd use it on herself, or on someone else?"

"I don't think she said."

"And Adele didn't ask?"

"I don't know. I don't think so."

"Revolver or automatic?"

"Revolver."

"Hers?"

"Yes. It's one I gave her. She was nervous and had to stay alone a lot at night. Her husband was away a lot of the time."

"All right. She threw the gun away. Then what?"

"Adele got her to promise to go on back to Kenvale and stay with her."

"Did she do it?"

"No."

"Why not. What happened?"

"We don't know. Adele drove on in her car. Milicent was right behind until they got to Kenvale. Then in the traffic, Adele lost her. It was getting dark and the headlights had been turned on. That makes it hard to watch a car behind, after you get in traffic."

"Adele lost her—so what? Did Milicent go to your house?"

"No. So far as I can learn, no one has seen her. Adele was watching the car in the rear-view mirror—other headlights cut in, and—well that's all."

"To whom has Adele told this?" Mason asked.

"I am the only one, so far. We want to know—"

Mason interrupted. "The deputy's getting ready to come back over this way. Does anyone know Milicent is missing?"

"No."

"When will they find out?"

"It may be some time. . . . I told Adele to tell the housekeeper Milicent was hysterical last night, that Adele gave her a sleeping tablet and put her to bed in the back bedroom upstairs—that Milicent isn't to be disturbed by anyone. That will stall things along until we can find her."

Mason said, "I'm not certain that what you've done is for Milicent's best interest."

"Why not? If they find out we don't know where she is—"

"I understand, but amateurs shouldn't try doctoring evidence. We haven't time to discuss it now. They're coming over this way. Get the deputy sheriff off to one side and tell him about that shortage."

Blane's face showed surprise. "Why, that's one of the things I wanted you to do—to keep that hushed up, to tell me how I—"

"You can't keep that hushed up," Mason interrupted. "Try to cover that up and let them catch you at it, and they'll blow the lid off."

"But I don't want—"

"Right now," Mason said, "I'm thinking of Milicent and you *should* be. Get the deputy sheriff off to one side, tell him you're giving him the information in strict confidence; that you don't want him to tell a soul."

"Well—all right—if you say so."

"Where's Adele?"

"At home."

"She know you sent for me?"

"Yes."

"Where's the nearest telephone?"

"Up the road about three miles there's a little settlement, a ranger station and—"

"Okay, go talk with the deputy. Here he comes now; then meet me at the Kenvale Hotel *as soon as you can get away from here.* Try to follow me within fifteen or twenty minutes."

The deputy sheriff was walking toward them. His manner was that of a man who has made up his mind to do something and wants to get it over with.

Mason said in a low voice, out of the corner of his mouth, as though coaching an actor, "Beat him to the punch. Beat him to the punch, Blane."

Blane raised his voice. "Oh, Jameson, I want to talk with you for a few minutes—privately, please."

The deputy glanced at the others, said, "Well, all right."

Mason turned to Della Street. "Come on, Della. This way." He led her around toward the back of the house, then along a well-defined trail running down a dry wash, deep enough so that they were invisible from the cabin. After they had gone a hundred yards, they scrambled up out of the wash, swung around to the place where Mason had parked his car.

Mason said, "I don't want them to hear the sound of the motor, Della. Put it in high, turn on the ignition, push the clutch pedal down. I'll start pushing it toward that grade. Let the clutch in when I tell you—after the car gets to going at a pretty good rate of speed. . . . Okay now, swing that wheel."

Mason pushed the car until it began to coast down the grade, then jumped in beside Della Street. When the car was running along at a good rate, he said, "All right, ease in the clutch."

The engine purred into smooth power.

"Make time up to that settlement," Mason said. "I want to telephone."

"I take it we're not conserving rubber?" Della asked.

"We're conserving a reputation," Mason told her.

They made the three miles of mountain road to the telephone in just a little over three and a half minutes. Mason found a telephone booth in the store, called Vincent Blane's residence in Kenvale, asked for Adele.

A few moments later, he heard a feminine voice on the line saying dubiously, "Yes, what is it, please?"

"This is Perry Mason. Know anything about me?"

"Why . . . yes."

"All right. No need to mention details. You knew your father was going to send for me."

"Yes."

"Know why?"

"Yes."

Mason said, "Your father told me about the upstairs bedroom—you understand?"

"The person who's supposed to be in it?"

"That's right."

"I understand."

Mason said, "I don't like it."

"Why not?" she asked.

"It's dangerous. We don't know what trumps are— yet. I want you to do something."

"What?"

"Go where you won't be questioned. Get out, and get out fast. Simply disappear."

"For how long?"

"Until I tell you to come back."

"How will you reach me?"

Mason said, "My secretary, Miss Della Street, will be registered at the Kenvale Hotel. Call her about five o'clock tonight. Don't mention any names over the phone. She won't mention names. If the coast is clear, she'll manage to let you know. If she doesn't let you know, it means the coast isn't clear. After five, keep calling her every few hours. . . . Got that straight?"

"Yes, Mr. Mason."

"All right, get started—and don't tell a soul where you're going. Fix things so you can't be traced. . . . And be certain to call Miss Della Street."

"I have it all straight," she said. "Good-by."

Mason hung up the receiver, waited a moment, then called his office in Los Angeles.

When the girl at Mason's switchboard answered, central said, "Deposit fifty-five cents for three minutes, please, including the Federal tax."

Mason fumbled in his pockets, opened the door of the telephone booth, called to the man behind the counter. "I've got a Los Angeles call in. My party's on the line. I need fifty-five cents. Can you give me some change?"

Mason waved a dollar bill. The man rang up NO SALE in the cash register, pulled out three twenty-five cent pieces, two dimes and a nickel, and came trotting over to the booth.

Mason thanked him, closed the door of the booth, dropped in the coins and heard the voice of Gertie, the tall, good-natured girl at the switchboard, saying, with her customary breezy informality, "Good Heavens, Mr. Mason, why didn't you just tell them to reverse the charge? Then you wouldn't have had to bother about the coins."

Mason chuckled. "Because, in the course of an investigation that may be made, the officers will wonder why I went tearing up here to put in a telephone call. Then they'll talk with the storekeeper and know my call was to my office in Los Angeles."

Gertie hestiated a moment, then said, "I get it, your *second* call."

"That's right. Only it won't occur to *them* there were two. Be a good girl, Gertie."

"Thank you, Mr. Mason. Shall we indulge in the usual

41

comments about the percentage there is in it, or have we talked long enough?"

Mason said, "We've talked long enough. You know all the answers anyway," and hung up.

6

■

At the hotel in Kenvale, Mason gave Della Street swift instructions. "Just before we turned off the main road, I noticed a road sign put up by the Auto Club bearing the words, *'Kern County.'* Look up the exact location of the county line and of that cabin. Then come back here and hold the fort."

"On my way," she said. "It shouldn't take long."

Mason made himself comfortable in the lobby of the hotel, watching the door, waiting for Vincent Blane. At the end of thirty impatient minutes, he went to a telephone booth and put through a person-to-person call for Paul Drake, head of the Drake Detective Agency in Los Angeles. The call was completed within a few seconds, and when Mason heard Drake's voice on the line, he said, "Perry Mason, Paul. I'm suspicious of telephones so you'll have to dot the *i's* and cross the *t's.*"

"Okay, go ahead."

"I'm in Kenvale. About twenty miles from here, in the mountains, a man by the name of Blane has a cabin. Blane's son-in-law, Jack Hardisty, got himself bumped off in that cabin sometime last night. Jameson, the resident deputy sheriff who's on the job now, is inclined to be decent. There are replacements coming from Los Angeles

42

who will be hard boiled. I'd like to get everything lined up before they clam up."

"What do you mean by everything?"

"Time of death, clues, means of death, motives, opportunities, alibis—and locate Milicent Hardisty, the widow of the victim."

Drake said, "Is that last job a bit of routine?"

"No."

"You mean it may be difficult?"

"Yes."

"That's the *i* I'm supposed to dot?"

"Also the *t* you're to cross. There's a probability it may have to be a double cross."

"I take it there's no use looking in the usual places?"

"Right—and don't be fooled by information to the contrary."

"Okay Perry, where will you be?"

"Kenvale Hotel, at least until we get things straightened out. If I'm not here, Della will be."

"Who's your client?"

"Vincent P. Blane."

"Any chance that he did it?"

"The police haven't said so."

Drake said, "That doesn't answer my question."

"You just think it doesn't."

Mason hung up the telephone, waited another five minutes, then impatiently called the Blane residence.

"This is Perry Mason, the lawyer," he said to the feminine voice who answered the telephone. "Is Miss Adele Blane there?"

"No, sir."

"You're the housekeeper?"

"Yes, sir. Martha Stevens."

Mason said, "Mr. Blane was to meet me here in the hotel. He's evidently been detained. Have you heard anything from him?"

"No, sir."

"Is Mrs. Hardisty there?"

"Yes, sir. She's here in the house, but there are strict orders that she isn't to be disturbed. She was hysterical last night, and had some sleeping tablets."

Mason smiled, said, "That's fine. I won't bother her. . . . Have there been any other calls asking for her?"

"Yes, sir."

"How many?"

"Oh, there must have been half a dozen."

"Friends?"

"No, sir. Strange voices who wouldn't leave names."

"Men or women?"

"Both."

Mason said, "All right, if you hear anything from Mr. Blane, directly or indirectly, call me at the Kenvale Hotel."

He hung up and was just leaving the telephone booth when the lobby door was pushed open explosively. A small group erupted into the lobby, Blane and Jameson in the lead. Blane's face lit up with relief as he saw Mason. Jameson kept at Blane's side as the pudgy, harassed businessman crossed over to the lawyer.

Mason kept his voice casual, as he said to Blane, "You seem to pick up more people as you keep traveling."

Blane's eyes held desperate appeal. "These are witnesses," he explained quickly. "Miss Strague and her brother and Mr. Beaton. They live up around there."

Mason said, "You folks look rather hot and flustered. How about coming up to my room where it's cool and where we can have a drink?"

The deputy said, "I'm afraid there isn't time for that, Mr. Mason. Mr. Blane has adopted a very peculiar attitude."

"What is it?"

"Miss Strague has found the weapon with which the

44

murder was committed. Mr. Beaton was with her at the time."

Mason, sparring for time, made a little bow to Lola Strague. "Congratulations. Evidently you did some high-class detective work. . . . May I ask where it was?"

"Lying in the pine needles on the other side of that rock near which Mr. Raymand says the clock was buried."

"We don't need to go into all that now," Jameson interjected hastily. "The point is, there's evidence linking this gun with Jack Hardisty's wife."

"Is that so?" Mason asked, his voice showing only casual interest. "What's the evidence?"

Blane nodded to Beaton.

Beaton interposed hurriedly, "Of course, gentlemen, I won't swear that it was a gun she had in her hand, but I drove past her last evening. She was standing on the main road, and had something in her hand. At the time I thought it was a wrench, that her car might have broken down. I was going to ask her if she needed help, but just then she drew her arm back and tossed this gun —if it was a gun—down into the canyon. Her face was contorted with emotion. She looked at me as I drove past, without showing the slightest sign of recognition. I doubt if she even saw me, although I raised my hat."

"What time was this?" Mason asked.

"Somewhere between six-fifteen and dark. Up in the mountains we don't bother much about time. I carry a cheap watch. Sometimes I wind it, and sometimes I don't. When it's running, I usually set it by the sun, so I'm not going to stick my neck out on a statement of time that could be twisted around by a lot of lawyers on cross-examination."

Beaton's eyes twinkled amiably at Mason, the network of crows-feet springing into quick prominence. "No hard feelings, Mr. Mason."

45

"None at all," Mason grinned. "I think you'd be a hard witness to cross-examine."

Beaton said, "Mrs. Payson was in the car with me. We were going in to Kenvale together. We went to dinner and a show. She may be able to tell you what time it was, although *she* didn't see Mrs. Hardisty toss the gun down in the canyon."

"You think this was after six?" Mason asked.

"I know it was after six-fifteen because Mrs. Payson was listening to a radio program that came on at six and went off the air at six-fifteen. She made me wait until the thing was over before she'd leave. . . . And that's as close as I can fix it."

"All this is beside the point," the deputy said. "I want to talk with Mrs. Hardisty. Blane acts as though he believed his daughter was guilty."

"Nothing of the sort," Blane retorted angrily. "I'm simply trying to protect my daughter's health."

"Well, you rushed to the telephone and got Perry Mason down here in a hurry," the deputy charged, also getting angry. "I wasn't born yesterday. I know what *that* means."

Mason smiled affably. "Well now, gentlemen," he said, "*I* wasn't born yesterday, but I'm not certain that *I* know what it means."

"It means Blane is trying to—"

"Yes?" Mason invited as the deputy stopped abruptly.

"I'm not sticking my neck out," Jameson said somewhat sullenly. "I'm just a resident deputy down here. There'll be someone on hand from the main office. . . . I've looked for them to be here before this. I—Here they come now."

The door was pushed open. Two men came barging over toward the group, moving with grim purpose like warships plowing through sea toward a convoy.

Mason said to the deputy, "Doubtless, you'll want to

46

explain the situation to these gentlemen. While you're doing that, I'll confer with my client."

He scooped his hand through Blane's arm, drew him off slightly to one side, said, "Okay, Blane, this is the pay-off."

When Blane spoke, he was so nervous his lips quivered. "It's her gun, Mason," he said. "I recognized it."

"What have you told them?"

"I've told them I would have to consult you before letting them know where my daughter was. . . . This is terrible, Mason. They'll find out that Milicent has disappeared now. There's no way we can stall it off any longer."

"You haven't any idea where she is?"

"No."

"Well, you've got to let them go to your house—and *then* bluff it out. Remember I'll be with you. When they find the darkened bedroom with a bed that hasn't been slept in, they'll start acting rough. When the going gets too tough for you, let me step in and handle it."

"All right—just so they don't jump on Adele."

"They won't."

"What makes you so certain of that?"

Mason smiled, "What did you think you'd retained counsel for? Go ahead, Blane, get it over with. . . . Here they come now."

The men from the Los Angeles office were hard boiled. They offered Blane none of the polite courtesies which the resident deputy had extended. "We want Mrs. Hardisty," the man who acted as spokesman said. "What's the idea that we can't see her?"

"I think there's been a misunderstanding," Mason interposed. "Mr. Blane knows that his daughter has been very much upset over another matter which has nothing to do with—"

"Well, we think it has a lot to do with it."

47

Jameson said hastily, "I've explained to these men what Mr. Blane told me. We'll try to keep it out of the papers."

"As I was endeavoring to explain," Mason went on suavely, "because of this unusual situation, Mr. Blane—"

"What's that got to do with where Mrs. Hardisty is now? Do you *know* where she is, Blane?"

Blane hesitated.

Mason said, "Go ahead, Blane. Tell them."

"She's at my house, asleep."

The spokesman turned to Jameson. "You know where his place is?"

"Yes."

"Okay, let's go."

"Got your car here?" Mason asked Blane, as the others turned away.

"Yes."

"All right, let's get there first."

Blane led the way to where his car was parked.

Mason settled down in the cushions, said nothing until Blane had parked the car in front of the house, then he said, as the officers drove up, "Remember to show surprise when they find no one in that bedroom."

They escorted the officers into the house. Blane said, "I'll go up and notify my daughter that—"

"No dice," the man from the Los Angeles office interposed. "This is a business, not a social call. We want to talk with Mrs. Hardisty before anyone talks with her, before *anyone* gives her a tip on what's happened. So suppose you just—"

"I insist," Blane said with simple dignity, "that I'm going to be there when you interview my daughter."

The Los Angeles deputy hesitated.

Mason said, "And, as attorney for Mrs. Hardisty, I am going to be on hand."

"Okay, I'm not going to have an argument about that.

48

I'm not going to bite her. . . . But one thing's definite: *I'm* going to do *all* the talking. If she answers my questions satisfactorily, all right. If she gets any coaching from you people, I'm going to take that into consideration in making my recommendations to the D.A. Now, show us the way to the bedroom."

Mason nodded to Blane, and Blane led the little group up the stairs and down a corridor to a closed door.

"This it?" the deputy asked.

Blane said. "Yes, this is the back bedroom."

The deputy reached toward the doorknob.

"Just a minute," Blane said. "My daughter is entitled to *some* courtesies."

Blane knocked on the door.

There was no sound from within the room.

The officer knocked, his knuckles beating a loud summons on the panels of the wood.

Mason was reaching for his cigarette case when he heard a key turn on the inside of the door, and a woman, who quite evidently had been in the process of dressing and had hurriedly thrown on a bathrobe, said, "What is it, please?"

"You're Mrs. Jack Hardisty?" the deputy asked.

"Yes. What is it, Father?"

The Los Angeles deputy said to Blane, "Okay, I'll handle it from here on."

Mrs. Hardisty showed her consternation. "Why, what's the matter?"

"Where's your husband, Mrs. Hardisty?"

"I . . . Why, I . . . Isn't he at Roxbury at the bank?"

"You know he isn't."

She was silent.

"Did you know he was short at the bank?"

Blane started to interrupt, but the officer pushed him into the background. "How about it, Mrs. Hardisty? Did you or didn't you?"

She glanced toward her father.

"Let's have a straight answer to the question, please. Never mind trying to get signals from anybody."

"I . . . Yes."

"That's better. When did you see him last?"

"Yesterday."

"What time yesterday?"

"I guess it was about one o'clock or one-thirty."

"Let's see if we can't do better than that, Mrs. Hardisty. You're familiar with the mountain cabin your father owns?"

"Why, yes, of course."

"You were up there yesterday afternoon, weren't you?"

"Yes."

"Why did you go up there?"

"I . . . I thought Jack might be up there."

"You went up there, then, to see your husband, didn't you?"

"Yes."

"And what time was that?"

"I don't know exactly."

"And you did see him, didn't you?"

"No."

For a moment there was a break in the rapid-fire tempo of the questions as the officer digested his surprise; then he returned to the attack, this time a little more savage, a little more grim. "Mrs. Hardisty, I'm going to be frank with you. Your answers may be very important—important to you. Now I want a *truthful* answer. You saw your husband up there at the cabin, didn't you?"

"No, I didn't. I didn't even go all the way up to the cabin. I . . . I had hysterics. I stayed down on the highway . . . Well, I walked up our road a ways. I don't know how far. I just went all to pieces—and then I came back to the main road and tried to quiet my nerves by walking, and I met Adele—"

50

"Who's Adele?"

"My sister."

"Why did you go to pieces? What was it you intended to do when you saw your husband?"

Mason interposed suavely, "I think that's far enough along that line, officer."

"*You* do?"

"Yes."

"As it happens, you don't have anything to say about it. I told you *I* was going to do the talking."

Mason said, "So far as questions of fact are concerned, that's quite all right. I have no objection to letting my client answer—"

"But who *is* this man?" Milicent asked in confusion. "What's this talk about me being his client?"

Mason said to the officer, "I'm going to give you every advantage. I'm not going to answer that question. I'm going to let you break the news to her in your own way, but I'm—"

"I'm doing this," the officer said angrily. "I don't *have* to do it here. I can load her in a car right now and take her in to the D.A.'s office. I've got enough on her."

"You haven't got enough on her to move her out of that room," Mason said.

"Don't you think I haven't. That gun—"

"What about the gun?" Mason asked.

The officer angrily turned back to Mrs. Hardisty, said, "Since the subject has come up, I'll ask you the question direct. Why did you take a gun up there with you?"

She was quite apparently stalling to cover her confusion. "I . . . take a gun . . . You mean—"

"I mean that you took a thirty-eight caliber revolver which your father had given you for a Christmas present up to the cabin with you when you went up to see your husband. Now *why* did you do it?"

51

Mason interposed meaningly, "The gun your father gave you for your *protection,* Mrs. Hardisty."

"I took it up because—because I was afraid of Jack."

The deputy said angrily to Mason, "Oh, no! *You* aren't going to say anything! You're going to give me every advantage to get at the truth. Then you go and push words in the mouth of your client. 'The gun your father gave you for your *protection.'*—All right, I'll tell you what *I'm* going to do. I'm going to take this woman to Los Angeles with me, and question her there."

"Going to arrest her?" Mason asked.

"If you want to force my hand, yes."

"All right," Mason said, "I'll force your hand."

"Very well," the deputy announced, "Mrs. Hardisty, you're under arrest. I warn you that anything you say may be used against you."

"Under arrest for what?" Mason demanded. "You can't arrest her without telling her the specific charge."

The deputy hesitated.

"Go on," Mason taunted. "If you're going to take her out of that room as being under arrest, you're going to arrest her on a specific charge. Otherwise she doesn't leave this house."

The officer hesitated another second or two, then blurted, "All right, I'll do it up brown. Mrs. Hardisty, I'm an officer of the law. I'm arresting you for the murder of your husband. As an officer of the law, I have reasonable ground to believe that you were guilty of that murder. Now you won't be permitted to talk with anyone. Get your things on. We're leaving for Los Angeles right now."

Mason said, "And, as this woman's attorney, I advise her not to answer any questions asked her by anyone unless those questions are asked in my presence."

The deputy said angrily, "I should have known better

than to have let you come along. I'll know better next time."

Mason smiled, "And if you'd tried to stop me from coming along you'd know better than to have tried *that* next time."

7

Mason stopped by the Kenvale Hotel to find Della Street waiting in the lobby.

"Find out about that cabin?" he asked.

"Yes. I went to the county assessor's office and got the thing definitely located."

"Just where?" Mason asked.

"It's in Los Angeles County, but as near as I could tell from making measurements on the map, the cabin is just about fourteen hundred feet from the county line."

"But the road to the cabin crosses the line into Kern County?"

"That's right. The private road to the cabin turns off just beyond the county line."

"How far beyond?"

"Not far—around two hundred feet."

Mason chuckled.

"What is it?" she asked.

Mason said, "If the murder was committed where the car was pushed over the grade, and the body was then brought back to the cabin, the murder was committed in Kern County. But if the murder was committed in the cabin, then, of course, it was committed in Los Angeles

53

County. Right now the officers may not know the answer to that."

"Isn't there some law that covers that, though?" Della Street asked suspiciously.

"Exactly," Mason said. "Section 782 of our Penal Code. . . . And *that's* going to make it nice."

"Come on, tightwad, loosen up."

"That section provides that when a murder is committed within five hundred yards of the boundary of two or more counties, the jurisdiction lies in either county."

"Then why the chuckle? In this case either county could take jurisdiction."

Mason said, "You'll see, if it works out—and I think it will."

"What happened out at the house?" she asked.

Mason ceased smiling.

"I sure led with my chin on that one. She was there."

"Milicent Hardisty?"

"Yes."

"But wasn't she supposed to be there?"

"That's what the officers supposed. Blane told me she wasn't."

"Was Blane lying to you?"

"I don't know. I don't think so. It certainly made me feel as though someone had kicked me in the stomach when she opened the door. There I was, standing helplessly by, letting the officers get hold of my client before I'd had any chance to talk with her. . . . Has Adele Blane called you up yet?"

"No."

"She will. I want to see her. She may as well come home now. Tell her that when she calls—only to be certain to see me first."

Della glanced at him, said, "You sound almost as though you'd arranged her disappearance. . . . What did they do with Mrs. Hardisty?"

"Put her under arrest and they're going to bury her."

"What do you mean by that?"

"Ordinarily prisoners charged with murder are taken to the county jail, but if the authorities have an idea they can do more with a prisoner by taking him to some other jail, they do so. . . . You can see the situation with Milicent Hardisty. I told her not to answer questions. Perhaps she will. Perhaps she won't. In any event, they know I'm going to try to see her. It's a ten-to-one bet that instead of taking her to the Los Angeles jail where I can find her, they'll take her to some other town in the county and hold her there. By the time I finally locate her, they'll have had plenty of time to work on her. That's what is known as 'burying a prisoner.' "

"Isn't that unethical?"

Mason grinned. "There are no ethics when you're dealing with the police. Or I should say when the police are dealing with you. *You're* supposed to be bound by ethics. The police don't have ethics. They act on the assumption that they're *'getting the truth,'* whereas you are *'protecting a criminal.'* "

"That doesn't seem right," Della said.

"Of course, you have to admit this. The police *are* trying to solve crimes. They sincerely believe that everything they do has a tendency to uncover the truth, that anything they're stopped from doing is a monkey-wrench in the machinery. Therefore they look on all laws which are passed to protect the citizen as being obstacles thrown in front of the police. . . . Well, I suppose I've got to go start proceedings for a writ of *habeas corpus*. It'll take me two or three hours. You stay here and run things while I'm gone."

"What do you want me to do?"

Mason said, "Harley Raymand for one. Get him to go back to that cabin and look around."

"Why?"

55

"I'm not entirely satisfied with some things."

"What, for instance?"

"Evidently Jack Hardisty wore nose-pincher glasses. I saw the marks on his nose where the supports dug in."

"Well?"

"He didn't have his glasses on."

"Wasn't he partially undressed?"

"Yes."

"Men don't go to bed with their glasses on."

"I couldn't see them anywhere in the room."

"He probably put them in his coat pocket when he undressed."

"Perhaps—but other things indicate he didn't undress himself."

"What?"

"The shoes."

"What about the shoes?"

"The shoes," Mason said, "looked as though Hardisty had just stepped out of a shoeshining parlor."

"What's wrong with that?"

"If Harley Raymand and Adele Blane are telling the truth, Hardisty got out of his car and walked around among the pine needles. That would make the shoes pretty dusty, but there's something else about the shoes that bothers me."

"What?"

"I noticed that they were put under the bed with the toes pointing *toward* the bed."

"Well?"

Mason said, "Nine persons out of ten sitting on a bed and undressing will take off their shoes and put them down so the toes are pointing away from the bed; but if another person puts shoes down by a bed where a person is sleeping, he'll almost invariably point the toes *toward* the bed."

56

Della thought that over, then nodded thoughtful acquiescence.

"Now, then," Mason went on, "if you had noticed the bottom part of Jack Hardisty's trousers, you'd have observed that there was a little mud on them—a dried, reddish clay—not much, but enough to show. Now it hasn't rained here in Southern California for a month. Jack Hardisty would hardly have carried mud around on his trousers for a month. . . . I want to get Harley Raymand to explore around and see if he can find some place where a stream of water runs through reddish clay."

"But if he walked in the reddish clay, why didn't it stick to his shoes?"

"That's exactly it. He either took off his shoes and socks, and walked in there barefooted, or else cleaned his shoes afterwards."

"Good Heavens, why?"

Mason grinned and said, "Perhaps ninety thousand dollars in cash would be the answer."

"Oh, I see. . . . Do you want me to point that out to Mr. Raymand?"

"Definitely not."

"Anything else?"

"Yes. Tell Raymand to make a search for that clock, keep listening for the sound of ticking. If he gets his hands on the clock again, have him bring it to me at once."

"Okay," Della Street said, "I'll start Raymand out. Any—"

"Yes. Here's something I want you to do with Paul Drake. It's going to be tricky, but he can put it across."

"What?"

"Under that section of the penal code, the jurisdiction lies in either Kern County or Los Angeles County. Now, if Paul Drake could get some newspaper reporter to put a bug in the ear of the district attorney of Kern County that this was going to be a spectacular case, with a chance for big notoriety and a possibility of political advancement for the district attorney who tries it—well, you know how it is. That's the sort of thing that prosecutors in small counties eat up."

"Then you want the case to be tried in Kern County?"

"No. I want each county to think the other is trying to steal the show."

"I'll tell Paul to fix it up. Anything else?"

"I think," Mason told her, "that will be enough."

8

Harley Raymand realized with some surprise that the events of the day had not dragged him down as much as he had anticipated. His sleep in the cool, crisp air at the mountain cabin had rested his nerves and given him the feeling that he was "over the hump."

The sheriff's office had been very thorough. The mattress and bedding had been removed from the bed and taken to Los Angeles for expert examination. Harley gathered there was quite a question in the minds of the authorities as to whether Hardisty had been shot while he was lying in the bed, or whether the body had been transferred to the bed within a short time after the murder had been committed. . . . And now Harley was working with definite objectives in mind: to find moist, reddish-brown clay—to find the clock—to locate the spade which had been in Hardisty's car, and, in general, to pick up any stray clues which might have been overlooked by the police—those things which a person actually living in a place might notice, but which would escape the attention of a more casual investigator.

Vincent Blane had asked him if it would make him nervous staying alone in a cabin where a murder had been committed. . . . Harley smiled every time he thought of that; he who had been trained to carry on while comrades were shot down all around him; he who had become so familiar with death that it had ceased to inspire him even with healthy respect, let alone fear, being afraid to sleep in a cabin simply because a man had been shot in it!

The rays of afternoon sunlight were once more slanting across from ridge to ridge while the valleys cradled purple shadows. Harley strolled across the pine-scented, sloping flat where the clock had been buried. Whoever had removed that clock had made a very cunning and thoroughly workmanlike job of replacing dirt in the hole, tamping it down, cleaning up each particle of surplus earth, and spreading moss and pine needles over the place.

Not only was there no sign of the clock, but Harley was forced to admit that if he, himself, had not seen the buried box at this particular place, he would have doubted the word of anyone who told him a clock had been buried there.

The moss and pine needles were a cushion under his feet.

The tall, straight trees caught the golden sunlight, cast long shadows. . . . Some sparkling object reflected the sun's rays with scintillating brilliance and a rim of color.

Harley moved over toward the rock outcropping, with the realization that the object reflecting the sun's rays must have come from a seam in the rock.

Upon approaching the rock, however, he could find nothing that could have caused the reflection. The seam in the rock held a threadlike line of pine needles which would furnish a background of dark green contrast to any metallic object which might have been there.

Puzzled, Harley retraced his steps to the point where he had first seen the shimmer of reflected sunlight, and moved back and forth, up and down, until suddenly he once more caught the glittering reflection. This time, he marked the place carefully and walked toward it without taking his eyes from it.

Just as he reached the rock, something urged him to turn.

Lola Strague was less than twenty feet behind him.

"Hello," she said with a little laugh, "what are *you* zig-zagging back and forth about?"

Slightly irritated, Harley said, "And may I ask what *you* were stalking?"

"Was I stalking?"

"You were very quiet."

"Perhaps your attention was concentrated on what you were doing, and you didn't hear me."

Harley became dignified. "Were you," he asked, "looking for me?"

"Not definitely."

"Then may I ask what you *were* looking for?"

She laughed. "I presume, when you come right down to it, I'm a trespasser, although the property lines aren't very clearly marked around here. No fences, or signs, you know. . . . And I found a gun here earlier in the day. That should give me the right to return."

"I'm not worried about the trespassing," he said, "but I had the distinct impression you were looking for something, and that you were being just a bit—well, furtive."

"Did you, indeed! That interests me a lot. Do you trust the impressions you form that way, or do you find they are sometimes misleading? I'm collecting data for an article I intend to write on the subject."

He said, "I trust my impressions. My first impression was that you were looking for something, just as my present impression is that you are stalling around, trying to avoid answering my question until you can think up just the right answer."

She laughed. "I guess your impressions are all right, Mr. Raymand. I'll be fair with you. I was looking for the clock."

"And why so interested in *it?*"

"I don't know. I'm always interested in the mysterious, in those things that aren't explained. . . . And now, since I've answered your question, I'll ask you one. What are *you* looking for?"

"Health, rest, fresh air and relaxation," he said.

Her eyes were laughing at him. "Go on."

"And the clock," he admitted.

"And why were *you* so interested in the clock?"

"Because I have an idea the police are half convinced that I'm lying about it."

"You had a witness, didn't you?"

"Adele Blane, yes."

Lola Strague made her next question casual—perhaps just a little too casual. "Where is Adele Blane now?" she asked.

Harley frowned, said, "I presume she's trying to get in contact with Milicent—Mrs. Hardisty, you know. That's her sister."

"I see," Lola said, making the words sound quite unconvincing. "Wasn't she up here last night?"

"She was up here with me yesterday afternoon."

"And she came back afterwards?"

"I don't know. I went to the hotel and slept."

The tall, slender girl moved over to the outcropping, adjusting her pliable young body to the irregularities of

61

the rock. Her eyes regarded Harley Raymand with disconcerting steadiness. "Are you going to join us up here, or are you just vacationing?"

"What do you mean?" he asked, managing to seat himself in such a position as to conceal the exact point in the rock seam from which he had caught the reflected light.

"Oh, you know. Are you going to live a leisurely life, or run in the breathless pursuit of success?"

"I don't know. Right now, I'm getting acquainted with myself, taking a breathing spell. I haven't blueprinted the future."

She picked up a little twig and traced aimless designs on the surface of the rock. "This war seems sort of a nightmare. It will pass, and people will wake up."

"To what?" Harley asked.

She looked up from her design tracing. "Sometimes," she admitted, "I'm afraid of that."

They were silent for a space of time, while Harley watched the creeping shadow of a pine limb move from her shoulder up to the lobe of her ear.

"Somehow," she said, "society got off on a wrong track. The thing people pursued as success wasn't success at all."

Harley kept silent, clothing himself in the luxury of lazy lethargy.

"Look at Mr. Blane," she went on. "He's an exponent of that system—driving himself. Now he's around fifty-five. He has high blood pressure, pouches under his eyes, a haunted expression. His motions are jerky and nervous. . . . You can't think that life was intended to be that way. He never relaxes, never takes a good long vacation; he has too many irons in the fire. And they say he isn't getting anywhere; that the income taxes are taking all he makes, and keeping his nose to the grindstone."

Harley felt that loyalty to Vincent Blane demanded speech. He aroused himself to say, "All right, let's look at Mr. Blane. I happen to know something about him. His parents died when he was a child. His first job paid him twelve dollars a week. He educated himself while he was working. He's responsible for two banks, one in Kenvale, one in Roxbury. He's put up a big department store. He gives employment to a large number of people. He built up the community."

"And what does it get him?" Lola Strague asked.

Harley thought that over, said, "If you want to look at it that way, what does it get *us?* He's a representative American, typical of the spirit of commercial progress which has changed this country from a colony to a nation."

"Are you," she asked abruptly, "going to work for him?"

"I don't know."

"Are you working for him now?"

"Is that—well, shall we say, pertinent?"

"You mean, is it any of my business?"

He shook his head. "I didn't express it that way."

"But that was what you meant?"

"No. I wondered if it might actually have some bearing."

"On what?"

"On—well, your attitude toward me."

Her eyes flashed quick interest, then were hastily averted as the end of the pine twig she was holding started scratching away at the rock again. "What were you doing out here?" she asked.

"When?"

"When I walked up just now."

"Looking at the place where the clock had been."

"And at something else on the rock," she said.

"Were you watching me?"

"Only just as I moved up. And when you sat down you acted as though you were concealing something."

He smiled at that, but said nothing.

"After all," she said, "I can sit here just as long as you can, if you're sitting on something to cover it up. It'll still be there when you get up."

"Of course, I could point out that you're trespassing."

"And eject me?"

"I might."

"In that event, you'd have to get up. I doubt if anyone has ever ejected a trespasser sitting down."

"And what makes you think I'm sitting here to conceal something?"

"I thought so when we started talking. I'm certain of it now."

"Why?"

"Otherwise, when I accused you of it, you'd have jumped up and looked around at the rock to see if there actually was anything to conceal."

"Perhaps I'm not as obvious as that."

"Perhaps."

"Very well," he said, "you win," and got up.

"What is it?" she asked.

"I don't know. Something was reflecting the light."

"There doesn't seem to be anything here."

"It must be a piece of glass. I can't understand anything else that—yes, there it is!"

"Looks like part of the lens from a pair of rimless glasses," she said, as Harley turned the curved piece of glass around in his fingers.

He nodded. "It must have fallen into these pine needles. They cushioned the shock and prevented it from breaking; also held it propped at just the right angle so it reflected the sun's rays just now."

"What do you make of it?" she asked.

Harley dropped the glass into his pocket. "I don't know. I'll have to think it over."

She laughed suddenly and said, "You're a cool one."

64

"Am I?"

"Yes."

He judged the time was ripe for a counter-offensive. "Why," he asked, "were you so upset when you learned Rodney Beaton was returning from town with Myrna Payson?"

Her face flamed into color. "That's an unfair question. You're insinuating that—"

"Yes?" Harley prompted as she ceased speaking abruptly.

She said, "It's a personal, impertinent and unfair question."

"You've been asking me questions," he said, "about my plans, and—"

"Simply being sociable," she interjected.

"And," Raymand said, smiling, "trying to find out something about my future moves and how long I'd be here. Hence, my question. Are you going to answer it?"

She caught her breath, preparatory to making some indignant comment, then seemed abruptly to change her mind. "Very well," she said with cold formality, "I will answer your question because apparently you think it's relevant and material. If you think I'm jealous, you're mistaken. I was merely piqued."

"There's a difference?" he asked.

"In my case, yes."

"And why were you piqued?"

"Because Rodney Beaton had stood me up. We had a date to go out and patrol the trails together."

"I'm afraid I don't understand."

She said, "Rodney is getting a collection of photographs of nocturnal animals. He has three or four cameras rigged with flashguns, and clamps them on tripods in strategic places on the trails. During the early part of the evenings he'll patrol the trails, finding the camera traps that have been touched off by passing animals. Then he'll put in fresh plates, reset the shutter, and put in a new flashbulb."

"And you accompany him?"

"At times."

"And last night he had given you some specific invitation?"

"Oh, it wasn't like that. It was just casual. He asked me if I was going to be doing anything, and I said no, and he said 'if you're around, we might take a look at the cameras,' and I told him I'd be glad to. That's what makes me angry. It wasn't a definite date—and he'd evidently forgotten all about it. If he'd made a definite date with me, and then broken it to go to town with that . . . that . . . with Mrs. Payson, I'd at least know where I stood. But it was casual and informal, and he simply forgot all about it. That puts me in the position of having to pretend that *I* forgot all about it, too. It's quite possible that Rodney will remember it later—and then it will be mutually embarrassing. And I think Mrs. Payson knew about it—and deliberately inveigled him into taking her to town. She's a widow, one of the—oh, let's not talk about her! Now then, that's the whole story. You see, it's a very commonplace affair. I think any young woman hates to be stood up. . . . But I don't want you to get the idea that I'm setting my cap for Mr. Rodney Beaton."

"Did I give you the impression that I thought that?"

She met his eyes fairly. "Yes," she said.

"While we're on the subject," he said, smiling, "since we've disposed of Rodney Beaton, what can you tell me about Myrna Payson?"

"Not much. She's a widow. She inherited some money. She's gone in for cattle ranching."

"Has a place up here?"

"She has a small ranch up here. She has two other ranches, and—well, *she* goes around with Rodney, taking care of the cameras quite frequently."

66

"Rodney seems to be very popular."

"He's a very interesting man, and—I don't know how I could describe it so you'll appreciate it, but there's a terrific wallop in this camera hunting."

"I don't get it."

"You set your camera, put in a flashbulb, string a black silk thread across the trail. If you're after animals the size of a coyote, you put it at a certain height. If you're looking for deer, you'll raise the thread. If you're after the smaller animals, you put it just an inch or two above the trail. Sometimes you string out three threads. You walk away, making a round of the other cameras, and come back at an interval of perhaps an hour. When you find the thread broken, the shutter tripped, and the flashbulb exploded, you know you've got a picture. Then you get down on your hands and knees and study the tracks in the trail to see what animal tripped the shutter. . . . Skunk pictures are usually cute. Deer pictures are hard to get, and quite frequently, deer photographed under those conditions seem angular and ungraceful. Foxes usually make beautiful pictures. Wildcats have a sinister look about them.

"Rod is a very expert photographer. He has infinite patience. He'll prospect for days to get just the right camera location—a smooth, fairly level stretch where there's no background to show—"

"Why no background?" Harley interrupted.

"Because Rod only wants the animal against a dead black background. He uses a small flashbulb and a wide-open lens. He says most flashlight pictures give an effect of unreality because they show garish foreground and black—but you must get Rod to show you his collection. It's wonderful."

"Does Mr. Beaton develop the films here?"

"Oh yes, he has a little darkroom in the cellar of his cabin. We go down there when we get back from our patrol and develop the films that have been exposed. That's when it gets exciting, seeing what you've got on the film, whether it's a good picture, whether the animal was facing the camera or facing away from the camera, or just trotting along the trail when it set off the flash-bulb."

"Ever get pictures of human beings?" Raymand asked.

"No, silly, of course not."

"What's to prevent someone walking along a trail and blundering into one of those camera traps?"

"Why—nothing, I guess, except that no one ever has done it so far. There's no reason for people to go prowl-ing around these hills at night."

"And Myrna Payson takes an interest in night pho-tography?"

Lola Strague became suddenly economical of words. "Yes."

"And there is a certain element of rivalry?"

"No."

"But you and Myrna Payson aren't particularly inti-mate?"

"I think I can settle that very quickly, Mr. Raymand. It's absolutely none of your business, but we're *quite* friendly. Up here, we all try to get along with one an-other, be friends, and—mind our own business."

"Ouch!"

"You asked for it."

"I did, indeed. What's more, I'm going to ask for more from time to time."

"If your questions are frank, you'll have to pardon me if my answers are also frank."

"Just so I get the information," Raymand grinned, "I don't care what sort of a verbal package it's wrapped in."

"I see. And precisely what information are you angling for?"

"I want to know why a good-looking young woman like Myrna Payson should be marooned up here—"

"She came up here a few weeks ago to look over her property. She intended to stay two days. It was just a trip of inspection."

"And she met Rodney Beaton?"

"Yes."

"And she has now been here for some several weeks, you say?"

"Yes."

"Then it took longer for her to investigate—"

"I don't know," Lola Strague interrupted irritably. "I'm really utterly incapable of reading Mrs. Payson's mind. I don't know what your object is, Mr. Raymand, but if you're up here trying to play detective, and are starting on the surmise that Myrna and I are engaged in some sort of a struggle for the affections or companionship of Rodney Beaton, you're . . . you're all wet. And now, if you'll pardon me, I'll be on my way. . . . Unless there are further questions?" Her manner was one of cold anger.

Harley said, "I'm simply trying to get the picture in focus in my mind. I—" He broke off to listen. "A car coming," he said.

She had caught the sound almost at the same time he had. They stood there wordlessly, waiting for the car to make its appearance, both yielding to a common curiosity, yet maintaining their dignified hostility.

Harley Raymand was the first to recognize the man who drove the car up out of the shadow-filled canyon to the gentle slope in front of the cabin. "It's Perry Mason, the lawyer," he said.

Mason saw them standing there, and swerved the car over to the side of the road, shut off the motor and came walking across to join them.

69

"Hello," he said. "You look very serious, as though you were engaged in a council of war."

"Or an altercation," Lola Strague said with a smile.

"Tell me, what have they done with Mrs. Hardisty?" Harley Raymand asked.

"I've got a writ of *habeas corpus* for her. They're going to have to bring her out into the open now. They've had her buried in some outlying town. . . . Were you people looking for something?"

"I came out here looking for the clock," Harley said.

"Find anything?"

"Not a sign. I've listened at various places—holding my ear to the ground. Can't hear a thing."

"You could hear it ticking fairly plainly when you first discovered it?"

"Yes. The sound seemed to carry well through the ground. It was quite audible."

Lola Strague regarded Harley Raymand with amused eyes. "Well," she asked, "are you going to tell him?"

Raymand reached his hand in his pocket. "While I was looking for the clock," he said, "I found a piece of glass. It looks as though it had been broken from a spectacle."

Mason took the piece of glass in his fingers, turned it around thoughtfully, said, "Just where was this, Raymand?"

Harley showed him.

Mason started looking along the needle-filled seam in the rock. "We should be able to find the rest of this. This is only about a half of one lens."

They searched the little fold in the rock carefully. Then Mason gave his attention to the surrounding ground. "That's mighty peculiar," he said. "Suppose a pair of spectacles were thrown against that rock and cracked into pieces. You'd naturally expect to find little pieces of glass around here on the ground. There doesn't seem to be a sign of anything, not even—wait a minute. What's this?"

70

He crawled forward on his hands and knees, picked up a wedge-shaped sliver of glass. "Looks as though this is also from a broken spectacle lens," Mason said. "And that seems to be the only other piece that's anywhere around here."

"What should I do with this piece that I've found?" Harley Raymand asked him. "Do you think I should report it?"

"I think it would be a good idea."

"To the sheriff's office?"

"Yes. Jameson, the resident deputy, is a pretty decent sort. You might get in touch with him. You can tell him about the piece you found. *I'll* tell him about the one I found."

Lola Strague smiled. "Much as I would like to hang around and wear my welcome out, I think I'd better be getting back. And, since I didn't find anything, *I* won't say anything to anyone."

Mason watched her walking down the trail, a slight smile twinkling at his eye corners. Then he turned to Harley Raymand, said, "I want to look around a little, and I'd better do it before sundown. . . . Where do cars customarily park up here?"

"Just about any place, I believe," Raymand replied. "I'm a little out of touch with things, but before I left, and when they'd have parties up here, people parked their cars wherever they found shade. There's eighty acres in the tract, which makes for quite a bit of individuality in parking automobiles."

Mason digested that information. "When I was here this morning, I noticed the deputy sheriff's car was parked under that tree. Did it stay in that one place?"

"Yes. Later on, when the Los Angeles men arrived during the first part of the afternoon and took the body away, they parked their cars right close to the porch on that side."

71

Mason strolled over to look at the tracks along the road, then walked leisurely to the back of the cabin. "This seems to be a fairly level place—"

"It's reserved for barbecues," Raymand said. "At least it was the last time I was a regular visitor here."

"Nevertheless," Mason observed, "a car seems to have swung around here, a car which left very distinct tire prints."

"That's right," Raymand agreed. "Those prints of two wheels certainly are distinct."

"The rear wheels," Mason pointed out. "You can see where they crossed over the tracks of the other wheels. . . . You don't know when those tracks were made, do you, Raymand?"

"No sir, I don't. I got up here quite a bit after dark last night, and—wait a minute. I know they *weren't* here yesterday afternoon, because I walked around back of the house to go to the spring. I'm quite certain I'd have noticed it if these car tracks had been here then."

Mason half closed his eyes in thoughtful contemplation. "Oh well, I guess the police have covered the ground. . . . Just ran by to see how you were making it, Raymand. I'll be at the hotel in case anything turns up."

9

Myrna Payson's ranch was some two miles beyond the point where the road turned off to the Blane cabin. Here the country changed to a rolling plateau, with little tree-filled valleys and several small lakes. In the distance, the peaks of mountains that bordered the plateau lifted crests that were some eight thousand feet above sea level.

Up here on the plateau, away from the shadows of the mountains, there was still enough sunlight, when Mason turned his car into the gate marked *"M Bar P,"* to turn the winding graveled road to a ribbon of reddish gold. An old-fashioned picket fence cast long, barred shadows. A sagging gate that hung disconsolately from one hinge reminded Mason somehow of a weary pack horse standing with its weight on three legs.

The house was a roomy, old-fashioned structure, weathered and paintless.

Mason parked his car, climbed three steps to a somewhat rickety porch, and, seeing no doorbell, knocked loudly.

He heard motion on the inside. Then the door was opened, and an attractive woman in the early thirties was sizing him up with curious eyes.

"Miss Payson?" Mason asked.

"Mrs. Payson. I'm a widow," she corrected. "Won't you come in?"

She had taken care of her figure, her skin, her hands and her dark hair. Her nose was perhaps a bit too upturned. Her mouth required makeup to keep the lips from seeming a shade too full. Her eyes looked out on life with a quizzical, slightly humorous expression, and she was quite evidently interested in people and things.

It was, Mason decided as he accepted her invitation and entered the house, an interest which would make this woman very fascinating. This was not the eager curiosity of the youngster, nor the exploitation of the adventuress, but rather the appraisal of one who has acquired a perspective, has lost all fear that events may get out of hand, and is quite frankly curious to see what new experiences life has to offer.

Mason said, "Aren't you a little afraid, being out here alone like this?"

"Of what?"

"Of strangers."

She laughed. "I don't think I've ever been afraid of anything or anyone in my life. . . . And I'm not alone."

"No?"

She shook her head. "There's a bunkhouse out here about fifty yards. I have three of the toughest bow-legged cowpunchers you ever saw. And you have, perhaps, overlooked the dog under the table."

Mason took a second look. What was apparently a patch of black shadows proved on closer inspection to be a shaggy substance that was taking in everything that was happening with watchful, unwinking eyes.

Mason laughed. "I will amend my statement about your being alone."

" 'Spooks' doesn't look formidable," she said, "but he's a living example of still water running deep. He never growls, never barks, but believe me, Mr. Mason, I have only to give him a signal and he'd come out of there like a steel spring."

"You know who I am, then?" Mason asked.

"Yes. I've seen your photograph in the papers, had you pointed out to me once or twice in night clubs. . . . I presume you want to ask me about what I saw when Rod and I went to town last night."

Mason nodded.

She smiled. "I'm afraid it won't do any good to ask."

"Why not?"

"In the first place," she said, slowly and distinctly, "I sympathize with that woman. I sympathize with her very, very much. In the second place, I wasn't interested in what she had in her hand. I was fascinated by what I saw on her face."

"What *did* you see on her face?" Mason asked.

74

She smiled. "And I know enough to realize that's not proper evidence, Mr. Mason. I don't think a court would let me testify to that, would it? Doesn't it call that opinion evidence, or a conclusion, or something of the sort?"

Mason smiled. "You're not in court, and I am very much interested in what you saw on her face. I don't know but what I'd be even more interested in that than in what she had in her hand."

Myrna Payson narrowed her eyes, as though trying to recall some vague memory into sharp focus. Abruptly she said, "But I haven't offered you a drink. How inhospitable of me!"

"No drink," Mason said, "not now, thanks. I'm very much interested in what you saw in Milicent Hardisty's face."

"Or a cigarette?"

"I have my own, thank you."

"Well now, let's see," Mrs. Payson said thoughtfully, "just how I can describe it. . . . It was a fascinating expression, the expression of a woman who has found herself, who has reached a decision and made a renunciation."

"That sounds rather definite and deliberate."

"Well?"

"The story, as I gathered it, is that Mrs. Hardisty was completely hysterical and emotionally upset."

Mrs. Payson shook her head. "Definitely not."

"You're certain?"

"Well, of course, Mr. Mason, when it comes to reading facial expressions, we all have our own ideas, but I've been interested in faces and in emotions. I have a very definite idea about Mrs. Hardisty from what I saw. And it's not anything I'm going to tell in court."

"Could you tell me?" Mason asked.

"You are acting as her lawyer?"

"Yes."

Mrs. Payson thought for a moment, then said, "Yes, I think I could tell you—if there were any reason why I should."

"There is," Mason assured her. "The authorities have buried Mrs. Hardisty. I can't get in touch with her. I'm called on to defend her for murder."

Mrs. Payson said, "Well, you'll laugh at me when I've told you, Mr. Mason."

"Why?"

"Because you'll say it's impossible for a person to learn so much of another's problems and decisions by a fleeting glimpse of a facial expression."

"I'll promise not to laugh," Mason said. "I may smile, I may doubt, I may question—but I won't laugh."

"On the strength of that promise, I'll tell you about Mrs. Hardisty. She had the expression of a woman waking up, of a woman who has definitely reached a decision, a decision to put something old out of her life and to go on with something new. I've seen that same expression two or three times before. I—I went through that experience myself once. I know what it's like."

"Go ahead," Mason said, as she hesitated.

She said, "Mr. Mason, I'll tell you something you can't use as evidence. It isn't worth a snap of your fingers anywhere. If you tell it to anyone, they'll laugh at you, but you can take it from a woman who knows her way around that Milicent Hardisty went out there to kill her husband. She went out with the deliberate intention of murdering him. Probably not because of the hurt he had inflicted on her, but because of the hurt he had inflicted on someone else. She came within an ace of killing him. Perhaps she even fired a shot and it missed. And then suddenly she realized the full potential effect of what she had almost done, realized what the gun she held in her hand really was. It ceased to be a mere means by which she could remove Jack Hardisty from her life forever, but became

76

the key which fitted the door of a prison cell. It became the symbol of a bondage to the law, something that would chain her to a cell until she was an old woman, until love had left her life forever. And she had this sudden revulsion of feeling, and wanted to get rid of that gun. She had a horror of it. She wanted to throw it so far she'd never see it again. And then she was going to the man she loved. And, regardless of consequences, regardless of gossip, regardless of conventions, she was going to live her life with that man. . . . Now, go ahead and laugh, Mr. Mason."

"I'm not laughing, not even smiling."

"And that," Mrs. Payson announced, "is all I know."

"That is what you would call the result of a woman's intuition?"

"That is what *I* would call applied psychology, the knowledge of character one gets when one has lived and gone through a lot—and I have."

Mason couldn't resist asking one more question. "How about Miss Strague?" he asked.

"What about her?"

"What do you deduce from *her* expressions?"

Mrs. Payson laughed. "Would that help you to clear Mrs. Hardisty?"

"It might."

Mrs. Payson said, "Lola Strague is a delightful girl. She's fresh, sweet, and she's spoiled. She waits on her brother hand and foot, but her brother idolizes the ground she walks on, and watches over her.

"She thinks I'm an adventuress; she's in love with Rodney Beaton; she thinks I have designs on him. She's somewhat amateurish in her little jealousies, and just a little hypocritical. She gets jealous, but she won't admit it, even to herself. She tries to rise above all the petty emotions. She pretends to herself that she's done so. And when she puts on that particular mask, she makes me

77

terribly ill, because then she's being a damned little hypocrite. But, in her inexperienced way, she's a very nice little girl. . . . However, I don't think she's the sort that Rodney Beaton would marry."

"And how," Mason asked, "do you feel toward Rodney Beaton?"

She looked him frankly in the eyes and laughed at him.

"Well, now let's see," Mason said. "What else can I ask you?"

"You seem to have taken rather a wide latitude."

"I've asked you just about everything I could think of. Could you swear that Mrs. Hardisty tossed the gun down the barranca?"

"I couldn't swear that she tossed anything down a barranca. I think I saw her arm move. I couldn't swear to it. I don't know what was in her hand. I was watching her face. I tell you I was completely and utterly fascinated with her face."

"How about Burt Strague?" Mason asked.

"What about him?"

"What do you think of him?"

She hesitated a moment, then slowly shook her head.

"Not going to answer that one?" Mason asked.

"Not all of it," she said. "There's someting about Burt Strague that just doesn't fit into the picture. He has a sister complex. He's intensely loyal, emotionally unstable; he has a swift, devastating temper; he's undoubtedly just what he says he is, and yet—and yet, there's something about him that—"

"Doesn't ring true?" Mason asked, as she hesitated, groping for words with which to express the idea.

"It isn't that," she said. "There's something about him —something that he's afraid of, something that his sister is afraid of, something they're fighting, some very dark chapter in his life."

"What makes you think that?"

"The way he's always watching himself, as though some careless word might betray something that must be kept secret at all costs. . . . There, I've told you more than I intended to tell you, and I presume you know why."

"Why?"

"Because I want to help Mrs. Hardisty. I wish all women could realize how much better it is to write off their emotional liabilities and turn to the future while there still *is* a future. Time slips through one's fingers so very imperceptibly, Mr. Mason, that it's tragic. When one is seventeen, twenty is getting old. When one is in the twenties, the thirties seems positively doddering, terribly distant. And the woman in the forties has to conceal her emotions; otherwise people laugh at her. . . . And there's a peculiar shifting viewpoint. When one is in the thirties, one looks at the thirties as being just the prime of life; when one's in the forties, one looks at the thirties with a feeling that they're still a little callow. Time is a clever robber."

"How does a woman of forty look to a man of forty?" Mason asked.

Mrs. Payson smiled. "She doesn't have a chance. A man of forty considers himself in the prime of life and starts ogling girls in the twenties. He reasons that other men of forty may be a little passé, but not him. He's 'exceptionally well preserved.' He's a man who 'looks ten years younger.' "

Mason grinned at her. "Well, how about the men in the sixties and seventies?" he asked.

Mrs. Payson reached for a cigarette. "I think," she announced laughing, "that you've got something there."

10

■

At the hotel Mason found Della Street waiting in the lobby.

"Hello," she exclaimed. "I'm starved! *What* do we do about it?"

"We eat," Mason proclaimed.

"That's swell. Paul Drake's here."

"Where?"

"Up in his room. They gave him a room next to yours, with a communicating door. . . . They say the hotel dining room is a fine place to eat, one of the best in the city."

"We can eat," Mason said, "on one condition."

"What's that?"

"That Jack Hardisty was killed before seven o'clock last night."

"But that's just the time Milicent was up there. You don't want the murder to have been committed while she was there, do you?"

"If it was," Mason said, "it's unfortunate, but there's nothing I can do. If it was committed later, it's also unfortunate, but there's a lot I'm going to have to do."

"What?"

"For one thing, I've got to take a chance—that the person to whom Milicent would turn when she was in desperate trouble, in whom she'd have utter and complete confidence, and who had recently been able to put two brand-new tires on his automobile, would be the family physician."

Della Street thought that over, said, "It sounds logical."

"Okay. Go telephone Vincent Blane. Make your question sound just as casual as possible. Ask him what physician in Roxbury could give us a certificate that Milicent is in a precarious nervous condition due to the strain of her domestic relations."

"Then what?" she asked.

"That's all. Just note the name of the doctor. Then come up to Paul Drake's room. . . . Is the local evening paper out?"

"Yes."

"Anything in it about Milicent?"

"Not a line. They haven't released a bit of information about the arrest."

"The story of the murder is in there?"

"Oh yes. Not a great amount of information, just the statement expanded and amplified and rehashed—the way they do with news nowadays."

"All right. Go put through that call. I'll run up to see Paul."

"Do you want me to telephone from my room or from the lobby?"

"Booth in the lobby. The girl at the switchboard might be curious."

Della Street nodded, moved over toward the telephone booth. Mason went up in the elevator, unlocked the door of his own room, crossed through the communicating door to the adjoining room, and found Paul Drake standing in front of the mirror just finishing shaving with an electric razor.

"Hello, Perry," Drake said, disconnecting the razor and splashing shaving lotion on his face. "What's news?"

"That's what I came up to find out."

Drake put on his shirt and knotted his necktie.

"Well?" Mason asked.

Drake said nothing for the moment, concentrating his attention on getting his tie knotted just right. He was tall, limber, loose-jointed, and his appearance was utterly at variance with the popular conception of what a detective should be. In repose, his face held a lugubrious lack of interest; his eyes, which missed nothing, seemed to be completely oblivious of what was taking place about him. Behind this mask a logical mind worked with mathematical certainty and ball-bearing speed.

"What's the matter?"

"That Milicent girl."

"What about her?"

"You told me to find her, that I could pass up all the tips that she'd be easy to find. You gave me a pretty broad hint that I'd hear she was in her house but that that was just a gag you'd thought up to hand to the cops. Well, I put a flock of men——"

"I know," Mason interrupted, "I was fooled worse than you were."

Drake looked at him, trying to read more meaning into the lawyer's words. "It *wasn't* a stall you'd thought up for the police?"

Mason merely smiled.

"It floored me," Drake went on. "I was looking in all the hide-out places, and here she was at her father's house, tucked safely in bed, with a housekeeper answering all inquiries by saying, 'Yes, she's here, but she can't be disturbed.'"

"And there she was," Mason said.

"Exactly."

"Well, Paul, you've crabbed from time to time that I gave you jobs that were too tough. This was an easy one. All you had to do to locate her was phone her father's house."

Drake said, "Don't give me any more of those 'easy' ones or I'll go nuts."

"What else have you done?" Mason asked.

"Think I've got some place with the Kern County idea. The D.A. over there could use a little publicity."

"What's he doing?"

"Nothing violent yet, but he's sitting up and taking interest. If we could dig up a spectacular angle on the case, I think he'd fall for it. . . . You know, the newspapers like to get an interesting handle they can tack onto a murder—the Tiger Woman Case, the White Flash Case, the Snake-Eyes Murder. . . . Thought maybe you could work out something with that buried clock that would be an angle. Then the city newspapers would go to town on it, and when that happened I think Kern County would move in."

"What time was the murder committed?" Mason asked.

"Can't tell you that yet," Drake said. "I've got a man working on that angle."

Mason frowned. "The autopsy surgeon must have made at least a preliminary report."

Drake said, "That's the queer part of it. They're not releasing anything based on a preliminary report. Makes it seem there's something in the case that doesn't fit."

Mason nodded.

Drake said, "You don't seem very enthusiastic about that, Perry."

"I'm always suspicious of the things in cases that don't fit," Mason said. "I've seen too many lawyers grab hold of some isolated fact that didn't fit and brandish it around in front of a jury. Then something would click and that particular fact fitted into a particular interpretation that hung the client."

When Drake was thinking, he always sought for complete bodily relaxation, propping himself against something or sprawling all over a chair. Now he placed an elbow on the back of a chair, then after a moment, sidled around so that he was sitting on the rounded overstuffed arm, his elbow resting against the back, his hand propping up his chin. "What I'm afraid of is that the D.A.'s office isn't going to pay any attention to that buried clock. They think it's a fairy story. If they play it down the newspapers won't play it up."

Mason said, "I can *almost* give them a theory on that clock, Paul."

Drake said, "Give me a theory that will hold water, and I'll show you some action."

"Ever hear of sidereal time, Paul?"

"What's sidereal time?"

"Star time."

"Are you kidding me?"

"No."

"Why is star time different from sun time?"

"Because the stars gain a day on the sun every year."

"I don't get you."

"The earth makes a big circle around the sun and returns to the place where it started once each year. The effect of that circle is to make the stars rise about two hours earlier every month, or a total gain of twenty-four hours in the twelve months. By keeping clocks that run about four minutes fast every day, astronomers can keep star time instead of sun time.

"Time really is nothing but a huge circle. You divide a circle of three hundred and sixty degrees into twenty-four hours, and you get fifteen degrees of arc that is the equivalent of each hour."

"You're getting too complicated for me," Drake said. "I don't get it."

Mason said, "It's simple enough, once you get the idea. What I'm trying to point out is that by using sidereal time, astronomers know the exact position of any given star at any given moment."

"How?"

"Well, they give each star a certain time position in the heavens, which is known as its 'right ascension.' Then, by knowing the right ascension, looking at a clock and getting the sidereal time, they can know the exact position of the star. That's the way they work the astronomical telescopes. They get the position of the star at a given moment, turn the telescope so that the angle is exactly right, set it for latitude on another graduated circle known as the star's *declination,* look in the finder telescope—and there's the star."

"All right," Drake grinned, "there's the star—so what?"

Mason said, "So, it's a newspaper headline."

Drake thought that over. "I believe you've got something there, Perry—if we could make it stick. What makes you think *this* clock was geared according to this sidereal time you're talking about?"

Mason said, "Look at it this way, Paul. Twice during the year, sidereal time must agree with civil time—once when it hits it right on the nose, and again when it's gained twelve hours, which would have the effect, on a twelve-hour clock, of—"

"Yes, yes, I know," Drake said. "I can figure that out."

"One of these times when sidereal time agrees with civil or sun time, is at the time of the equinox on September twenty-third."

"And then the clock goes on gaining four minutes a day?" Drake asked.

"That's right."

"But this clock was twenty-five minutes *slow.*"

"Thirty-five minutes fast," Mason said, smiling.

"I don't get you."

"You've forgotten that our time has been advanced an hour. Therefore, our war time is an hour ahead of sun time, so that a clock that was twenty-five minutes slow on our war time would be thirty-five minutes fast on our sun time. . . . That gives us something to think about."

"Something to think about is right," Drake said. "If we can tie this murder in with astrology, or even astronomy, we'll give it so much notoriety the district attorney of Kern County will grab at it like a hungry dog grabbing a bone."

Mason said, "Well, it's an angle to think over. All it is, is just a publicity gag for the newspapers, but it'll give them a handle—a tag line."

"I'll say it will," Drake said. "When can I go to town with that, Perry?"

"Almost any time."

Della Street's knock sounded on the door. "Everybody decent?" she called.

"Come on in, Della."

Della Street entered, grinned a salutation at the detective, and walked across to slip a folded piece of paper into Mason's hand.

Drake, whose eyes apparently were centered with fixed interest on some object at the far end of the room, said, "You're ruining that girl, Perry."

"How so?"

"It's the legal training. She's getting so she doesn't trust anyone. You tell her to get some information, and she knows you'll be in here talking with me, so she writes it out on a piece of paper and slips it to you."

Mason laughed, said, "She knows you have a one-track mind, Paul. She doesn't want to distract it." He unfolded the paper.

Della Street had written merely a name on a sheet of paper torn from her notebook. *"Dr. Jefferson Macon, Roxbury."*

Drake said, "There's a story going around that Hardisty had been dipping into funds at the bank. I suppose you're not going to tell me about that. You—"

The telephone rang.

Drake said, "This is probably one of the boys with a report." He picked up the receiver, placed it to his ear, said, "Hello," and then let his face become a mask while he digested the information which was distinguishable to the other occupants of the room only as harsh, metallic noises emanating from time to time from the receiver.

"You're certain?" Drake asked at length. Then, evidently being assured that there was no doubt about the matter, added, "Stay where you are. I may call you back in about five minutes. I'll want to think this over."

He hung up the receiver, turned to Mason and said, "The report of the autopsy surgeon shows Jack Hardisty was killed sometime after seven o'clock, probably around nine o'clock. The time limits are fixed as being between seven o'clock and ten-thirty."

Mason pushed his hands down deep in his trousers pockets, studied the pattern on the faded hotel carpet intently, suddenly snapped a question at the detective. "Was the fatal bullet in the body, Paul?"

The question jarred expression into Drake's face, shattering the mask of wooden-faced disinterest with which the detective customarily masked his thoughts. "Perry, what the devil put that idea in your mind?"

"Was it?" Mason asked.

"No," Drake said. "That's the thing the autopsy surgeon can't figure. That's one of the reasons he held up his report until he'd made a double check. The man was undoubtedly killed with a bullet, probably from a thirty-eight caliber weapon. The bullet didn't go clean through the body—*and the bullet isn't there!*"

Mason nodded slowly, thoughtfully digesting that information.

"You don't seem surprised," Drake said.

"What do you want me to do—throw up my hands and say 'my, my'?"

Drake said, "Bunk! You can't fool me, Perry. You anticipated that very thing."

"What makes you think so?"

"Your question."

"It was just a question."

"And I'll bet this is the only murder case in which you ever asked it."

Mason said nothing.

"Well," Drake told him, "in any event that lets Milicent out."

"What does?"

"The fact that the murder took place after she left the cabin."

Mason shook his head slowly. "No, Paul, it doesn't let her out; it drags her in. I'm sorry, but I'm having to pass up dinner. Take Della—on the expense account."

Drake said, "There are times, Perry, when you get some very commendable ideas."

"Do I know where I can reach you, in case anything turns up?" Della Street asked Perry Mason.

He nodded.

"Where?"

The lawyer merely smiled.

Della said, "I get you."

"And I *don't*," the detective protested.

Della Street placed her fingers on his arm. "Never mind, Paul. We're going to dinner—on the expense account. . . . Do your dinners include cocktails, Paul?"

"They always have when they've been on an expense account," Drake said, "although Perry probably doesn't know it."

Mason grinned, took the sliver of glass from his pocket.

"A piece of a spectacle lens, Paul," he said, handing the sliver to the detective.

Drake turned it over in his fingers. "What about it?"

Mason started for the door. "That's what I'm paying you for, Paul."

11

Roxbury's main street seemed strangely surreptitious with its unlighted neon signs, its shielded illumination, making the figures of pedestrians appear vague, shadowy and unreal.

Perry Mason, driving slowly along, counted the intersections to find the cross street that he wanted, turned abruptly to the right, ran his car for a block and a half, and stopped in front of a white stucco, red tile, pretentious house. The sign on the lawn which said "DR. JEFFERSON MACON" was hardly visible, now that the street lights had been extinguished.

Mason climbed a flight of short steps, found a bell button, and pushed it. A broad-beamed middle-aged woman with unsmiling countenance opened the door and said, "The doctor's evening hours are nine to ten."

Mason said, "I want to see him upon an urgent private matter."

"Do you have a card?"

Mason said impatiently, "Tell him Perry Mason, a lawyer, would like to see him at once."

The woman said, "Wait here, please," turned on her heel and marched with slow, deliberate steps down a corridor, pushed open a door and banged it shut behind her, the explosive sound of the closing door conveying definite disapproval.

Mason had been standing for almost a minute when she returned, coming toward him with the same slow, deliberate steps—heavy-footed, wooden-faced.

She waited until she had assumed exactly the same position which she had been in when Mason first saw her—evidently her answering-the-door stance. "The doctor will see you."

Mason followed her back down the corridor, through the door and into a small, book-lined room, near the center of which, in a huge black leather chair, Dr. Jefferson Macon was stretched out, completely relaxed.

"Good evening," he said. "Please be seated. Pardon me for not getting up. The exigencies of my profession are such that I must ruin my own health safeguarding the health of others. If I had a patient who lived the life I do, I'd say he was committing suicide. As it is, I have been forced to make it a rule to relax for half an hour after each meal. . . . Kindly state what it is you wish. Be brief. Don't be disappointed if I show no reaction whatever. I'm training myself to relax completely and shut out all extraneous affairs."

Mason said, "That's fine. Go ahead and relax all you want. Did Milicent Hardisty spend all the night here last night, or just part of it?"

Dr. Macon jerked himself into a rigid sitting posture. "What—*what's that?*"

He was, Mason saw, a man approaching fifty, firm-fleshed, steady-eyed, slender. Yet there was in the man's face that grayish look of fatigue which comes to those who are near the point of physical exhaustion from the strain of overwork.

Mason said, "I wanted to know whether Milicent Hardisty spent the entire night here or only part of it."

"That's presumptuous. That's a dastardly insinuation! That—"

"Can you answer the question?" Mason interrupted.

"Yes, of course. I can answer it."

"Then what's the answer?"

"I see no reason for giving you any answer."

Mason said, "She's been arrested."

"Milicent—arrested? You mean the authorities think— why, that's shocking!"

"You knew nothing of it?" Mason asked.

"I certainly did not. I had no idea the police would be so stupid as to do anything of the sort."

Mason said, "There's some circumstantial evidence against her."

"Then the evidence has been misinterpreted."

"Go right ahead," Mason said, motioning toward the deep cushions of the chair. "Lie right back and relax. I'll just ask questions. You keep on relaxing."

Dr. Macon continued to sit bolt upright.

Mason said, "Everyone's acted on the assumption that Hardisty's death occurred early in the evening. Quite possibly ten or fifteen minutes before deep dusk. A report's just come in from the autopsy surgeon. They held it up until they could make a double check, because it didn't agree with what the police thought were the facts."

Dr. Macon stroked the tips of his fingers across his cheek. "May I ask what the report indicated?"

"Death between seven and ten-thirty," Mason said. "Probably, around nine."

"Did I understand you to say probably around nine o'clock?"

"Yes."

"Then that—then Milicent couldn't possibly have been connected with it."

"Why?"

"She was . . . she was home at that time, wasn't she?"

"How do you know?"

Dr. Macon caught himself quickly and said, "I don't. I was only asking."

"What time were you up there?"

"Where?"

"Up at the Blane cabin."

"You mean that *I* went up there?"

Mason nodded.

Dr. Macon said somewhat scornfully, "I'm afraid I don't appreciate your connection with the case, Mr. Mason. I know who are are, of course. I would like to meet you under more favorable—and I may say, more friendly —circumstances; but I am afraid you are definitely barking up the wrong tree. I am, of course, enough of a psychologist to appreciate the technique of a cross-examination in which startling questions are propounded without warning to an unsuspecting witness and—"

Mason interrupted him to say, apparently without feeling, "I may be mistaken."

"I'm glad to hear you say so."

"Whether I am or not," Mason said, "depends on the tires on your automobile."

"What do you mean?"

"An automobile left tracks up at the Blane cabin. I don't think the significance of those tracks has occurred to the police—as yet. The Los Angeles deputies took it for granted the tracks were made by the local authorities. It evidently hasn't occurred to the local authorities to check up on them."

"What about them?"

"They were the tracks of *new* tires."

"What if they were?"

Mason smiled. "Perhaps in your position, Doctor, you haven't as yet appreciated the seriousness of tire rationing, and therefore have dismissed it from your mind."

"I'm afraid I don't—"

"Oh, yes you do. You're stalling for time, Doctor. You recently had two new tires put on the back wheels of your automobile. Undoubtedly you had to get those tires through the tire rationing board. There's a complete record of installation, application for purchase, and all that. As soon as I saw the *new* tire marks, it occurred to me that I was dealing with a police car. When I found out it couldn't have been a police car, I simply started running down the other angles. It isn't everyone who could possibly have *two brand-new tires* on his automobile, you know."

"And that investigation brought you to me?"

Mason nodded.

"I suppose you realize," Dr. Macon said, with frigid formality, "that you are making a most serious charge."

"I haven't made any charge yet but I'm going to make one in a minute—as soon as you quit stalling around."

"Really, Mr. Mason, I think this is uncalled for."

"So do I. I'm trying to help my client."

"And who is your client, may I ask?"

"Milicent Hardisty."

"She has retained you?"

"Her father did."

"She is—you say she is charged with—"

"Murder."

"I can't believe it possible."

Mason looked at his watch. "You've got to start seeing people at nine o'clock, Doctor. Time's limited. I took a short cut getting here. I saw the tracks of two new tires and jumped at conclusions. The officers will go at it more methodically. They can't afford to play hunches. They'll probably make a cast of the tire marks, check with the tire rationing board on all permits for new tires, check with dealers for sales, and eventually they'll get here. I'm simply leading the procession."

93

Dr. Macon shifted his position uneasily. "I take it that anything I may say to you will be entirely confidential, Counselor."

"Guess again."

"You mean it won't?"

"That's right."

"But I thought you said you were representing Milicent Hardisty."

"I am."

"I—"

"I'm representing her, and no one else. Anything *she* tells me is confidential; anything *you* tell me is something I use or don't use, depending on *her* best interests."

"If she has an alibi for—well, from seven o'clock on until midnight, that would absolve her from any connection with the crime?"

"Probably."

"I—" Dr. Macon's voice dissolved into a somewhat dubious silence.

"Make up your mind," Mason said.

Dr. Macon said, "I want to tell you a little story."

"I'd rather you'd answer a little question."

He shook his head impatiently. "You have to understand the preliminaries, the steps by which this thing came into existence."

"Tell me about the thing that came into existence, and we'll talk about the steps later."

"No. I can't do that. I must go about it in my own way, Mr. Mason. I insist."

Once more Mason looked at his watch.

Dr. Macon said, "I will be brief. The modern physician, in order to serve his patients, must know something of their emotional natures, something of their backgrounds, something of the problems which confront them —the emotional crises, the—"

"I know all that," Mason said. "Tell me about Mrs. Hardisty."

"As soon as she came to me I realized there was some deep-seated worry, some lack of mental harmony. I suspected her domestic relations."

"And asked questions?"

"Not at once. I first went about getting her confidence."

"Then what?"

"Then I questioned her."

"What did you find out?"

"That, Mr. Mason, is confidential. I can't betray facts learned from a patient in making a diagnosis."

"Then why mention them?"

"Because I want you to realize that my knowledge of Milicent Hardisty is much more complete than yours could possibly be."

Mason settled down comfortably in a chair, lit a cigarette. "Because you investigated her mental condition in connection with your diagnosis?"

"Yes."

"Don't kid yourself," Mason said. "A lawyer does just as much probing into minds as a doctor does. What's more, a lawyer is better equipped and better trained to do it. You probably won't admit that. It doesn't make any difference whether you do or whether you don't, particularly since I haven't as yet had an opportunity to talk with Milicent Hardisty.

"Now you want to stall around for time, lay a foundation for impressing me, and put yourself in the position where you can tell me what you want to tell me, and hold out what you don't want me to know. If you think you can get away with it, go right ahead. It's going to take a little more time, but when we get done we'll understand each other that much better. You go right on with your prepared speech, and when you get finished, *I'll* do a little probing."

95

Dr. Macon smiled. "I'm afraid, Counselor, that you underestimate the facilities at the command of a trained physician. I know Milicent Hardisty much better than you could ever hope to know her by what you lawyers call cross-examination."

Mason gave himself to the enjoyment of his cigarette, made no comment.

Dr. Macon's professional bearing gradually reasserted itself. With the manner of a physician telling the patient just what the patient should know for his own good, and withholding everything that was not necessary for the patient to understand, Mr. Macon said, "Milicent Hardisty became a patient of mine. She had implicit trust in me. She confided in me. I came to know her innermost secrets. I was able to do her some good. I can tell you this much without betraying any confidence. She had devoted too much attention to her career, to the serious things in life. That over-emphasis on work left her with a secret hunger to be the center of attraction with some particular person —not a platonic attraction, but a sex attraction. For that reason she didn't question, even in her own mind, the motives of Jack Hardisty when he began rushing her off her feet in a whirlwind, impetuous courtship. Even if she *had* questioned his motives, I doubt if a realization of his duplicity would have stopped her. She was too thrilled with the novelty of having some man woo her, making of his courting not an intellectual pastime but a violent emotional activity.

"Jack Hardisty was shrewd enough to realize all that. Milicent has a good mind. She had in the past tried to appeal to persons upon an intellectual plane. Jack Hardisty decided the way to impress her was to sweep her off her feet, to bring ardor and passion to his wooing. It succeeded admirably."

Mason dropped ashes from the end of his cigarette into Dr. Macon's ash tray, said nothing.

"I'll tell you this—that after Vincent Blane established Jack Hardisty in business, Hardisty repaid his benefactor by embezzling money." Dr. Macon paused, dramatically.

Mason merely nodded.

Dr. Macon was obviously disappointed that his information came as no surprise. He frowned for a moment, then said, "Oh yes, the father retained you. Naturally, he told you about that."

"Go on," Mason said.

Dr. Macon thought for a minute, then began talking again, this time with more swift certainty. "I knew that Mrs. Hardisty was approaching a very definite crisis in her life. I knew that she had been unhappy for a long time. She had kept on, merely to preserve a semblance of happiness, and because she hesitated to make public confession that Jack Hardisty's interest in her had been financial. I think you will appreciate the feeling."

Mason made no comment.

"Late yesterday afternoon, when she failed to appear at my office to keep an appointment for a treatment, I took steps to ascertain that she was all right. As a result of those steps, I found that her husband had gone to Kenvale, and from there up to a mountain cabin owned by Mr. Blane. I learned that Mrs. Hardisty had followed him. I feared that, under some emotional unbalance, Mrs. Hardisty might suffer a nervous shock which would permanently impair her nervous and emotional stability."

"What did you do?" Mason asked.

"I started out to find Mrs. Hardisty."

"What time?"

"I would prefer to tell this in my own way, Mr. Mason. Your questions can come later. I believe you mentioned you wanted to probe my mind," and Dr. Macon's smile was icy.

"Go right ahead," Mason said, "pardon me. Simply because time is short I thought I could expedite matters.

97

But if you want to rehearse your story as you make it up, so as to be certain it's bomb-proof, go right ahead."

Dr. Macon said, "I am *not* making up this story. Whatever slight hesitancy you may notice is because I don't know exactly how much I can safely tell you without betraying confidential communications, and——"

"Never mind all that," Mason interrupted. "Go on with the story. What happened?"

"I drove toward the cabin in search of Mrs. Hardisty, that's all."

"Find her?"

"Yes."

"Go on," Mason said. "Tell it your way."

"I didn't find Mrs. Hardisty *at the cabin*. I found her in Kenvale. She was, I believe, following her unmarried sister, who was driving in a car ahead."

Dr. Macon paused for an appreciable interval. His face showed satisfaction; his eyes were triumphant. "I believe that about covers it. . . . I found Mrs. Hardisty in a serious nervous and emotional state. I kept her with me until approximately ten o'clock in the evening, until her nerves had responded to treatment. Then I drove her back to Kenvale, administered a hypodermic just before she entered the house, and told her to go to bed at once and to sleep late."

"That all of it?" Mason asked.

"That's enough, isn't it? I know that she was with me until after ten o'clock. I personally administered a hypodermic and know that immediately after taking that she would go to sleep and remain asleep for almost twelve hours."

"Finished?" Mason asked.

"Yes, sir. I have finished."

"All right," Mason said. "Now we'll start probing."

"Go right ahead."

"I believe you said you decided to go up to the cabin

98

in order to rescue Milicent from an experience which would disorganize her nerves and emotions."

"Substantially that. As usual with laymen, you have garbled the medical exactitude of expression; but we'll let it stand."

"And you found Milicent at Kenvale?"

"Yes."

"What time?"

"Well . . . let me see. . . . I should say that it was about —a man doesn't consult his watch under such circumstances, you know, even though attorneys are very fond of asking for exact time."

"Approximately what time?"

"Oh, it was sometime after six—perhaps around half past six."

"As late as seven?"

"I don't think so, yet it might have been."

"And not before six o'clock."

"No."

"And when you left your office, looking for Milicent, you knew that she was up at the cabin?"

"Yes."

"You mentioned that certain sources of information advised you on that point?"

"Well, yes. I secured that information."

"How?"

"I can't make any statement as to that."

"Why?"

"It would be betraying a confidence."

"Whose?"

"That's beside the point."

"A patient's?"

Dr. Macon thought over the question. A little gleam flashed in his eye, then disappeared. "Yes. The information came from a patient."

"And you realized that because Mrs. Hardisty was up

99

at the cabin and because Jack Hardisty was up there, there was a certain element of danger involved."

"What do you mean by danger? You must be more explicit, Counselor. You may mean danger to my patient's health, or physical danger, or—"

"That it was dangerous to the health of your patient to be up at the cabin."

"Yes."

"Then," Mason said with a smile, "how did it happen that immediately after you found her in Kenvale, in place of getting her as far away from the cabin as you could, you transported her right back up to that cabin?"

Dr. Macon's lips tightened. "I didn't say that."

"I'm saying it."

"I don't think that's a fair inference from what I said."

"It's not only a fair inference from what you said, but it's definitely indicated by your tire marks. Your automobile was up at that cabin."

"You haven't identified my tire marks. You haven't even seen my machine."

Mason said wearily, "Quit stalling. Did you or did you not take your car up to that cabin? Did you or did you not take Milicent up to that cabin after you found her in Kenvale?"

"I don't have to answer that question."

"You don't have to answer any of my questions," Mason said. "But those questions are going to be asked you by the police."

"There's a good chance the police may not even come to me."

"About one chance in a million."

"I don't agree with you."

"It doesn't make any difference whether you agree with me or not. You're going to be called on to answer that question. You're dead right in saying I have no authority to make you answer it. Does that mean you're afraid to answer it here and now?"

"I simply refuse to answer that question."

"Why? Because the answer might incriminate you?"

"I give you no reason. I just don't have to answer that question, and I refuse to, that's all."

"No argument about that. Naturally, when you become afraid to answer questions, I am free to draw my own conclusions."

Dr. Macon stroked his chin nervously. "I took Milicent up there for certain reasons—connected with her health. It was a part of the treatment I had worked out for her. And I think you will agree with me, Counselor, that the minute I say *that,* no authority on earth can make me divulge what that treatment was or why I knew it was indicated."

"I don't think your medical exemption is that broad," Mason said, "but we'll let the answer stand for the minute. It is, of course, predicated upon the fact that you are her physician and that you are making that statement in that capacity."

"Certainly."

"How long have you been in love with her?" Mason asked.

Dr. Macon winced perceptibly, then said, as he made an attempt to regain his composure, "I suppose there is no limit to the insinuating, insulting questions—"

"You *are* in love with her, aren't you?"

"That is neither here nor there."

Mason said patiently, "It's very pertinent, Doctor. You tell a story which gets you into a position where you have to rely on your professional immunity to keep from answering interrogations. In other words, you have to show that *what* you did was done as a physician.

"Now, as the character of the physician merges into

101

that of the lover, the immunity of the physician vanishes."

"That is a matter we will leave with the police," Dr. Macon said with dignity.

"All right," Mason went on, "we'll get back to your story and my probing. You state that you gave Mrs. Hardisty a hypodermic which would put her to sleep."

"Yes."

"How soon would it take effect?"

"Within a very few minutes."

"Ten minutes?"

"An effect would be noticeable within that time, yes."

"She'd be asleep within half an hour?"

"Definitely."

"She couldn't have pretended to go to bed and then got up, taken a good strong cup of coffee or a caffein capsule and—"

"Definitely not," Dr. Macon interrupted.

"And you gave her that hypodermic just before she entered her house?"

"Yes."

"Acting as her physician?"

"Yes, of course."

"Not as her lover?"

"Mr. Mason, I'll thank you to—"

Mason silenced him with an upraised hand.

"You don't have to answer the question if you don't want to, Doctor. Just don't get steamed up about it."

"It's an insulting question, and I refuse to answer it on that ground—and on that ground alone."

"All right. You gave that hypodermic while she was sitting in the automobile and before she entered the house."

"Yes."

"How long have you been practicing, Doctor?"

"Something over twenty years."

"And during that time, have you *ever* given any other patient a hypodermic under similar circumstances?"

"What do you mean?"

"If you were acting as her physician, and solely in that capacity, you would naturally have gone into the house with the patient. You would have ordered her to prepare herself for bed. After she had got in bed, you would have administered a hypodermic. Then you would have waited a few minutes to make certain the hypodermic had taken effect, and then left the house, leaving instructions with whoever was in the house as to the care of the patient."

Dr. Macon's eyes avoided those of the lawyer.

"This business of sitting out in front of a house giving a woman a hypodermic, telling her to go in and put herself to bed, and then driving off, smacks of something furtive, something secretive, something that is highly irregular."

"Under the circumstances, I thought it was best to administer the hypodermic in that way. I reached that decision as a physician because of her symptoms, and I refuse to be questioned on that point."

"There was no reason why you weren't welcome in Mr. Blane's house?"

"Well . . . I don't think Mr. Blane approved of me as a physician for his daughter."

"Why?"

"I'm sure I couldn't tell you."

"It wasn't because he had some doubt as to your professional qualifications?"

"Certainly not."

"Then it must have been because of the personal relationship which was being built up."

"I prefer not to go into that."

"I can see that you might. . . . Well, there you are, Doctor. There are enough holes in your story right now

103

to start you sweating, and I can think up a dozen more angles of attack."

"Then you don't believe my story?"

"It's incredible. It's unconvincing. It's contradictory. You can't make it stand up. You can't explain why you took her to the cabin, or why you gave her that hypodermic out in the car."

"I don't have to."

"Not to me, perhaps, but if you're telling a story to protect Milicent, it's something that *has* to stand up."

"What makes you think I am telling this to protect Milicent?"

"Because it's a fair inference that you met Milicent; that you went back up to the cabin with her because you knew Hardisty was up there; that you and she wanted to submit some proposition to Hardisty; that Hardisty was killed with a bullet from Milicent's gun, fired either by you or by Milicent; that you then extracted the bullet from Hardisty's body so it couldn't be traced to Milicent's gun."

"Absurd!"

"Well, we'll try another angle, then. Milicent Hardisty went up to the cabin. She met her husband up there. They had an argument. She accused him of a lot of things and insisted that he turn over to her the money and negotiable securities he had taken from the bank. He refused. She threatened him with the gun. There was a struggle for the possession of the gun. Jack Hardisty got shot, but death was not instantaneous. Milicent, in a frenzy, started running down the road from the cabin, hardly knowing what she was doing. Her sister, Adele, met her on the road. Milicent, in a panic, concealed her gun somewhere, or threw it away. Adele saw where this was. . . . Jack Hardisty was badly wounded. Milicent and Adele put him to bed. They then telephoned a frantic appeal to you. You dashed up to the cabin, examined Hardisty and found that he was dead. He had died between the time he was put to bed and the time of your arrival. You then, swayed by your love for Milicent, proceeded to try to fix things up so that the murder was hopelessly obscured. You ran Hardisty's car over the grade. You removed the fatal bullet with your surgical instruments and took care to see that *it* would never be found. Adele may or may not have been in on the whole business. She probably was. You intended to deny any knowledge of what had happened, or that you had any connection with it. But the fact that I traced you through those automobile tires gave you a terrific jolt. . . . Now then, Doctor, let's hear what you have to say to that."

Dr. Macon shifted his position, said nothing.

At that moment, knuckles tapped gently on the door. The woman who had let Mason in opened the door and said apologetically, "I beg your pardon for disturbing you, Doctor, but a Mr. Jameson and Mr. McNair want to ask you some questions."

Mason said to Mr. Macon, "There it is. Jameson's the resident deputy at Kenvale, and Thomas L. McNair is a deputy from the district attorney's office. So you see, Doctor, you didn't have as much time as you thought you had. . . . Now let me tell you something. If Milicent Hardisty fired the bullet that killed her husband, either accidentally or in self-defense, or because he was just a rat who needed killing, now's the time for you to say so, and I'll see that she gets a fair break. But if you're trying to cover it up; if you think you can match wits with the law and come out on top, you're going to wind up by getting her convicted of first-degree murder. . . . Speak up."

Dr. Macon said, "I am not afraid of the law, Mr. Mason."

The lawyer studied him. "That's the worst of you doctors. Your training makes you too self-reliant. Just because you can advise patients on diet, you think you know how to advise 'em on everything. A lawyer wouldn't think he could snip out an appendix. But you're taking it on yourself to think out Milicent's defense to a charge of murder —and I think it's a lousy defense."

Dr. Macon said, with calm, professional dignity, "I have nothing to add to the story I have told you, Mr. Mason, and nothing to retract from it. Show the gentlemen in, Mable."

"Just a minute," Mason said. *"Just* a minute! Come in here, Mable, and close that door."

She hesitated a moment, then obeyed.

Mason said, "If those two find me here, they'll crucify you. The mere fact that I'm talking with you will make them think Milicent or Adele sent me to you. Is there any other way out?"

"Not out of this room. Where are they waiting, Mable?"

"In the hallway—and I don't think they'll wait long."

Mason said, "Tell them the doctor is busy with an emergency patient; that he'll see them just as soon as he completes the dressings." Then he turned to Dr. Macon. "Bandage up my head, Doctor. Leave one eye so I can see and that's all. Put my arm in a sling, spill on some disinfectants, and time things so they'll pass me in the corridor on the way in."

Dr. Macon nodded to the housekeeper, said to Mason, "Loosen your necktie and open your shirt."

The physician's hands moved with swift, deft skill. He wound bandage around Mason's head, placed his left arm in a sling, ripped wide adhesive tape into narrow ribbons, anchored the bandage with strips of tape, and sprinkled on antiseptic.

"All ready?" he asked Mason.

Mason's voice, coming from beneath the bandage, sounded strangely muffled. "Okay, Doctor. I'm warning

106

you for the last time—don't try to cover up. You can't get away with it."

Dr. Macon was crisply confident. "I can handle this situation very nicely," he said. "One of the things you fail to take into consideration, Counselor, is that a doctor is trained to keep his wits in an emergency."

Before Mason could reply, Dr. Macon threw open the door of the little den, said in a loud voice, "Show the gentlemen in, Mable."

Mason, his hat in his hand, walked out of the office, stooping slightly so as to disguise his figure.

Jameson and McNair passed him on the way in, keeping well over to one side so as not to brush against Mason's arm. Apparently they gave him no second glance.

Behind him, Mason heard Dr. Macon say, "Good evening, gentlemen, what can I do for you?"

The housekeeper held the outer door open for Mason.

"Good night," the lawyer muttered.

The woman made no answer, indignantly slammed the door as soon as Mason reached the porch.

12

■

Paul Drake was waiting for Mason in the lobby of the Kenvale Hotel. "We've located Adele Blane, Perry."

"Where?"

"San Venito Hotel, Los Angeles. . . . That is, she *was* there. We've located her, and lost her again."

"How come?"

"The locating was easy," Drake said, "just a matter of leg work. We covered all the garages here. Didn't find anything. Didn't expect to. We checked all the garages at

Roxbury and found her car stored in the Acme Garage. The Acme Garage is near the bus depot. We checked on the time the car had been stored, and then started checking on the buses that left within an hour of that time. We found that a woman who answered Adele's description had gone to Los Angeles, traveling without baggage. I put operatives on the job, covering all the hotels near the Los Angeles bus terminal. We had a good description, and acted on the assumption that she'd been checking in without baggage. My operative finally located her at this little hotel. It's within about four blocks of the bus depot. She's registered under the name of Martha Stevens."

Mason knitted his brows. "That name's familiar, that's—"

"Housekeeper," Drake interposed.

"That's right. . . . Why would Adele Blane register under the name of her father's housekeeper?"

"Don't know," Drake said. "I can tell you one thing, Perry. . . . Martha Stevens isn't just any old housekeeper. She really rates, both with Vincent Blane and with the children. Incidentally, she gives Vincent Blane his hypodermics."

"What hypodermics?"

"Insulin."

"Is Blane diabetic?"

"Uh huh. Has to have an insulin shot twice a day. He can, of course, take them himself when he has to, but it's a lot more convenient to have someone else do the jabbing. . . . Martha does it."

"She's a nurse?"

"No. Milicent is, you know—or was. Milicent must have taught her how. . . . What did you find out just now, anything?"

Mason said, "Fat's being poured into the fire."

"How come?"

"The name on the paper Della handed me just before

108

I went out was that of Dr. Jefferson Macon, who lives at Roxbury."

Drake's eyes narrowed. "Milicent's physician?"

"Yes."

Drake snapped his fingers in exasperation. "*I* should have thought of that. What gave *you* the lead, Perry?"

"Tracks of new tires up at the cabin."

"Oh, *oh!*"

Mason said, "He's one of those calm, competent physicians and surgeons. He's been in love with Milicent for some time. Evidently knows pretty much about what's going on. . . . He got a tip that Hardisty was up at the cabin, and Milicent was going up, so he started out after Milicent, claims he met her on the outskirts of Kenvale. The evidence substantiates that part of it. What I'm afraid of is that he went *back* to the cabin with Milicent. The thing that bothers me most is that there must have been a note from Milicent to him, and there's just a chance that note may not have been destroyed."

"What gives you the idea of the note?" Drake asked.

"The time element. If Milicent had telephoned him that she was going to the cabin, Dr. Macon would have dropped everything and dashed up there after her, arriving a few minutes after she did. The way things look at this time, and from where I stand, Milicent must have written Dr. Macon a note. Someone delivered it—perhaps Martha Stevens. . . . Where's Della?"

"Upstairs."

Mason strode over to the room telephones, got Della Street on the line and said, "Just back, and going out. You haven't heard anything from Adele Blane?"

"No."

"Stick around. If she calls, have her keep under cover until I can get in touch with her. There's another angle to this thing. It doesn't look so good."

"See the doctor?"

109

"'Yes."

"Okay. I'll wait right here."

Mason hung up the telephone, walked back to Drake. "How did your man happen to lose her once he'd found her?" he asked.

"Adele?"

"Yes."

Drake said, "It's just one of those things, Perry. My man doesn't *think* that she was wise to him, but she *may* have been. She walked out of the hotel, evidently looking for a taxi, although there was nothing to tip off my operative that that was what she was doing. He tagged along fifty or seventy-five feet behind her. She was headed toward a taxi stand, as it turned out. Then, just as she was crossing a street, a taxi drew up, she flagged it, the signal changed, and they were gone. My man jumped on the running board of a private car, told the driver to follow the taxi. It just happened the driver didn't see things that way. He pulled over to the curb and started to argue. My man jumped off and tried to grab another cab and this motorist claimed it was a hold-up, and let out a squawk for the police. By the time the thing got straightened around, there was no chance of finding Adele Blane. . . . Those things happen in this business. . . . We're keeping the hotel covered, of course. She hasn't checked out. She'll be back."

Mason said, "That Martha Stevens business is the thing I can't understand. It worries me."

Drake said, "Want to go find this housekeeper and shake her down?"

Mason nodded. "My car's outside. Let's go, Paul."

13

∎

Perry Mason slid his car to a gentle stop in front of the Blane residence.

"Looks dark," Drake said.

"The lights may be shielded," Mason observed, putting on the emergency brake. "Let's take a chance."

They walked up the echoing cement, pounded up the stairs to the porch. The sound of the doorbell was a sepulchral echo from the interior of the house.

Mason and Drake exchanged glances.

They rang twice more before giving up.

"Perhaps it's her night off," Drake said.

"Uh huh, we'll talk with Vincent Blane about her."

"Where are you going to find him?"

Mason said, "Ten to one there's a directors' meeting at that bank in Roxbury, and Blane is sitting there at the directors' table, very affably and suavely discussing ways and means and alibis."

"Want to bust in on him?" Drake asked.

"Why not?"

"Okay. Let's go."

While they were driving along at a thirty-five-mile-an-hour pace that seemed as awkward as the three-legged gait of a crippled greyhound, Drake said, "I can't get over Adele registering under the name of Martha Stevens. Why the devil didn't she think up a name?"

"Two reasons," Mason said.

"You're two ahead of me. I can't even think of one."

"One of them is that just in case anything ever came

up Adele might have fixed it up with Martha Stevens to swear that *she* was the one who occupied the room."

Drake said, "Well, it's an idea, but I don't get enthusiastic over it."

"The other one," Mason pointed out, "is that someone was going to meet Martha Stevens at the San Venito Hotel. Adele knew about the rendezvous, and decided to double for Martha Stevens. . . . Or else she's a stand-in to hold things in line until Martha can get there."

Drake shifted his position nervously. *"Now* you've got something, Perry. That last sounds more like it. I'll bet Martha Stevens is on her way to that hotel right now."

Mason said, "On a hunch, Paul, let's telephone your office from Roxbury. Send down a couple of operatives to check on the hotel, give them a description of Martha Stevens. Tell them to stick around and see what happens."

Drake said, "Step on it. It's going to take a little while to get men on the job. You can't pick up good operatives these days just by asking for them."

Entering the outskirts of Roxbury, Mason said, "While we're about it, we may as well drive by Hardisty's house. I want to see what the place looks like. . . . You know where it is?"

"I have the address," Drake said, pulling a memorandum book out of his pocket. "I haven't covered it personally. I've been busy on this other stuff."

"Okay. Let's hunt the place up. What's the address?"

"453 D Street."

Mason said, "Let's see how the streets run. Probably the letter streets are either north and south or east and west. . . . What street is this?"

Drake craned his neck out the car, said, "I can't tell. The sign is right next to the street light."

"There's a spotlight in the glove compartment. I'll slow down so you can take a look at the next one."

Drake gave vent to his feelings. "A detective's nightmare, these ornamental lamp posts with brackets for street names. You can't possible read these signs at night. You're looking at a black object silhouetted against a bright light. Cities have been buying those things for the last twenty-five years. What good does it do to advertise that it's a friendly city, thank you for your patronage and ask you to call again, when they're storing up ill will by sticking signs where strangers can't see 'em?"

"Why don't you go before a luncheon club and make a speech?"

"Some day I'm going to. It'll be *some* speech!"

"In the meantime take a look at this one," Mason observed slowing the car.

Drake tried to shield his eyes, said, "It's no use." He took the spotlight Mason pushed into his hand, directed the beam against the sign and said, "This is Jefferson Street."

"Okay. We'll turn to the right and see if we pick up the lettered streets."

The next street was A Street. Mason ran swiftly across B and C Streets to D, and turned left. Drake, with the aid of Mason's flashlight, began picking up numbers.

"This is the six-hundred block, two blocks more. About the middle of the block on the right-hand side. . . . Okay, Perry, take it easy now. . . . That looks like the place right ahead. There are lights in the windows."

Mason slowed the car to a scant fifteen miles an hour, crept past the lighted house, turned the corner to the right.

"Circling the block?" Drake asked.

"Yes. I want to take another look at it. What do you make of it, Paul?"

"Darned if I know. Lights are on and the shades are up. You can look right into the place, but there doesn't seem to be any sign of life."

113

Mason kept the car at the fifteen-mile-an-hour pace as he circled the block. "It *may* be a trap, Paul."

Drake said, "If no one's home, let's not go prowling around."

"On the other hand," Mason observed, "it *might* be that Adele Blane is in there. It's not apt to be Milicent Hardisty; it *can't* be Jack Hardisty. . . . Oh well, let's go see."

"Promise me you won't go in," Drake pleaded. "If no one's in there, and lights are on and perhaps the door unlocked, let's not stick our necks in a noose."

Mason said, "We'll see what it looks like."

They swung around the corner, back into D Street. Mason shifted into neutral and coasted up to the curb. He switched off the motor and lights and for a moment the two men sat in the car looking at the house.

"Front door's open a crack," Mason said. "You can see light around the edges."

"Uh huh."

"Of course, Paul, it may be that Vincent Blane has just stopped by. He may have a key."

"I tell you, Perry, it's a trap of some sort."

"Well, let's go up on the porch."

"Promise you won't go in?"

"Why all the holding back, Paul?"

"Because they'd accuse you of trying to find evidence and planning to conceal it. After all, Perry, we're playing this whole thing pretty much in the dark."

"I'll say we are," Mason agreed as they walked up the steps to the porch.

"Front door is open, all right," Mason said pressing a thumb against the bell button.

The jangling sound of the bell came from the interior of the house, but there was no other sign of life or motion.

Drake, looking through the front window, said suddenly, "Oh, Perry! Take a look here, will you?"

Mason moved over to his side. Through the open window could be seen a massive, antique, mahogany writing desk. A slanting door dropped down to form an apron for writing, back of it were a series of pigeonholes.

The splintered lock on the writing desk told its own story. Papers, strewn about the floor, had apparently been pulled out from the pigeonholes, hastily unfolded, read and discarded in a helter-skelter of confusion.

Drake said, "That settles it, Perry. Let's get out while the getting's good."

Mason hesitated a moment, standing in front of the window, then said with evident reluctance, "I guess that's the only sensible thing to do. If we notify the police, they'll always be suspicious we pulled the job, and then notified them after we had found and concealed what we wanted."

Drake turned and started eagerly for the stairs on the porch. Mason paused long enough to push against the front door.

"Don't do it, Perry," Drake pleaded.

Mason said, "Wait a minute, Paul. Something's wrong here. There's something behind the door. Something that yields just a little yet blocks the door—it's a man! I can see his feet!"

Drake, standing at the edge of the porch said, "All right, Perry, there's nothing we can do. Telephone the cops if you feel that way about it. We just won't give our names when we phone, that's all. Let them come and see what it's all about."

Mason hesitated for a moment, then squeezed through into the room.

Drake said with angry sarcasm, "Sure, go ahead! Stick your neck in! Leave a few fingerprints! You aren't in bad enough already. It won't hurt *you* to discover a couple more corpses, and when I try to renew *my* license another black mark more or less won't make any difference."

Mason said, "Perhaps there's something we can do, Paul," and peered around at the object behind the door.

The man who lay sprawled on the floor was somewhere in the late fifties. A spare individual with high cheek bones, a long, firm mouth, big-boned hands and long arms. His slow stertorous breathing was plainly audible once Mason had entered the room.

Mason said, "Oh, Paul, take a look. He's not dead, just knocked out. . . . Don't see any signs of a bullet wound —wait a minute, here's a gun."

Mason bent over the weapon. "A short-barreled .38," he said. "There's an odor of powder smoke. Looks as though it might have been fired. . . . But I still can't see any bullet wounds."

Drake said, "For the love of Mike, Perry, come on out of there. We'll telephone the police and let *them* wrestle with it."

Mason, completely absorbed with the problem of trying to deduce what happened, said, "This bird has a leather holster on his belt. Looks as though it was his gun. He may have been the one who did the shooting and then perhaps he got slugged. . . . Yes, here's a bruise up on the left temple, Paul. Looks as though it might have been done with a blackjack or—"

A siren sounded with that peculiarly throbbing sequence of low notes which comes before and after the high-pitched scream. A blood-red spotlight impaled Paul Drake on the porch, swept past him to throw a reddish light through the half-open front door.

Drake said with what was almost a groan, "I should have known it!"

A voice from the outside barked a gruff command. "Come out of that! Get your hands up!"

There were steps. Paul Drake's voice was raised in rapid explanations. Mason moved around the man's feet to appear at the half-open front door.

Two men, evidently local officers, carrying guns and five-celled flashlights, tried to hide nervousness behind a gruff exterior. "What's coming off here?" one of them demanded.

Mason said, "I'm Perry Mason, the lawyer. Milicent Hardisty is my client. I stopped by to see if she was home. We saw the lights and came up on the porch. As soon as I looked in the house, I saw something was wrong."

The second man said in a low voice, "It's Mason, all right. I've seen him before."

"How long have you been here?" the first officer asked.

"Just a matter of seconds," Mason said. "Just long enough to look inside. We were just starting to telephone for the police."

"Oh yeah? *This* guy was coming down off the porch when we spotted him with the light."

"Certainly."

"There's a telephone right here, ain't there?"

Mason said scornfully, "And if we'd used it, you'd have bawled us out for obscuring fingerprints."

"What's happened?" the officer asked.

Mason said, "I don't know. A man inside appears to have been slugged. There's a gun lying on the floor."

"Your gun?"

"Certainly not."

"You do any shooting?"

"Of course not."

"Hear any shot?"

"No. I'm not certain any were fired."

"Somebody telephoned headquarters," the officer said, "said that a shot had been fired in the Hardisty residence, and it looked like a murder."

117

"How long ago was this?" Mason asked.

"Seven or eight minutes."

Mason moved back through the half-opened door. "I don't see any evidences of a bullet wound," he said, "but there's a bruise on the left temple."

The two officers herded Drake in through the door, and then looked down at the unconscious figure.

"Shucks, that's George Crane," one of the men said.

"We'd better get him up off that floor," Mason said, "and see what can be done for him. Who's George Crane?"

"Merchant patrol, deputy constable. A good sort, does a little private work on the side."

Mason said, "We could lift him up on that couch."

"Okay. Let's do it. . . . Wait a minute; who's this man with you?"

"Paul Drake, head of the Drake Detective Agency."

"We'll take a look at his credentials first," the officer said.

Drake extracted a leather wallet from his pocket, passed it over. The men opened it, turned the cellophane-faced compartments, one at a time, looking at the cards. The leader said, "I guess you're okay," and handed the wallet back to Drake. They holstered their guns, snapped flashlights to their belts, then bent over the unconscious man on the floor. Mason and Drake helped them lift him to the couch. Almost immediately the eyelids fluttered, the tempo of the breathing changed, the muscles of the arm twitched.

Mason said, "Looks as though he's coming around. Find the bathroom, Paul; get towels soaked in cold water, and—"

"Just a minute," the officer in charge said. "You boys are staying right here with me, both of you. Frank, *you* get that wet towel."

The officer prowled around, found the bathroom. They

heard the sound of running water, then he was back with cold towels.

George Crane opened his eyes, stared groggily, then suddenly flung himself to a sitting position and started flailing about him with his arms.

The officers said, "Take it easy, George. Take it easy. You're okay."

Recognition came into the man's eyes.

"You're all right," the officer repeated soothingly.

"Where is she?" George Crane asked.

"Who?"

"The woman who slugged me."

"A woman?"

"Yes."

The officer looked questioningly at Mason, who shook his head.

The officer turned back to Crane. "There wasn't any woman, George, not when we got here. What happened?"

Crane raised a hand to his sore head, pulled down the wet towel, felt with exploring fingers along the line of the bruise on his temple, said, "The deputy sheriffs left me in charge until they could get a key to that writing desk, or a warrant to bust in, one or the other."

"Who has the key?" Mason asked.

"Mrs. Hardisty, I guess, but Mr. Blane said he thought her sister might also have a key. She has a key to the house."

"What happened?" the officer asked.

Crane pressed the towel back against his bruised head, said, "I left the place dark. Sort of thought someone might start prowling around and I could do a little good for myself by catching them red-handed. Nothing happened. I was sitting out here on the porch—and all of a sudden I knew someone was on the inside. I peeked through the window, cautious-like. I could see a woman

119

standing in front of that desk with a little flashlight playing on the stuff in the pigeonholes.

"The front door was locked. I figured she must have got in through the back door. If I tried to come in through the front, she'd put out the flashlight and make a run for it—so I sneaked around real quiet to the back. . . . Sure enough, the back door was open. I started pussyfooting through the house, heading for the front of the place. I must have tipped my hand. First thing I knew she was right in front of me. I had my gun in my right hand. I tried to grab her with my left, and she hit me on the right arm with a blackjack. I had the gun half raised when she cracked down. The jerk that came with the blow pulled the trigger on the gun—and that's all I remember."

"Did you hit her?"

"I don't know. . . . I don't think so. I wasn't aiming, just had the gun half up."

"Why didn't you use your flashlight?"

"I'm telling you I wanted to catch her red-handed. I thought she was still in the front room. I was pussyfooting through, not making no noise."

The officer said, "The trouble with you, George, is that you're half deaf. You *thought* you weren't making any noise, but—"

"Now that will do! I don't have to take any criticism from *you!*" George Crane interrupted angrily. *"You* ain't so smart. How about the time you were after the two burglars in the hardware store, and—"

The officer interrupted hastily, "Keep your shirt on, George. No one's criticizing you. We were just trying to find out how it happened. What time was this?"

"I don't know, rightly. Right around nine o'clock, I guess. What time is it now?"

"About fifteen or twenty minutes past nine."

"I guess it was right around nine, then."

"Someone telephoned in they heard a shot. Wouldn't leave a name. You don't know who that was, do you, George?"

Crane said irritably, "From the time I was halfway through the house, I don't know anything."

"You were over by the front door when we found you," Mason said. "Do you have any idea how you got there?"

Crane looked at him suspiciously. "Who are *you?*"

"We're the persons who found you," Mason said, smiling.

"Milicent Hardisty's lawyer," the officer explained.

Instant suspicion appeared in Crane's eyes. "What were *you* doing here?"

"We called to see if Mrs. Hardisty was home."

Crane started to say something, then apparently changed his mind, glanced significantly at the officers.

The officer in charge said, "I guess that's all. We know where we can get you two if we need you. . . . How about it, George, can you describe this woman?"

George Crane said pointedly, "Not while these guys are here."

The officer smiled. "I reckon he's right at that, boys."

Drake needed no second invitation. "Come on, Perry."

They walked out of the house, across the front porch, and down to where Mason had left his car parked. Drake said in an undertone, "Feel like running before they start shooting? It's an even-money bet they'll grab us before we get to the car."

Mason laughed, said, *"We're* okay, Paul. Something else is bothering me."

"What?"

"I'd just like to know if Adele Blane's car is still at the Acme Garage."

Drake said. "We can soon find out. That garage is just one block over from the main drag. My man says you can't miss it."

Mason, starting the motor, said, "I'm suspicious of the things you can't miss. . . . Wonder who it was that telephoned in about that revolver shot."

"I don't know, and I don't suppose they're going to give *us* any information in case they do find out. . . . Swing to the left at the next corner, Perry, and then turn to the right."

Drake said, "Better let me go in, Perry. Two of us will make him suspicious. There's a way of handling these things."

Drake entered the garage, was gone for about five minutes, came back, jerked open the door of Mason's car, slid in beside the lawyer and slumped down on the seat.

"Well?" Mason asked.

Drake said, "Adele Blane took her car out exactly forty-five minutes ago."

Mason slammed the car into gear.

Drake, slumping dejectedly over against the corner of the seat, said, "One thing about a guy who works on your cases, Perry, he never needs to get bored. . . . Where are we going now?"

Mason, putting the car rapidly through the gears, said, "This time I'm going to *try* to get an interview before the police do."

"With Adele?" Drake asked.

"With Adele," Mason said, pushing the throttle down to the floorboard.

14

■

Utter silence surrounded the mountain cabin. The steady hissing of the gasoline lantern was the only sound that reached Harley Raymand's ears. There was no wind in the trees. The air was cold and still with that breathless chill which polishes stars into glittering brilliance.

It was, of course, absurd to think that the aura of death could make itself felt. Harley Raymand had seen death strike around him, to the right and to the left. He had trained himself to disregard danger. And yet, try as he would, a feeling persisted that gradually grew into a nervousness—a feeling that murder was in the air.

Those other deaths he had witnessed had been violent, full-blooded deaths in the heat of combat. Men, seeking to kill, had in turn, been killed. It was a fast game played in the open, and for high stakes—victory for the winner and death for the loser. But this was something different: a cold, sinister, silent death that struck furtively in the dark and then vanished, leaving behind only the body of its victim.

Harley realized that nine-tenths of his uneasiness was due to the feeling that he was being watched, that someone was keeping the cabin under a sinister surveillance.

He slipped out through the kitchen to the tree-shaded barbecue grounds, climbed the three long steps to the rustic porch, walked around to the front of the house, and stood by the porch rail, looking out at the stars.

Something flickered. A mere wisp of light that shone

like a fitful firefly in the trees, and then was gone. Harley waited, tense, watching. He saw the light again. This time it was stronger, sufficiently powerful so that he could see shadows cast on a pine tree. He knew then that someone was picking a surreptitious way through the forest, using a flashlight only at intervals.

Harley flattened himself in the shadows, and waited.

After some three minutes he saw two figures come out in the open. For a moment they were silhouetted against a beam of light flashed against the white granite outcropping. Then the flashlight was extinguished and all was darkness.

Harley thought he could hear the faint hiss of cautious whispers. Noiselessly he left the porch. Moving slowly, with the night stealth he had learned as part of his military training, he approached the rock.

The flashlight came on once more, shielded by cupped hands, throwing a spot of illumination on the ground at almost the exact spot where he had discovered the clock.

He was close enough to hear the whisper. "This is the place."

There was something vaguely familiar about that whisper. It was a woman's voice. Hands were scraping away at the ground. Harley caught a glimpse of those hands. Long, tapering fingers, slender, graceful hands and wrists—

"Adele!" he exclaimed.

The flashlight went out. There was a little scream, then a nervous, almost hysterical laugh, and Adele Blane said, "Harley! You scared ten years' growth right out of me. . . . Are you alone?"

"Yes. Who's with you?"

"Myrna Payson. . . . Harley, what happened to the clock?"

"I don't know. We couldn't find it. It isn't there."

"You searched for it?"

"Yes. . . . How did you get here? Why didn't you come to the cabin?"

"I went to Myrna's. We drove down to the first hairpin turn, left the car there and took a short cut. There's a trail over the ridge, only about half a mile of good walking. . . . I'm keeping myself out of circulation. . . . But if anyone offered me a hot drink, I could certainly use one."

"Got tea, coffee and chocolate," Harley said. "Why doesn't Myrna Payson say something?"

Myrna threw back her head and laughed. "What do you want me to say? As far as the hot drink is concerned, I'll say yes."

"Let's go up to the cabin," Adele suggested. "You'll have to keep the curtains drawn, Harley. I don't want anyone to know where I am."

"Why?"

"It's a long story. I can't tell you now. Harley, we've simply *got* to find where Jack hid that stuff he stole. It's around here somewhere. That's why he came up here with that spade. . . . And I keep thinking the clock has something to do with it."

"Well, let's go to the cabin and talk it over. There's no use looking at night."

"I suppose not. I thought that clock would be here, and I could tell something from that. I'd been telling Myrna about it. She felt it was the best clue of all."

"That's one of the first things they looked for."

"You told them about it?"

"Yes."

"And they didn't find it?"

"Not only that, but they can't find any evidence that anything was *ever* buried there."

"I wasn't sure you were still here," Adele said. "That's

125

why I was being so furtive. There's no one else in the cabin, Harley?"

"No."

"No one must know I'm here. Understand? Not a solitary soul."

"It's okay by me."

They entered the lighted cabin. Myrna Payson frankly sized up Harley, grinned, and said, "Hello, neighbor. You remember me? I'm the cowgirl who has the ranch over on the plateau. The cattlemen all think I'm going broke because I'm a 'fool woman'; and when I go to town, women look askance at me because I'm living 'all by myself, cooking for three cowboys.' On the one hand, I'm a fool; and on the other, a fallen woman. Pay your money and take your choice."

"And a darned loyal friend," Adele interposed.

Myrna Payson settled herself in a chair, thrust out high-heeled riding boots, fished a cloth sack of cigarette tobacco from her shirt pocket, and started rolling a cigarette, "Adele won't admit it, but I think she's wanted by the police, and concealing her will make me a real, sure-enough criminal."

Adele said, "Don't joke about it, Myrna. It's serious."

"I'm not joking," Myrna said, spilling rattling grains of tobacco into the brown paper.

"I have some cigarettes here," Harley said, reaching for the package of cigarettes.

Myrna said, "Drop one of those tailor-mades, and it will start a fire, but I never saw a fire started with a rolled cigarette. What's more, you can carry enough tobacco in a sack to really last you. . . . Well, we seem to have lost the clock. What's next, Adele?"

"I don't know," Adele admitted.

"Did you just drive up?" Harley asked Adele.

"I left my car in Roxbury. I got it out of the garage an

hour or so ago, and drove up to Myrna's ranch. She was out. I sat around twiddling my thumbs, waiting for her to come back."

"Went to town after provisions," Myrna explained. "Got back about half an hour ago and found Adele camped on my doorstep. She wanted to have reinforcements while she looked for the clock."

Adele laughed nervously and said, "Not only reinforcements, but a witness. Otherwise someone might think I'd planted the clock myself."

Myrna said practically, "You could have done it ten times over while I was in town."

"Myrna! *What* are you talking about?"

Myrna scraped a match on the sole of her shoe. "Don't lay your ears back, dear. I was just talking the way the police would."

"I don't like the police," Adele said.

"Don't blame you," Myrna said through a cloud of smoke. "I don't like them myself. Not as an institution. They're too nosey. I—"

She broke off abruptly as the sound of an automobile horn came to their ears. A moment later they heard the throbbing of a motor.

Adele said, "I *musn't* be found here, Harley."

"Why?"

"I can't tell you. I just *can't* be questioned right now. I'm keeping out of sight. You and Myrna are going to be the only ones who know. If anyone comes here they mustn't find me."

"How about Mrs. Payson?" Harley asked.

"We can't both hide very well," Adele said, "and—yet it wouldn't look right for her to be here with you. . . . What time is it, Harley?"

"Around ten thirty."

"Good Heavens!" Adele said.

Myrna Payson drew in a deep drag of smoke, exhaled slowly. Her words came lazily through the cigarette smoke, "It's all right, Adele. I haven't any reputation left, anyway. Go on and duck. Here they come."

They heard steps on the porch. Rodney Beaton's voice called, "Hello, the cabin! Are you still up?"

Adele slipped silently through the hallway into the bedroom.

Harley said reassuringly to Myrna Payson, "I won't have to invite him in—"

"Nonsense," she said. "I've come over for a visit. We're just talking, that's all. Invite him in as far as I'm concerned."

Harley went to the front door, threw it open, said, "Come on in, Beaton, and—"

He broke off as he saw that Rodney Beaton was not alone. Lola Strague was with him. Harley regained his verbal composure, said affably, "Why hello, Miss Strague. Come on in. Mrs. Payson and I were getting acquainted. I've been away so long that I hardly know the country any more."

Myrna Payson said easily, "Hello, Lola. Hello, Rod. I've been trying to get Harley to tell me about the war. He won't talk."

Harley noticed the tension between the two women, saw Lola Strague barricade herself behind a wall of watchful hostility. Myrna Payson, on the other hand, seemed thoroughly at ease, completely relaxed, but nevertheless gave the impression of being on her guard. Rodney Beaton was embarrassed, but Harley couldn't tell whether it was because he had found Myrna Payson visiting the cabin at such an hour, or because he didn't care to have Myrna know he had been out with Lola Strague.

"Is . . . anything wrong?" Harley asked somewhat awkwardly.

Rodney Beaton recovered his self-possession, laughed, "Heavens no! I forgot you don't realize my nocturnal habits. We've been out tending cameras."

"Any luck?" Harley asked.

Lola Strague accepted the chair Harley held for her, but sat stiffly erect. Beaton sprawled comfortably and informally. Myrna Payson continued to sit with her legs, incased in whipcords, extended in front of her. She was lounging easily in the chair, thoroughly enjoying herself so far as appearances were concerned.

Beaton said, "I've got three negatives to develop."

"Know what animals you've got?" Harley asked.

"No, I don't. I used to look for tracks, but now I've found it's a lot more fun just to develop the negatives."

"You have more than one camera?"

"Oh yes. I've got half a dozen scattered around."

"Don't you frighten the game away when you make the rounds?"

"No more," Beaton said. "I have a new system now. I go around and set the cameras after it gets dark. Then I climb up on a point where I have good observation, settle down, and wait. When one of those flashbulbs goes off it makes quite a flare, illuminates quite a bit of territory. I can tell, of course, what camera it is. I make a note of the location of the camera and the time the flashbulb was discharged. After I've waited two or three hours, I go around and pick out the plates, reset the cameras, go to my cabin, and develop them."

"And leave the cameras set?"

"Yes, I leave them until morning."

"I don't see why you watch them in the evening then."

"So I can pick up the first batch of plates and reload the cameras that have been set off before midnight. . . . Usually the best time is about four o'clock in the morning, but on the other hand I've had some very nice pictures around ten or eleven o'clock. . . . We were driving by on our way home and thought we'd drop in just to see—well, to see if you wanted anything, or—well, if you were all right."

Myrna Payson said with her slow drawl, "I reckon we all felt the same way. It would give me the creeps staying alone in a cabin where a murder had been committed. Harley says it doesn't bother him any."

Harley realized that his visitor had twice referred to him by his first name, so he laughed and said, "After all, if I were afraid, I'd hardly admit it to Myrna."

Lola Strague said somewhat stiffly, "Well, I think we'd better be going. It's really rather late for visiting, you know. I—"

Steps pounded up on the porch. Knuckles beat impatiently against the front door.

Myrna Payson said, "Well, it looks to me as though you're going to have a convention. I thought we were all here."

Harley started for the door. Before he had taken two steps Burt Strague's impatient voice called out, "Hey, Raymand! Is my sister in there?"

"Oh, *oh*—he's got the shotgun," Myrna Payson said.

Harley flung open the door.

Burt Strague, his voice sharp with anger, said to his sister, "Oh, there you are."

"Why, Burt! What's the matter?"

"Matter! Where on earth have you been?"

"Why, out with Rodney."

Burt repeated after her scornfully, "Oh yes, *out with Rodney!*"

Rodney Beaton moved forward. "Any objections?" he asked.

Lola managed to get between her brother and Rodney Beaton. "Burt!" she said, "don't be like that! What on

130

earth *is* the matter with you? I left a note telling you where I was going."

"Think again. You mean you *intended* to leave a note, but forgot to do it."

"Why Burt! I left it on the mantel, in the usual place."

Burt said irritably, "It wasn't there when I got there. I've been worried to death about you. . . . I'm sorry, Rod, if I seem to be a little brusque, but I've been worried."

"Burt, I've told you a dozen times that you're not to worry about me," Lola Strague said tartly. "I'm able to take care of myself."

"Oh, yes. A murderer's hanging around the country and I'm not supposed to worry. . . . Well, skip it. I've certainly been combing these hills for you, prowling the trails, looking all over. Incidentally, Rod, I walked through one of your camera traps down there by the fallen log where you got the picture of the squirrel."

"Tonight?" Rodney Beaton asked.

"Uh huh. Set off the flashlight. You probably got a good picture of me. As worried and annoyed as I was, I couldn't help but laugh when that flashlight burst into illumination, thinking about how you'd feel when you made the rounds of your camera traps, got what you thought was a swell deer picture, started to develop it and saw me plodding along the trail."

Beaton looked at his notebook. "That flashbulb exploded at nine-five," he said. "Do you mean to say you've been wandering around all the time since then?"

"I've been all *over* these mountain trails, I tell you. I even went up to the old mining tunnel."

Lola Strague became indignant. "What did you think *I'd* be doing in that old mining tunnel?"

"I didn't know," he said. "I got to the point where I was just a little bit crazy. I couldn't find you anywhere. . . . Just as a point of curiosity, where *were* you?"

"Out on that point where Rodney painted the picture of the sunset," Lola said. "From there we can look down on the valley and tell whenever a flashlight goes off."

Rodney Beaton said, "It's my new system. Beats blundering around over the trails, and scaring the game to death."

"And you mean to say you were up there *all* the evening?" Burt Strague asked, suspicion once more apparent in his voice. Rodney Beaton flushed.

"And you didn't hear me whistle? Why, I walked past that trail whistling that whistle I always use to call Lola!"

"Sorry," Beaton said somewhat stiffly.

"We didn't hear you," Lola said, then added hastily, "but of course, we weren't particularly listening for you. We weren't expecting to hear a whistle."

Myrna Payson laughed, said as though closing the subject, "Oh well, the lost is found, so why worry about it?"

The strained silence of tension settled on the room. Quite apparently Burt Strague wanted to say something, yet was managing with difficulty to restrain himself for the moment. Rodney Beaton, while retaining his poise, yet maintained toward Burt Strague the attitude of an annoyed grown-up dealing with an impudent child.

"Well," Myrna said, laughing and trying to make her voice casual, "someone say something."

No one did.

It was apparent that when that silence was broken, friendships would also be broken. Lola Strague was perhaps the only one who had it in her power to ward off what was coming, and for some reason she seemed incapable of doing so at the moment.

It was against that background of a silence charged with static hostility that Adele Blane's scream, high-pitched with terror, caught everyone by surprise.

Rodney Beaton whirled. "Good Lord, Raymand! That came from the room where Hardisty was murdered."

Myrna Payson, without a word, got to her feet, started running toward the closed door which led to the bedroom. She had taken no more than three steps when the door burst open. Adele Blane, her hair streaming back from her head, her eyeballs glistening in the light of the gasoline lantern, her mouth stretched open to its fullest capacity, screamed into the corridor.

Behind her there was a glimpse of a shadowy figure; another figure darted across the field of illumination from the doorway. An arm lashed out in a blow. There was the sound of a brief struggle.

Myrna Payson caught Adele in her arms, said, "There, there, Honey. Take it easy."

So imbued was Adele with the idea of flight, that she struggled to free herself, still screaming.

"What is it, Adele?" Rodney Beaton asked.

Harley Raymand said nothing. He pushed past the others, ran down the corridor which led to the bedroom. After a quick glance at Adele, Rodney Beaton crowded into the corridor behind him. Burt Strague took a hesitant step, then paused and turned to his sister. "Look here, Lola, you—"

She turned her back on him, and by that gesture shut off the unfinished sentence.

Harley Raymand went through the door of the bedroom, recoiled for a moment as the beam of a powerful flashlight stabbed him full in the face with blinding brilliance.

The voice of Jameson, the deputy sheriff, sounded crisp and competent. "It's all right, Raymand," he said. "We've just put Dr. Macon under arrest, and while we're here, we'll pick up Miss Adele Blane as a material witness."

Raymand fell back in sheer surprise. Jameson pushed his way into the corridor. Behind him an assistant deputy was wrestling the handcuffed, and still struggling Dr. Macon toward the doorway.

Jameson said to the chalk-faced Adele Blane, "And the next time, Miss Blane, you play the police for a bunch of suckers, you might remember that we're not *entirely* dumb."

15

In the midst of the excitement the arrival of Perry Mason and Paul Drake went unnoticed. Not even after Mason had pushed open the door of the cabin did anyone take immediate notice of him.

Dr. Macon had quit struggling against the grip of the handcuffs. Jameson, smilingly triumphant, was exhibiting the small black object which he held in the palm of his hand. "I'm calling on all of you," he said, "to witness that this is the bullet which Dr. Macon was trying to remove from the place where he had hidden it. I'm going to make a small scratch on the back of the bullet, so that we'll have a definite means of identification. . . . Do you care to make a statement, Doctor?"

Dr. Macon simply shook his head.

"And you, Miss Blane," Jameson said. "You, I believe, saw him enter through the window?"

She nodded.

"And do you care to make a statement at this time, telling what you saw, and explaining how you happened to be in that dark bedroom, apparently hiding from—"

Perry Mason stepped forward. "I don't think Miss Blane cares to make *any* statement at the present time," he said. "As you can plainly see, she's upset and frightened."

Jameson apparently saw Mason for the first time. "*You* again?"

Mason nodded and smiled.

"How the devil did you get here? We've had the place under surveillance."

Mason said, "Mr. Drake and I just arrived."

"Oh."

"And since I'm here, I'd like to talk with Miss Blane."

It was Jameson's turn to smile. "Unfortunately, Mr. Mason, we're taking Dr. Macon with us, and Miss Adele is going along as a material witness. Your arrival was opportune, but I'm afraid, Mr. Mason, it was just a little too late to save your client from sticking her head in a noose."

Jameson nodded to the deputy who was assisting him. "All right," he said, "let's get them out of here. And," he added after a moment during which he sized up the possibilities of the situation, "let's get them out of here fast."

It was as Dr. Macon and Adele were being hustled through the door, that Mason said to Paul Drake in an undertone, "Notice the reddish clay mud on Rodney Beaton's shoes."

Adele Blane flashed Mason an appealing look.

Mason surreptitiously lowered his right eye, raised an extended forefinger to his lips.

Jameson said to Rodney Beaton, "You have a car here, Beaton. Our car is parked down at the foot of the grade. Take us down there, will you please?"

Beaton said laughingly, "I suppose that's a request which is a command."

"We *could* commandeer your car," Jameson agreed, smiling. "We thought perhaps you'd prefer to do the driving."

"Come on," Beaton said.

Jameson lost no time in hustling his prisoners out of the house, taking care to give them no opportunity to talk with Perry Mason. The lawyer, holding himself completely aloof, stood over by the stone fireplace, leaning against the mantelpiece, smoking a cigarette.

At the very last moment Lola Strague said, "I'm going along with you, if you don't mind, Rod."

Beaton turned questioningly to Jameson.

"She was with you when you drove up?" the deputy asked.

"Yes," Beaton said.

"Okay. Bring her along."

Burt Strague started to say something, then checked himself, watched the others out through the front door, across the rustic porch, down the steps, and into the car.

After they had gone Myrna Payson said, "Well, despite our isolation, we manage to have a little excitement now and then."

"I presume Adele Blane came with you?" Mason asked.

She said, "That's your privilege, Mr. Mason."

"What is?"

"To presume anything you like."

Mason turned to glance questioningly at Harley Raymand.

"Really, Mr. Mason, I'd rather not," Raymand said.

"Okay," Mason announced.

Burt Strague said abruptly, "I don't like it. I don't like the way they're dragging Sis into this thing."

"Into what thing?" Mason asked.

"They've been out setting Rodney Beaton's cameras," Burt Strague said, *"but* they've been somewhere else."

"I noticed," Mason observed, "there were bits of a reddish clay soil on Rodney Beaton's shoes."

"Well, what of it?" Burt Strague asked suspiciously.

"I was just wondering where he might have picked up that reddish clay."

Burt Strague remained sullenly silent.

Mason went on after a moment, "There were traces of a similar clay on the bottoms of the trousers Jack

Hardisty was wearing when his body was found here in the cabin."

"You mean that clay might be a clue?" Burt Strague asked.

"It *might* be," Mason said.

"Oh well, that's different. I wasn't going to say anything if your inquiry was just idle curiosity, or an attempt to involve my sister, but I can tell you where Rod must have got that clay mud."

"Where?"

"Up at the mouth of the mining tunnel, back here in the mountains about half or three-quarters of a mile."

"That mud is *in* the tunnel?" Mason asked.

"No. It's on the trail about fifty or a hundred yards in front of the mining tunnel. It's where some of the dirt from the dump is softened up by drainage water that seeps out of the tunnel. The upper trail goes directly through it."

"I thought you said you were up there tonight," Raymand said.

"I was. I went by the lower trail. There are two trails up to the mining tunnel. I think originally there were old mining shacks on these cabin sites around here, and the men cut roads up to the mine. Those roads have gradually disintegrated until now there are only trails left."

"The upper trail goes from here to the tunnel?" Mason asked.

"Yes."

"And the lower trail?"

"That's more from the other side, over back of where Rodney Beaton has his cabin. . . . I went up there tonight, looking for my sister. Beaton's got cameras scattered around over all those trails. I touched off one of his flashguns tonight."

Mason said, "I think I should like to see that tunnel and go over the trails. Could we do it tonight?"

Strague hesitated. "I don't think Rodney would like it," he said. "He has his cameras set to pick up some game pictures. He hates to have the game disturbed at night. . . . However, if it's important—"

Mason said, "It's important. But under the circumstances, we'll wait and ask Beaton how he feels about it when he returns."

Myrna Payson said, "Oh bosh. Let's not put off any investigations simply on account of some pictures—unless, of course, you want to talk with Mr. Beaton."

Mason smiled. "I think we'll put it off until Mr. Beaton returns. Here he comes now."

In the moment of silence which followed, they could hear the sound of Rodney Beaton's automobile coming back up the grade to the cabin, and a moment later, Beaton and Lola Strague rejoined the little group.

"They played that pretty slick," Beaton said. "Had their car concealed down there, and kept the cabin under surveillance. They evidently knew when you and Adele came in, Myrna, but they didn't want to close the trap just then. They were waiting for additional game to walk in. I think they had an idea Dr. Macon might show up and try to tamper with some of the evidence. . . . Anyone know what actually happened in there?"

No one said anything.

"I gathered," Beaton said, "that Adele came with you, Myrna; that when she heard us coming she hid in that back room. It was dark in there, and when Dr. Macon showed up, he slipped in through the window and tried to remove the evidence he'd left there. . . . I presume that's the so-called fatal bullet they caught him taking away."

Lola Strague said, "Poor Adele. I don't blame her for being frightened to death."

Myrna Payson said nothing.

Mason said, "A matter came up while you were out, Beaton, that I think might well be discussed."

"What?"

"A certain reddish clay soil on your shoes."

Beaton looked at his shoes, said, "Yes. That's from up by the tunnel."

"I thought you said you weren't up there," Burt Strague said sharply.

Beaton regarded him for a moment with unwinking scrutiny, then said, "Not *in* the tunnel, youngster. As you probably know, that's on the upper trail about a hundred yards from the mouth of the tunnel. We went past there to cut down to the other trail to change the films in that camera. Incidentally, that's the one you tripped off when you walked through the trap."

"Then why didn't you meet me coming up the trail?" Burt Strague asked.

"Because we waited a while after the flash before we went down to the camera," Lola Strague said sharply.

"And I *do* wish, Burt, you'd either snap out of it or go home! After all, I'm free, white and twenty-one. I certainly don't need you to chaperone me, and I see no reason for airing these little grievances in front of—"

Mason said smoothly, "Well, as far as we're concerned, that's entirely outside the question. What we're interested in is a patch of red clay that was on Jack Hardisty's trousers when the body was found. Also there's some indication that a deliberate attempt was made to remove all traces of that mud from his shoes. I had asked Harley Raymand to look around here and see if he could find a place where the trail was muddy. I felt that it must have been near a creek bed or a spring, because it hadn't rained for a while, and—"

Beaton interrupted. "You should have asked me, Mr. Mason. Raymand isn't entirely familiar with the back country. I could have told you in a minute. There's only one place anywhere around here where there's that type of mud; that's on the upper trail to the tunnel."

"Do you suppose," Mason asked, "we could take a look at it?"

"Sure. . . . But what would Jack Hardisty have been doing up there?"

As Mason made no answer, the significance of the situation apparently dawned on Rodney Beaton, and he gave a low whistle. "So *that's* it. Anybody been in that tunnel recently?"

They exchanged glances and head shakes.

"There's just a chance," Beaton said, "we might find something there."

Drake asked, "How about flashlights? Do we have plenty? I only have one, and—"

"I carry extra batteries and an extra bulb for mine," Beaton said. "Being out in the mountains at night as much as I am, I can't afford to take chances. . . . How about it, are we all going?"

Harley Raymand was the only one who hesitated; then, as he reached for the knob on the gasoline lantern, he smiled and said dryly, "It looks as though we're all going."

16

∎

The little group strung out along the mountain trail. Flashlights, sending forth beams of light, looked like some weird procession of fireflies twisting a tortuous way through the night.

Rodney Beaton in the lead said, "Here's the place, Mr. Mason."

Mason inspected the muddy stretch in the trail.

Beaton went on to state, "This peculiar red clay came from the inside of the tunnel. It was brought out here and dumped when the tunnel was being excavated. There's a seepage of water that trickles down from the mouth of the tunnel. It keeps this patch of clay moist."

"Can you tell anything about these tracks?" Mason asked.

"Not much. You can see my tracks and Miss Strague's. Here are some deer tracks, and here's where a coyote has crossed over, but there are a lot of older tracks in the trail. Tracks made prior to the time Miss Strague and I came over it."

"Let's take a look inside the tunnel," Mason suggested.

They climbed a sharp incline to the mouth of the old tunnel.

"Know how deep this goes?" Mason asked.

"Only a couple of hundred feet," Beaton said. "They drifted in along a vein, and then lost their vein."

The inside of the tunnel was filled with musty, lifeless air. The smell of earth and rock had permeated the atmosphere.

"Gives me the creeps," Myrna Payson said. "I never could stand the inside of a tunnel. If it's all the same with you, I think I'll wait outside."

"I'll keep you company," Lola Strague said. "I feel somewhat the same about tunnels."

Burt Strague hesitated for a moment as though trying to find some excuse to stay with them, but Lola said sharply, "Go on in, Burt. Stay with the men."

Rodney Beaton, Burt Strague, Harley Raymand, Paul Drake and Perry Mason entered, walked to the far end of the tunnel. It was Rodney Beaton's flashlight that showed the significant excavation at the end.

"Looks as though someone had been getting ready to bury something here," Beaton said, indicating a shallow hole in the loose rock fragments which marked the end of the tunnel.

"Or," Mason said, "as though something had been buried and then dug up again."

Beaton became thoughtfully silent.

Drake glanced quickly at Perry Mason.

Mason swung his flashlight around the face of the tunnel. "Don't see any shovel here," he said.

All the flashlights explored the face of the tunnel.

"That's right," Burt Strague said, "there *isn't* any shovel."

"What's more," Mason pointed out, "this excavation wasn't made with an ordinary shovel. It was made with a garden spade with a six-and-a-half- or seven-and-a-half-inch blade. . . . You can see an imprint here of the whole blade."

Beaton bent forward. "Yes," he said, "and—"

Mason touched his shoulder. "I think," he announced, "we'll leave this bit of evidence just the way it is. Come on out—and let's try to keep from touching anything."

They walked silently out of the tunnel, explained the situation to Lola Strague and Myrna Payson.

Mason said, "I'd like to take a look at this lower trail that goes down by Beaton's cabin. . . . I take it that this mining tunnel is in Kern County."

"Oh yes," Beaton said. "It's well over the line."

"About how far?" Mason asked.

"Oh, I'd say a good half mile. Why? Would it make any difference?"

"It might," Mason conceded enigmatically.

Beaton said, "I'd better lead the way from here on. I reset the camera that caught the picture of Burt Strague on the trail. And if you don't mind, we'll circle around when we come to that point."

Beaton went first down the trail, walking with long swinging strides, moving with an easy rhythm that covered ground rapidly.

After almost three hundred yards of walking down a good trail, Beaton slowed his pace, said, "The camera's right ahead. There it is."

His flashlight played on a camera set on a tripod, a synchronized flashbulb attached to one side of the shutter.

"How is that tripped?" Mason asked.

"I use a small silk thread stretched across the trail," Beaton said.

"And I blundered right through it," Burt Strague observed.

"Yes, here are your tracks," Raymand said, "—and you certainly were moving right along."

He indicated the tracks of Burt Strague's distinctive cowboy boots, tracks swinging along with the even regularity of a man hurrying along a mountain trail.

Burt Strague said impulsively, "I was worried about Sis. . . . I guess I acted a little foolish tonight, Rod. Forgive me, will you?"

Beaton's big hand shot out and clasped Burt Strague's. "Forget it. Your sister's rather a precious article, and I don't blame you for wanting to keep an eye on her."

17

■

MURDER MAY HAVE ASTROLOGICAL BACKGROUND! DID STARS CONTROL DESTINY OF JACK HARDISTY?

JURISDICTIONAL PROBLEM TEMPORARILY HALTS MURDER CASE.
AUTHORITIES OF KERN COUNTY INVESTIGATING NEW EVIDENCE INDICATING MURDER MAY HAVE BEEN COMMITTED IN ABANDONED MINING TUNNEL.

Swiftly moving developments today characterized the Jack Hardisty murder case as one of the most baffling that has ever confronted local authorities.

Late yesterday afternoon, it was pointed out by the sheriff's office that the buried clock which Harley Raymand, an Army man invalided home, claims to have discovered near the scene of the murder, was set to what is known as sidereal, or star time.

Astronomers state that sidereal time is distinctly different from civil time, gaining a whole twenty-four hours during the course of a year. If, therefore, as now seems probable, the murderer of Jack Hardisty chose a moment for perpetrating his crime which would be under the most auspicious stellar influences, authorities feel they have a very definite clue.

The Bugle has commissioned one of the leading astrologers to cast the horoscope of Jack Hardisty. Jack Hardisty was born on July 3rd, which according to astrologists, makes him a *'Cancer,'* and astrologists point out that persons born under the sign of Cancer are divided into two classes—the active and the passive. They are thin-skinned, hypersensitive, and suffer deeply from wrongs, real or fancied. They are at times irrational in their emotions, and subject to ill health.

With recent developments indicating that the crime may have been committed either in Kern County, or so near the border of Los Angeles and Kern Counties that either county may have jurisdiction, the district attorney of Kern County is launching an independent investigation . . .

18

■

WATCHMAN SLUGGED IN HARDISTY HOME

FRAGMENT OF BROKEN SPECTACLE FIXES JURISDICTION IN MURDER CASE
MYSTERIOUS WOMAN SLUGS DEPUTY SHERIFF GUARDING HOME

Developments in the Hardisty murder case moved today with bewildering rapidity.

A person who is in close touch with the situation, but who wishes his name withheld, stated positively that Jack Hardisty had in his possession, at the time of his death, a large sum of money. There is a rumor that this money may have been removed from a Roxbury bank, where Hardisty had been employed up to the time of his death.

The sheriff's office, making a search of the Hardisty residence, was confronted with an antique locked desk. Because this was valuable as an antique Vincent P. Blane, the father-in-law of the victim, insisted that the lock should not be forced, but that officers should get a key either from Mrs. Hardisty or from Adele Blane. An attempt was made to secure a passkey, but because the antique writing desk had been recently fitted with a most modern lock, all efforts to open it in the usual routine manner proved futile.

Placing George Crane, a deputy constable and merchant patrol of Roxbury, in charge, police started trying to locate a key which would fit the lock. Mrs. Hardisty, who has steadfastly refused to make any statement concerning the case, finally consented to permit the authorities to use her key in opening the desk.

Shortly before nine o'clock, however, the telephone at police headquarters in Roxbury rang insistently. The voice of a man whom the police have not as yet been able to identify, advised them that he had heard the sound of a revolver shot at the Hardisty residence. Officers Frank Marigold and Jim Spencer, making a quick run to the scene, found George Crane unconscious from a blow with a blackjack administered a few minutes earlier by some unidentified woman at whom Crane had taken a shot, and whom he may have wounded. It was reported that Mrs. Hardisty's lawyer and private detective were also on the premises at the time. They were permitted to leave the premises without being searched. The writing desk had been forced open, and papers lay in a litter of confusion over the floor (see photograph on page three).

Coincident with this development, police have found evidence which definitely establishes the place where the crime was committed. Near a granite rock, some seventy-five yards from the Blane cabin where Hardisty's body was found, police found the broken fragment of a spectacle lens. A test by competent experts shows that was a fragment from Jack Hardisty's glasses—glasses which incidentally were not found on the body of the dead man.

In the face of this information, the district attorney of Kern County has stepped to one side, and jurisdiction will be held in Los Angeles County. . . .

19

Perry Mason threw the newspaper aside impatiently. Della Street's eyes met his. "You almost made it, Chief."

Mason said, "Almost doesn't count—not in this game."

"I notice that you were 'permitted to leave the premises without being searched.'"

Mason said bitterly, "Sure, that's a swell way of insinuating to the public that Paul Drake and I walked in and picked up ninety thousand bucks of stolen money, that we're going to use it as our fees. It's a nice little example of police innuendo."

"Can't you do something about that?"

Mason shook his head. "There's nothing libelous in the statement. We *were* permitted to leave the premises unsearched. That's the fact. I probably should have demanded that they search us, but we were so anxious to get out of there while the getting was good, that I didn't give the matter very much thought."

Della said, "Well, if the murderer did rely on astrology in order to pick an auspicious moment for committing the crime, he did a darn good job. This case certainly seems to be jinxed. First it's one thing and then it's another."

Mason lit a cigarette. "Trying a lawsuit is like changing a flat tire. Sometimes the jack works perfectly, the rim comes off, the new tire goes on, and you're on your way so smoothly that you hardly know you've had a flat. Sometimes everything goes wrong. The jack won't work, and when you finally get the car up, it rolls off the jack, the old tire sticks, the new rim won't go on. . . . And this is a case just like that, where everything has gone wrong to date."

"You've seen Mrs. Hardisty?"

"Yes."

"What does she say?"

"Nothing. Absolutely nothing."

"You mean she won't talk to you—as her attorney?"

"She won't say a word. Not only to the police, but to me."

"And how about Adele?"

"Adele Blane was hiding because she knew that her sister had written Dr. Macon a note that was what is known as indiscreet."

"Indiscreet in the Victorian or the legal sense?" Della Street asked with a smile.

"Both."

"And she's told that to the police?"

"I don't know what she's told the police. I doubt if even *she* does. They got her talking, and I understand she made some contradictory statements. However, I doubt if they got *very* much out of her."

"Dr. Macon?"

"Dr. Macon is in love. He's one of those self-reliant surgeons who has been trained to tackle anything—and he *may* have killed Jack Hardisty."

"We're not representing him?" Della Street asked.

"Definitely not," Mason said. "We're representing Mrs. Jack Hardisty, and she's the *only* one we're representing. She's probably in love with Dr. Macon, knows some evidence that incriminates him, and therefore won't say a word, even to me.

"Another thing that bothers me is the cocksure attitude of the district attorney's office. I understand a new deputy is going to try it—a chap by the name of Thomas L. McNair. He's supposed to be a legal whirlwind. Came out here from the east somewhere, and has one of the most brilliant trial records of any young lawyer in the country. A percentage of nine convictions out of every ten cases tried—and for some reason or other, the district attorney's office is laughing up its sleeve, just lying in wait for me."

"And that's why you think this case is going to be one of those that will be like the flat tire that goes wrong."

Mason nodded moodily. "Something," he said, "is in the wind. There are certain angles of this case about which I know nothing. . . . You've always told me that it would be better for me to stay in my office and wait until cases came to me as other lawyers do, instead of getting out on the firing line. Well, this is once you can see how it works. From the start I've been one jump behind, and I *know* from the way they are acting, the district attorney's office is virtually certain of getting a conviction of both defendants."

"Who's representing Dr. Macon?" Della Street asked.

Mason grinned. "Dr. Macon. Trust the old self-reliant

149

surgeon for that. He's going to rush right in where angels fear to tread—"

The door opened somewhat explosively. Paul Drake, too excited even to bother with the formality of knocking, entered Mason's office. "They've got you, Perry!" he announced.

"Who has?"

"The D. A."

"On what?"

"That Hardisty case. They've got a dead open-and-shut case, a lead-pipe cinch. You'd better try to cop a plea."

"Has there been a confession?"

"No. But they've uncovered some evidence that makes it tighter than a drum. I don't know just what it is, but it has to do with a hypodermic syringe. I've found out that much. The district attorney let down the bars to one of the newspaper boys. He told this reporter that he just wanted to see your face when the evidence came in. He said in all the other cases you've tried, you've known in advance what the evidence was going to be, that this time, you're going to have the props knocked out from under you."

"Under those circumstances there's only one thing to do."

"What's that?"

Mason grinned. "Trust to cross-examination."

Drake said, "I think you'd better try to cop a plea, Perry. I don't think the district attorney will let you. He's been laying for you for a long time, and this time he thinks he has you where he wants you. But you *might* manage a plea."

Mason said, "I don't think I could get a plea. I wouldn't even try, unless Milicent Hardisty confessed to me that she was guilty and asked me to. . . . What have you found out about the sliver of spectacle lens, Paul?"

Drake's face showed a surprise. "Why," he said, "I thought the D. A.'s office had that all sewed up."

"What do you mean?"

"They've checked that piece of lens Harley Raymand gave them, and it matches up absolutely with Jack Hardisty's prescription."

"And how about the piece you have?"

"Why, it'll be the same of course."

"You mean you haven't had it tested?"

"No."

Mason said, "Have it tested."

"But, Perry, it'll be the same."

"How do you know it will?"

Drake thought the question over for a second or two, then grinned and said, "I'm just acting on the assumption that it will, I guess, Perry."

Mason nodded. "Have it checked, Paul."

20

The selection of the jury in the case of The People of the State of California *vs.* Milicent Blane and Jefferson Macon consumed a day and a half. At two o'clock in the afternoon of the second day, the jurors, having been sworn to try the case, settled back comfortably in their seats and looked expectantly at the district attorney.

Thomas L. McNair, the new, brilliant trial deputy, walked over to stand in front of the jurors to make his opening statement.

"Ladies and gentlemen of the jury, I will make no detailed statement of what we intend to prove. I shall let the evidence itself speak for the prosecution. I have long thought that it was presumptuous for a district attorney to tell intelligent men and women what the evidence means, or what he expects it to mean. I shall, therefore, merely content myself with showing that on the first day of October, of the present year, the defendants murdered Jack Hardisty, the husband of the defendant, Milicent Hardisty. I shall leave you, ladies and gentlemen, to deduce what happened. I will call as my first witness, Frank L. Wimblie, from the coroner's office."

Mr. Wimblie, having been duly sworn, testified to routine matters, the finding and identification of the body, the taking of photographs showing the position and condition of the body. He was followed on the stand by Dr. Claude Ritchie, one of the autopsy surgeons.

Dr. Ritchie, having duly qualified, testified that he had examined the body of Jack Hardisty; that death had been caused by hemorrhage and shock produced by a bullet wound which had been fired into the back of the decedent, entering just to the left side of the spine, ranging downward from behind the shoulder blade. The bullet had not been found in the body.

McNair sought to emphasize this point, so that the jury would be certain to get it. Despite the fact that he had, of course, known of this peculiar feature of the case for weeks, he managed to put surprise into his voice. "Did I understand you correctly, Doctor? The fatal bullet was *not* found in the body?"

"That is right. The bullet was not found."

"May I ask why?"

"It had been removed."

"It could not have dropped out?"

"Impossible."

"And it didn't go entirely through the body?"

"No, sir. There was no wound of exit."

McNair glanced significantly at the jury. "Now, Doctor, did you discover any other unusual condition in connection with your examination of that body?"

"I did."

"What was it?"

"A drug had been administered."

"Indeed! Can you tell us the nature of that drug?"

"In my opinion it was scopolamine."

"What is scopolamine, Doctor?"

"It is a drug which remains in the mother-liquors in the preparation of hyoscyamine and atropine from henbane seed, and those of Datura Stramonium."

"Of what use is scopolamine?"

"Among other things, scopolamine is used to detect, or rather to prevent, falsehoods."

"Can you explain that, Doctor?"

"Yes. Mixed with morphine, in proper proportions, scopolamine has the power of submerging certain inhibitory areas of the brain, yet at the same time leaving intact the patient's memory, hearing and powers of speech. In fact, the memory is sharpened beyond the normal conscious memory. Cases are on record in which persons under the influence of scopolamine have confessed to minor traffic crimes which had been completely forgotten during their ordinary everyday existence."

"And you state that this drug has a tendency to prevent lies?"

"That is right. Henry Morton Robinson cites, in *Science versus Crime,* experiments performed upon subjects under the influence of scopolamine in which they were urged to tell falsehoods and attempted to do so. They were incapable of falsifying their statements."

McNair glanced at the jury, then turned once more to the doctor. "What can you tell us, Doctor, about the *time* of death?"

"The time of death was between seven-thirty and ten o'clock in the evening of October first."

"Those represent extreme limits, Doctor?"

"Those represent extreme limits, yes, sir. If I were to express it according to the law of averages, I should say that the chances were about one in fifty that the man met his death between seven-thirty and seven-forty-five; that there was about one chance in fifty that he met his death between nine-forty-five and ten o'clock; I would say that there were about thirty chances out of fifty that the man met his death between eight-forty-five and nine o'clock in the evening."

"From the nature of the wound, was death instantaneous?"

"I would say not. I would say that the patient lived for perhaps five minutes to perhaps an hour. On an average, I would say probably a half hour. I am basing that answer upon the extent of the internal hemorrhage."

McNair turned to Perry Mason. "You may cross-examine."

Mason waited until the doctor's eyes turned to him, then asked, "Could you tell whether the decedent had been killed while he was in bed, or placed in bed after he had been shot?"

Dr. Ritchie said frankly, "I can't tell—that is, I cannot answer that question positively. You will understand that I am a physician and not a detective. I make certain *medical* deductions from the state of the body. That is all."

"I understand, Doctor. By the way, were there any powder burns upon the skin of the decedent?"

"No, sir."

"Did you examine the decendent's clothes?"

"Yes, sir."

"Did you notice whether there was any bullet hole in the coat the decedent had been wearing?"

"Yes, sir. There was such a hole."

"The coat, then, had evidently been removed *after* the shot was fired."

Dr. Ritchie smiled. "As I have stated, Counselor, I am not a detective. That inference is for the jury, not for me."

McNair's smile was almost a triumphant leer.

Mason nodded. "You are also a professional gambler, Doctor?"

Dr. Ritchie's smirk was lost in indignation. "Certainly not! That is an unwarranted question."

It was Mason's turn to smile. "Your making up of a list of chances, Doctor, indicated a knowledge not usually possessed by the physician. May I ask if your 'book' on the time of death based on the number of chances out of fifty is merely a casual estimate, or founded on mathematical calculations."

Dr. Ritchie hesitated while he mentally canvassed the possibilities of standing up to a cross-examination on the laws of probability. "An offhand estimate," he admitted sheepishly.

"And an estimate entirely outside the medical field?"

"Only in a manner of speaking."

"You have never had any experience in making book or determining the mathematical laws of chance?"

"Well . . . no."

"So you made an offhand estimate which is probably erroneous?"

"Well, it was a guess."

"So you were willing to make a guess, and swear to it as a fact?"

"Well, it was an estimate."

Mason bowed. "Thank you very much, Doctor. That is all."

Judge Canfield, somewhat by way of explanation, said to the jury, "Mr. Perry Mason is representing the defendant, Milicent Hardisty. Dr. Jefferson Macon is acting as his own counsel. I will, therefore, ask Dr. Macon if he has any questions on cross-examination."

"Yes," Dr. Macon said. "How did you determine the presence of scopolamine?"

"I relied principally upon the bromine test of Wormley, although I used both Gerrard's test and Wasicky's test."

"And it is your contention," Dr. Mason asked indignantly, "that I administered scopolamine to this person in order to make him talk and answer questions before he was murdered?"

Dr. Ritchie turned slightly toward the jury to deliver his answer. "That, Doctor," he said, "is your own suggestion. I am drawing no inferences. I am merely testifying to the facts that I found."

Dr. Macon muttered, "That's all."

"My next witness," McNair announced, "will necessarily be a hostile witness. I dislike to call him, but there is no alternative. I will call Vincent P. Blane, the father of the defendant, Milicent Hardisty."

Blane took the stand. His face showed plainly the effects of worry, but he was still very much master of himself, poised, courteous, dignified.

"Mr. Blane," McNair said, "because of your relationship to one of the defendants, it's going to be necessary for me to ask you leading questions."

Blane inclined his head in a courteous gesture of understanding.

"You knew that your son-in-law, Jack Hardisty, had embezzled money from the Roxbury Bank?"

"Yes, sir."

"There had been two embezzlements, I believe?"

"Yes, sir."

"One of ten thousand dollars?"

"That is the approximate amount."

"And when you refused to hush that up, Hardisty embezzled some ninety thousand dollars in cash, and advised you that if he was going to be short, he would make his embezzlement worth while; that if you kept him from going to jail and made good the ten thousand dollars he would return the ninety thousand dollars?"

"Not in exactly those words."

"But that was the gist of it?"

"The facts of the matter are, that before the bonding company would issue a bond on Mr. Hardisty, it required certain guarantees. The upshot of the matter was that I virtually agreed with the bonding company that if it would issue the bond, I would indemnify them against any loss."

"And did you ever recover the ninety thousand dollars?"

"No, sir."

"Or any part of it?"

"No, sir."

"That is all."

There was no cross-examination.

"I will now call another hostile witness," McNair said. "Adele Blane."

Adele Blane, plainly nervous, took the witness stand, was duly sworn, gave her name and address, and looked somewhat apprehensively at the vigorous young trial deputy who seemed to have that peculiar quality of focusing the attention of the entire courtroom upon himself.

"You are familiar with the location of the mountain cabin owned by your father, and in which the body of Jack Hardisty was found on October second, Miss Blane?"

"Yes, sir."

"And you were at the cabin on the afternoon of October first?"

"Yes, sir."

"Did you see Jack Hardisty there?"

"Yes, sir."

"What time?"

"I can't tell you the exact time. It was sometime after

four o'clock, and, I think, before four-forty-five, perhaps around four-twenty."

"And that is the best you can do so far as fixing the time is concerned?"

"Yes, sir."

"And you saw Jack Hardisty drive up?"

"Yes, sir."

"He stopped his car?"

"That's right."

"Did you see him take anything from his car?"

"Yes, sir."

"What?"

"A spade."

"Could you identify that spade if you saw it again?"

"No, sir."

"Were you alone at the time?"

"No, sir. A Mr. Raymand was with me."

"Mr. Harley Raymand?"

"That's right."

"And what did you do immediately after seeing Jack Hardisty at the cabin? Just describe your moves, please."

"Well, I drove back to Kenvale with Mr. Raymand. I took him to the Kenvale Hotel. I—"

"Just a minute," McNair interrupted. "Aren't you forgetting something? Didn't you see the defendant, Mrs. Hardisty, prior to that time?"

"Yes, that's right. I met her in an automobile."

"And where was she going?"

"I don't know."

"She was, however, driving on the road which led to the mountain cabin?"

"Well, yes."

"And you had some conversation with her?"

"Yes."

"You and Mr. Raymand?"

"Yes."

158

"And she asked if her husband was up at the cabin?"

"I believe so, yes."

"And you told her that her husband was up there?"

"Yes."

"And she promptly started her car and drove away in the direction of the cabin?"

"Well—well, yes."

"You know she went to the cabin, don't you, Miss Blane?"

"No, sir. I don't think she did go to the cabin."

"You left Mr. Raymand at the hotel, and turned around and speeded up the road to the cabin, didn't you?"

"Yes."

"Now, please tell us, Miss Blane, just what you found when you arrived at the cabin—or rather, just before you came to the road which turns off to the cabin."

"I found my sister."

"The defendant in this case?"

"Yes."

"What was she doing?"

"She was standing near an embankment."

"Did you notice any evidences of emotional upset—any external evidences?"

"She was crying. She was partially hysterical."

"Did she make any statement to you about a gun?"

Adele Blane looked around her, as though she were actually in a physical trap, instead of merely being on the witness stand under oath to tell the truth, and faced with the probing, searching questions of a vigorous prosecutor.

"Did she say anything about a gun?" McNair repeated.

"She said she had thrown her gun away."

"What were her exact words? Did she say she had thrown it down the canyon, on the brink of which she was standing?"

"No. She said she had thrown it— I can't remember."

"Did she say why?"

Adele looked appealingly at Perry Mason, but Mason sat silent. It was not the silence of defeat, but rather the silence of dignity. His eyes were steady. His face might have been carved from stone. His manner was confident. But, where the ordinary lawyer would have been throwing objections into the record, would have been storming and ranting, fighting for time, seeking to keep out damaging evidence, Mason was merely silent.

"Yes," Adele Blane said. "She told me why."

"What did she say?"

"She said that she was afraid."

"Afraid of what?"

"She didn't say."

"Afraid of herself?"

"She didn't say."

"Obviously," McNair said to the witness, "if she had been afraid of her husband, she would have kept the gun. Throwing it away means only that she was afraid of herself. Isn't that the way you understood her, Miss Blane?"

Mason came to his feet then, quietly, confidently. "Your Honor," he said, "I object to the question. It is argumentative. It is an attempt on the part of counsel to cross-examine his own witness. It calls for a conclusion of the witness. I have made no effort to prevent the *facts* from getting before the jury. Nor have I objected to the leading questions asked of this witness. But I do object to argumentative, improper questions such as these."

McNair started to argue, but Judge Canfield gestured him into silence. "The objection," he said, "is sustained. The question is clearly improper."

McNair pounced back on the witness, resuming his attack with a redoubled fury, convincing jurors and spectators, as well as the witness, that here was a man who

160

could not be stopped, who was only stimulated by rebuffs to fight harder.

"What did your sister do after that?"

"She got in her car."

"Where was her car?"

"It was parked a short distance up the road."

"You mean by that it was parked on the main highway?"

"Yes."

"It was not parked on the side road which led up to your father's cabin."

"No."

"And then what did she do?"

"Followed me back to town."

"At your suggestion?"

"Yes."

"And then what happened?"

"When I got to Kenvale, I missed her."

"You mean that she deliberately avoided you?"

"I don't know. I only know that she didn't follow me to the house."

"And what did you do? Where did you go?"

"I went to Roxbury."

"Yes," McNair said, somewhat sneeringly, "you went to Roxbury. You went directly to the home of the defendant, Dr. Jefferson Macon. You asked for the doctor, and were advised he was out on a call. Isn't that right?"

"That is substantially correct."

"And you waited for Dr. Macon to return, did you not?"

"Yes."

"And when did he return?"

"At approximately ten-thirty."

"And what did you say to the defendant, Dr. Macon?"

"I asked him if he had seen my sister."

"And what did he say?"

161

"Just a moment," Judge Canfield said. "The jury will be instructed that at this particular time, any statement testified to by this witness as having been made by Dr. Macon will be received in evidence only as against the defendant, Macon, as a declaration made by him. It will not be binding upon the defendant, Hardisty, or be received as evidence against her. Proceed, Miss Blane, to answer the question."

She was close to tears now. "He said he had not seen my sister."

"Cross-examine," McNair snapped at Mason.

"No questions," Mason said with calm dignity.

Then McNair apparently went off on a detour. He began introducing evidence concerning the spade which belonged to Jack Hardisty. A witness testified that he had seen Hardisty using a spade in the garden. Was there anything peculiar about that spade, anything distinctive, McNair asked? And the witness stated that he had noticed the initials J. H. cut in the wood.

With something of a flourish, McNair sent an attendant scurrying to an anteroom. He returned with a spade which was duly presented to the witness for identification.

Yes, that was the spade. Those were the initials. He was satisfied that that was the identical spade he had seen in Jack Hardisty's hands.

There was no cross-examination.

McNair looked at the clock. It was approaching the hour of the afternoon adjournment. Obviously, McNair was looking for some peculiarly dramatic bit of evidence with which to close the first day's evidence.

"Charles Renfrew," he called.

Charles Renfrew proved to be a man in the early fifties, slow and deliberate of speech and motion, a man who quite evidently had no terror of cross-examination, but considered his sojourn on the witness stand with the

162

satisfaction of a man who enjoys being in the public eye.

He was, it seemed, a member of the police force of Roxbury. He had searched the grounds about the house where the defendant, Dr. Jefferson Macon, had his residence and his office.

McNair said, "Mr. Renfrew, I am going to show you a spade which has been marked for identification in this case, and ask you if you have seen that spade before."

"That's right," Renfrew said. "I found that spade—"

"The question was whether you had seen it before," McNair interrupted.

"Yes, sir. I have seen it before."

"When?"

"That day I made the search, October third."

"*Where* did you see it?"

"In a freshly spaded-up garden patch back of the garage on Dr. Macon's property."

"And you're certain this is the *same* spade you found at that place at that time?"

"Yes, sir."

McNair's smile was triumphant. "You don't, of course, know how this spade was transported from that mountain cabin to Dr. Macon's residence?"

Mason said, "Objected to, Your Honor, assuming a fact not in evidence as well as calling for a conclusion of the witness. There is no evidence that *this* was the spade Jack Hardisty had in his car."

McNair said instantly, "Counsel is right, Your Honor, I'll prove *that* tomorrow. In the meantime, I'll withdraw this question." He flashed a smile at the jurors.

Once more there was no cross-examination.

McNair went rapidly ahead. Rodney Beaton told of seeing the defendant, Milicent Hardisty, standing near the edge of a barranca by the roadway, some object in her hand, her arm drawn back. He couldn't swear, he admitted, that she had actually thrown this object down the barranca. She might have changed her mind at the last minute. He also testified that the next day he and Lola Strague had been searching the vicinity of the granite outcropping. They had found a thirty-eight caliber revolver pressed down in the pine needles. He identified the gun.

Mason made no cross-examination.

Lola Strague, called as a witness, also told of finding the gun, and identified it. Then McNair, with a dramatic gesture, introduced in evidence records that showed this gun had been purchased by Vincent P. Blane two days before Christmas of 1941.

At that point McNair looked at the clock significantly and Judge Canfield, taking the hint, announced that it had reached the usual hour for the evening adjournment.

McNair left the courtroom wearing an expression of complete self-satisfaction wreathed all over his countenance. His exit was punctuated by brilliant flashes as news photographers took action shots for the morning editions.

21

■

McNair started his second day of taking testimony with a technique that left no doubt he was deliberately building this case upon a series of dramatic climaxes. Court attachés and jurors, who had become accustomed to the conventional dry-as-dust method of building a murder case from accusation to conviction, began to throng the courtroom, attracted by this dynamic personality, who was, for the moment, presenting so colorful a figure.

William L. Frankline was McNair's first witness of the day. Frankline, it seemed, was the deputy who had been with Jameson at the time Dr. Macon had been surprised at the Blane cabin, and Frankline testified in detail to steps they had taken to place the cabin under surveillance, and to seeing Adele Blane and Myrna Payson enter the cabin. Subsequently, Rodney Beaton and Lola Strague had arrived, and Adele had secreted herself in the dark bedroom where the body of Jack Hardisty had been found. Thereafter, Burt Strague had put in an appearance. Some minutes later, a skulking figure had been seen prowling around toward the back of the cabin. Having ascertained that the bedroom was dark, and apparently deserted, this figure had forced the window and entered the room. At that point the witness and one William N. Jameson, also a deputy sheriff, had approached the window, and at a signal simultaneously switched on flashlights, which had disclosed Adele Blane rushing screaming from the room, and the defendant, Dr. Macon, in the act of taking a bullet from its place of concealment behind a picture which hung on the wall of the bedroom. The bullet had been taken from Dr. Macon's hand as the handcuffs were put on him, and subsequently marked with a distinctive scratch for identification. And the witness unhesitatingly identified the bullet which McNair showed him as being that bullet.

"Cross-examine," McNair said to Perry Mason.

Mason regarded the witness thoughtfully. "You say that when you turned on your flashlights you saw this man in the act of removing a bullet from behind a picture?"

"Yes, sir."

Mason said, "In other words, you saw his hand behind the framed picture. When you jerked the hand out you found there was a bullet in it, and from that, you deduced that he was removing a bullet from behind the picture. Is that right?"

"Well—you might put it that way."

"And for all you know," Mason said, "the defendant, Macon, instead of taking something out, may have been—" Mason broke off abruptly as his eye caught the smirk on McNair's face. "I'll withdraw that question," he said calmly, "and there are no further questions of this witness."

McNair was suddenly furious. He started to get up, apparently to make some objection, then dropped back into his chair. He frowned thoughtfully.

Mason drew toward himself a pad of paper, scribbled a note. "McNair wanted me to force Frankline to admit that Macon might have been putting the bullet *in* instead of taking it *out*. Something fishy here. Hold your hat."

He walked over to hand the note to Della Street.

Judge Canfield looked at Dr. Macon. "Does the defendant, Macon, have any questions?"

"No questions."

"Any redirect, Mr. McNair?"

"No . . . no, Your Honor. That's all." McNair seemed definitely nonplussed, but a moment later he called Dr. Kelmont Pringle.

Dr. Pringle qualified himself as an expert criminologist, laboratory technician, a specialist in forensic medicine and toxicology, and an expert on ballistics.

"Handing you the bullet which has previously been identified and received in evidence," McNair said, "I will ask you if you examined that bullet and made certain tests with it."

"I did."

"I now hand you a thirty-eight caliber Colt revolver, which I am asking at this time may be marked for identification. I will ask you, Doctor, if you fired any test bullets through that gun."

"I did."

"And did you, with the aid of a comparison microscope, compare them with the bullet which I have just handed you?"

"I did."

"And were the bullets fired from this weapon of the same general description as the bullet which you hold in your hand, Doctor?"

"Yes, sir."

"Now then, Doctor, by the aid of the comparison microscope, did you determine whether or not this bullet which you hold in your hand had been fired *from this very weapon* to which I have directed your attention?"

"I did."

"Was that bullet so fired from this gun, Doctor?"

There was the trace of a frosty twinkle in Dr. Pringle's eyes. "It was not!"

Judge Canfield looked down at McNair's smiling countenance, glanced at Perry Mason, leaned forward on the bench, said, "I beg your pardon, Doctor. Did I understand the answer to be that the bullet was *not* fired from that weapon?"

"That is right," Dr. Pringle said. "The bullet definitely was not fired from this weapon."

Dr. Macon settled back in his seat with the relaxation which comes with relief from a great tension.

There was no expression whatever on the face of Milicent Hardisty.

Perry Mason kept his eyes fastened steadily on the witness.

"Now then," McNair went on, "since it appears that the bullet was *not* fired from this .38 revolver which I have handed you, Doctor, I will ask if you made any further examination of that bullet or found out anything further in connection with it?"

"Yes, sir. I did."

"I direct your attention, Doctor, to certain reddish-brown stains appearing on the bullet, and, at one particular place, to a certain bit of dried reddish material."

"Yes, sir."

"What is that material, Doctor?"

"It is animal tissue which has become dehydrated by exposure to the air."

"And these reddish-brown stains, Doctor, what are these?"

"Those are blood."

"Have you made tests with that tissue and with the blood?"

"Yes, sir."

"And have your tests definitely ascertained whether that is or is not blood?"

"Yes, sir. They have. It is blood."

"Now, Doctor, please listen carefully to this question. Assuming that, on the first day of October, nineteen hundred and forty-two, a man was killed by a bullet fired from a thirty-eight caliber revolver, is there anything about this bullet which would enable you, as an expert, to tell whether or not this particular bullet which you are now holding in your hand was the fatal bullet which brought about the death of this individual on October first, nineteen hundred and forty-two?"

"Yes," Dr. Pringle said. "There is something about this bullet which would enable me to answer that question."

"Will you please state to the jury just what that is, Doctor?"

"I tested the blood on that bullet both by the precipitin

test and by microscopic measurement with a micrometer eyepiece."

"And what did you find?"

"I found that the erythrocyte was one thirty-five hundredth of an inch in diameter."

"What is the erythrocyte, Doctor?"

"The red blood corpuscle."

McNair turned abruptly to Mason. "Do you have any cross-examination?"

Mason hesitated, then said, "Yes."

He regarded Dr. Pringle with a frown. "Doctor, that is a most peculiar way to give your testimony."

"I answered questions."

"You did, indeed. You volunteered no conclusions."

"No, sir. I was asked, at this time, only for facts."

"You stated that you convinced yourself the diameter of the red blood corpuscle was one thirty-five hundredth of an inch."

"Yes, sir."

Mason paused for a moment, then went ahead cautiously. "Doctor, I am not absolutely certain of my information, but it seems to me that the red blood corpuscle of the human being is one thirty-two hundredth of an inch in diameter."

"That is right."

Mason shifted his position.

Judge Canfield leaned abruptly forward, resting his elbows on his desk, looking down at the witness. "Doctor, I want to eliminate the possibility of a misunderstanding. Do I understand from your testimony that the red blood corpuscles of the blood on this bullet were one thirty-five hundredth of an inch in diameter?"

"Yes, sir."

"And that those of a human being are one thirty-two hundredth of an inch in diameter?"

"That is right."

"Then do I understand, Doctor, that the blood on this bullet was *not* human blood?"

"That is correct, Your Honor."

Judge Canfield looked at the district attorney with an expression of exasperation on his face, settled back in his cushioned chair and said to Mason, "Proceed with the cross-examination, Counselor."

"Then, since the blood on this bullet was not human blood," Mason said, "did you determine what blood it was?"

"Yes, sir. It was the blood of a dog. The erythrocyte of a dog measures one thirty-five hundredth of an inch, and, of all the domestic animals, its size is the nearest to that of the human. I satisfied myself by the precipitin test that the blood on this bullet was that of a dog."

"Then," Mason went on, feeling his way cautiously, "you would state, would you not, Doctor, that under no possible circumstances could this bullet have been the fatal bullet which brought about the death of Jack Hardisty?"

"Yes. This bullet has had no contact with human flesh. This bullet has been fired into a dog."

Mason said abruptly, "That is all."

McNair smiled and bowed at Mason. "Thank you, Counselor, for clarifying my case for me."

Judge Canfield, plainly irritated, started to make some comment, then checked himself. After all, Perry Mason could very well take care of himself.

"That's all for the present, Doctor," McNair said. "I'll call my next witness, Fred Hermann."

Fred Hermann came forward and took the witness stand. He, too, it seemed, was on the police force at Roxbury. He was of the stolid, phlegmatic type. Appearing as a witness in this case was, to him, merely another chore which interfered with his daily routine. He acted as

170

indifferent and bored as though he had been called to court to testify in connection with some routine misdemeanor arrest he had made the night before.

When he had given his name, age, residence and occupation, McNair asked him, "You are familiar with the witness, Renfrew, who was on the stand yesterday?"

"Yes, sir."

"Did you accompany him to the office and residence of the defendant, Dr. Jefferson Macon, on the third day of October of the present year?"

"Yes, sir."

"Were you with him when he discovered the spade?"

"Yes, sir."

"I will show you that spade which was introduced in evidence, Mr. Hermann, and ask you whether you have ever seen it before."

The witness took the spade, turned it over slowly, methodically, deliberately, in his big hands, handed it back to the prosecutor. "Yes, sir," he said, "that's the one."

"And where was it that this spade was found?"

"On the north side of the garage. There was a little garden patch there and some freshly dug earth."

"And what did you do with reference to that earth," McNair asked, glancing triumphantly at Perry Mason.

"We started digging."

"And how deep did you dig?"

"About three feet."

"And what did you find?"

Hermann turned so that he was looking at the jury. "We found," he announced, "the body of a big dog. There was a bullet hole in the body, but we couldn't find any bullet; that had been removed."

McNair was smiling now. "Your witness," he said to Mason.

"No questions," Mason announced.

Judge Canfield, looking at the clock, said, "It's time for the noon recess. Court will reconvene at two o'clock."

There was a swirl of activity on the part of spectators as Judge Canfield retired to his chambers. Newspaper reporters, rushing forward, took flashlight photographs of McNair, showing him smiling triumphantly. They had Dr. Pringle pose for them on the witness stand. They did not ask Perry Mason for photographs.

22

Perry Mason and Della Street sat in the curtained booth of a little restaurant around the corner from Mason's office, eating a luncheon which consisted mostly of tea and cigarettes.

"I don't get that about the dog," Della Street said.

Mason said, "The thing works out mathematically from the district attorney's point of view. Dr. Macon met Milicent as she was coming back from the cabin. She told him about the new embezzlement, about Jack Hardisty having ninety thousand dollars in cash that he was using as blackmail. Dr. Macon suggested that they return to the cabin, that he give Hardisty a hypodermic of scopolamine that would make him talk, and betray the hiding place of the stolen currency."

Della Street sipped her tea. "I understand that, all right," she said. "According to that theory they must have gone back and give him a hypodermic. After that he became violent and one of them shot him. But where does the dog come in?"

172

"Don't you see? Dr. Macon would know that they'd recover the fatal bullet, that they'd check it with Milicent's gun, that then they'd have a dead open-and-shut case. So he extracted the bullet and hid it."

"But how could he shoot it into a dog after—"

"He didn't. McNair's betting that Macon got another gun of the same caliber, killed a dog with it, removed the bullet, buried the dog, and intended to conceal the bullet in the cabin in such a place that it would be found sooner or later. When the authorities found it, they'd think they'd discovered the fatal bullet where it had been concealed by Dr. Macon. They'd test it and find, to their surprise, that it *didn't* fit Milicent Hardisty's gun."

"Then Dr. Macon was putting the bullet behind the picture, instead of taking it out, when he was apprehended?" Della Street asked.

"Exactly," Mason said, "and I almost led with my chin by asking on cross-examination if he might not have been putting something *in* instead of taking something *out*. . . . I caught myself just in time on that one."

"What gave you the tip-off?"

"Something in the way McNair was watching me, some expression on the witness' face. . . . But I walked right into that dog business. I had to. I was in a position where I either had to stop my cross-examination, which would have made it look as though I were afraid of the truth, or go ahead and bring out the point which crucified my client."

"Why didn't McNair bring it out under direct examination?"

"Because it hurts my case more when I bring it out on cross-examination. . . . Those are sharp tactics, and I'm going to get even with him."

"How?"

"I don't know *yet*," Mason admitted.

Della Street stirred the few grounds of tea in the bottom of the tea cup. "I could almost cry," she confessed. "—You can see what happened. If Milicent Hardisty didn't kill her husband, Dr. Macon at least thinks she did, and tried to protect her. In doing it, he dragged them both into the mess. . . . Or Dr. Macon killed him, and Mrs. Hardisty is trying to protect him. Either way we're licked—and McNair is so sneering, so soaked up with triumph, that he just makes me *sick*. I'd like to pull his hair out, a handful at a time. I'd like to—" Rage choked her words.

Mason smiled, "Don't get excited, Della. Use your head instead. . . . There's one discrepancy in the evidence that I doubt if McNair's thought of."

"What is it?"

Mason grinned at her. "Wait until he puts Jameson on the stand."

"I don't get it."

"I don't think anyone's thought of it," Mason said, "but I'm going to make them do a lot of thinking about it."

"But you can't possibly work out any theory that will get Milicent Hardisty acquitted—can you?"

"I don't know," Mason said somberly. "Perhaps not, but I can mix the case up so that a lot of that supercilious smirk will come off McNair's face and—"

Mason broke off as he heard Paul Drake's voice asking the proprietor, "Is Perry Mason eating in here today?"

Mason pulled back the curtain of the booth. "Hello, Paul, what have you got?"

Paul Drake entered the booth. His face wore a grin. Under his arm he carried a small package wrapped in newspaper and tied tightly with a string.

Della Street moved over so he could sit down beside her. Drake put the package on the table.

Almost instantly a faint but unmistakable sound of steady ticking became apparent.

"The buried clock?" Mason asked.

Drake nodded.

"Where did you get it?"

"Harley Raymand found it buried just under the surface of the ground, about ten feet from the edge of the rock where it had been concealed the first time."

"How far from where the broken spectacle lens was found?" Mason asked.

"Not very far. . . . Harley Raymand tied up the package and wrote his name across the wrapper. I wrote my name just above his, and tied it up in another wrapping. . . . Do you want to open it in court?"

Mason thought it over for a moment, then said, "We'll put Harley Raymand on the stand, and let him identify his signature. . . . We've got to do that before the clock runs down. It's a twenty-four-hour clock, isn't it, Paul?"

"Yes."

"And what time did the clock say—that is, was it slow or fast or—"

Drake said, "The darned clock is two hours and forty-five minutes fast."

Mason pulled a piece of paper from his pocket and did some rapid figuring. "That puts it almost exactly on sidereal time, Paul. As I get it, sidereal time would be about three hours and forty-five minutes fast today, but our time has been moved up an hour on account of the war. That means the clock is almost exactly on sidereal time."

Drake gave a low whistle. "Perhaps that tag about the stars wasn't just a pipedream, Perry. Why the devil should a man want a clock that keeps time with the stars —and why should it be buried around in different places?"

Mason's grin was gleeful. "That, my boy, is a question we'll try to dump in the lap of Thomas L. McNair."

"They won't let you put it in the case, Perry."

Mason said, "I know they won't, but they'll have a hard time keeping me from putting it in the minds of jurors."

23

■

As court reconvened at two o'clock, Thomas L. McNair sat at the table reserved for counsel for the prosecution, his face wearing a smile which just missed being a smirk.

Judge Canfield said, "The Jurors are all present, and the defendants are in court, gentlemen. Are you ready to proceed, Mr. McNair?"

"Just a moment, Your Honor," Mason said, getting to his feet. "At this time I wish to ask permission of the court to introduce some testimony out of order."

"Upon what ground is the motion made, Mr. Mason?"

"Upon the ground that the evidence is, in its nature, perishable. It will not keep until I have an opportunity to put it on in regular order."

"Why not?" McNair demanded truculently.

Mason turned to him with a little smile. "It's rather difficult to explain that without going into the nature of the evidence, Counselor."

McNair said sneeringly, "Go ahead and explain it. I'd like to know what evidence you have that is, as you so aptly term it, perishable."

Mason turned back to Judge Canfield. "It is a clock,

176

Your Honor. A clock which was found buried near the alleged scene of the crime. It—"

"And what does a clock have to do with it?" McNair interrupted sarcastically. "Good Heavens, Your Honor. Here we have a plain open-and-shut murder case, and counsel for the defendant comes into court with a clock which was buried near the scene of the crime. It's incompetent, it's irrelevant, it's immaterial. It can't possibly be introduced in evidence."

Mason said, "Of course, Your Honor, I will connect it up at the proper time; otherwise, the jurors can be instructed to disregard it."

"But what is perishable about a clock?" McNair demanded. "You've got the clock. I guess it will keep, won't it? I never heard of a clock spoiling. You might pickle it in alcohol."

There was a well-defined titter from the courtroom. A few smiles appeared on the faces of the jurors, and McNair grinned gleefully at these smiling faces.

Mason said, "The *clock* will keep, but the *time* shown on the dial of the clock won't. If the Court please, I am advised that this clock is now exactly two hours and forty-four and one-half minutes faster than our Pacific War Time. And inasmuch as our Pacific War Time is advanced one hour, that makes the clock exactly three hours, forty-four and one-half minutes ahead of our sun time."

Judge Canfield frowned. "And exactly what is the possible significance of that fact, Mr. Mason? In other words, why should that evidence be preserved?"

"Because," Mason said, "as of this date, sidereal time is exactly three hours, forty-four minutes, thirty-nine and one-half seconds in the advance of civil time. It is, therefore, plainly apparent that this ordinary alarm clock has been carefully adjusted so that it is keeping exact sidereal time, and inasmuch as I understand it is a twenty-four-hour clock, unless it is received in evidence, and the jury given an opportunity to note the time shown on the dial, the clock will have run down, and this valuable bit of evidence will have been destroyed."

"And what possible connection can the stars have with this murder?" McNair demanded.

Mason said, "That, Your Honor, is one of the things I will connect up when it comes time to put on my case. All I am asking at the present time is permission to identify this clock so that the testimony may be preserved while it is available."

Judge Canfield said, "I will grant your motion."

Harley Raymand, being duly sworn, testified that he had first found the buried clock on October first, the date of the murder. That at that time, the clock, according to his best recollection, was some twenty-five minutes slow. That he had again found it on October second. That he had thereafter made search for the clock and had failed to find it again until approximately eleven o'clock on the morning of the present day when he had happened to hear a ticking noise; that he had listened carefully, located the spot in the ground from which that ticking was heard, and had uncovered what appeared to him to be exactly the same clock, in exactly the same box. That at this time, however, the clock was some two hours and forty-five minutes fast, as compared with his own watch.

"What did you do with this clock?" Mason asked.

"I wrapped it up in a package, wrote my name across the wrapping at the suggestion of Mr. Paul Drake. I then delivered the package to Mr. Paul Drake who also wrote his name directly above mine."

Perry Mason asked, "Open this package, which I hand you, and see if it is the same package which you so gave to Mr. Drake."

The jurors were leaning forward in their seats.

178

"Your Honor," McNair said, "not only do I object to the introduction of this evidence at this time as being out of order, but I object to it as incompetent, irrelevant and immaterial."

Judge Canfield said, "The Court has already ruled on the motion permitting Mr. Mason to put on the evidence at this time, and out of order. The Court will reserve a ruling on the objection that it is incompetent, irrelevant and immaterial until the defendant presents his case. Or, to put the matter in another way, the Court will admit the evidence temporarily, subject to a motion on the part of the prosecution to strike it out in the event it is not properly connected up."

"That," Mason announced, "is all I ask, Your Honor."

Harley Raymand unwrapped the package, took out a small wooden box. He opened this box and disclosed an alarm clock ticking competently away.

Mason made some show of taking out his watch and comparing it with the dial of the clock, then he turned to consult the electric clock at the back of the courtroom. "May we call to the attention of the jury at this time, that the clock is apparently two hours, forty-four minutes and forty seconds fast."

Judge Canfield said, his voice showing the interest he was taking, "It will be so noted for the record."

McNair, plainly irritated that the smooth progress of his case had been interrupted, said, "Your Honor, I would like to reserve my cross-examination of this witness until after the Court has finally ruled whether the evidence is admissible."

"So ordered," Judge Canfield said. "Has any test of this clock been made for fingerprints, Mr. Mason?"

Mason said suavely, "Apparently not, Your Honor. I would like very much to have the Court instruct the fin-

179

gerprint expert from the sheriff's office to make proper tests."

"That will be the order," Judge Canfield said. "Now, Mr. McNair, do you wish to proceed with your case?"

"Yes," McNair said truculently. "Now that we have disposed of the horoscopes and the astrology, we might get down to brass tacks. I will call Mr. William N. Jameson as my next witness."

Jameson, duly sworn, testified to finding the body of Hardisty in the cabin. Testified also to matters of technical routine, identifying maps, photographs, and presenting all the groundwork necessary in murder cases.

Gradually, however, having disposed of these details, McNair once more started building to a dramatic climax. "Did you," McNair asked, "on the second day of October of this year, have occasion to go to Roxbury with me?"

"Yes, sir."

"And where did you go when you arrived in Roxbury?"

"To the place where the defendant, Dr. Macon, has his office and residence."

"Did you see Dr. Macon at that time?"

"I did."

"Who else was present?"

"You and Dr. Macon, that's all."

"And, following that interview, did you have occasion to examine Dr. Macon's automobile?"

"I did."

"Who was present at that time?"

"No one. You were talking with Dr. Macon. I slipped out and went through his car."

"What did you find, if anything?"

"Dr. Macon's surgical bag was in the back of the automobile. I looked through it. In a little leather medicine case which held a lot of small bottles, I found a bottle which seemed to be filled with cotton. I took out the cork and pulled out the cotton. Concealed in the cotton was a piece of paper."

McNair looked at the clock. "Any writing on this piece of paper?"

"Yes, sir."

"Would you recognize this piece of paper if you saw it again?"

"Yes, sir."

McNair said, with a smile, "I am offering the paper at this time for identification. Tomorrow, I will introduce handwriting experts to show that the writing on the paper is in the handwriting of the defendant, Milicent Hardisty. In the meantime, purely for the purposes of identification, I wish to read into the record the message which is upon this paper."

"No objection," Mason said, as Judge Canfield regarded him with a puzzled frown.

McNair read:

"Dearest Jeff:

Jack has done the most awful thing. I couldn't believe him capable of such perfidy, such dastardly treachery. He is up at the cabin. I am going up there for a show-down. If the worst comes to the worst, you won't see me again. Don't think too badly of me. I can't see why men like him are permitted to live. . . .

There is no use my trying to tell you how much you have meant to me, Jeff, or what you have done for me. No matter what happens, I will feel that I am always close to you and that you will be close to me.

I am hoping that I can get Jack to see the light, and right, at least in part, the great wrong he's done my father. For what he has done to me, I do not

181

care. I can stand that. It will be humiliating, but I can take it. But I can't take what he has done to Father, lying down. As this may be good-bye, I want you to know how very, very much you have meant to me. Your kind patience, your steady faith, your friendship, and the more which lay behind all this have been inspiration and sustenance to me. Good-bye, my dear.

Yours,
Milicent."

McNair handed the paper to the clerk of the court with a flourish. "Please mark this for identification," he said, "as the prosecution's exhibit."

McNair turned to Perry Mason, glancing triumphantly at the clock, to note that once more the papers would have an opportunity to record a dramatic finish to the afternoon session.

"Is that all of your direct examination of this witness?" Judge Canfield asked.

"Yes, Your Honor. It is approximately four forty-five, and—"

Judge Canfield ignored the hint. "Cross-examine," he said to Mason.

For a moment there was a flash of consternation on McNair's face. It was quite apparent he had hoped Judge Canfield would adjourn court, and there was a sympathetic glint in the eyes of His Honor as he glanced at Perry Mason.

Mason faced the witness.

"You worked up this case, Mr. Jameson?" he asked.

"What do you mean by that?"

"You endeavored to uncover evidence in it?"

"Yes."

"You did everything possible to unearth significant facts which might be considered as clues?"

"Yes."

"Did you look down in that canyon to see if you could find the weapon which the defendant, Milicent Hardisty, is said to have thrown down there?"

Jameson smiled. "That was hardly necessary."

"And why not?" Mason asked.

"Because her gun was found—where she had tried to hide it after the murder."

"I see," Mason said. "Therefore, it wasn't necessary to look for a gun she might have thrown down into the canyon."

"That's right."

"In other words, having found Mrs. Hardisty's gun, there was no use searching for any other."

"That's right."

"You knew Mrs. Hardisty told her sister she had tossed her gun over an embankment?"

"She *claimed* that," Jameson grinned.

"And as an officer looking up facts in the case, you checked that statement by looking in the place she had indicated?"

"No, by looking in the place she actually hid the murder gun."

"You don't *know* it was the murder gun?"

"Well . . . of course—it was the gun she must have used."

"And you are willing to swear there is no gun lying on the steep slope where Mrs. Hardisty told her sister she had thrown *a* gun?"

"I couldn't *swear* that, but I'd bet a million dollars on it."

Judge Canfield said sternly, "The witness will answer questions and refrain from extraneous comments."

Mason smiled. "You don't *know* this is the gun that killed Hardisty. You don't *know* Mrs. Hardisty put the gun where it was found, and, as an officer, you have never checked Mrs. Hardisty's story that she had thrown the gun which was in her purse down that steep slope. Is that right?"

"Well, I—do you mean, Mr. Mason, that the defendant had *two* guns?"

"*I* don't mean anything," Mason said. "I'm merely asking questions. I am trying to find out what investigation was made."

"Well, we didn't look in the bottom of the canyon, or along the slope."

"So, for all you *know*, Mrs. Hardisty *may* have thrown a gun in the bottom of the canyon."

"Well, yes."

"And that gun *may* have been the thirty-eight caliber revolver which fired the bullet which the witness Pringle states had been used to bring about the death of a dog."

"Well . . . I wouldn't say that."

"The question is argumentative," McNair objected.

"I think it's within the bounds of legitimate cross-examination, however; bearing in mind that counsel is entitled to show bias of the witness," Judge Canfield ruled, "the objection is overruled. Answer the question."

"Well . . . I—oh, I suppose she *could* have shot a dog and buried it at Dr. Macon's house, and then driven up to the top of the canyon and thrown the gun away," the witness said, with an attempt at sarcasm.

"And," Mason observed, "by the same token, she could have driven up a little farther, killed a dog near the cabin and thrown the gun away. Then Dr. Macon could have found the dog, carried it home and buried it near his garage, couldn't he?"

"Well, I don't think it happened that way."

"Oh, you don't *think* it happened that way?"

"No."

"So what you want this jury to do is to return a verdict

of guilty of murder in the first degree, predicated on the way you *think* the thing must have happened."

"Well, not exactly that."

"Pardon me. I must have misunderstood you. That was what I understood to be the effect of what you said, the position you had adopted."

"Well, there wasn't any dog up at the cabin."

"How do you know?"

"Well, there was no evidence that a dog had been up there."

"And just what would you expect to find in the line of evidence that would convince you a dog *had* been up there, Mr. Jameson. Speaking as a detective, what evidence would you say a dog might leave behind that would tell you he had been there?"

Jameson tried to think of some answer, and failed.

"Come, come," Mason said. "It's approaching the hour of adjournment. Can't you answer the question?"

"Well . . . well, no dog was up there."

"And how do you know?"

"Well, I just *know* he wasn't."

"What convinced you?"

"There's no evidence a *dog* had been up there."

"That," Mason announced, "brings us right back to the point where you stalled before. What evidence would you expect to have found?"

"Well, there weren't any footprints."

"Did you look for footprints?"

"Yes."

"For a dog's footprints?"

Jameson smiled. "Yes, sir."

"And that was before there had been any evidence connecting a dog with this case?"

"Well, I guess so, yes."

"But you were looking for a *dog's* footprints?"

"Well . . . well, not exactly."

"Then you *weren't* looking for a dog's footprints?"

"Well, not for a dog's. We were looking the ground over."

"And did you notice any dog's footprints?"

"No, sir."

"How about a coyote's prints? Is that what those tracks were?"

Jameson thought for a moment and said, "Well, now wait a minute. . . . Now, come to think of it, I'm not going to swear there *weren't* any dog's footprints, Mr. Mason."

"And you aren't going to swear that there *were* any?"

"Well, no."

"In other words, you didn't look for a dog's footprints?"

"Well, not particularly. Come to think of it, the footprints of a coyote are so much like—no sir, I'm not going to swear one way or another."

"You have already sworn both ways," Mason said. "First that no dog was up there, second that you looked specifically for a dog's footprints, third that you *didn't* look for a dog's footprints, fourth, that a dog *may* have been up there. . . . Now, what is the fact."

Jameson said irritably, "Oh, go ahead, twist everything I say around—"

"The witness will answer questions," Judge Canfield admonished.

"What," Mason asked suavely, "is the fact?"

"I don't know," Jameson said.

Mason smiled. "Thank you, Mr. Jameson, and *that* is all."

Judge Canfield glanced at the clock, then down at the discomfited McNair. "It appears," the judge said slowly and deliberately, "that it has *now* reached the time for the afternoon adjournment."

Perry Mason paced the floor of his office, head thrust forward, thumbs pushed into the armholes of his vest. Della Street, sitting over at her secretarial desk, watched him silently, her eyes filled with solicitude.

For nearly an hour now, Mason had been pacing rhythmically back and forth, occasionally pausing to light a cigarette or to fling himself into the big swivel chair behind his desk. Then after a few moments he'd restlessly push back the chair, and once more begin his pacing back and forth.

It was almost nine o'clock when he said abruptly, "Unless I can think of some way of tying in the astronomical angle of this case, I'm licked."

Della Street welcomed the opportunity to let words furnish a safety valve for his pent-up nervousness. "Can't you let the clock speak for itself? Surely it isn't just a coincidence that it's keeping perfect sidereal time."

"I could let the clock speak for itself," Mason said, "if I could get it introduced in evidence; but how the devil am I going to prove that it has anything whatever to do with the murder?"

"It was found near the scene of the murder."

"I know," Mason said, "I can stand up and argue till I'm black in the face. 'Here's a buried clock. It was found near the scene of the murder. First, the day of the murder, second, the day after the murder. Then it disappeared until weeks later when we're trying the case'— and Judge Canfield will look at me with that cold, analytical gaze of his, and say, 'And suppose all that is true, Mr. Mason. What possible connection does all that have with the case?' And what am I going to say to him then?"

"I don't know," Della admitted.

"Neither do I," Mason said.

"But there must be someone connected with the case that is interested in astrology."

Mason said, "I'm not so darned sure. That astrological angle was a good thing to use as a red herring to try and get the Kern County district attorney interested, but a person doesn't have to know sidereal time in order to play around with astrology. A person wants sidereal time for just one purpose: that is, to locate a star."

"Please explain again how you can locate a star by a clock," she said.

Mason said, "The heavens consist of a circle of three hundred and sixty degrees. The earth rotates through that circle every twenty-four hours. That means fifteen degrees to an hour. . . . All right, astronomers divide the heavens into degrees, minutes and seconds of arc, then translate those degrees, minutes and seconds of arc into hours, minutes and seconds of *time*. They give each star a so-called right ascension, which is in reality nothing but its distance east or west of a given point in the heavens, and a declination, which is nothing but its distance to the north or south of the celestial equator."

"I still don't see how that helps," Della Street said.

"An astronomer has a telescope on what is known as an equatorial mounting. The east and west motion is at right angles to the axis of the earth. As the telescope moves, an indicator moves along graduated circles. Once you know the right ascension and declination of a star, you only have to check that against the sidereal time of that particular locality, swing the telescope along the graduated circle, elevate it to the proper declination, and you're looking at the star in question. . . . Now, you tell

188

me what on earth that has to do with the murder of Jack Hardisty."

"I can't," she said, and laughed.

"Neither can I," Mason said, "and unless I can find some way of doing it, I'm damned apt to have a client convicted of first-degree murder."

"Do you think she's guilty?"

Mason said, "It depends on what you mean by being guilty."

"Do you think she killed him?"

"She may have," Mason conceded. "But it wasn't cold-blooded, premeditated murder. It was an accident, something that came about as a result of some unforeseen development. . . . But she *may* have pulled the trigger."

"Then why doesn't she tell the complete circumstances?"

"She's afraid to, because in doing that she'll implicate someone else. . . . But what we're up against, Della, is a double-barreled crime."

"How do you mean?"

"How does this look? Jack Hardisty takes that money up to the tunnel. He buries it. Someone gives him a dose of scopolamine, he talks, and under the influence of the drug babbles his secret. That person goes up and gets the money; or else goes up and finds that some other person has been there first and got the money."

"And you don't think that was Milicent Hardisty?"

Mason shook his head. "If Milicent Hardisty or Doctor Macon had found that money, they'd have gone to Mr. Blane and said, 'Here you are. Here's the money.' That's what all the trouble was about. They were trying to get that money back because it was going to put Blane in a spot if he had to make it good."

"Yes. I can see that," Della Street admitted.

"Therefore," Mason said, "some third party intervened. Someone has the ninety thousand dollars, and is hanging onto it. And just as sure as you're a foot high, that clock is connected with it in some way, and simply because I can't find out what the connection is before court convenes tomorrow morning, I'm letting a damned whippersnapper, smart-Aleck deputy district attorney nail my hide up against the side of the tannery."

"It isn't as bad as that," she protested. "You've certainly got them worried about that gun now."

Mason nodded almost absently, said, "The gun is a red herring. It's a little salt in an open wound, but that clock—damn it, Della, that clock *means* something!"

"Can't we tie it in with something else?" she asked. "The piece of broken glass from the spectacle lens, for instance. Couldn't you—"

Paul Drake's knuckles pounded three knocks on the door, then after a pause, two short sharp knocks.

"Paul Drake," Mason said. "Let him in."

Della Street opened the door. Drake, grinning on the threshold said, "You've got them all churned up, Perry. They're up there prowling around that canyon with spotlights, flares, floodlights, flashlights, and matches. Jameson swears he's going to go into court tomorrow morning and prove to you that there isn't a gun anywhere in the whole damned barranca."

Mason nodded absently, said, "I thought he'd do that. I may have some fun with him on cross-examination, but that isn't telling me how the clock ties into the case."

"Astrology?" Drake suggested.

Mason said, "That astrological angle is interesting, but it's nothing we can sell Judge Canfield."

Drake said, "Don't be too certain. I've just found out something about Mrs. Payson."

"What about *her?*"

"She's a student of astrology."

Mason gave that matter frowning consideration.

"I'm going to tell you something else," Drake said.

"You'll remember that when we got the oculist's report on that sliver of broken spectacle lens, he said he thought it was from Jack Hardisty's spectacles, the same as the other piece was. Well, I checked with *another* oculist, and *he* says you were right. Remember you weren't at all certain that it was from the same—"

"Never mind that," Mason interrupted. "What's the latest?"

"It's a pretty small sliver to check on, Perry. That first man was afraid to say it wasn't Hardisty's because the sheriff had the big chunk, and said it was. . . . Well, anyway, I've stumbled onto an oculist who has made some very delicate and complete tests. He says this piece isn't from Hardisty's spectacles, but that the piece the sheriff has is made to Hardisty's prescription. That means there were *two* broken spectacles.

"Now, according to this oculist, the normal eye has a certain power of adjustment, or what is known as accommodation. It's really an ability to change the thickness of the lens of the eyeball, which has the effect of bringing objects into focus—just the same as you move the lens of a camera in and out, in order to focus it on some object."

Mason nodded.

"That power is lost as a person becomes older. At the age of about forty, a person needs bifocals; at about sixty, he loses the power of accommodation altogether. Of course, some persons are more immune to the effects of age so far as the eye is concerned, but on a general average. an optician can tell the age of a person pretty well from the correction of his eyeglass. Now, this oculist tells me that just making a guess—not something he'd be willing to swear to under oath, but making a darned close guess—that the spectacle lens came from the glasses of a person just about thirty-six years old.

"Now, Jack Hardisty was thirty-two. Milicent Hardisty

is twenty-seven, Adele is twenty-five. Harley Raymand is twenty-five, Vincent Blane is fifty-two, Rodney Beaton is about thirty-five, but he doesn't wear any glasses. He's one of those chaps who have perfect eyes. . . . But here's something you haven't considered. Myrna Payson seems to be thirty or so, but she *may* be a lot older. She doesn't ordinarily wear glasses, but she may wear 'em when she's reading—or when she's checking astronomical time in connection with a buried clock."

Mason flung himself into his big creaking swivel chair. He melted back in the chair, rested his head against the cushioned back. closed his eyes, then said abruptly, "Done anything about it, Paul?"

Drake shook his head. "The idea just occurred to me. Somehow I hadn't considered her in connection with those glasses and the clock."

"Consider her now, then," Mason said without opening his eyes.

"I'm going to," Drake said, getting to his feet. "I'm starting right now. Is there anything else?"

"Nothing else," Mason said. "Only we've got to tie up that sidereal time angle tight by tomorrow morning. I think McNair is going to throw the case into my lap sometime tomorrow. Then I'll have to start putting on evidence. I haven't any to put on. The only thing I can do is to use that clock to inject such an element of mystery into the case that McNair will have to take notice of it."

"Can't you do that anyway?" Drake asked.

"Not unless I can get the clock introduced into evidence." Mason said, "and how I'm going to prove that sidereal time has anything to do with the murder of Jack Hardisty, is beyond me. The more I cudgel my mind on it, the more I find myself running around in circles."

Drake started for the door. "Okay," he said, "I'm going up and do a little snooping around Myrna Payson's cattle ranch."

"Watch out for her," Della Street said, laughing. "She oozes sex appeal."

Drake said, "Sex appeal means nothing to me."

"So I've noticed," Della Street observed.

Drake had reached the door when he paused, took a wallet from his pocket, opened it and said, "I've got something else here, Perry. I don't think it has a darn thing to do with the case, but I found it out there by the rock, not over twenty-five yards from where the clock was first found. . . . See what you make of it."

Drake opened an envelope he took from the wallet, and handed Mason a small circular piece of black paper, not quite the size of a silver dollar.

Mason inspected it, a puzzled frown drawing his eyebrows together. "It seems to be a circle carefully cut from a piece of brand-new carbon paper."

"That's it," Drake agreed, and "that's all of it. You can't make another darn thing out of it."

Mason said, "The circle was carefully drawn. You can see where the point of a compass made a little hole here. Then the circle was drawn and cut with the greatest care. The carbon paper had evidently never been used, otherwise there'd be lines on it or the imprint of type."

"Exactly," Drake agreed. "Evidently someone wanted to make a tracing of something, but never used the circular bit of paper—it's about the size of a small watch. It probably doesn't mean a darn thing, Perry, but I found it lying there and thought I'd better bring it along."

"Thanks, Paul. Glad you did. It may check up with something later."

Paul Drake said, "Well, I'll be on my way. Be seeing you."

Mason remained tilted back in the swivel chair for nearly five minutes after Paul Drake had left, then he straightened himself, drummed his fingers on the edge of the desk for a few moments, then shook his head.

"What's the matter?" Della Street asked.

"It doesn't click," Mason said. "It just doesn't fit. The clock, the glasses, the stars, the—" Abruptly Mason broke off. He frowned, and half closed his right eye, staring fixedly at the far wall of the room.

"What is it?" Della Street asked.

"Martha Stevens," Mason said slowly.

"What about her?"

"She's thirty-eight."

"I don't get you."

"Thirty-eight," Mason said, "wears spectacles. A practical nurse, trained in the giving of hypodermics, because she gives Vincent Blane his insulin shots. . . . *Now*, do you get it?"

"Heavens, yes!"

"And," Mason went on, "the night after the murder when Adele Blane disappeared, she went to the San Venito Hotel and registered as Martha Stevens. . . . We never found out why."

"Do you know now?" Della asked breathlessly.

Mason said, "I know what *might* have been a reason."

"What?"

"Martha Stevens had a date with someone at the San Venito Hotel. She couldn't keep it. Adele went there and registered under the name of Martha Stevens, so she could meet whatever person was to call on Martha Stevens."

"Who?" Della asked.

Mason hesitated for a moment, drumming with his fingers on the edge of the desk. Abruptly he picked up the telephone, and gave Vincent Blane's number in Kenvale.

After a few minutes, he said, "Hello. Who is this speaking please? Oh, yes, Mrs. Stevens. . . . Is anyone home except you? . . . I see. Well, Mr. Blane wanted you to take his hypodermic syringe—the one he uses on his insulin shots—to the office of the Drake Detective Agency. You can just leave it here. He wanted you to catch the first interurban bus and bring it in. Do you think you can do that? . . . Yes, right away. . . . No, I don't know, Mrs. Stevens. All I know is that's what Mr. Blane asked me to notify you. He's feeling rather upset—the strain of the trial and all—yes, I understand. Thank you. Good-by."

Della Street looked at him curiously. "What good does that do?" she asked.

Mason pulled open a drawer in his desk, took out a bunch of skeleton keys.

"It gives us an opportunity to go through the room of Martha Stevens, and do a little searching along lines that probably haven't occurred to the police. . . . And perhaps steal a pair of glasses."

"That comes under the head of burglarious housebreaking?" Della Street asked.

Mason grinned. "In view of the fact that I'm employed by the owner of the house, and might be considered to have his implied permission, there's a technical question as to the burglarious intent."

"Would the district attorney appreciate such a technicality?"

"I'm afraid he wouldn't. Hamilton Burger, the district attorney, or Thomas L. McNair, the brilliant trial deputy, would hardly think there was anything to differentiate the act from burglary—*if I got caught.*"

"Can't you get the evidence in the regular way?"

"There isn't time. If I can find some peg on which to hang the evidence of that clock, I've got to know about it tonight. And if I can't find anything, the sooner I know that, the sooner I can start on some other approach."

Della Street walked over to the cloak closet and took her hat down from the shelf.

"Where," Mason asked, "do you think *you're* going?"

"Along."

Mason grinned. "Okay. Come on."

25

■

Vincent Blane's house went back to an ancient day of architecture when huge frame houses garnished with gables, ornamental half turrets and balconies sprawled over spacious grounds, in an era of tranquillity, financial security and happiness.

Mason surveyed the big spaciousness of the house. "I presume," he said, "it will be one of the rooms in the back."

"Probably on the ground floor," Della said. "Let's try the back door first."

"No," Mason said. "The back door will be locked from the inside, and have the key in it. The front door will have a nightlatch. We can work it with one of these passkeys—if we're lucky."

They waited until the street was deserted, then slipped up to the dark porch. Della Street held a small fountain-pen flashlight while Mason ran through his bunch of skeleton keys, looking for the right one.

"Here's where we give another statute a compound fracture," Della Street said. "I was afraid our law-abiding rôle was getting too irksome."

Mason selected a key he thought might do the work, and

inserted it tentatively in the lock. "We're doing it in an emergency to clear a client who may be innocent."

"If she's innocent," Della Street said spitefully, "why doesn't she tell you the true story of what happened?"

"Because she's afraid to. The truth looks too black. She—" The lock clicked back in the middle of the explanation. Mason opened the door, grinned and said, "Did it with the first key. That's an omen, Della."

The house was warm, with an aura of human occupancy. There was a comfortable, lived-in aroma clinging to the rooms, the faint after-smell of good cigars and well-seasoned cooking—the mellow feeling which clings to huge wooden houses and is almost never found in fireproof apartments.

Mason said, "Okay, we'll head for the back of the house. There are back stairs. I remember seeing them that day when the officers came to get Milicent Hardisty."

Della Street said, "Her room might be at the head of the back stairs. At any rate, it'll be a good place to start."

Within five minutes they had found it. A room on the second floor, at the extreme back of the house.

"It's pretty hard to make a search with flashlights," Della Street said.

Mason nodded, boldly walked over to the light switch, and clicked it on. "Neighbors," he announced, "get suspicious when they see the beam of a flashlight playing around a room, or even impinging against the drawn shades, but they think nothing of it when lights are on. . . . Just make certain the shades are all drawn, Della."

Della Street went around the room pulling shades.

"All right," Mason said, "let's get to work."

"What are we searching for?" Della Street asked.

Mason grinned. "That's the beauty of it. We don't know, we—" He broke off abruptly. "What was that, Della?"

Della Street said, "Someone tossed gravel up against the window."

Mason frowned. "Sit tight. See what happens."

A moment later more gravel was thrown against the window.

"Do I dare to switch out the lights, and take a peek at whoever is below?" Della asked.

Mason thought for a moment, then said, "Give it a try, Della."

He switched out the lights. Della Street drew back the window shades, stood against the dark window, looking down into the back yard.

After a moment she moved back from the window and said with an odd catch in her voice, "It's a man. He beckoned to me, and then moved up to the back porch. He's standing there waiting, as though expecting me to let him in."

For a long moment Mason deliberated this new development, then he said with sudden decision, "Okay, Della. We let him in."

"But we can't afford to be caught here, and—"

"We let him in," Mason repeated. "It's a hunch. Maybe Martha Stevens' boy friend. . . . Come on, Della, unlock the back door, and don't say a word. I'll be standing directly behind you. See what he does."

With the aid of the flashlight, they negotiated the back stairs, crossed the kitchen. Della Street unlocked the back door, Mason switched out the flashlight, stood directly behind her. As the door opened, a slender man, wearing a reefer-type overcoat, pushed his way into the room and slipped a familiar arm around Della Street's waist. "Cripes," he said, "thought I wasn't going to get away. Give us a kiss."

Mason's flashlight snapped on.

The man frowned at the annoyance of the flashlight, then caught a glimpse of Della Street's face and jumped back as though he'd been shot. "Say, what's the idea?" he demanded.

Mason said with every assurance of authority, "Come on up," he invited.

"Where to?"

"Martha's room."

"Say, who do you think *you* are?"

Mason said with every assurance of authority. "Come along, my man, I want you to answer questions about what happened the night Jack Hardisty was murdered."

Every bit of resistance oozed out of the man as though he had been hit hard in the solar plexus. "Who . . . who *are* you?" he asked, his shoulders drooping, the coat seeming suddenly much too large.

Mason merely clasped an authoritative hand on the man's arm. "Come on."

Silently they climbed the stairs, entered Martha Stevens' room. Accusingly, Mason turned to regard the frightened man. He fixed him with a steady, penetrating scrutiny that he used at times effectively in his cross-examination.

"All right," he said, at length. "Let's have it."

"Where's Martha?"

Mason said, "Martha's having a chance to tell her story to a Los Angeles detective. You can tell yours *now.*"

The man fidgeted uneasily. "I haven't done anything."

Mason merely smiled.

The man settled down in a chair, his body seemingly trying to hide behind the heavy folds of the sagging coat.

Mason said, "We haven't got all night. . . . What's your name?"

"William Smiley."

"Where were you," Mason asked, "when Martha Stevens broke her glasses?"

"I was right there."

"How did they get broken?"

"This guy lunged at her."

"You mean Hardisty?"

"Yes."

Della Street quietly extracted a notebook from her purse, unscrewed the cap from a small fountain pen, and started making shorthand hieroglyphics.

"Why did you go up to the cabin to meet Hardisty in the first place?" Mason asked.

"It was Martha's idea. She'd been reading the dope in this magazine about how this drug made people talk. Hardisty had been dipping into funds, and Blane was going to have to make good, so Martha figured that by giving him a shot of this drug, we could make him talk his head off, and get the money back.

"She knew she was going to have to use force. That's where I came in. . . . I didn't like it. I didn't want to. She'll tell you that herself."

"I know," Mason said sympathetically, glancing from the corner of his eye to see that Della Street was keeping up with the conversation. "Just tell me what happened, so that I can check it with Martha's story."

"Martha won't lie, she'll tell you the truth."

"I know," Mason said soothingly.

"Martha and I would have married, only Blane doesn't want a married housekeeper. He always said he never hired a couple that was any good. Either the man was good and the woman wasn't, or the other way around. . . . Well, Martha and I was going together secret-like. This thing came up, and she called on me."

"Where did you get the hypodermic?" Mason asked.

"One she used to give Blane his shots for diabetes."

Mason waited for the other to go on.

Smiley, recalling what had happened, became less hostile. "Okay," he said in a nasal, somewhat whining voice as though he were accustomed to registering complaints which did no good, "what was there for *me* to do? I had to go through with it. Martha got the gun for me."

"What kind of a gun?" Mason asked with a significant glance at Della Street.

"A thirty-eight. It was Mrs. Hardisty's gun. Mrs. Hardisty was spending part of the time over here. She kept that gun in her suitcase. Martha got it and gave it to me. We went up to the cabin. Hardisty was there, all right. He'd parked his car and was standing right by this big granite rock. He had a spade in his hands, like he was going to dig. I wanted to try talking with Hardisty, to be reasonable about it, but Martha was all business. She gave him the works right away."

"Shot him?" Mason asked.

"No. Don't be silly! *I* had the gun. She told him she was going to give him this hypo, that it would make him tell the truth, and not to try getting rough. I cut down on him with the gun, and made him get his hands up. He was scared, but not *too* scared."

"And what did Martha do?"

"She gave him the hypo."

"And then what?"

"Then, I guess he came to the conclusion that I wouldn't shoot. Anyway he made a swing at Martha, and clipped her one that knocked off her glasses, and it gave her a jolt."

"And you shot?" Mason asked.

"Not me, brother. I got sore when he pasted Martha. I hauled off and hit him."

"With the hand that was holding the gun?"

"No. I tossed the gun away when I pasted him. . . . Damn little shrimp, hitting a woman. I should have broken his jaw. As it was, I knocked him down and he broke his glasses—we thought we'd picked up all the pieces. Guess we missed some."

"And then what happened?" Mason asked.

"He wouldn't talk for a while, then finally he got to talking. At first I thought that magazine article was on the up-and-up. He said he was just about ready to call the whole thing off and go to Blane and make a clean breast of it. He said that he didn't have the nerve for a job like that, that every time he hid the stuff he was afraid the police would find it. He said he'd hid it in his house first. Then he'd got nervous and gone up to the tunnel with it, buried it in the end of the old mining tunnel. That had been only an hour or so ago, but he'd got nervous before he'd driven half a mile and began thinking of other and better places. He said after he'd hidden the stuff in the tunnel it seemed like any school kid would have picked the tunnel as a place to look.

"Of course, it's easy to look back now and see what this guy was doing to us. Martha had made the mistake of telling him this drug was going to make him tell the truth. Maybe it would have if we'd given it a chance, but he out-foxed us. He pretended it had taken effect before he even felt it, and sent us on a wild-goose chase."

"You mean you went to the tunnel?" Mason asked.

"Sure. We fell for it, hook, line and sinker. We left him there at the rock, and Martha and I went up to the tunnel. We took his spade along to dig with."

"And you dug?"

"I'll say we dug. I haven't shoveled so much dirt in a year—and the lousy crook had the swag right there in his car all the time. He just outsmarted us, that's all."

"What did you do when you realized he'd been lying to you?" Mason asked.

"We came back to see if we could question him some more. Naturally, we couldn't find him. He'd dusted out, lock, stock and barrel, as soon as he got rid of us. So then we came on back home."

"Exactly where was it that you met Hardisty?"

"Right by that big granite rock. He was there with the spade. Looked like he was getting ready to do some digging. If we'd only laid low we could have caught him red-handed. It was this hypo that queered things, gave him his chance to slip one over on us."

"And this was before dark?"

"Sure. It was late in the afternoon, but it was light, all right."

"While you were driving up, did you meet Adele Blane on the road?"

"She drove right past us just before we made the turn off to the cabin," Smiley said, "but she didn't see us. She had some fellow with her."

"Did you see anything of a clock that was buried near that—"

"Nope," Smiley interrupted. "I read about that buried clock. It doesn't make sense to me. Why would Hardisty want to bury a clock?"

For a long moment there was silence, then Mason said, "You came back to this house with Martha Stevens?"

"Nope. We were afraid there might be a kickback on that dope business. She put me on the interurban. I went in to Los Angeles. She was to meet me there the next night at a hotel. She'd registered, all right, but she went out again and didn't come back. I called there and hung around for a while, but she never did show up."

"And you didn't go back to recover your gun?" Mason asked.

"No. I just chucked it away when he hung one on Martha. Then after I got him licked and he got started talking, I forgot all about the gun. As soon as he said he'd buried the stuff in the tunnel, Martha and I fell for it. We beat it up there. I did want to take him with us, but he acted dopey and just sat down all caved-in like, and his eyes got glassy. Martha pushed the spade at me

203

and said to come on, that she knew where the tunnel was. . . . Shucks, the guy had never been near the tunnel. I tell you he had the dough right there in the car with him."

"Did you go into the cabin when you got back from the tunnel?" Mason asked.

"No. We saw Jack Hardisty's car was gone, so we took it for granted he'd beat it. We left the spade up there, got in our car and came back."

"How long were you up at the tunnel?"

"I don't know, maybe an hour and a half from the time we left until we got back. It was pretty dark when we got back to the cabin."

"How did it happen you didn't pick up the gun, if you picked up the broken glasses?"

"We picked up the glasses right after the fight. You know how a person picks up glasses as soon as they get broken. Martha was picking up pieces of glass almost as soon as he'd knocked 'em off."

"Who picked up his glasses?"

"I did. I put 'em in my pocket. There was just one big piece knocked out of his. I was afraid to give 'em to him, sort of afraid they might be evidence."

"And you knew the gun was found later on?"

"Oh, sure. I read the papers about the trail and all that, and Martha's told me stuff. . . . How come Martha hasn't told you this?"

"Where were you working?" Mason asked.

"Turret Construction Company—defense work. Been there for six months."

"You read in the papers about Hardisty's body being discovered in the cabin?"

"Sure."

"Do you know whether he was in the cabin when you got back from the tunnel?"

"No I don't. His car was gone—and I was getting an

awful case of cold feet. You know, jabbing a man full of a drug—"

"I know. Where did Martha get this drug, do you know?"

"She told Mrs. Hardisty she wanted to get it. I don't know what excuse it was she gave to Mrs. Hardisty, or what she said she wanted it for. I think she told Mrs. Hardisty the old man wanted it, or intended to use it, somehow. . . . Anyhow, Mrs. Hardisty was friendly with a doctor, and she said she could get it. I don't think Hardisty's own wife even knew he was short. Martha found out about it listening to Blane talking on the long distance phone with the bank directors over at Roxbury."

Mason said abruptly, "You haven't told anyone anything about this?"

"No."

"Not a soul?"

"Not a soul."

Mason said, "Well, I think Martha Stevens will be home pretty quick. You can wait here, if you want."

"Not me. I don't like to come in the house unless Martha's here. I don't think the old man would like it. I saw the light up here and threw a little gravel against the window pane. That's our signal. . . . I'll go out and wait around outside, until Martha gets here. You don't think it will be long?"

"No, I don't think it will be long," Mason said.

Della Street closed her notebook, dropped it into her bag, screwed the cap on the fountain pen, glanced at Perry Mason. He shook his head, almost imperceptibly.

The three of them walked out of the house. Mason said, "Well, good night, Smiley."

"Good night, sir."

Mason helped Della Street into the automobile.

"Couldn't you have used him somehow?" she asked in a low voice.

205

Mason said, "If he ever told that story in front of a jury, Mrs. Hardisty would be out of the frying pan and into the fire. This is one of those cases where they throw everything at you except the kitchen sink. . . . You can begin to understand now why Milicent is keeping her mouth shut, why Dr. Macon doesn't dare to say a word. Dr. Macon thinks she did it."

"Are you sure?"

"It's a cinch," Mason said. "Remember, she went to him for the scopolamine. Remember, she was a trained nurse before she was married. Dr. Macon thought she wanted to try this drug on Jack Hardisty. Evidently there'd been a magazine article on it. . . . He probably thinks Milicent is lying to protect her father as well as herself."

"But if they had Milicent's gun, what gun was it that she threw away?"

Mason said, "It wasn't what *she* threw away, it was what *I* threw away."

"How do you mean?"

"The only point I had to argue to a jury," Mason went on, "was that *if* Milicent Hardisty had thrown her gun down an embankment, that same gun couldn't very well have been found beside the big granite rock. . . . I couldn't keep my big mouth shut. I had to take what seemed to be a minor discrepancy at the time, and use it to heckle Jameson. Now Jameson is up there searching for that gun, and if he finds it—Well, if he finds it, we're not only licked, we're crucified—unless I can figure out some way I can get that damned clock introduced in evidence."

"Well, there's one thing," Della said. "You know what happened now."

Mason's eyes were thoughtful. "I'm not so certain that I do."

"What do you mean by that? That Smiley was lying?"

206

Mason said, "One bit of evidence bothers me."

"What?"

"Hardisty's trousers. The red clay mud showed that he *had* been up at the tunnel—and someone took off his shoes, removed every bit of mud on the shoes, polished them, put them by the bed—and forgot to inspect the cuffs on his trousers."

Della Street's eyes were wide. "Then . . . then Smiley must have been lying?"

"Or telling the exact, unvarnished truth," Mason said.

26

■

Thomas McNair seemed more debonair than ever as he took his seat in court the next morning. The crowded courtroom buzzed with whispered conversation. The jurors solemnly filed in and took their seats. And then, Hamilton Burger himself, a barrel-chested figure whose every movement suggested a bulldog tenacity, entered the courtroom and took his seat beside McNair.

Mason knew they were moving in for the kill. They'd rush the case to a quick, unexpected conclusion, and then toss it into his lap, let him try floundering around, searching for a weak link in the chain of circumstantial evidence which gripped the defendants.

Deputy sheriffs escorted the defendants into the courtroom. Dr. Macon, with his face set in a fixed mask to conceal his feelings. seated himself with motions that were stiff with self-discipline. Milicent Hardisty dropped into her chair, almost immediately propped an elbow on the arm of the chair, and rested her head against the up-raised hand. Her attitude was that of tired dejection. She only wanted to get it over with as soon as possible.

Judge Canfield emerged from his chambers. The people in the courtroom arose as with one motion. After the judge seated himself, a gavel pounded counsel and spectators back to their seats.

"People *versus* Macon and Hardisty," Judge Canfield said with a crisp, businesslike efficiency. "Both defendants are in court, and the jurors are all present, gentlemen. Proceed with the case."

McNair went nimbly ahead producing witnesses who identified the molds of tire tracks which had been found at the Blane cabin, then expert witnesses who testified as to the make of the tires which had made those tracks, testified to checking the molds against the tires on Dr. Macon's car.

And then Hamilton Burger, the district attorney, took over with ponderous dignity, with the lumbering efficiency of a big-gunned battle wagon swinging into action. "We wish to recall William N. Jameson," he said.

Jameson, looking slightly weary about the eyes, but full of spirit, took the stand.

"You have already been sworn," the district attorney rumbled. "Now, Mr. Jameson, I am going to direct your attention to the fact that yesterday on cross-examination, counsel asked you if you had made any search of the spot near where the defendant, Milicent Hardisty, had been standing when she was seen by witnesses to throw a gun, or an object resembling a gun, into a canyon. And you testified, I believe, that you had made no such search."

"That is correct."

"Do you now wish to change that testimony?"

"Not the testimony. At the time I answered the question, my testimony was correct, but since then I've made a very careful and exhaustive search of the locality."

208

"When was that search made?"

"Last night."

"When did it start?"

"At about six o'clock."

"When did it terminate?"

"At about two-thirty this morning."

"Why did you terminate your search?"

"Because I found the object for which I was looking."

"Did you indeed! And what was that object?"

"A thirty-eight caliber Colt, police positive, double-action revolver, with all six chambers loaded, the gun bearing the number one-four-five-eight-one, and also bearing thereon two somewhat smudged latent fingerprints, which however, are readily identifiable as the fingerprints of the defendant, Milicent Hardisty."

Hamilton Burger was too dignified to smirk triumphantly at Perry Mason as McNair would have done. He said simply, "Your witness, Mr. Mason."

"No questions," Mason snapped.

Hamilton Burger seemed somewhat surprised. However, he promptly called a representative of the sheriff's office, who testified that some five years ago an application had been duly made by a citizen of Kenvale to carry a concealed weapon for the purpose of protection. The weapon was described as the Colt police positive, thirty-eight caliber, double-action revolver, bearing the number 14581.

"You have that application with you?"

"I have."

"Did any person witness the signing of that application?"

"Yes, sir. I did."

"It was signed in your presence?"

"It was."

"And I will ask you who signed that application?"

"Mr. Vincent P. Blane," the witness said, and then

added gratuitously, "the father of the defendant, Milicent Hardisty."

Hamilton Burger moved with the slow dignity of a steam roller as he got up and walked over to the witness. "I will now ask that this application to carry a firearm be received in evidence as an exhibit on behalf of the People, and marked by the clerk with the appropriate exhibit number."

Judge Canfield glanced at Perry Mason. "Any objection on the part of the defendant, Hardisty, Mr. Mason?"

Mason managed a bold front for the jurors. "None whatever," he said.

Hamilton Burger said with that ponderous manner which was so characteristic of him, "Your Honor, I would like to recall Rodney Beaton for a few questions. I think the Court will appreciate the position in which the prosecution finds itself. Due to the finding of this second weapon, the finding of the so-called first weapon, or prosecution's exhibit A, becomes relatively more important. . . . That is, the circumstances surrounding the finding assume an added significance."

Judge Canfield said, "The court will permit you to recall the witness, Counselor."

Burger bowed his head gravely. "Rodney Beaton, come forward, please."

Rodney Beaton arose from his position near the back of the courtroom, advanced to the witness stand.

Once more it was Hamilton Burger, himself, who did the questioning. "Mr. Beaton, you have previously been interrogated concerning the finding of a weapon which has been produced in evidence as the People's exhibit A. I call your attention, Mr. Beaton, to that exhibit, and also to the fact that the cartridge in one of the cylinders has been discharged. I'm going to ask you if, when you and Miss Lola Strague found that weapon, you noticed anything in connection with that discharged cartridge?"

Beaton said, "I noticed that it had been freshly fired."

Burger shook his head. "That is a conclusion. You are not, I take it, an expert on firearms?"

Beaton smiled. "I think I am."

Burger showed some surprise. "What has been your experience?"

"I've been a collector of firearms for several years. I held a State championship as a revolver shot for two consecutive years. I have shot thousands of rounds in revolvers of different types. I have studied the effects of different loads, different shapes and weights of cartridges, both by consulting the available data of firearm and cartridge manufacturers, as well as by practical observations of my own."

Hamilton Burger's face showed great satisfaction, "And as a result of your knowledge, do I undestand you to say that this weapon had been recently fired?"

"Within twenty-four hours," Beaton said positively.

"How can you tell?"

"By the smell of powder fumes in the barrel. There's a certain subtle change in odor after a weapon is fired. For the first few hours there's a decided acrid odor, which later gives way to a more metallic smell."

"Now, you have pointed out on the map, People's exhibit C, the approximate spot where this weapon was found. Can you state anything in connection with the physical appearance of the ground?"

Beaton said carefully, "The weapon, when Miss Strague and I found it, was lying in some pine needles, which in turn were on a rather soft stretch of ground. The weapon was indented in the ground, as though it has been stepped on."

"Were there any marks of struggle?"

"The pine needles would not hold clear-cut footprints,

211

but there was a certain scuffing of the pine needles in the immediate vicinity. I'm accustomed to studying tracks in connection with my photographic activities. A deer in deep pine needles will leave a certain scuffed-up track, and I thought for a while these were deer tracks, but I changed my mind when—"

"Never mind your conclusions, Mr. Beaton. Simply state the physical appearance of the pine needles."

"Well, they were scuffed up."

"You may cross-examine," Burger said to Perry Mason.

"What brought you to this particular place," Mason asked, "at the time you discovered the gun?"

"Miss Strague and I were prospecting for a camera location. For some time I had been planning to set up one of my camera traps at a spot immediately to the south and west of the granite outcropping. A careful study of the tracks of animals, however, convinced me at the last minute that there was a better location for the camera to the south and east of this rock outcropping."

"At approximately the point where the weapon was discovered?"

"Yes, sir. I was making a survey there, preparatory to placing the camera there."

"And previously you had made a survey of the point to the south and west?"

"That's right."

"And on this particular occasion, when you and Miss Strague found this weapon, you took notice of the tracks, Mr. Beaton?"

"Yes, sir."

"And you state that you have made it a point to notice tracks?"

"Yes, sir. I consider myself something of a naturalist. In getting night photographs of nocturnal animals, one

212

must necessarily place cameras with some degree of skill—at least if first-class photographs are to result."

"During the time that you were making a survey of this locality, did you see any clock, or did you hear the ticking of any clock, or did you—"

Hamilton Burger was up on his feet, clearing his throat importantly as he arose. "Your Honor," he interrupted, "it seems that—no, Your Honor, pardon me Counselor, finish the question."

"Or," Mason asked, "did you notice any indication that the ground had been disturbed in any way?"

"Your Honor," Hamilton Burger said, "this is objected to as incompetent, irrelevant and immaterial, as not proper cross-examination. If the defendants wish to get any evidence concerning a clock into this case, it will be necessary for them to introduce it on their *own* case and as part of that case. Furthermore, it appears that an attempt at this time to drag an alarm clock into this case, and to enshroud it with some sinister significance, is merely an attempt to confuse the issues and the jurors. I challenge counsel to point out to the court at this time any possible theory on which this clock can have anything to do with the murder of Jack Hardisty."

Burger sat down.

Mason smiled and said, "At this time, Your Honor, I am only cross-examining the witness to test his recollection, and to determine the nature and extent of the search he made at that time."

"As cross-examination directed for that purpose, the question will be permitted, and the objection is overruled," Judge Canfield said.

"No, sir. I saw no sign of any buried clock, I heard no ticking of any clock. I saw no indication that the ground had been disturbed."

"Subsequently, Mr. Beaton, while you were on the

ground, did you have any of the witnesses point out to you a spot at which a clock had been found?"

Both Hamilton Burger and Thomas McNair were on their feet. It was Thomas McNair, forceful, dramatic, rapid in his conversation, who managed to get the first objection into the record. "Your Honor, we object. That is absolutely incompetent. It is an attempt to drag another issue into this case. It calls for hearsay evidence. It is an attempt to prove an incompetent fact by asking a witness about a conversation."

Hamilton Burger cleared his throat, added importantly, "It is a matter which has, at no time, been touched upon in direct examination, Your Honor. No claim is made that the question even relates to the same general locality, concerning which the witness testified."

Judge Canfield nodded his head. "It would seem that this objection is well taken, Counselor," he said to Mason.

"I would like to be heard upon it, Your Honor."

"Very well."

Mason looked at the clock. "This, Your Honor, is a crucial point in the case. I think, if the Court please, I can get some authorities on the matter if I am given a little time. After all, some of the events of the morning, while known in advance to the district attorney, have naturally taken the defense entirely by surprise. The Court will note that this testimony about the second gun is at complete variance to the situation as heretofore disclosed by the testimony."

"But that was outlined, anticipated and even suggested in your cross-examination yesterday, Mr. Mason."

There was a smile in Mason's eyes as he said, "And the witness offered to bet me a million dollars there was no second weapon to be found in that barranca. In the absence of the million-dollar payment, I should be entitled to sufficient time to investigate the new legal situation disclosed by this abrupt switch in the testimony."

"Very well," Judge Canfield said, smiling. "Court will take a recess until two o'clock this afternoon. If you wish to look up authorities, Mr. Mason, please bear in mind the point made by the prosecution, that this is an attempt to prove an extraneous fact by hearsay evidence. Not only does the Court consider the fact itself to be extraneous and irrelevant, but the question, as framed, called upon the witness to relate some action he had taken in connection with a statement made by some other person."

"But Your Honor will note," Mason said, "that the question relates to an activity *on the part of this witness*. The *reason* for that activity is embodied as a part of the question. I think we are entitled to show the activity, and, having shown that, the reason for it, as it might tend to show bias on the part of the witness."

Judge Canfield frowned thoughtfully, then shook his head.

Hamilton Burger said, "If the Court please—"

"The Court will recess until two o'clock," Judge Canfield said, "and all arguments will be heard at that time. In the meantime, there is nothing to be gained by a further discussion. However, the Court will consider that it is incumbent upon Mr. Mason to produce authorities in support of his question. Failing in that, the objection will be sustained. I think that clarifies the situation and the position of the Court. We will recess until two o'clock."

■

27

Back in his office, Mason held a hurried conference with Jackson, his law clerk, Della Street and Paul Drake.

"Find me some authority," he said to Jack, "which even squints at the doctrine that hearsay evidence may be brought out on cross-examination to show the *reason* which actuated the witness. . . . There *must* be some authority somewhere—such, for instance, as a question, Didn't you go to a certain place, because so-and-so told you that such-and-such was the case?"

Jackson nodded, vanished into the law library.

Mason, frowning, said, "Unless I can drag that clock in on cross-examination, I'm not going to get it in. And the way things look right now, I'm not going to get it in on cross-examination."

"Did you think you could?" Della Street asked.

Mason said, "I'm sparring for time. Burger intended to rest his case. Judge Canfield would then have given me until two o'clock to put on my case. As it is now, we'll start arguing at two o'clock. I can talk for ten or fifteen minutes. Then let's suppose Judge Canfield rules against me, and *then* Burger rests his case. The Judge will then give me another continuance until tomorrow morning before I have to start putting on my case. I'll gain that much. . . . Damn it, Paul, that clock means something, and yet I can't even get it into evidence unless I can find out *what* it means."

"We can't get anywhere with Mrs. Payson," Drake said. "She's interested in astrology, but she's interested in a lot of other things. Astrology, it seems, doesn't have so much to do with astronomy, and like lots of women who talk about the signs of the zodiac, she doesn't know a damn thing about the stars themselves."

"You're certain?"

"Yes. I've pumped her."

"She might have been holding out on you."

"I don't think so."

Mason said, "Hang it, Paul. That clock wasn't set on sidereal time just as an accident. It wasn't—" He broke off abruptly.

"What's the matter?" Drake asked.

Mason said, "An idea, that's all . . . but— shucks, Paul!"

Mason picked up the telephone, said to the girl at the switchboard, "Gertie, get me the county clerk's office. I want the deputy who has charge of exhibits in the case of People *versus* Hardisty and Macon. I'll wait on the phone."

Mason held the telephone, his fingertips drumming the desk. After a few moments he said, "Hello. This is Perry Mason talking. That alarm clock which was introduced into evidence . . . Is it still running? It is. How fast is it running? . . . Check that accurately, will you? Let me have the exact time shown on it at a certain precise moment."

Mason took out his watch, laid it on the desk in front of him, said, "Okay, let me have it right now."

He marked down the figures on a pad of paper, frowned thoughtfully at them, then said after a moment, "Yes, that's all. Thank you."

He dropped the receiver back into place, said, "That's strange."

"What is?" Della Street asked.

"In the first place," Mason said, "that's a twenty-four-hour clock. We can count on somewhere around thirty-six hours to a winding. It will vary somewhat, depending upon the condition of the spring and the make of the clock. However, it's still running strong. That indicated it was wound up shortly before it was discovered. But the interesting thing is that *the clock hasn't gained a minute since yesterday.*"

"Well?" Della Street asked.

"Sidereal time," Mason said, "is almost exactly four minutes faster each day. It lacks just two or three seconds of that. It—" Abruptly he threw back his head and began to laugh.

"What is it?" Della Street asked.

Mason's laughter became uproarious. "The joke," he said, "is on me. I'm laughing at myself. We baited a trap and then walked into it ourselves."

"I don't get you," Drake said.

Mason said, "It goes back to the quotation about the engineer being hoist with his own petard. . . . Della, tell Jackson not to make any further investigation. We won't need those authorities. . . . Now give me half an hour to get my thoughts straightened out and we'll walk into court and give Mr. Hamilton Burger and his fresh assistant, Mr. Thomas L. McNair, a jolt they'll remember as long as they live! The solution of this whole mystery has been staring me right in the face, and I've been so blind I couldn't see it!"

28

■

It was five minutes past two, and Judge Canfield glanced down at Perry Mason. "Are you ready to submit authorities in support of your position, Counselor?"

Mason smiled. "No, Your Honor. I've decided to abandon my position. I will withdraw my question."

Hamilton Burger plainly showed his surprise. McNair sneered openly. "Very well," Judge Canfield said without giving any indication of his feelings, "Proceed."

"Just a few more questions of the witness," Mason said. "Mr. Beaton, you have testified that you are an expert tracker."

"Well, not exactly, but I have given considerable attention to the study of tracks."

"Yes. And you have set up several cameras at various points of vantage in the vicinity of your cabin, and in the vicinity of the Blane cabin where this murder was committed?"

"Yes, sir."

"Referring back, Mr. Beaton, to the time when the witness Jameson discovered Dr. Macon at the Blane cabin. You were there at that time?"

"Yes, sir."

"Prior to that time, where had you been?"

"I had been out watching my cameras, making the rounds, as I call it."

"Alone?"

"No. Miss Strague was with me."

"And Burton Strague, Miss Strague's brother, subsequently joined you at the cabin?"

"That's right."

"And stated he'd been looking for you all over the mountain and that his search had been fruitless?"

"Yes."

"And further stated that he'd walked through one of your camera traps, in connection with that search?"

"Yes."

"And told you which camera it was?"

"Yes, sir."

"And what was the time that he said he walked through that trap?"

"I don't know if he said. I know what time it was, however, because I made a notation when the flashbulb exploded."

"You were where you could see it explode?"

"Yes, sir. I saw the flare of light."

"And you customarily note such times?"

"You mean make notations of the time the lights flare up?"

"Yes."

"Yes, sir, I do."

"And yet, when it came to fixing the time when you saw the defendant, Milicent Hardisty, throwing a gun away, you weren't able to fix it very accurately, were you?"

The witness smiled. "My watches, Mr. Mason, are set sometimes by guess. When I make a note of the time a picture is taken, I do it for my own convenience, not because the standard time makes any difference. It is only the relative time. In other words, I wish the data for my own files. I want to know the relative time. That is, how long after the camera was set, before it was exposed, and things of that sort."

"Yes," Mason said, "so that your watch may at times be as much as half an hour off standard time?"

"I would say so, yes."

Mason said, "Now, did you develop the picture that was taken when Burton Strague walked through the camera trap?"

Again Beaton smiled, "I did, yes, sir."

"You don't happen to have a print of that picture with you, do you?"

"No, sir. I haven't."

"But you did make a print of it?"

"Yes, sir. I did."

220

"And what did it show?"

"It showed Burt Strague walking along the trail."

"Did it show his face plainly?"

"Yes, sir."

"Was it turned toward the camera, or away from it?"

"Toward the camera."

"Was he walking rapidly?"

"He was walking right along, yes, sir."

"Did the background show plainly?"

"No, sir. There is little or no background in any of my shots. I purposely select camera locations in places where a low-power flashbulb and a wide open lens will give me a picture of the animal against a black backdrop."

"What lens is on the camera with which this picture was taken, Mr. Beaton?"

"You wish a technical description?"

"Yes."

"On this particular camera it is a Taylor-Hobson-Cooke anastigmat of six-and-one-quarter-inch focal length, having a speed of F 3.5."

Mason took from his wallet the carbon paper disk Drake had discovered. "Would you say it was about the diameter of this circle of carbon paper?"

Beaton became quite excited. "May I ask where you got that?"

Mason smiled. "Please answer my question first."

"Yes. I would say it was about that—"

Hamilton Burger arose with ponderous dignity, said, "Your Honor, I have hesitated to object, because I felt that I wanted the defendants to have all the latitude possible. I realize that argument on an objection takes up more time than permitting irrelevant questions to be asked and answered. However, if this line of examination is going to continue, I shall certainly object—"

"Just a few more questions, and I am finished," Mason said.

Judge Canfield started to say something, then checked himself, muttered curtly, "Very well, Mr. Mason, proceed."

"Now then, as an expert tracker," Mason said, "did you have occasion to examine Burt Strague's tracks in the trail?"

"Yes, I noticed them."

"And did they indicate anything concerning the speed at which he was walking?"

"Really, Your Honor, I *must* object to this," Hamilton Burger said. "This is purely irrelevant. It is not proper cross-examination."

"I can assure the Court it is very pertinent," Mason said. "It tests the recollection of the witness, and it is proper cross-examination as to his qualifications. The Court will remember that the prosecution sought to qualify this witness as an expert on guns and tracks."

Judge Canfield said, "The objection will be overruled. It's proper cross-examination as to the qualifications of the witness as an expert tracker. The witness will answer the question."

"The tracks were spaced rather far apart, and showed he was moving right along," Beaton said.

"And the tracks were regularly spaced?"

"Yes."

Mason smiled at the witness. "And did you notice anything unusual about that, Mr. Beaton?"

"What do you mean?"

"About the fact they were regularly spaced?"

"Why no."

Mason said, "In other words, Mr. Beaton, as an expert tracker, when you see the tracks of a human being walking along a trail, going through a trap which trips a camera shutter, and at the same time suddenly explodes a brilliant flashbulb, you'd naturally expect these tracks to show the man had jumped back, or to one side, wouldn't you? You'd hardly expect to find his tracks moving regularly along at evenly spaced intervals, would you?" Sheer incredulous surprise twisted the muscles of Rodney Beaton's face.

"Can't you answer that?" Mason asked.

"Good Heavens!" Beaton exclaimed. "I never thought of *that!*"

"As an expert tracker, you've noticed what happens with wild animals when they set off a flashbulb, haven't you?"

"Yes, of course. It's—I can't understand it, Mr. Mason."

"But you're certain about the tracks?"

"Yes, sir. I'm certain. I noticed them particularly, although the significance of what I noticed didn't occur to me until just now."

"Exactly," Mason said. "I'll ask you one more question and I am finished. The nature of those photographic traps which you rig up is such that when any strain is put upon a black silk thread stretched across the trail, the picture is taken?"

"Yes, sir."

"And one final question," Mason said. "Wouldn't it be possible for a man to set an alarm clock to the tripping mechanism of your shutter, take a picture at any predetermined time? In other words, at any time the alarm should go off?"

Both Hamilton Burger and McNair were on their feet, both objecting at once. Judge Canfield heard their objections with a frosty smile, said calmly, "Objection overruled. Answer the question."

Beaton, seeming somewhat dazed, said, "Yes, sir. It could be done."

Mason said, "I think that's all, Mr. Beaton. . . . Oh, by the way, I believe the time you noted for the taking of the picture of Burton Strague was at approximately the same time the house of Jack Hardisty in Roxbury was being burglarized, and the night watchman, George Crane, was slugged?"

"I . . . I believe it was. I hadn't, of course, thought of it in that connection before."

Mason bowed with exaggerated courtesy to the two prosecuting attorneys who sat staring, open-mouthed, at the witness. "Have you gentlemen any questions on redirect examination?" he asked.

Burger semed as one in a daze. He turned his eyes from the witness to Mason, then leaned forward to indulge in a whispered conference with McNair.

"Your Honor," Hamilton Burger said, after a few moments, "this is a *most* remarkable development. It not only puts a completely new interpretation upon much of the evidence in this case, but it opens up possibilities that—if the Court please, we'd like an adjournment until tomorrow morning."

"No objection," Mason said.

"Granted," Judge Canfield snapped.

29

■

Back in his office, Mason opened a drawer in his desk, took out a bottle of rare old cognac, three large snifter glasses, said to Paul Drake and Della Street, "Well, now we can relax. At last I've got that damn clock off of my mind."

"I don't get it," Drake said.

Mason laughed. "Suppose, Paul, we had found an

alarm clock buried in the ground near a point where a man intended to plant a camera to take nocturnal pictures. Suppose we'd further found that one of the persons in the case relied upon a picture taken at night to establish an alibi. What would we have thought?"

Drake said, "Well, of course, if you put it *that* way."

"That's the only way to put it," Mason said. "Those are the simple facts. Too many times we overlook the simple facts in order to consider a lot of extraneous complications which merely confuse the issue. I was responsible for it, Paul. It should be a lesson to me. I tried to work in a lot of stuff about sidereal time in order to get the district attorney of Kern County interested. Naturally, that stuff got into the newspapers, and naturally the murderer read all about it. Therefore, when he got ready to let me discover the clock, it was only natural he would set it on sidereal time."

"But why would he want you to discover it?"

"Because I had started confusing the issues and he thought it would be a good thing to confuse them still more."

"Just what do you think happened?" Della asked.

Mason said, "I can't give you all the details, but I could make a pretty good guess. Vincent Blane had a magazine article lying around his house about how scopolamine would make witnesses talk, confessing crimes which they were really trying to conceal. Naturally, Vincent Blane read it; Martha Stevens, his housekeeper, read it; Adele Blane read it, and Milicent Hardisty read it. Probably all of them thought of that article when it became known that Jack Hardisty had embezzled another ninety thousand dollars and hidden it. . . . Martha Stevens got her boy friend, went so far as to make a practical test. Martha got Milicent Hardisty to procure the drug for her, and then surreptitiously borrowed Milicent Hardisty's gun. Remember, Martha learned of the second embezzlement from overhearing Blane's telephone conversation.

"Milicent didn't learn about the ninety thousand embezzlement until the day of the murder. When she found it out, she was furious. She obviously knew her husband was going to the cabin, and decided on a showdown. She couldn't find her own gun, but her father had a gun that was in the house. She picked it up and started up to the cabin. That, however, was *after* Martha and Smiley had gone to the cabin. She parked her car near the turn-off to the cabin and then became hysterical, and the very force of the nervous storm served to calm her and give her a sane perspective on what she was about to do. She went back and threw the gun away, met Adele, started back to the house. Dr. Macon picked her up in Kenvale. She told him about what had happened. Macon wanted her to go back to the cabin, either to remove some evidence indicating she had been there, to find the gun she had thrown away, or because he didn't entirely believe her story and wanted to check up on what had happened. . . . They got to the cabin well after dark, unwittingly passing Martha and Smiley in the dark on the road, found Jack Hardisty dying. Milicent said she knew nothing about it. You can hardly blame Dr. Macon if he didn't believe her."

"But who killed him?" Della Street asked.

"Martha Stevens gave him a hypodermic of scopolamine," Mason said. "When Jack told them about hiding the money in the tunnel, he wasn't faking. He was telling them the simple truth. They went up to the tunnel, and the money wasn't there. That means someone must have beaten them to it. That person must have removed the money almost as soon as Hardisty had buried it, and then gone on down to the cabin. We can reconstruct what happened then. He found Jack Hardisty drugged and talkative, telling the absolute truth under the influence of

226

the drug. He found the car in which Martha and Smiley had driven up, and of course, Hardisty's car was there also. Hardisty's glasses were broken. He was probably sitting on that big rock outcropping, and the gun which Martha had surreptitiously taken from Milicent Hardisty was lying there on the pine needles where Smiley had thrown it when he hit Hardisty.

"Now this newcomer must have been a friend of Hardisty's; more than a friend—a partner, an accomplice. And he must have been planning to kill Hardisty for some time."

"How do you know that?" Della asked.

"The evidence shows it. When he'd planted that alarm clock the first time, he intended to use it to manufacture an alibi. But he didn't use it because that day Beaton didn't put the camera in that location, and, instead of staying to watch the cameras that night, he took Myrna Payson to a movie."

"But why would this partner want to kill Hardisty?"

Mason smiled. "Put yourself in his place. Hardisty had got caught. Hardisty was going to jail. He was Hardisty's accomplice—and if he had Hardisty out of the way, he'd not only seal his lips but be ninety thousand to the good with no one ever suspecting. . . . The first embezzlement had been a scant ten thousand. That represented money they'd 'borrowed,' probably to finance a mining venture or horse races or stock gambling. The ninety thousand embezzlement was an attempt at blackmail, and it didn't work.

"Put yourself in Burt Strague's position. Jack Hardisty was going to the penitentiary. If Jack talked, Burt Strague would also go up as an accessory. He had intended to make away with Hardisty if he could do so safely. That's why he first planted the alarm clock where he expected Rodney Beaton was going to set up one of his cameras. He was arranging in advance to give himself an alibi. . . .

He came on Jack Hardisty, drugged. Jack Hardisty probably told him he had left some incriminating evidence in that writing desk, evidence that showed the original embezzlement had gone into a joint venture with Burt Strague. And he also told Strague that Martha Stevens had drugged him and that he'd told them where he'd left the money, that he was tired of it all, that he didn't have the nerve to go through with it. When Martha and her boy friend returned from the tunnel, Hardisty was going to tell them everything."

"Where was Milicent all this time?" Drake asked.

"At that particular moment she was probably just parking her car at the turnoff, and starting to walk to the cabin. However, she never did get there. She had hysterics, went back to the road, threw the gun she'd taken with her—her father's gun—away. She then met Adele, went back as far as Kenvale, met Dr. Macon, talked with him and finally returned to the cabin at Dr. Macon's suggestion. Probably Macon wanted to find that gun—and he may have doubted if Milicent's recollection of what had happened while she was hysterical was entirely accurate.

"When he arrived he found Hardisty in bed, dying from a gunshot wound. He naturally assumed Milicent, in her hysteria, had gone a lot farther than she remembered, and that a merciful amnesia had blanked the worst part of what had happened from her mind. That frequently happens in hysteria. In fact *Legal Medicine and Toxicology* by those three eminent authorities, Gonzales, Vance and Helpern, mentions hysteria as an authentic cause of amnesia. So you can begin to see Dr. Macon's position. He felt certain the woman he loved had killed her husband, probably in self-defense, had become hysterical and the hysteria had erased the memory from her mind.

"But to get back to Burt Strague and Hardisty. There

228

was an argument. Hardisty blurted out some things he shouldn't have said. Burt Strague shot him, probably in a struggle. Then, alarmed, he got the wounded man up to the cabin and into bed. He realized Hardisty was dying. He knew that the mud on Hardisty's shoes would show that he'd been to the tunnel. Naturally, he cleaned the shoes, because Burt had removed the money buried there in the tunnel almost as soon as Hardisty had driven away, and he wanted Martha and Smiley to think Hardisty had lied about the tunnel.

"Burt Strague knew that Martha Stevens and her boy friend would very shortly return from their fruitless search of the tunnel. He jumped in Hardisty's automobile, drove it down the grade and off over the embankment. That got rid of the automobile. . . . He didn't have a chance to dispose of some of the other evidence, as he would have liked to. Not until the next morning did he get a chance to dig up his clock—and he had to burglarize the writing desk in the Hardisty residence. That was a ticklish job. When it came to doing it, he relied on the alibi he had already cooked up."

"But how could he have left his picture in the camera," Della Street asked, "if he wasn't actually there?"

"Very easily," Mason said. "With his own camera, he took a flashlight picture of himself walking along the trail. He kept that undeveloped negative in reserve. When Rodney Beaton set up his camera, which was probably right after dark, Burt, taking care to avoid tripping the string which would release the shutter, went up and left tracks in the trail. Then he unscrewed the first element of the lens, inserted the carbon paper disk, replaced the lens, and substituted his exposed film for the one that was in that camera. Remember that it was dark by this time, and he could work by a sense of touch without needing a darkroom. He buried his alarm clock, adjusted the mechanism so it would trip the string and shoot off the

229

flashbulb at the proper time, and then beat it for Roxbury. Remember his slender build. He dressed himself in his sister's clothes, slugged the guard, broke open the desk, got what he was after, returned to the mountains, removed the carbon paper disk from the lens, then went to the Blane cabin, and told the story of having searched all over for Rodney Beaton and his sister. . . . Those are the high points. You can fill in the details."

"But why was the clock twenty-five minutes slow when it was first found?" Drake asked.

Mason grinned. "Because, in order to make the thing work right, Burt Strague wanted to have his alarm clock synchronized with Rodney Beaton's watch, and Rodney Beaton's watch was notoriously inaccurate, so Burt made an excuse to get the time from Beaton and then set his own watch accordingly, and subsequently set the alarm clock according to that time. . . . Once the clock was discovered, we might have tumbled to what it was all about if it hadn't been for the fact that I, myself, mixed the case up by injecting this angle of sidereal time. Having done this to fool the police and the district attorneys of Kern and Los Angeles Counties, I then proceeded to get fooled by it myself, because the murderer promptly picked up my idea and adopted it as his own. . . . And now, we're going to quit talking about the case and have a drink of good old brandy."

"What will they do?" Della Street asked.

"They'll figure the thing out, give Burt Strague the third-degree, and probably get a confession," Mason said. "Strague is something of a weakling, an introvert —the type that is emotional. He won't be a hard nut to crack. I feel sorry for his sister, though. She couldn't have known anything about it, and she's a nice kid. . . . Well, here's to crime."

The door from the outer office opened. Gertie said,

"Mr. Vincent Blane is here. He says he must see you at once."

"Show him in," Mason said.

As Vincent Blane entered the office, Mason took another glass from the drawer of his desk.

"You're just in time," Mason said.

Blane was so excited he could hardly talk. "He confessed," he said. "They got him. He told them all about it, and where he hid the ninety thousand he hijacked from the mine—and about planting that picture. It was an alibi so he could get into Jack's home and—"

Mason said, "I'm sorry, Mr. Blane, we just finished a post-mortem on the case, and decided we weren't going to talk about it until we'd had one good drink."

Vincent Blane seemed somewhat annoyed for a moment, then he grinned and dropped wearily into the big overstuffed leather chair. "At times, Mr. Mason," he said, "you get some remarkably fine ideas. If there's enough of that stuff in the bottle, let's make it *two* good drinks."

DICK FRANCIS

"The Best Thriller Writer Going!"*

_____ 78913 BLOOD SPORT $1.25

_____ 78945 DEAD CERT $1.50

_____ 80139 ENQUIRY $1.50

_____ 80088 FLYING FINISH $1.50

_____ 78884 FORFEIT $1.50

_____ 80109 FOR KICKS $1.50

_____ 80142 NERVE $1.50

_____ 78967 ODDS AGAINST $1.50

_____ 78872 SLAYRIDE $1.25

_____ 80437 KNOCKDOWN $1.50

*The Atlantic

Available at bookstores everywhere, or order direct from the publisher.

TV'S TOP COP!

_____ 78487 #1—SIEGE $1.25

_____ 78488 #2—REQUIEM FOR A COP $1.25

_____ 78817 #3—THE GIRL IN THE RIVER $1.25

_____ 78865 #4—THERAPY IN DYNAMITE $1.25

_____ 78912 #5—DEATH IS NOT A PASSING GRADE $1.25

_____ 78960 #6—A VERY DEADLY GAME $1.25

_____ 78996 #7—TAKE-OVER $1.25

_____ 78998 #8—GUN BUSINESS $1.25

_____ 80045 #9—THE TRADE-OFF $1.25

Available at bookstores everywhere, or order direct from the publisher.